CW01214357

This Rough Magic

By Deanna N.J. Rice

KDP

Cover photo courtesy of Svetlana, of Pexels

Copyright, Deanna N.J. Rice

2022

To mum and dad, for supporting me in all my crazy ideas and schemes over the years.

To Matt, for pushing me to make this happen.

To my friends, who read this over and over again half a dozen times and provided feedback.

I love you all.

CHAPTER ONE

Viola stifled a yawn behind the counter of her father's bookshop. It had been one hell of a day and she was tired. She hadn't slept well, waking up in the early hours after having a strange dream; she thought she remembered a battle of some sort. She'd been in a field and all around she heard screams and the clash of steel against steel. She thought she could recall bursts of flame, bright flashes of light and a hideous, high-pitched laugh. The details of everything, however, were rather hazy. She assumed it came from watching movies too late at night. Regardless, it left her feeling uneasy.

That uneasiness had only increased a few hours later. She was a grad student at the local university and, while riding the public transportation bus to school, she looked up from her book to see a young man staring at her from a few seats away. At first, she was intrigued. He wore a pair of red Converse, jeans and a red plaid shirt buttoned up over a black t-shirt. His hair was dark with blue tips, gelled to stick up in all directions in a sexy-messy sort of way. His eyes were a bright hazel, and they were staring directly at her, as a small smile played across his lips. She'd met his gaze and smiled back shyly, expecting him to say something. He never spoke, just stared at her as the bus rumbled along the road. She grew increasingly uncomfortable and when the bus stopped at the school, she realized he was following her across campus. She quickly made her way to Brooker Hall, home of the English department, and ducked into her office, pulling the door closed behind her.

  The whole encounter, combined with the discomfort left over from her dream that morning, had kept her on edge most of the day. She'd only finally started to feel a bit better after lunch and a ride home with her best friend, Liz. She told the story of the strange man on the bus and Liz decided that the best way to recover from such a day, and to start off the weekend, was a trip to their favorite bar. Viola was inclined to agree.

  After dropping off the majority of her school things, she grabbed a pile of essays that needed grading, tucked them into a bag and headed out the door to get to her father's shop. She worked as a Teaching Assistant at the university but put in a few hours at the bookstore to help her father, and because she just loved being surrounded by books. And so it was that she found herself grading essays at the counter, while a hipster sat in the corner, sipping on an overpriced coffee from the shop down the street, glaring over his laptop at the two little old ladies seated on the nearby couch, talking loudly about the knitting and quilting books they had piled on the table in front of them. She realized that she'd been staring at an essay, not taking in anything while reliving the day's events in her memory. If she kept this up she'd never finish grading. She ran a hand through her hair, as though the physical action would somehow clear her head and set to reading.

She raised an eyebrow as her phone buzzed briefly on the counter, alerting her that she had received a new text message. She slid her finger across the screen to unlock it and saw the message was from Liz.

How's the shop?

She looked up to make sure no one was coming to the counter before she began typing a response.

Glorious. Dad's at some town meeting about the owner of that lobster company wanting to expand. There's this hipster author here getting pissed at old ladies for talking too loudly about crafting projects, though! - Viola

Oh, man...that sounds fantastic. Meanwhile, I'm about to set these quizzes on fire. - Liz

Well, Spring is here but it is still a bit chilly at night. You can use them for warmth. - Viola

The two older ladies approached the counter, each with a couple of crafting books and magazines in their arms. Viola rang up their purchases, bagged their items and wished them a good night, trying not to laugh as the hipster author heaved a huge and overdramatic sigh of relief at their departure. She picked up the items they had decided not to buy and placed them back on their appropriate shelves. Returning to the counter, she was just about to reach for her phone to see if Liz had responded, when the bell over the door announced the entrance of another customer. She turned to greet the new arrival and dropped her phone, sending it skittering across the floor toward the creepy guy from the bus, who had just walked through the door. She stood frozen as he picked up the phone, brought it over to her and placed it in her hand.

"Here you go," he said, smiling widely.

"Um...th-thanks."

"No problem. Where's your fantasy section?"

She directed him to the back wall of the store and watched as he moved towards the bookshelves. Fumbling, she unlocked her phone, ignored the text Liz had sent to her and immediately typed out a new message.

Creepy guy from the bus just walked in. What do I do?!

Mere seconds passed before the phone buzzed again, all the while her heart was pounding, and she kept glancing between the creepy stranger in the back of the store and the one other person, the writer, praying he was deeply involved in whatever scene he was currently writing.

Shit, seriously??!!!! I'm leaving now!!! Be there soon!!! - Liz

Please HURRY!!!! - Viola

Liz didn't live very far away, she would no doubt be here within ten minutes, but Viola did not want to be by herself in the store with this strange man.

The pile of essays lay behind the counter, forgotten, as she spent the next few minutes looking back and forth between her phone, the hipster, the creepy fantasy lover and the clock. As it always does when one is excited or scared, it seemed ages between each tick of the minute hand. After what felt like an hour of waiting, she looked up at the plain, black and white clock hanging above the door to see that only about five minutes had passed since her last panicked text to Liz.

Uuuuggghh, where are you???!!!! - Viola

I'm on my way, keep your knickers on! - Liz

She looked toward the back of the store to check that Mr. Creepy wasn't doing something…well, creepy. He seemed to have found a book that piqued his interest, and was leaning against the shelves, reading. He was, however, facing the front of the store and, therefore, her direction, so she wondered if he was truly engrossed in the book's pages or if he had been staring at her while she typed to Liz. The ends of his blue-tipped hair were falling forward, blocking his eyes from her view. The sound of a zipper brought her attention back to the front of the store, where the hipster was starting to pack up his laptop. A tidal wave of fear crashed around her, her heart pounding and breath quickening. She did not want to be alone in the store with this strange guy. She felt her body starting to tremble and grasped her phone tightly. She tried to text Liz again but her shaking fingers were failing and betraying her at the worst possible moment. The bell over the door jingled suddenly and her head shot up in a panic to watch the writer walk out the door. A moment later, another noise from the back of the store made her swing her head that way once more. The stranger from the bus had just put his book back on the shelf and was now walking slowly toward the counter with a small smile on his face, which Viola was unable to read. She felt the panic rising within her and was just about to take off running when the bell jingled once more and in walked a damp-haired Liz, with makeup only half done.

"How's it goin', then," Liz asked, loudly. Her eyes found the strange blue-haired guy coming up one of the aisles and locked onto him. "I was getting ready at home but then I thought you might like some company. Mind if I hang here for a while?" She plopped her makeup bag and purse down on the counter, pointedly, as if to show the stranger she was here to stay.

The man's smile twitched for a moment and he veered toward the door rather than the counter. He said nothing as he passed by the two girls, acting as though he hadn't just been heading toward Viola. That settled it in Vy's mind; if he couldn't speak to her in front of Liz, if he had to wait for her to be alone, he was definitely up to something sketchy. As the door swung shut behind him Viola heaved a huge sigh of relief and sank onto the stool behind the counter.

"Oh, thank God!"

"That was the guy?" Liz turned around to watch him walk by the front windows. "He's quite a looker. Damn shame he has to also be a creeper." She turned back to Viola. "You're white as a sheet! What happened?! Did he say anything? What did he do?!"

Viola was still shaking as she ran her fingers through her copper curls. "No, he just looked at a book. He was on his way up to the counter when you walked in. I was just about to get the hell out of here."

Liz stepped up behind the counter and put an arm around her. "Bollocks! You're shaking like a jumpy chihuahua. Do you still have that Keurig in the back?" Viola nodded. "Good. I'm gonna make you a cuppa; or at least what serves as one under the circumstances. I'll leave the door open, okay? I'll be able to see if that creepy bloke comes back in, all right?"

Viola nodded again, and Liz went out to the back of the store. After a moment or two Viola could hear the hum of the Keurig as it brewed a nice, hot cup of tea. Meanwhile, she stared out the windows, making sure the man wasn't going to come back around the corner and into the shop again. By the time Liz was approaching the front of the store and Viola could smell the chai, she was starting to calm down a little. Her trembling was starting to slow down, at least.

"There, drink that. It'll help." Liz handed her the mug she had given to Viola for her birthday; a solid black mug with the words "this might be tequila," in silver lettering printed on the side. The warm mug felt comforting in her hands and the spicy aroma of the chai was soothing to her nerves.

Vy laughed softly. "How very English. All things can be fixed with tea."

"It's always worked for me," Liz, a native Brit, winked.

Viola sipped her tea while Liz grabbed her makeup bag and moved to the couch to finish putting on her face.

"Thank you for getting here so quickly, Liz. I really appreciate it."

Liz set up a mirror on the coffee table and waved her comments away. "Think nothing of it; there will inevitably be a day when I need to be saved from a creeper. I know you'll be there for me. Though, as you know, I hate leaving the house without having my face on. Be aware that this was a very serious personal sacrifice on my part," she finished, while brandishing an eyeliner pencil in Vy's direction. "Bloody creepers." She threw the eyeliner back into her bag with a bit more force than was necessary, then rummaged around for a moment before pulling out a tube of mascara. "Oh! By the way, I hope you don't mind but I invited Liam to come out tonight. He's that guy we met at the café a few weeks back."

"Oh sure, that's fine! How's that going, by the way? You two official yet?"

"Not really. Still just kind of seeing each other occasionally. Haven't even done anything good yet," she grunted. "Though, I'm hoping to change that tonight." She grinned wickedly over the top of her mirror. Viola rolled her eyes, then took a deep swig of tea before trying to get organized for closing.

Shortly past eight, Viola began getting the store ready to close at nine. She finished putting away the books people had decided not to buy or had left lying on shelves; she took a cloth and wiped down the coffee tables to get rid of any rings left on the wood and finally locked the door at nine o'clock. After she finished getting her face and hair together, Liz offered to vacuum the carpets while she cashed out the register and printed out the daily reports.

"Y'know," Liz started, as they stood on the sidewalk together while Viola locked up for the night, "you've had a bloody awful day. I'm buying your first drink and I expect, nay, I *demand* you be completely pissed by the end of the night!"

Viola laughed out loud, finally starting to feel more like herself. "I have never understood that one. How does 'being pissed' translate to being drunk in England, when over here it means you're super angry?"

"Oy! You don't hear me tearing your bastardized version of English apart, do you? Leave my proper language alone, dammit!"

They carried on this way, teasing each other and laughing, as they walked down Main Street, heading toward their favorite bar, Rum Runners. It was a decent place to hang out on the weekend, mainly full of college students. Upon entering, the bar was to your left, with several tables of varying size filling up the center and sides of the room. A medium-sized dance floor took up a portion of the back, with the DJ's booth just behind it, easily accessible to make song requests. The bathrooms were down a little hall to the left side of the dance floor. The place was mostly dark, the only lights coming from behind the bar and the rotating, colored lights of the dance floor. On Saturday nights, it was one of *the* places to be and finding an open table was nearly impossible. Luckily, Friday nights didn't get busy until around ten o'clock and the girls could make out two to three tables that remained empty.

The music was loud, of course; dance tunes with lots of bass, so Liz had to yell over it, and the sound of people talking and laughing. "Go grab us a table and I'll get you your drink!"

Vy nodded and headed toward the empty table against the right wall, located next to the dance floor. It was the perfect spot to laugh at the antics of drunken people attempting to dance and failing miserably. A middle-aged married couple usually hit the bar on Friday nights and spent the majority of their time dancing. It was cute but at the same time they were definitely lacking in the dance moves department. One night the girls had the pleasure of witnessing a particularly great performance by a guy who had obviously had too much to drink and was doing some sort of airplane move, his arms stretched out to his sides, "zooming" around the dance floor. As they were leaving that night, they also saw him "zoom" into the glass door on his way out. Thankfully, he didn't injure himself badly or break through the glass, but the two girls did not envy the headache he undoubtedly woke up to the next day.

Liz zig-zagged her way around people, heading over to the table with a glass of clear drinks with a lime wedge and ice in each hand. She placed one of them in front of Vy. "Here, drink that. That'll help you forget that creepy bloke!"

"Uuuh...what is this, exactly?"

"That is a gin and tonic. Great way to start a night of drinking!" Liz brought the glass to her lips, took a large sip and swallowed. "Aaaaaaah, that's the stuff! Lord, I needed this!"

Viola took a second to sniff at her drink before taking a small sip. It was bubbly, limey and tasted like she was drinking liquid pine needles. It was…odd. But it wasn't bad. And it was a drink. She shrugged her shoulders and took another, bigger sip. "Do you suppose our favorite dancers are here tonight?"

"I hope so! This has been a long week for both of us, we need a good laugh!"

The next hour passed rather uneventfully as they talked, laughed and watched as more and more drunks made their way to the dance floor. The older couple eventually arrived and attempted to dance like all of the cool kids surrounding them. Liz powered through several drinks while Vy tried to pace herself a bit more and maintain at least some level of sobriety. Someone had to be able to get them home, after all.

After downing her fourth drink, Liz slammed the glass on the table, grabbed Vy's hand and pulled her out to the dance floor. Viola was not one to dance much in public. She wasn't terrible at it, but she certainly wasn't going to win 'Dancing with the Stars,' so when she was in public and dragged onto a dance floor, she mainly just bobbed or swayed back and forth in time to the beat. Nothing fancy. She also did her best to hide in the corner, hoping no one would notice her or her pathetic attempts.

"Now, I don't want to alarm you, but you have another guy staring at you," Liz said over the music.

"What?! Not again! Where is he? Is it the creeper?!"

"No, no! Not the same guy as before. He's sitting at the bar, close to the bathrooms."

Viola positioned herself so that she could look in the direction of the bar and bathrooms. Sitting in one of the stools at the bar was a man in his mid to late twenties, with sandy hair and, from what she could see, dark eyes, with a decent build that looked like he worked out but wasn't so built that she'd have to wonder if he was hopped up on 'roids. He was wearing jeans, sneakers and a close-fitting black t-shirt that appeared to be bearing a character from some tv show, though in the dark she couldn't tell what it was. He was leaning back against the wall, his right hand laying on the bar, fingers wrapped loosely around a beer bottle, the other hand resting on his lap, clutching his phone. His eyes were facing forward toward the dance floor, focusing on her and Liz. He didn't seem overtly creepy but, as she had experienced earlier that day, it wasn't always so easy to tell. He saw the two girls looking in his direction, lifted his beer, smiled and nodded, then took a drink.

"How do you know he's looking at me," she asked. "I mean, he could be staring at you!" Given that she was still wearing the outfit she wore to school that day, a navy sweater and black scarf with white polka dots paired with jeans, and that Liz had changed into a low-cut shirt and skirt that fell above her knees, she thought this was more likely.

"Nope. Dude's definitely staring at *you*. I noticed him looking towards our table a couple of drinks ago. The last time I went up for drinks I watched him, and he kept staring at you. Didn't look at me once. Good lookin' bloke, too. Dude is *built*. I'm kinda jealous, to be honest."

The song ended, and they went back to their table, Vy feeling butterflies flapping around in the pit of her stomach. "Great. Another one, just what I needed today!"

"Maybe this one isn't a nutter," Liz ventured.

"I mean, he's sitting in the corner staring at a random girl he's never met. That's a bit nutty."

Liz shrugged. "Well, I guess you'll get the chance to find out. He's on his way over here."

Viola looked in the direction Liz was gesturing and saw the man coming towards them. After her experience today, she was understandably concerned by this stranger's approach.

"Hello, ladies. I don't seem to know anyone here tonight. Would you mind if I sit with you?" He had a deep, melodious voice that reminded Vy of Benedict Cumberbatch. She hoped to God this guy wasn't going to be creepy, because that deep rumbling bass was warm and soothing and more than a little sexy.

"No, of course not! Have a seat!" Liz gave her a look that seemed to say, 'don't worry, I'll be here, and we'll make sure he's okay.' Liz introduced herself and Viola.

"Thanks," he said, plopping down into a chair. "My name's Nate, I just moved here from the Chicago area."

The fact that he was talking, unlike the other guy, made Vy feel slightly better about the situation. Enough so, that she found her shaking to be at a minimum and that she could converse back with him. "Oh wow, you're a long way from home! What brought you to Maine?"

He shrugged while taking another swig of beer. "I dunno, really. I just...wanted something that the city couldn't offer me anymore. What that is, I don't know, but I decided to leave and start somewhere new. As for the location, to be honest, I basically just opened a map and put my finger on it while my eyes were closed, and I picked Maine. I've never lived near the ocean before, so I decided to go with a coastal town."

"Huh. Random, but exciting," Liz exclaimed.

He chuckled, "yah, it is a bit random but I'm glad I ended up where I did. It's very beautiful here." As he spoke his last sentence, his eyes shifted from Liz to look pointedly at Viola, who smiled shyly and took a rather long draught from her whiskey sour as she looked out onto the dance floor. She could feel Liz's gaze burning holes into her face as she felt the color rise in her cheeks.

"So, Nate, I see you're a *Doctor Who* fan."

Viola turned back at the mention of her favorite show and suddenly realized that the character on his shirt was none other than her favorite Doctor, as played by David Tennant.

"Oh, **huge** *Doctor Who* fan! I've loved it since I was a kid! And you two," he asked.

"Viola here is basically obsessed with it and me, well...I *am* English."

"Fair enough," he laughed.

"Is Tennant your favorite Doctor," Viola asked him.

"Definitely," he nodded. "He was in the first episode I ever watched, '*Blink*.'"

"Ooooh, that's such a great episode," she gushed. "I first saw him in one of the library episodes. Instantly fell in love with the show!"

The two of them launched headfirst into a conversation about their common interest. Liz easily could have contributed but remained quiet so the two of them could talk. Nate seemed harmless and Viola was enjoying the conversation, and barely even noticed when Liz excused herself to go meet Liam at the door, leaving her alone with their new friend.

CHAPTER TWO

Viola and Nate had been talking for quite some time on a variety of geek-culture topics. They had started with their mutual love of *Doctor Who*, then went on to discussing other favorite shows, movies and books. It turned out they had quite a lot in common and she was beginning to feel very hopeful, indeed. Nate had just made a hilarious joke regarding *the Doctor*, *Harry Potter* and *Twilight* and she was having a difficult time catching her breath due to how hard she was laughing.

"Hey, we should grab a coffee or something sometime," Nate said. "It would certainly be easier to hold a conversation than it is here!" He gestured to the DJ's box, indicating the loud music blasting throughout the bar.

She smiled back, still recovering from her fit of laughter. "Yah, definitely! That'd be great!"

"OH MY GOSH, YOU GUYS!!" Liz collapsed suddenly into the chair beside her. "Viola, oh my God, you won't believe it!"

Viola exchanged a look with Nate, who looked away and took a drink of his beer, in an attempt not to laugh at her incredibly drunk friend.

"Seriously, like, I'm not even kidding. Liam is the greatest guy on the bloody planet! No offense, you're great too," she slurred, looking towards Nate. He just shrugged and began shaking with silent laughter as he brought his bottle back up to his lips. "I'm gonna go marry him, tonight!"

"Whoa, whoa, whoa, calm down Liz!" Vy couldn't help giggling as she tried to make sense of her friend's nonsense. "Y'know, I haven't even met him yet, who is this guy?" She turned toward the busiest section of the bar, trying to determine which was Liam.

Liz pointed toward the bar, though she seemed to have a difficult time keeping her hand steady. "The bloke with the green hair. Isn't he delicious?"

Liam was very difficult to miss in the crowd. His hair was, indeed, very green; a green so bright and so neon it was most certainly not a shade readily found in nature. His hair was cut fairly short, but just long enough to be kept kind of messy and spikey, with a few pieces falling just above his eyes. He wore a black band t-shirt under his half-zipped black hoodie, over which hung a large, silver cross on a long chain. Another chain hung down from his belt loop and up into the pocket of his black jeans. The arms of his hoodie were pulled up slightly on his arms and Viola could see a couple of tattoos peeking out from beneath the fabric. He was sauntering toward their table, following the drunk Liz. He stretched his hand out to shake Nate's hand and then Viola's.

"'Sup? I'm Liam. Lizzie here has told me about you guys," he said, putting his arm around Liz.

"Uh...hi, Liam. Nice to meet you. I'm Viola. Liz was just telling us about you, actually."

She watched as Liz wrapped her arms around Liam's middle. Liz had never seemed like the particularly cuddly type but here she was, draping herself around this fellow.

"We're probly gonna hang around here for a bit longer and then Liam's gonna take me to his place. He lives with his sister," Liz slurred out. She put her hand on Vy's shoulder and leaned in slightly, as if she was about to impart the life-changing wisdom of the gods. "His sister has a corgi. I fecking *love* corgis!!!" She looked, for a brief moment, as if she was going to weep with joy. She then leaned in a little closer to her and whispered, not as quietly as Viola would have liked, "I'm probly finally gonna shag him tonight. He's sooo hot, right?!"

Vy was absolutely mortified and shut her eyes, in an attempt to pretend she wasn't really there, and her friend didn't actually just say that in front of Nate. When she opened her eyes, she could tell, even in the darkness of the bar, that Nate was red-faced with the effort of keeping the laughter from exploding out of him.

"Do you really think that's a good idea," she asked. "I fear you might not be in the most...competent states right now? Y'know...impaired decision-making skills and whatnot?"

Liz snorted. "Nah, nah, I'm good. I drank more than this when I was in Dublin a couple o' years ago. This is nothin'. I know what I'm doin' but thanks for taking care of me, *mum*."

Viola had learned a long time ago that Liz, even though she appeared giggly and drunk, actually held her alcohol fairly well. Maybe it was a British thing, or maybe it was just a Liz thing. Once she'd set her mind to something she didn't back down and Viola knew that no amount of protesting would stop her now.

"Okay, well...if you must." As Liz stood back up, intent to turn around and leave with Liam, Viola grabbed her arm and pulled her back. "Be safe," she said, looking at her pointedly, "and text me. Often. I want to know that you're okay."

"Will do, guvnah!" Liz threw a salute in her direction and grinned. "I'll keep you posted on things. A *play-by-play*, if you will."

"Uh, yah, that's okay. Just...y'know...in a couple hours or something, okay?" Liam gave Vy his address, which she typed into her phone. Always good to know where your friend is going. And she had a sneaky suspicion Liz might need a lift to her car in the morning.

"Okay, will do! Seeya later, Vy!"

"Bye!"

She and Liam turned to head out, walking so close together, they looked like some strange, two-headed, mutated beast. Viola was turning back to Nate to apologize when Liz suddenly yelled to her across the bar. "I HOPE *HE* HAS A CORGI, TOO!!!"

She shook her head and turned back to Nate, who had given up entirely on keeping his laughter in check and was letting it out in huge, rumbling guffaws. "I am so, so sorry. She's a little...out there."

"I think she's hilarious," he said, wiping tears from the corners of his eyes. "Oh man...seriously, though, you're okay with her going home with that guy?"

"Yeah, they've been seeing each other for a little while now. It's not like she just met him tonight. And she is more than capable of taking care of herself. Besides...she's probably not really that drunk."

"Really? She seemed pretty far gone..."

"She did, but I've seen her put away more drinks than that. And like she said, she did a legitimate pub crawl in Dublin during her undergrad. She's got one hell of a tolerance! I guarantee you she's probably mostly just buzzed."

He chuckled again, shaking his head. "Well, if you think she'll be all right… Sorry to disappoint, by the way, I don't have a corgi," he quipped, grinning widely.

Vy couldn't help but laugh. "That's very disappointing, indeed!"

There was a moment of awkward silence as Vy struggled to find words. She wasn't entirely sure she wanted to leave Nate just yet, as they'd been having such a good time, but it was also getting quite late, and she wanted to head home and get some sleep after her particularly long and strange day.

"Well, I... I guess I should probably be heading home, then," she said awkwardly.

"Yah, I should do the same, " he said. "Let me walk you out." He picked up her coat from the back of her chair and held it out for her. She thanked him and slid her arms into the sleeves, shrugging on her tan jacket. They worked their way through the bar, which had filled in with more people as the night wore on, and headed out the door. Without the tight crowds and the loud music, the night outside was infinitely more peaceful, despite the annoying humming in their ears from being inside the loud, noisy bar for so long.

"It was great meeting you tonight, Nate. I hope we can get that coffee sometime soon."

"Definitely. I look forward to it," he smiled back at her. "Do you live far from here?"

"Not terribly far, no. It's about a twenty-minute walk or so from here. I don't mind walking it usually but not this late at night."

"Sure, I understand. I wouldn't want you walking home in the dark like this, anyway." He gestured down the street. "Taxis should be coming down the street any minute. They always park just outside the bars at closing, which isn't too far away. It'll be easier to get a cab further away from the bar, though, before all the drunks start bursting out of the doors. If you go further up the sidewalk, they'll see you first."

"Oh, what a great idea," she said. "Thanks!"

"Here, I'll walk with you, and we can chat some more while we wait."

"Sounds great!" They started walking slowly down the sidewalk together. Rum Runners was located about halfway down a busy section of Main Street. This side of the street housed a few bars, a barber shop, salon, a small jewelry store and plenty of shops appealing to tourists eager for an overpriced coast-themed souvenir. They took their time, looking in all the windows and seeing what each shop had for sale. Many of them were full of lighthouses, starfish, lobster traps and netting arranged in a decorative manner, with white Christmas lights adding an element of sparkle to the display.

Her phone buzzed in her pocket and she pulled it out to see that Liz had sent her a picture of Liam's house and mailbox number, along with three more pictures of the corgi, who was absolutely adorable. The number matched what Liam had given her earlier. Good. She felt a little better now that she had an address and pictures.

As they neared the end of the street, approaching the corner, Nate suddenly grabbed her hand and gently pulled her into an alley way between buildings. "Um…what -", she started to speak but quieted as he pressed her softly against the brick wall behind her. He tucked a lock of curly, red hair behind her ear, then leaned his face in closer to hers. She could feel his hot breath tickling her face. Her heart was pounding but she closed her eyes and waited to feel his lips pressed against hers. A few seconds passed and nothing happened. Then suddenly she heard him begin to snicker. She opened her eyes and looked into his; but they weren't the eyes she had grown accustomed to in the bar. They were different. His eyes had seemed darker in the bar, a chocolate brown. Yet now they seemed to be more amber in hue, and there was something sinister hidden in their depths.

"Nate? What's going on?" She felt the familiar sensation of fearful butterflies flapping their wings in the pit of her stomach. This was happening far too often today.

His laughter evolved from a soft snicker into a chuckle and before long he was bent over, howling with it, while she stood, back against the cold brick wall, in a state of confusion.

"Nate??!! What the hell?!"

He let one last peal of laughter ring out, then suddenly he was standing up straight again, his hand clutched around her throat, keeping her pinned against the wall. "I'm not Nate," he growled. "My name is Tarak. What a gullible little bitch you are, Viola," he sneered.

"What," She asked, the terror making her voice shaky and weak. "I don't under-"

"SHUT UP!" He slapped her face, bringing a tingling pain to her cheek. "It has been *maddening*, having to put up with you and your ridiculous friend all night. You've both been driving me crazy!" She began trembling violently and tears born of fear began to pool in her eyes. She thought she could feel something warm trickling down her cheek from where he'd hit her. He leaned in closely and began to whisper softly in her ear, seeming to revel in her fear-quickened breathing. "But now, I get to show you the truth. I know the queen wanted you for herself, but I think I deserve the satisfaction. Your death shall be long, painful and torturous. Just like tonight was for me." He pulled back ever so slightly, and she saw that his eyes had indeed changed from their warm, dark hue to a glowing, golden yellow.

   She wrapped her hands around the wrist that was holding her against the wall and struggled to tear it away as she let out a scream that echoed down the alleyway. He just chuckled again, saying "Really, dearie? It's just about closing time at all the bars in this town. Right now, that street is full of drunken idiots yelling, laughing and hollering for taxis." As if to illustrate his point, a scream rang out from down the street, followed by a couple of loud *whoopwhoops*. He grinned and used his free hand to poke her nose softly, in time with each word. "No. One. Can. Hear. You." He was right; even if someone did hear her scream, it would be lost amongst the cries of the happy, intoxicated revelers. He backed away slightly, still grinning as sobs began to wrack through her lungs and throat. "I'll be rewarded for this, you know. That should settle your mind a bit; to know that your sacrifice will bring great reward and recognition to your dear Nate," he sneered.

A strange snapping sound began to fill the alley and Viola struggled to find the source. When Nate..or...Tarak's body began to jerk and move in strange ways, she realized it was the sound of bones snapping and reforming. In the midst, his grasp around her neck loosened. She knew it was the perfect chance to slip away but when she tried, she found that she couldn't move. She watched, frozen in place by fear and awe, as the man in front of her began to change. Hair began growing from every part of his exposed skin, some poking out from underneath his shirt. His face and limbs began to elongate, and it looked as though the transformation caused him intense pain. He completely let go of her throat to wrap his arms around his middle, while at the same time, he lifted his head and opened his mouth to scream. Doing so revealed his teeth, which were growing longer and sharper by the second. He lifted his arms, and she could see that his fingers had lengthened, the nails growing into claws, which he used to rip his clothes and shoes into shreds, exposing the canine bone structure forming beneath them. He finally dropped to all fours, panting, while she stared in horror at the gigantic, black wolf now standing before her. Its face turned toward hers, the gleaming yellow eyes staring at her, teeth bared in a snarl. It stood still like that for a few moments, catching its breath from the transformation, before it began to growl; a deep, terrifying sound that she could feel as much as hear. It slowly began to walk closer to her, it's claws scratching the asphalt each time it stepped forward, the growl continuing to rumble through its chest.

  Self-preservation told her to run but she knew there would be no point. She wasn't athletic, wasn't into sports, and this thing was built for speed and strength. It would overtake her within seconds. She tried to look around the alley for something she could use to defend herself but aside from bits of trash scattered along the ground and a large dumpster at the back end, there was nothing. She closed her eyes and dug her nails into the bricks behind her, trying to mentally prepare herself for the horrors that were to come. She heard the volume of the growl increase as the scrape of the nails began to come faster. She could once more feel hot breath on her face and she inhaled air to let out one last scream, which was stopped short when there was a sudden THUD and the creature let out a horrific whine.

  She opened her eyes, expecting to see the wolf's open mouth mere inches from her face, instead she saw the strange guy from the bus crouching in the middle of the alley a few feet away from her. He was staring straight ahead, glaring at something off to her left. She turned her eyes in that direction and saw the wolf getting up from where it had been thrown against the dumpster, leaving a huge dent in the dark green metal. It raised itself up on its gigantic paws, shook off the blow and faced off against the newcomer. The growl started up again and the wolf sprinted from the ground, rushing toward the man, who quickly jumped up and over the wolf just in time. Viola stared, open mouthed, at the height to which the man's jump had allowed him to climb. He landed and immediately spun around to face the wolf, who had skidded to a halt, turned around and was rushing the man once again. This stranger from the bus crouched down and moved his arms in front of himself, as if he was scooping something up. Viola thought she could see his lips moving but couldn't read what he was saying from this distance. In the next instant the ground in front of the man's feet shot up into the street. It was as though a spike of earth had erupted from the ground, the top of which came up to the man's chin. The wolf's reflexes were much too fast, however, and he darted around the spike, his claws raised in perfect position to open several bloody gashes on the man's arm.

   The blue-haired man staggered back, clutching his arm while the beast let out several short barks that sounded much like laughter, as he lapped at the scarlet beads dripping from his claws. The fur on his back bristled as he shuddered with pleasure. The stranger glared at the creature, mumbled a few indecipherable words under his breath, then smiled wickedly as he held his hands up. Moments later, they burst into balls of flame. He took a few slow steps toward the wolf, which seemed to shrink back a little at the sight of fire. He flicked his wrists and began shooting fireballs at the creature, who did his best to dodge them, though the occasional flame licked at his sides and fur, eliciting whines as he ran around the narrow alley. The man brought both of his hands together to send out a fire ball that was doubled in size. The wolf dodged out of the way and leapt towards him, only to crash down on a second earthen spike the man had just created, the point burying itself deep into his flesh, killing the creature instantly.

   Viola, still pressed against the brick wall further down the alley, watched as the man stretched out his arms and lowered them to the ground, the earthen spike growing shorter and disappearing into the ground below, a crack in the pavement the only sign of its existence. He gently turned the wolf's body over, so it was lying on its back, snout pointed to the dark sky above. He whispered some sort of incantation over the body, which returned to the form of the man she had met in the bar. He stroked the man's hair softly, then stood, his teary gaze falling on Viola. He wiped at his eyes and walked toward her. With a sad smile, he put his hand on her shoulder.

"Hello, Viola," he spoke softly and slowly. "My name is Vince. I'm sure you have a lot of questions for me."

The alcohol paired with terror-induced adrenaline pounding through her veins was too much for her body to handle. The last thing she saw before she blacked out was this strange man holding out his arms to catch her as she fell.

CHAPTER THREE

As she swam in and out of consciousness, Viola could hear voices that sounded vaguely familiar. There were moments when she opened her eyes and could sense, rather than see, that she was in a vehicle. They were moving; there were two people in the front seats, both of whom sounded like someone she knew, but in the fog of unconsciousness and the darkness inside the car, she couldn't say for sure to whom the voices belonged. Occasionally, there were busts of light in the foggy darkness, which she thought must have been streetlights, but she soon drifted off again and the lights were forgotten. She thought she could feel something warm, a blanket, over her body. Then, the darkness claimed her again.

When she woke fully from her faint, she began taking stock of her surroundings, rejoicing that she was finally capable of full comprehension. She was curled up in the backseat of a vehicle with a coat or something thrown over her to keep her warm. She was alone, the two occupants from earlier having left the now stationary vehicle. Through the closed doors and windows, however, she could hear hushed voices. There were two of them; both male. One seemed to have a deep, older quality to it while the other sounded younger and slightly higher in pitch. They were talking quietly, almost in whispers, no doubt assuming she was still asleep, and she struggled to hear much of anything that could help identify the speakers. She couldn't make out the words they were saying but it sounded as though the older man was upset about something. She had no idea where they were; all she could see out the windows, from her position, was the outline of trees in the darkness.

   Slowly, so very slowly, she began to lift herself up to see if she could learn anything more about either their location or the identity of her kidnappers. As she gradually raised herself up into a sitting position, she could see their darkened silhouettes sitting on the hood of the car, talking. They were facing away from her, making it impossible to see any facial features that might be recognizable. Keeping her eyes on the two figures the entire time, she slowly and carefully maneuvered herself around in the back of the car. After making sure she was hidden behind the passenger seat, she looked out the windows, hoping to figure out where they had taken her. To her left, she could see a large hill, covered in trees, sloping down toward the lights of the city and the ocean beyond. Out the passenger side she could see that they were parked outside the open, wrought-iron gates at the entrance to a large, dark, Victorian mansion, towers reaching toward the open sky above. She recognized it immediately as the old, abandoned hotel, Sugar Maple Inn, on top of Maple Hill, not far from the university. If she could just get around the old inn and over the next hill, she could get to the school and reach one of the emergency sirens placed throughout campus. Pressing a button at one of the stations would have the campus police speeding toward her location in seconds. She just had to get there in time.

Peeking around the edge of the seat once more, she saw that the two men were still engrossed in their inaudible conversation, not looking back in her direction. She slowly and carefully pulled upwards on the lock button, releasing the door lock, then peeked around the seat again. They were still talking animatedly and hadn't heard anything. As she worked to slowly open the door, snippets of their conversation became more distinct.

"Nearly killed her," the slightly higher voice was saying, "- should have been informed earlier, then this wouldn't have happened."

"Well, what did you expect me to do," the other man hissed. Keeping her eyes on them, she blindly felt around for the door latch and slowly pulled it towards her, trying to make as little noise as possible. The latch gradually released as she applied more pressure to the handle, until she was able to push the door open slightly. They must have been very focused on their conversation, indeed, because neither seemed to notice the small click the door made as it opened. She took one last look, then carefully shifted her body on the seat to be in position to get out of the car. Her plan was to open the door just enough to slide out and sneak off quietly without them noticing, then disappear in the tall grass, unmowed for years, that surrounded the inn. Once she reached the house she could take off at a run and hopefully lose the men in the darkness of the woods beyond.

"I tried, okay?! We'll just have to take her to –" She didn't hear where they planned to take her because as she pushed the door open ever so slightly it let out a horrible, loud creaking sound and the conversation at the front of the car ceased abruptly. She didn't stop to look around at them but instead launched herself out of the car and took off running. Bolting towards the hotel grounds, she heard a stream of curses coming from behind her, followed by the sounds of quickened footsteps and two voices calling her name.

"Viola, wait!"

"We just want to talk!"

"Viola!!"

"Vy-vy!! *Stop*!!!"

She froze in her tracks suddenly, just beyond the old iron gate. She turned around quickly, her thoughts a mixture of anger, confusion and fear. She stared into the eyes of the man who had just used her childhood nickname.

"*Dad*?! What the hell?!"

CHAPTER FOUR

"What is *happening* right now?!"

Viola was standing just on the other side of the iron gate, looking back and forth at her father and the strange boy from the bus and the alleyway, all the while feeling confused beyond description. How did these two know each other and what were they doing, taking her out in the middle of nowhere?!

Her dad took a couple of steps toward her and tried to calm her down. "Don't worry, Vy-vy. Everything's okay." The moonlight washed out all the shades of his graying red hair and beard, making him look older in the dim light. "This," he said, gesturing to the young man beside him, "is Vince. I've known him for years. He's a good guy and you don't need to be scared of him." Vince inclined his head toward her in acknowledgment while she just stared at him, still trying to reach some level of understanding.

"Okay, that's fantastic. Nice to meet you, Vince," she barked sarcastically. "Now, tell me why the hell I just woke up in the backseat of a strange car in the middle of fucking nowhere, with no idea how the hell I got there?!" She usually tried to keep her cursing to a minimum around her father, but the confusion and anger was catching up with her now that the fear was subsiding. "And *why* is my father hanging out with some creepy guy who stared at me all morning on the bus and stalked me through campus?! And how did he magically appear in the alleyway just as some freaky werewolf guy was about to kill me?! What in the actual *fuck* is happening?!"

Vince stepped forward cautiously, not wanting to upset her any further. "Your dad and I have known each other for a few years, now. After you were attacked in the alley, I called him and told him what happened. He met us in the alley and helped me clear things up and get you in the back of my car."

"Hold on, wait a minute. You're telling me that was real? The alley was real; like…*actually* real?" She took a moment to run her hands over her face, something she did whenever she was incredibly confused or frustrated. She liked to think it calmed her down and helped to clear her head. Didn't seem to be working very well at the moment, though. "I thought that was just some weird dream I had while I was unconscious in the backseat, something brought on by too much alcohol."

"I'm afraid not," he said. "That was Tarak, shape-shifter. He's a member of the race of faerie."

She stared at him for a moment with a look of incredulity, one eyebrow raised. "I'm sorry, the what? 'The race of faerie?' Seriously?" He nodded and she snorted in response. "Dude, what kind of drugs are you *on*?"

"He's not on anything, Vy. It's the truth," her dad chimed in, "I know it's hard to believe but all the faerie stories, the fantasy...it's all based on truth. There really are faeries, magic does exist and," he paused for a second or two, trying to collect himself. "And... you are one of them."

Vy stared at her father in silence for several moments, unable to comprehend what he was saying. "Sorry, what?"

"It's true, sweetie. Come on, we'll show you," he said, gesturing to the abandoned hotel behind her.

"What does a dilapidated old building have to do with the fact that you two are completely mental," she demanded.

"Just come in with us," Vince said as he gently pushed past her and onto the hotel grounds. "You'll believe it all, then." He started up the long path toward the building, followed by her father, who paused for a moment to put his hand on her shoulder in a reassuring gesture, then continued on his way.

She stood by the gate for another moment or two, watching them walk toward the old building. It was falling apart, and she wasn't sure if it was entirely safe to go inside it. There were windows missing, rotting wood everywhere and the entire structure was surrounded by tall, overgrown grass and bushes. She shook her head, ran her fingers through her hair and then reluctantly began following the two men. At the very least, she needed to make sure her father, who had apparently lost his mind, made it out safely.

The two men turned right just before the steps leading up to the entrance, and proceeded through the tall, brown grass and weeds. She followed behind, the tops of the overgrown lawn brushing against her legs, just above her knees. Liz was a fan of horror movies and would always make Viola watch them with her and as she walked, she couldn't help but think of how many films featured abandoned and decaying buildings in the middle of nowhere. As she passed by the darkened, broken windows on the side of the great house, she half expected some apparition, hideous monster, or a man wearing a grotesque mask to reach out from the blackness within to pull her inside. The only sound to be heard was that of the grass rustling and crunching under their feet. As she looked around, Viola realized she didn't see or hear any animals scurrying through the underbrush; not even the hooting of owls in search of prey disturbed the eerie quiet.

  The pounding of her heart slowed a bit as she passed by the back end of the house, finally getting away from those dark windows and their secrets. They were entering the substantial gardens located behind the old inn. If she thought the grass out front and on the sides of the building was tall and wild, they didn't hold a candle to the forgotten gardens. Through the dim light, scattered in between the grasses and weeds, she could pick out the shapes of flowers that insisted on growing each year, despite the lack of anyone to care for them, entangled amongst twisting weeds and shrubs that had been left to grow as they pleased, almost completely taking over what must have once been a beautiful garden. She could see her father and Vince making their way along the path, walking toward an ivy-covered archway ahead of a silent and crumbling stone fountain in the middle of the garden. She looked down at her feet as she carefully picked her way over the broken stones, tangled weeds and vines that made up the pathway. Looking up, she caught a quick glimpse of the two men a few steps ahead of her, just about to pass through the archway and she immediately tripped over an upturned rock. She managed to land on one foot and did a sloppy, bent-over half-run for a few steps while she regained her center of gravity. Her hands brushed against the tangle of ivy as she took her final balancing step through the archway. She balked when her foot hit the ground on a perfectly shaped and polished stone tile, the sequins on her ballet flats shimmering in the evening light.

  She slowly stood up straight, eyes open wide, trying to comprehend what she was seeing. The garden in front of her was not the dark, creepy mess of overgrown weeds which had surrounded her a moment before. Instead, the path at her feet was unbroken, winding its way through a lush patchwork made of hundreds of varieties of flowers. She saw roses in every color, tulips and carnations next to brightly colored lilies and orchids and still dozens upon dozens of blossoms she couldn't name. The hedges were trimmed to perfection and though it was night, the entire garden was lit by several orbs of varying colors, which seemed to hover in the air above the path. Beyond the gurgling fountain in the center of the garden, stood the large house she had just walked past. The glass in the window frames was no longer shattered and a warm light poured from every window; the paint was no longer faded and chipped, but crisp and pristine. It looked cozy and inviting; a far cry from the haunted-looking husk of a house she'd just passed by.

"Wha..." She tried to form a sentence; she really did. Unfortunately, she couldn't seem to speak.

She turned around to look behind her and on the other side of the archway she had just passed through she could see the grim, dilapidated house and weedy excuse of a garden beyond. She scrunched her eyes shut as hard as she could, shook her head, even slapped herself to see if she could wake up from this crazy dream. All to no avail. When she opened her eyes and faced forward again, she still saw the beautiful flower garden and pristine house. It was as though she'd passed through a mirror, the real world was the dark, dreary, overgrown mess behind her and before her lay the lush, verdant garden of the world on the other side of the looking glass. Yet there were no giant caterpillars smoking on pipes to offer her wisdom or explanations. Her father and Vince stood a few steps ahead, both with similar expressions of amusement on their faces.

"I know this is incredibly confusing, Vy," her dad soothed, "but believe me when I tell you that everything is fine. We are safe. Just follow us into the house and we'll explain everything, okay?"

Vince bent his elbow and held his arm out for her, which she took, gladly accepting the friendly gesture. She still wasn't sure she trusted him but given the larger matters she was currently trying to understand, she appreciated the comfort he was offering. She gripped his arm tightly as they followed a short distance behind her father, all the while staring wide-eyed at her surroundings, taking in each and every detail while not understanding any of them. The trio walked toward the large Victorian, which was now pristine in the moonlight and glow of the garden lights. The blue paint was no longer faded and the white trim on the house showed no signs of yellowing from age and years of neglect. The silver weather vane reflected the moonlight, producing a magical glittering effect atop the turret on the right side of the great house. She and Vince followed behind her father, who led them up the steps and onto the wrap-around porch, stopping at the blue door. He knocked firmly and after a few moments the door swung open, revealing a very short man sporting a long red beard.

The man looked all three of them over, a serious and rather grumpy expression on his face. After a few moments his scowl lifted, and he grinned brightly. "Charles! I 'aven't seen the likes o' you in a dog's age!" Vy watched him lunge toward her father and give him the kind of hug reserved for old friends. The two men separated, and the smaller man reached up to put his hand on Vince's shoulder. "Welcome back, Vince. We missed ye." At last, he turned his gaze toward Viola. "An' who is this lovely young lass," he asked, taking her hand in his to place a small kiss on the back.

"This is my daughter, Viola," Charles started. "Vy, this is Fulrin Hammerfist, an old friend of mine and your mother's."

Still overwhelmed and very much confused, she was operating on autopilot. "Nice to meet you."

Fulrin's eyes had widened at the mention of her name and he released her hand, staring at her wide-eyed for a moment or two, before turning back to her father. "Now, why would ye be comin' out this way, then?"

This time it was Vince who spoke up. "She was attacked tonight, Fulrin." Vy was confused by the tone he used to say this, it was dark and heavy with a meaning she didn't understand.

"Well, then...I s'pose it's time." The dwarf looked up and stared intently at her for another moment before continuing. "Follow me. I'll take ye to Lady Rosalyn."

He stood aside, giving them room to enter the house. To her right, a staircase led to the upper levels, and straight ahead was the main hallway. The trio followed Fulrin down the long hall of the house, all the while Viola's head was turning right and left, taking in the grandeur of the house's interior. She had never been inside the old Sugar Maple Inn but had always admired it, often imagining what it must have been like when it was still a popular vacation spot for Victorian ladies and gentlemen. Perhaps it was a trick of her mind, an illusion brought on by the madness of this evening, but it seemed to her that the house was much bigger on the inside. The hallway seemed as long as a hall in one of the school buildings on campus. Her earlier confusion and fear were replaced by pure awe as she stared around at the largest and most beautiful house she had ever seen. Everything gave off a feeling of warmth - oriental rugs of deep red and gold stretched across the hall floor and up the stairs, gas lamps flickered from ornate, golden sconces on the walls, adjacent to classical paintings in gilded frames. She heard voices all around, sounds of laughter and amusement, the sound of a grand party with friends.

Viola tried to peek inside rooms as they passed and though she could see very little through the open doors, she saw several people playing cards, having conversations; in one room a stage seemed to have been set up for a play. A couple of faces looked back at her, wide-eyed, as they tapped their arms of their friends, gesturing for them to look toward her. She turned away, face burning as she felt their stares. Fulrin took them down the main hallway to the back of the house and directed them into the last room on the left, where they paused outside as he rapped on the door. From the door across the hall came the sounds of clanging pots and instructions being called out. Judging from the muffled cacophony of metal pots and pans, and the delicious smells emanating through the gap under the door, Viola surmised that the kitchen lay just on the other side.

  The door on which Fulrin had just knocked swung open and he started through, beckoning them to follow. They entered the dining room, a long wooden table stretching across the room, with matching dark wooden chairs, the seats covered in flowery, blue upholstery. At the far end of the room, seated at the head of the table was one of the most beautiful women Viola had ever seen, being guarded by two men who stood on each side of her. She was dressed in a pale blue gown, the bodice a shimmering satin which ended at the empire waist and was replaced with yards upon yards of the lightest, softest, flowiest of fabrics, which seemed to go on forever. Wavy blonde hair framed her face, which was bright and welcoming with a smile that reached her crystal blue eyes as she spread her arms in welcome.

  "Good evening! Please, take a seat," her voice was high and musical, like the tinkling of a bell, as she gestured to the many empty chairs at the table. Fulrin, Vince and her father all took places near this mysterious woman, so Viola took a seat to the right of her father, not wanting to be too close to this new person. "Are you hungry? I know it is quite late, but I find it is always easier to discuss matters of importance when there is something delicious and comforting to go along with it." She turned and nodded to one of the two men standing still beside her, who then gave a small bow and walked to the door they had just entered from, opening it to allow a cart of food to be brought into the dining room. Viola hadn't been particularly hungry when they all sat down but the smells that began dancing in front of her nose, as a man dressed in a white chef's uniform began transferring trays from cart to table, were just intoxicating. There was a silver platter of cold meats and cheeses, followed by a tray containing an herb-crusted, roast chicken; beside that, on a matching tray, a glazed ham. Next came bowls of steamed vegetables, garlic mashed potatoes and gravy, golden loaves of crusty bread, and to finish it all off was the tallest cake Vy had ever seen, covered in perfectly smooth, impeccable white frosting and fresh fruits. Next to each of those sitting at table was placed a glass of water, a goblet of some sort of golden liquid and a simple, white, overturned teacup, waiting to be filled with tea or coffee.

    Vy was hesitant to take anything, still unsure of what was happening. She was beginning to wonder if perhaps she was still at the bar and someone had drugged her and maybe this was all in her head. Fulrin, however, greedily tucked in, helping himself to thick slices of meat, a mountain of potatoes and shovels full of vegetables. Her father and Lance soon followed suit. The woman seated at the head of the table seemed to be waiting for everyone else to serve themselves. After her father gave her a strange look, she began adding small amounts of food to her plate. She barely had time to register that she had just tasted the best mashed potatoes on the planet when the strange woman began to speak.

"Viola, I know you have questions, the answers to which are going to be very hard to believe but everything I'm going to tell you is the absolute truth." She took a dainty sip of the golden liquid before continuing, as though she had quite the long story to tell. "First, I must introduce myself. My name is Rosalyn and I am the interim leader of what you would recognize as the fey folk, or faeries." At this point, Viola had quite convinced herself that she had been drugged. She began to mentally replay the evening at the bar, trying to figure out when she might have left her drink unattended. "I know this might be difficult to accept; all your life you've been told that faeries and the like do not exist. Well, I can tell you, this couldn't be further from the truth. The fact of the matter is, dear, that all these creatures exist. Magic is real. And you can wield it."

Vy had stopped eating. She was not capable of doing anything besides attempting to process what this woman was saying to her. She looked around at everyone sitting at the table, her gaze finally stopping on her father's face, who was looking at her with an honest, open expression.

"What the hell is this," she asked him. "Why are we here?"

"Just as she said, Vy. Lady Roselyn *is* telling you the truth."

Shaking her head, she tried to wake herself up or dispel the hold the possible drugs had on her. "This is ridiculous. I don't understand what in the world is going on right now." She felt the pressure of her father's hand rest on her shoulder in an attempt to comfort and reassure her.

Roselyn gave her a moment to process before beginning to speak again. "Magic has existed since the world came into being, though not everyone can use it. Centuries ago, there was a great war between those who could wield magic and those who could not. The people who were not born with magical ability were stirred to take arms against us, saying it was unfair to them, that at any time we could use our magic against them, and they would have no way to defend themselves."

Vy put her head in her hands and laughed to herself. "Okay, sure...I'll play along. Weren't they justified in that way of thinking?"

"To an extent, yes." Rosalyn paused and took another delicate sip from her glass. "Certainly, there were some magic wielders who were tricksters and interacted with the others in ways they shouldn't have. However, the vast majority of us would never do such things; we prefer to use our magic to help non-magical beings in any way we can. It truly serves no benefit for us to trick and torture others."

"And what about all those tales of faeries doing terrible things to humans? What about the creatures who tricked humans into being imprisoned, serving faeries for eternity? Or...changelings?" Vy had decided to just go with it, it seemed there was nothing she could do to wake herself from this dream state.

Roselyn nodded, a look of shame on her face. "It is true, there are several species of faerie that are rather more mischievous than others; they revel in causing trouble and witnessing the consequences. That's where a large number of the villains in your fairy tales come from. Though, I guarantee it, there are far more good-natured faerie creatures than bad. We can discuss the different species at a later time. Right now, we must address magic and your ability to wield it"

"You said that only some can use it. Why is that," Vy asked. "Don't wizards have apprentices to whom they teach all of their spells?"

"Only those who have the spark of magic within them. Those who are not born with the magic inside of them would be unable to control it. There were many who attempted to teach humans how to use spells and enchantments, but this rarely ended well. Magic is incredibly powerful. It is, in essence, the energy of the world around us. Some are born with a connection to that energy and are gifted with the ability to use that energy for their own purposes. Those who are not born with that connection, well...trying to harness that energy and wield it would be devastating. The energy would be too much for their bodies and minds to handle.

That much borrowed energy, contained within a vessel that couldn't sustain it, would burn them up inside; they would either go mad or be killed by it; usually both."

Vy had discovered the golden liquid in the glass before her was some kind of honey wine, perhaps a mead. This certainly seemed like a great time to commence further alcohol consumption. "So, how did this epic war of yours end," she asked, taking a deep swig.

Rosalyn's lips pressed together in a thin line. It was obvious she could tell Vy didn't believe a word she was saying. Still, she continued with her story. "Well, the non-magics were being led by a terrible woman called Melarue. She fanned the flames of their discontent and they declared all-out war against us, attacking our people every chance they could. Eventually, we were forced to raise an army to face them. We met on a vast expanse of open field. Our own leader, Evelina, tried to explain to Melarue that much of her anger was due to the energy she had borrowed and stolen from magical beings who tried to teach her their ways, but she refused to listen. She demanded war and we were forced to give in to her." She paused for a sip of mead, less dainty and more needful than her previous intakes. It looked as though this conversation was driving her to drink, as well.

Meanwhile, this was starting to sound rather familiar to Vy, as it was rather reminiscent of the dream from which she'd awoken this morning. "There were many casualties on either side, so many needless deaths," continued Rosalyn. "In the end, Evelina and Melarue found each other on the field and though Evelina tried desperately to dissuade Melarue from her actions and to end the terrible war, Melarue was resolute. She demanded to fight Evelina, who, in the interest of peace and her people, was forced to consent. Their battle was fierce, and many stopped fighting to watch what transpired between them, knowing the future depended upon the outcome of their fight. They both mortally wounded each other and with her last breath Melarue spoke a curse, declaring she would return at a future time to finish what she had started." Vy was now completely enthralled by Rosalyn's words; this *was* her dream.

"With the speaking of that curse, she died. Not, however, before Evelina had made her way over to the woman. Evelina was caught in Melarue's spell before she too, succumbed to her wounds. Then both women disappeared from the battle field. We spent the next several years unraveling the spell Melarue had cast and began to understand that the two of them would one day return to us. And, if Melarue was reborn with the same kind of burning hatred in her heart, we knew we'd be facing battle once again."

Vy found she could no longer sit in silence and interjected the moment Rosalyn paused for breath. "I dreamt this." Everyone turned toward her and stared, causing her voice to take on a bit of a nervous tremor as she continued. "I had a dream last night that is so like what you just described. I can't remember most of it but some of the details that stuck with me…that's what happened." She noticed the faerie leader's lips begin to stretch into a small smile. "Why? Why did you just describe my dream?"

"That wasn't a dream, Viola. That was a memory. A memory buried deep in your subconscious, only available to you when the time was right."

"What are you saying?"

Rosalyn leaned into the table, staring intently into Viola's face. "Viola, the spirit, the energy, the very *essence* of Evelina resides within you. *You are Evelina.*"

CHAPTER FIVE

Viola was utterly flabbergasted. It seemed everyone around her had lost their minds, leaving her to deal with the real-world implications. And yet, this entire evening was becoming far too much to endure and with each passing moment she became more and more convinced that this wasn't the effects of something added to her drink. In which case, there were only two reasonable explanations for what was happening: either everyone around her had completely gone 'round the bend or everything they were saying was true.

"You're mad, all of you," she shrieked, looking around the table. "This is absolute, complete and total madness!" She pushed away from the table, determined to leave this place as quickly as possible, furious with her father, while simultaneously worried about his mental state. She heard him say her childhood nickname, attempting to stop her. "No, Dad. I'm gone." She heard a small pop as she pulled the door open revealing Rosalyn standing before her, smiling. "Wha?" Turning back, she looked toward the seat at the head of the table, where the woman was still sitting, wearing that same smile. "How..?"

Rosalyn smiled brightly, "I can do many things you've never seen before, Viola, and with some training you can do them, too. That," she said, nodding her head toward the door, where her image remained, "and so much more." Upon closer inspection, Vy could tell that the woman standing in the doorway before her wasn't real. There was a slight golden shimmering around her edges, as though she was being viewed on an old television screen. Vy watched as the shimmering intensified, the image flickered and began to fade away before her eyes. After a moment's hesitation, she turned back to face the dining room, meeting Rosalyn's gaze as she spoke. "Evelina was the most powerful of us all in her time. *You* are Evelina. When you have accepted this and learned to use your abilities properly, you will once again be infinitely powerful. Once you have achieved your potential, you will be able to take your rightful place as queen."

Overwhelmed and rather terrified, Vy sank into the nearest chair and was silent for several moments, contemplating. Before they had started with Shakespeare, her mother had read faerie stories to her when she was a child. While she had believed them then, spending her afternoons searching for evidence of their existence, her belief in all things magical had gradually ebbed away to nothing. School, work and adulthood had taken over and replaced all things magical and fantastic with things like rent, bills and wages per hour. Now, at twenty-six, she was seated in a room full of others who were far more experienced and knowledgeable than she, telling her that everything she had known to be true was false. She was struggling to believe it, but she had just witnessed Rosalyn disappear and reappear in front of her.

"I just…" she started then paused, reaching for just the right words. "This doesn't make sense. None of it makes any kind of sense. I have to be dreaming."

Her father's chair scooted against the hardwood flooring as he pushed away from the table and made his way over to her. Pulling a chair around to face her, he sat down, taking her hands in his own. "You're not dreaming. I know, Vy. This is quite a lot to take in. I had a difficult time accepting this when I first learned of this world's existence, but I assure you, everything she's saying is true. I don't have an ounce of magic in me, but your mother was quite the powerful faerie."

"Mum was a faerie?! Like…wings and everything?"

Nodding and chuckling, he said "Not all faeries have wings but yes, your mom had a set. She showed them to me a few times and they were iridescent and sparkled in the moonlight." His eyes drifted as he lost himself in wistful reminiscing. "They were beautiful. Most of the time they were hidden by use of a glamour, a sort of…enchantment faerie creatures can use to alter the perception of their appearance."

Vy studied her father's hands gently grasping her own while she processed, then turned toward Lady Rosalyn again. "Let's say I believe everything you're telling me. Hypothetically, of course. How do you know I'm this reincarnation of your faerie queen...thing?"

"Typically, magical ability doesn't manifest itself until around the ages of twelve to sixteen in humanoid magical beings. Only the most powerful will show signs of that ability from infancy. You were one of the few children throughout history who have displayed such signs."

"Not possible," Vy said, shaking her head and looking toward her father for validation. "I wasn't doing any crazy magic tricks or anything when I was a kid. So…guess I'm not your girl!" She gave them all a wry smile, knowing she'd finally proven them wrong and could get back to her normal life again.

"Well…actually…"

She swiveled her head to look toward her father, who was gazing sheepishly back at her. "When you were just a few days old, your mother walked into your nursery in the morning to find you spinning the butterfly mobile that hung above your crib. You were cooing happily and were slowly moving your tiny little hand in a circle in the air, controlling the speed of the mobile. Every few days we would find you doing that. As you learned to crawl, move around and play, you would make your teddy bears and dolls dance around in your play pen." He chuckled, reminiscing. "You thought it was hilarious. You'd giggle and giggle."

She stared at him in silence for a moment, disbelieving. "But what about later? When I was five, or seven, or ten? I don't remember *anything* weird or out of the ordinary."

"That's where we came in," Rosalyn piped up. "You see, only the strongest, most powerful magical beings display their ability at such an early stage of life. Magic usually manifests in one's teens or early twenties. When you began to exhibit signs of magic at such an extraordinarily young age, your parents brought you here. We soon realized that you were the reincarnation of Evelina. In order to keep you safe we crafted a special, homespun magic to keep your magic dormant for a while. A sort of," she paused, searching for the right words. "A kind of magical lock, let's say. But recently we've sensed that lock beginning to fail. And with our growing concerns surrounding Melarue and her attacks, we began sending a guard to keep an eye on your safety." At this she gestured to Vince.

Vy looked across the table to the young man, seated next to Fulrin. Both were sitting quietly, allowing her the space she needed to accept this overload of information. They both gave her a small, encouraging smile. She felt exhausted; mentally, physically and emotionally. It had been one hell of a day.

She pulled a hand from her father's, rested her elbow on the table and leaned her forehead against the palm of her hand. "This is just too much."

Lady Rosalyn stood, nodding and walked across the room toward them. "Quite right. Why don't I have Vince drive you both home? I'm sure you have quite a bit to discuss." Viola nodded, gratefully, as Rosalyn crouched beside her, arm around her shoulders. "Take some time to process this, then come back and we'll sort it out further. Perhaps on Monday. How does that sound?"

Viola wanted to say no; this was all just too bizarre, but looking into Rosalyn's open, kind face with her wide, trusting bright green eyes, she couldn't bring herself to do so. Instead, she nodded in silent affirmation.

Rosalyn smiled brightly and clapped her hands together. "Splendid!" She then went about arranging their transportation back home with Vince and for Viola's return visit on Monday. Rosalyn said she would have liked to get started right away but thought Vy would appreciate an extra day to cope and recover from the events of this evening. Throughout this discussion Vy remained seated, in an exhausted daze, nodding when she needed to do so but not doing much else, until it was time for them to leave. Rosalyn and Fulnir lead their party back to the front of the house and as she walked, Vy noticed that several people and creatures were poking their heads out of doors. She assumed they were all quite eager to catch a peek of their supposed returned queen. Some looked at her with abject awe, while others bore expressions she couldn't quite read. They seemed suspicious, irritated, perhaps even angry. She couldn't think why.

Pausing on the porch outside, she said, "I just have to ask one more question." Everyone turned to look at her, as she gestured toward the house and expansive garden. "What about all this? It should just look like an old run-down Victorian Inn."

"More magic," winked Vince, speaking for the first time in the past hour or so. "Anyone else who looks on this house will only see the decrepit old inn but if you've been touched by magic, the path to this realm will open itself up to you and grant you passage."

He had noticed when her eyebrows furrowed at the word, realm. "It's a bit complicated but where we are now is a sort of world within a world, almost like a mirror of the other side. Walking through the archway in the gardens allows you to walk from one reality to another. Many of the people you see here in the house tonight have lives on the other side. They've adapted over the years and have taken to living half of their lives as humans do; they have jobs, wear suits, go to the gym, have caffeine addictions and whatnot. But sometimes, they need to feel that connection to their own people, sometimes they need to get away from those skyscrapers, stressful jobs, busy cities; so, they come here, this tiny little bubble universe where they can remove their glamours and be who they truly are, without fear of scaring the locals to death."

"But it's hidden?"

"O' course," Fulrin piped up. "The last thing we be needin' is alla those non-magic folks findin' us and coming in ta bother us. Asking for wishes, spells, curses. Too much damn greed an' fightin' out there, I say! We don't need any o' that here!"

She smiled at him and had to admit that she found the dwarf to be quite charming, in his own way. "But suppose a *non-magic*," she said, adopting their term, "was to walk under the archway. Wouldn't they be able to get here?"

Vince shook his head. "They wouldn't walk beneath the arch. This particular glamour works in two ways. First, it hides the truth of what this place really is, and second, it instills a feeling of discomfort to any non-magics who might find themselves wandering along the estate. Basically, it makes them want to avoid the house. The magic is strongest near the arch but radiates outward, encompassing the grounds and the house, itself."

Vy pondered for a moment. "So…is that why it looks like it's home to murderers and vengeful ghosts?"

The entire group burst out laughing, Fulrin's deep guffaws the loudest of them all. Through their chuckling, both Vince and Rosalyn confirmed that her theory was correct; the seemingly dilapidated and dangerous façade of the house kept unwanted guests away from the area.

They said their goodbyes and the trio left the house, heading back through the beautifully lit gardens. As they neared the archway again, Vy felt butterflies take wing inside her stomach. Taking a deep breath, she shut her eyes tight, stepped through the archway and found her footing on the other side. Sure enough, when she opened her eyes, she was staring at the back of an old, neglected Victorian manor in desperate need of repair. Her father and Vince were standing a short way ahead of her, amused smiles on their faces as she collected herself. She quickly turned around, half expecting to see another Victorian on the other side of the archway, beautiful and crisp, well-tended, surrounded by the most beautiful of gardens. Rather, all she saw were more weeds, broken benches and a rotting wooden archway covered in overgrown vines. The only hint that something was off, was a slight shimmering around the edges of the archway, similar to that which she'd seen on Rosalyn's image earlier. She mentioned it and as they walked back in the direction of Vince's car, he explained that it was a sign indicating the presence of magic, only visible by those with a touch of magic in their blood.

   Vince drove them to her father's house on the other side of town. She had decided not to stay alone at her apartment tonight, after everything that had happened. There was silence in the car as they made their way through the early morning streets, but she didn't mind; she was a tad preoccupied. She thought of all she had learned of her mother, of her supposed former life, of the magic she'd witnessed. Those ancient curses terrified her. She wasn't entirely sure she wanted anything to do with this madness but also didn't see any way of escaping it, short of running away. She wouldn't do that. She didn't think so, anyway. As terrified and overwhelmed as she was by everything that had happened, there was another thought that kept pushing at the back of her mind, something that actually made her unbelievably happy: magic was real, and she was going to learn how to use it.

CHAPTER SIX

When Vy woke up the next morning, she was briefly shocked to find herself in her old bedroom. Even though she'd spent half her childhood and the entirety of her teenage years sleeping in this room, she'd quickly grown accustomed to sleeping in her apartment. Waking up to angry-looking musicians looking glaring back at her from the posters tacked all over the walls was slightly jarring. After adjusting to her surroundings, she shifted to lay on her other side, though she knew it was highly unlikely she'd be able to fall back to sleep. Upon waking her head was immediately filled with memories that rushed back to the forefront of her mind. Memories of dark, dingy alleys and sharp teeth, mixed with images of soft, flowing fabric and creatures out of a fantasy novel. She pressed her palms to her eyes and rubbed the sleep from them, hoping the memories would disappear along with it. Perhaps, she hoped, when she opened her eyes again, she would find herself in her apartment bedroom and those memories, both good and bad, would have been from the influence of some movie or book to which she had fallen asleep.

Nope. Those angsty musicians in their black clothes were still there, frowning at her from the walls. She knew it probably wouldn't happen, but part of her had still hoped it might work. Resting her forearm across her eyes, she tried to block out the light and considered staying in bed for another hour or two before finally dragging herself back into this new reality. At that moment, however, the smell of brewing coffee found its way under the door and began to permeate the air in her old room. Charles Campbell took his coffee very seriously, roasting and grinding the beans himself, and the smell of the fresh coffee was intoxicating. And was that…bacon? She sniffed and her stomach grumbled in response. Time to get up, she thought to herself. Her dad's breakfasts were always amazing, and Heaven knows she needed the caffeine. Throwing off the covers, she pulled on the clothes she'd worn yesterday and pulled her hair back into a loose ponytail. Less than five minutes later she padded her way into the kitchen.

"Hey, Vy-vy! Breakfast is almost ready so go ahead and take a seat." Charles was in the middle of flipping eggs over in the skillet. Vy poured herself a cup of coffee, raided the fridge for creamer and grabbed the dish of cooked bacon from the counter, taking both over to the table in the corner of the kitchen. Her dad had already deposited plates and utensils on the table, so she added a couple slices of bacon to her plate and sipped her coffee as she waited for her dad to make his way over. She wondered what their morning conversation would be like. Either way, it wouldn't be a very long chat, as the bookstore opened in an hour and a half and her father needed to leave in a half hour to get things ready to open.

Two short minutes later, he approached the table bearing a platter of eggs, his homemade hash brown potatoes, and toast in one hand and a jar of apricot preserves in the other, Vy's favorite kind of jam. After setting them on the table, he darted back into the kitchen to grab his own coffee mug then returned to sit down and eat.

"Been a while since we had a proper breakfast together, eh?" He was obviously trying to ease the awkward silence growing between them.

"Yeah, this is great." She smiled back at him, reassuringly. Any minute now he would eventually address the events of last night. She was torn. On the one hand she wanted to know more. On the other, she still hoped it was a dream conjured by an over stimulated and inebriated imagination. They both put a little bit of everything on their plates. As Vy was spreading the preserves across a slice of toast, her father finally broke the silence.

"Listen, Vy." He paused, trying to find the right words. Here we go, she thought. "I hope you're not mad about my not telling you who you really are. Your Mum and I agreed that we would tell you everything when you were ready."

Vy started at this, her egg-laden fork paused a centimeter away from her mouth. "And you waited until now? I mean…I'm in *grad school*, Dad!"

"I know, I know." He sighed. "I guess part of me hoped Rosalyn was wrong about you; that you could have a normal life."

They chewed on their breakfast slowly and silently for a few moments, giving Vy a chance to think.

"How long have you known," she asked.

"You were two. Your Mum had gone to the store for a couple of things and I'd stayed home with you. You were sitting on the living room floor, completely enthralled by *Sesame Street* or *Eureka's Castle* or something like that. I got up to take dinner out of the oven. I was gone…not even two minutes. And when I came back you had toddled over to the plant we had in the corner of the living room. It was just a small fern, but you were playing with the leaves and I watched as tiny little flower buds started to sprout along the leaves you were touching." He chuckled softly. "I knew what it was of course, that it was magic. The night I proposed your mother told me what she was."

"That didn't freak you out?"

"I thought she was joking. Then she performed some magic for me and turned off her glamor, exposing her wings. There was no way I could deny it after that." He paused, smiling at the memory. "And yes, I definitely freaked out. I hurried home and didn't talk to her for several hours. But in the end, Vy, I loved your mother more than any discomfort I might have felt at her abilities.

"And when we found out we were pregnant with you, we discussed the possibility of you inheriting her magic. Relationships between magics and non-magics do happen, and they are beginning to happen more often. Sometimes the children of these matches exhibit magical ability. And sometimes they don't."

"So, it could have gone either way with me." She'd managed to finish her breakfast while he'd been talking and was now slowly working on the last of her coffee, enjoying the warmth from the mug beneath her cool palms.

"Right. But after you made the mobile move while you were in your crib, we knew you'd inherited your mother's abilities. After the fern incident she knew something was different about you and it began to worry her. Enough that your mother insisted we take you to Rosalyn, so she could look at you."

"Why? I would think she'd be happy I'd inherited her abilities."

He claimed the last slice of bacon and chewed on it in between sentences. "Well, as your mother explained to me, magic might make brief appearances in early childhood but it's usually small things. Making your mobile move on its own was one thing but making plants grow and flower was slightly more advanced magic. Far too advanced for a two-year-old, anyway."

"Why is that?" She supposed she should start learning as much as she could about this magic thing, since apparently it was part of her life now.

He shrugged as he took a swig of coffee to wash down the bacon. "Not entirely sure but I think it's something to do with the level of development in the brain and body. By the age of ten or twelve, you've developed a solid understanding of the world around you and about that time you also start maturing physically. The magic just sort of...pops up along with the rest of that."

"I suppose that makes sense," she mused. "So, what did you do then, if you were having concerns about it?"

"As I said, after the fern incident we took you to Rosalyn. She and the wisest members of her council looked you over, had you perform a few tests; they took a bit of blood, coerced you into displaying your ability, used magic to detect any anomalies in you and…" He paused here, his eyes wandering away from her face.

"And?"

"And everything pointed to you being the reincarnation of their leader, Evelina," he said, sighing. "Something about your magical signature being a match for hers. To be perfectly honest, I'm not sure I understand it all. There's a kind of science to their magic that is beyond me."

After several silent beats, Charles sighed deeply, placed his utensils on his plate and looked toward her with a most serious expression. "There's something else I need to tell you, Vy. Something about your mother." He ran a hand over his stubbled face before beginning. "Vy, your mom…she wasn't sick. She was taken. Most likely by Melarue's forces."

Viola had been in the middle of a sipping on coffee when this announcement came, and she choked on it for a few moments before being able to speak "What?!"

He nodded, sheepishly. "I'm sorry I never told you. You were just so young when it happened, and I couldn't bring myself to lay all of this on top of the loss of your mother."

"How?" Vy was struggling to form strings of words but single words seemed easy enough and still got her point across.

"She was out shopping. You and I had stayed home because you were sick with a cold. When she didn't come home, I bundled you up and we went out to search for her. We looked for hours, then went home, in the hopes that she'd made it back while we were out. When she wasn't home by dinner time, I called the police. They searched for days and could find nothing, then suddenly, probably a week later, she was found in the river. The police said she must have gone for a walk and fell into the water, but I knew that couldn't be the case.

"Soon after that, Rosalyn sent a messenger to us. A pixie tapped on our window one evening and told me that your mother had been attacked. We weren't sure exactly by whom, chances are Melarue was already sending out forces trying to find you. So, I decided it was safer for us to move here, closer to Rosalyn and the other magics. I wanted to make sure you would be safe. I couldn't lose you, too."

They sat in silence for several moments, Vy attempting to process as she nursed the last dregs of coffee, her father doing the same. Eventually, she forced herself to speak. "I don't blame you, Dad. I understand why you would want to keep that from me. It would have been far too much for me to handle at that age."

He let out a deep sigh of relief and Vy realized he'd been holding his breath.

"I'm glad you finally told me, though. I'd rather know the truth about what happened." She paused for another moment, deciding to move on with present-day concerns. "Do I really have to fight this Melarue person?"

"I don't know," he said, running a hand through his graying hair. "Rosalyn, her council…even your mother, after your identity had been revealed, seemed to think so. But Vy-Vy," he said, reaching across the table to take hold of her hand. "This is all your choice. You don't *have* to do anything. If you want, you can forget all of this and just walk away; have a normal life. But should you decide to do this, you won't be alone. You know that, right? I'll be there with you every step of the way. Along with everyone else you met at the house last night, plus the others who live in the town. You don't have to do *any* of this by yourself."

"Okay, Dad." She tried to sound more confident and accepting than she felt but she wasn't sure if the attempt was successful. Fortunately, before he could say anything else, his cell phone alarm went off, signaling that it was time for him to leave for work. "Oh, dammit! How is it this late already?!"

"Time flies when you're having fun, as they say," she said, trying to laugh it all off and break the tension. "Don't worry, I'll take care of this." She gestured to the table laden with their dirty breakfast dishes. "Then I'll head home to shower and grab some clothes and be at the store to work. Probably around ten, if that's okay?"

"Of course." He headed for the door, stopping to slip his coat over his frame. "You okay, Vy?"

"It's a lot to take in but I'll be fine, Dad. Promise." She smiled at him with a confidence she didn't feel, until he felt reassured and left for the store. She picked up all the dishes from the table and placed them in the sink, along with the dishes he'd used to cook. She'd wash them as quickly as she could then head home. Had it really only been 24 hours since she'd left her apartment to head to school? It felt like weeks.

CHAPTER SEVEN

A pile of ungraded essays lay forgotten on a corner of Viola's desk as she scoured the university's online library search engine, looking for anything she could find regarding faerie tales and magic. The majority of texts available in the university library were fantasy novels or art books. Surprisingly, there were also a few faerie-themed role-playing game books. Scattered throughout the mostly unhelpful results were a few gems which contained detailed descriptions of various creatures she had never bothered to pay much attention to in the past. After the conversation with her dad on Saturday, she had decided that if she was going to be part of this world, she should educate herself on every facet of it. Just as she was about to view a digital edition of a book promising ways to protect yourself from mischievous fey folk, she heard a loud crash as someone burst into the room behind her.

"Where the hell have you been, Shakespeare?!" Liz had given Viola this nickname the first day they met, after she'd spoken her name and told how her mother had chosen it based on her favorite play by the Bard.

Viola turned around to look her friend in the eye and was taken aback by her appearance. Liz had the dark circles of someone who had barely slept the previous night. Her hair was pulled back into a hasty ponytail, wisps of black hair escaping and dangling by the sides of her face. The black smudges around her eyes indicated she had slept in her eyeliner.

"Hey Liz! What are you doing here?" She quickly minimized her browser to hide her research. "I didn't think anyone would be around campus today!" Until she'd arrived at the near-empty university this morning, she'd completely forgotten that this particular Monday was a campus-wide day off so students could study for their finals. Though, more than likely, most of them were drinking and partying heavily rather than studying.

"What do you mean? What the hell are *you* doing here?! This is a day of sleeping in and drinking Bloody Mary's in the hope of getting over your weekend hangovers," she whined, flopping into a chair at the desk beside Viola's. She leaned back in the chair and rested her head against the wall. "I went by your apartment, didn't see your car so I drove by the book shop. Finally figured you must have been here, of all places."

"Why didn't you just call or text?"

Liz lifted her head to look pointedly at Vy. "Check your bloody phone."

Vy pulled her phone from her pocket to see it had been set to silent and that she had missed five calls and around a dozen texts from Liz. "Oh. Uh....sorry?"

"Sorry?! What happened to you on Friday? I expected graphic details of your passionate night with tall, dark and handsome! I was rather disappointed, to be honest."

Vy closed the cover of her laptop and began packing everything, computer and essays, back into her bag. "Nothing happened." She had prepared a lie for Liz, not expecting her friend to believe the truth of what actually happened. "We got into separate cabs and went to our own homes."

"Wha-at??!!!" Liz threw her arms into the air in exasperation. "What the hell happened?! You two were making eyes at each other the entire time! When I left to meet Liam, you were enthralled with each other. I expected more, dammit!"

"I dunno...I guess we just didn't click quite as well as I would have liked?"

"Ugh!" Liz seemed deeply disappointed with the whole situation. "Well, we can go out again this coming weekend. Maybe he'll be there again, and you'll hit it off better, or we can find you a new man." She paused for a moment. "Shame, though. Liam said he thought the guy seemed cool."

"Oh, ho! And how is Liam? You two have a good time the other night," she asked, latching her bag, grateful for the chance of topic. "I noticed I didn't receive a text from you at all yesterday. And I was home all day!" She'd slept late on Sunday and spent the day in her apartment, still trying to process. Her dad had called her and they'd talked a bit more but she'd just needed some time alone to think.

"Well...I didn't do anything remotely resembling work all weekend, so there's that." Liz pushed herself out of the chair with great effort. "Honestly, I'm a bit sore."

"Well, that was rather more than I needed to know," Vy said. Liz grinned back at her wickedly. "Please, spare me the details." She shouldered her messenger bag and both girls started toward the office door.

"Vy, I think I really like this guy," she said. "I mean, he's hot, funny, smart. He's studying marine biology, y'know. Absolutely loves water. Y'know, we got into the shower this morning and-"

"That is *quite* enough of that, thank you!" Vy was now exceedingly thankful for the study day and a nearly empty building. She could feel the color rise slightly on her cheeks, despite the silent hallway. Liz had a habit of not caring what she said around other grad students. Or anyone else, for that matter. Vy, on the other hand, didn't like drawing any more attention to herself than was necessary.

"Oh, come on, Vy! I'm just dying to tell you about it! My God, you should've seen his -"

"NOPE! Done! So very done."

Liz let out a cackle which reverberated through the empty corridor. "You're too much fun. Anyway, Liam and I are heading to The Lobster Trap down by the waterfront. Can you believe this kid has lived here for three years and hasn't tried lobster yet?"

"Terrible. What kind of Mainer is he?"

"Right?! That's what I said! Do you want to come with us? They have those bacon-wrapped scallops you're mad for." Liz was digging deep into her violently red purse, searching for her car keys.

"I'd love to, Liz, but unfortunately I have plans today."

"You never have plans for Mondays. *No one* does anything on Mondays. What are you on about," Liz asked, looking puzzled.

"Yeah, I know. Dad asked me to go over and have lunch with him today. It's been a year but I think he's still struggling with the adjustment of me moving into my own place. Empty nest and all, y'know?"

"You two could join Liam and I," Liz suggested.

Vy looked at her pointedly. "Yes, because I want to bring my dad on a super weird, super awkward double date thing where you and your new man are feeding each other bits of sea creatures and sucking the melted butter off each other's fingers. Hard pass!"

"Meh," she grumbled. "Fine. Figures your dad wants his little girl to spend time with him just after I finally meet a decent guy in a bar." The jingling of her keys as she liberated them from the deep, dark depths of her purse filled the quiet hall with a few seconds of tinkling music. "Well, I want you to meet him properly sometime. You'll like him! And maybe we can find someone for-"

BANG!!

A cry of pain rang out as she kicked open the heavy door of the building, only to have it swing into a young man on the outside, who immediately doubled over, clutching his face.

"Oh, holy shit! Monty, I'm so sorry! Are you okay?!" Liz and Viola both rushed forward to come to the man's aid.

"Hnn ug fuum wiz!" With his hands over his face, his words were terribly muffled and distorted. The girls each had their hand on one of his shoulders, ready to help with whatever he might need.

"Sorry? What was that," Liz asked, gently.

"Ugh!" He pulled his hands away from a very red and painful looking nose before repeating what he'd said. "What the fuck, Liz?!"

"I know! I'm so sorry! The whole campus is empty, so I didn't expect anyone to be out here! Is it broken?! It isn't bleeding, is it?! Are your glasses okay?! Can we do anything to help?!" Liz was speaking frantically, very quickly and in a particularly high-pitched voice. Evidently, the more concerned she was, the higher in pitch her voice became. Liz and the man confirmed that his nose wasn't bleeding and was not, in fact, broken. It just hurt like hell. Concerned as she was with his well-being, Vy couldn't help but notice the looks of the man in front of her. She had never seen a man so beautiful. His dark hair was arranged in the tousled style so popular nowadays, looking slightly messy but simultaneously gorgeous and put-together. There was a faint shadow of stubble along his chin and jawline. He wore a dark blue and white checkered button-up shirt under a dark blue suit jacket, complete with pink bow tie, slim-fitted jeans and black shoes. A pair of thick-framed black glasses rested on his nose. And his eyes. Vy was losing herself in those eyes. They were an icy shade of blue that made her run both hot and cold at the same time. She had no idea who he was but, as cliché as it sounded in her own head, she'd happily drown in those icy blue pools forever.

"Mission Control to Viola! Come in Viola!"

She realized suddenly that Liz had been talking to her. "What?! Sorry, I was...somewhere else."

"Yeah...evidently. Do you have any Advil or Tylenol or anything?

Vy thought for a moment. She was feeling incredibly jittery with this man standing so near her, it made connecting coherent thoughts rather difficult. "Yes, actually, I believe I do have something." She rummaged through her purse for a moment or two before pulling out a half-empty bottle of pain relievers. Opening it, she dumped several pills into the palm of her hand and held them out to the man. "Here you go!"

"Thanks, I appreciate it." His voice was deep and velvety. Viola felt herself melt into a puddle as he gratefully took the pills from her hand.

"No problem," she said, rather breathily.

Liz looked at her strangely for a moment, took in all the information she needed from Vy's facial expression, then raised one knowing eyebrow. "Viola, this is Montgomery Stevens. He's a grad student in the history department. Monty, this is my good mate, Viola Campbell; she's in English."

Montgomery stretched out his hand to shake hers. "Viola, huh? Like from *Twelfth Night*."

Gorgeous and he knew Shakespeare. Vy tried not to allow the thoughts and feelings starting to nudge at her to fill her brain. No. No, this was a bad idea, don't even start. "Exactly, yes. My mother had a bit of an obsession with Shakespeare."

"One that she passed down to her kid," Liz interjected. Monty looked at her rather quizzically.

"Uh, yes." *Girl, what the hell is wrong with you*, she screamed at herself internally. "Yes, I'm...studying Shakespeare."

His smile was warm and dazzling. "What a coincidence," he offered. "My area of research happens to be Elizabethan England."

"Oh, wow! That's great!" She could feel Liz's eyes darting back and forth between them as they spoke. There was a moment of semi-awkward silence and smiling between them before he took the initiative to break it.

"Well, I should probably go take a couple of these," he said, gesturing to the pills in his hand, "and get to work on the essay for Sawyer tomorrow."

Liz gasped beside them. "Oh, bloody hell, I completely forgot about that. I have about ten more pages to write!"

"Better get on it, then," he chuckled. "Sawyer grades harshly enough without papers being late." He turned back to Viola again. "We should meet up sometime and talk about all things

English and Shakespearean. The coffee on campus is terrible but there's a great little coffee shop down on Main Street. They make pretty decent soup and sandwiches, too."

The butterflies fluttering in her stomach began dancing a tango. "Yes, absolutely. I'd love that. Uh, my office is on the first floor, room 102."

"Great! I'll stop by sometime."

"I look forward to it," she smiled. "It was nice meeting you, Montgomery, though I apologize for the unfortunate circumstances leading up to it." *About damn time you actually construct a proper sentence*, she thought.

Laughing, he replied, "not exactly my favorite way of meeting people, no, but it was memorable, so there's that! It was wonderful to meet you, Viola. And please, call me Monty. Most everyone else does. Montgomery sounds like the grand title of a stuffy old man." He smiled down at her for a moment then stepped to her left side, heading toward the door. After a few steps, he turned back, saying, "see you in class, Liz. And learn how to open a door in the future, eh?" He smiled at Vy once more before heading inside the building. Vy watched him go until he was lost in the shadows of the dimly lit hallway, then turned back to Liz, who was standing with her arms crossed in front of her chest, one eyebrow raised, and the left corner of her mouth drawn up into a smirk.

"What?"

"Oooh...nothing, nothing at all." Her smirk widened into a grin. "Just looks like ol' Nate from the other night has been forgotten."

Vy snorted, rolled her eyes and turned away, walking toward the parking lot. "Oh, bullshit!"

"Bullshit nothing, woman!" Liz jogged to catch up to her. "You were like a dog staring at a thick, juicy cut of steak back there. I might have to call the caretaker to clean up the drool you left on the ground. Someone might slip and break their neck!"

"Okay, fine," Vy snapped. "Yes, he is freaking gorgeous! But I'm not ready to get involved with anyone again after that last asshat. Besides, he probably barely took notice of me anyway, so it doesn't even matter!"

"Vy, he asked you to lunch. Did you not notice this?"

"To talk about research. It's not like it's a date or anything."

Liz snorted, furrowing her eyebrows in Vy's direction. "Girl, you are just not confident enough in yourself. Let me tell you something about Montgomery Stevens," she said, as they neared their two vehicles. "He just spoke more words to you than he's spoken to anyone in the entire history department. He's the kind of guy who doesn't want to deal with people unless they're worth bothering with and you, my dear, were just invited out to lunch with him. So, start feeling awesome about yourself!" Vy was completely speechless, filled with shock at the lecture from her friend, and with the giddy joy that only comes from a new crush. "Okay," Liz started, "I need to go meet Liam and finish an essay, and *you* need to go see your dad and tell him about your soon to be boy-toy." She popped her keys into her driver's side door and continued, before Vy had the time to open her mouth in protest. "Have a good time with your dad and tell him I said hi. I'll see you tomorrow, hot stuff!" With that she launched herself into her car and shut the door, knowing Vy was still working on a response. She grinned and waved madly as she drove out of her parking spot.

  Vy waved back, feeling rather conflicted after what Liz had just told her. Monty was unbelievable gorgeous, interested in the same historical period as she was, and she was certain that buttery voice of his could lull raging grizzly bears into a peaceful calm. However, her last relationship had not ended well, and, not to mention, the last guy she'd shown interest in had turned out to be a shapeshifter that had nearly killed her. She wasn't entirely sure she wanted to jump into that madness again. As she also got into her vehicle, she couldn't help feeling a wave of guilt wash over her, drowning out the thoughts of her non-existent love life. She hated lying to her best friend. It was a terrible feeling, but she didn't see how she could tell Liz the truth without sounding completely insane. Heaving a deep sigh, she started the engine and pulled out of the parking lot, heading not toward her father's house, or the book shop, but to the other side of town, toward Sugar Maple Inn.

CHAPTER EIGHT

Viola parked her car in the shadows of the overgrown trees which edged the driveway, locking her doors after ensuring her computer bag was tucked safely into her trunk. She made the trek passed the old house which, during daylight, managed to look only slightly less ominous than it had two days before. She paused for a moment, closing her eyes and trying to settle the familiar fluttering in the pit of her stomach, before stepping through the archway. Opening her eyes again, she stared open-mouthed at the garden on the other side. In the darkness the other night, she had been unable to see just what an expanse of land made up the grounds of the estate. The garden was just as beautiful as it had been the first time she had seen it, though she missed the colorful glowing lights that must only be present in the dark of night, but beyond the gardens was a large, green field, surrounded entirely by a lush wood that seemed to go on for miles. She made a mental note to go exploring at the earliest opportunity.

After marveling at the landscape for a minute or two, she walked the rest of the way up to the door and rang the bell. Fulrin answered and welcomed her back warmly. "Miss Viola," he said, bowing deeply, "come in, please!" They exchanged pleasantries and she agreed to follow him. He led her a short distance down the hall toward a door on the right. As they passed by doorways in the hall, she once again saw several creatures seated or milling about inside. A few of them looked up as they walked by, some with expressions of awe or curiosity, yet others seemed to look at her with suspicion, as they had during her first trip through the house. At least, she hoped it was just suspicion. She frowned, bewildered, and started to speak to them, to ask what was wrong, but they turned away and went back to what they were doing. She shook her head and pushed it from her mind. Beyond the door where Fulrin led her, was a beautiful room with love seats and chairs arranged so they faced a white fireplace. Two small dark wooden tables stood in between a chair and a love seat. The upholstery and curtains were of a soft burgundy which matched well with the green wallpaper and Oriental rug on the floor, white vines curling around its edges.

Seated in one of the love seats was Rosalyn, her deep purple dress fanned out across the upholstery, her blond hair piled on top of her head in dozens of ringlets. Her smile immediately brightened the room as she greeted Viola. "I hope you're doing well today. I'm so happy you came back." Vy nodded and smiled, unsure of what to say. Rosalyn smiled back and rang for tea, which was brought in momentarily. "I hope you and Charles had a good talk about all of this," she said, gesturing to the room.

"A little bit. We didn't have a whole lot of time, but we'll get together again to discuss it some more." She breathed in the warm aroma of the fruity tea. She wasn't entirely sure what it was, perhaps pomegranate or raspberry but it was warm and comforting, which is everything tea should be. "I must admit, this is all still a bit messy and a lot to handle but I'm working on coming to terms with everything."

Rosalyn nodded, suggesting that she understood. "It *is* quite a lot to take in, but we are all here to help you absorb everything. As a matter of fact," she began with a small smile on her lips, "today I'm going to introduce you to someone. He is one of our wonderful instructors who teaches everyone who is new to magic usage. He should be here any moment."

"What kind of magic will I be able to do?"

"It is rather difficult to list off all the possibilities and limitations of magic. Every individual has their own strengths and weaknesses. There are those, like your instructor, who have spent many, many years studying magic and how different people react to its presence, whether there is a link between magical specialties and races, gender and so forth."

"It sounds very much like our kinds of science. I didn't realize magic was like that."

"Oh yes, there's much more to it than you realize. For instance -." She was cut short at the sound of the door opening. Into the room walked a young man, who, Vy realized, must be an elf, for he had the classic look of otherworldly beauty, gracefulness and long, pointed ears. His hair was like silver moonlight and he kept it long and rather unkempt. He wore simple clothing, a loose white tunic and brown tweed pants, both held close to his middle with a belt of brown leather. Viola felt as though she'd been dropped into the middle of a Tolkien novel.

"Ah, there you are! Viola, this is Tamnaeuth. He will be your new magic instructor," she exclaimed, beaming.

The youth smiled and gave Viola a deep and graceful bow. "Pleasure to meet you, my Lady. I am honored to be your teacher."

"Nice to meet you, as well, Tam...Tamen..Tarm." She struggled to form his name on her lips, feeling incredibly embarrassed. She felt awful, but he was chuckling brightly.

"Do not feel badly, my lady. My name can be hard to pronounce for those who are not accustomed to the elven tongue. Please, call me Tam if it is easier for you."

"I'm so, so sorry. I'll try to work on that but thank you, I'll use Tam for the time being."

"As you wish, my lady." He turned toward Rosalyn and bowed to her, as well. "If you are finished, I am ready to start Lady Viola's lesson." he said, bowing once more.

"Absolutely, Tamnaueth. She is yours!" Rosalyn put her hand on Vy's shoulder. "I wish you good luck with your first lesson, Viola. Come back to see me when you've finished, and we shall arrange a time for your next lesson."

Viola followed Tam out the door, though she had no idea where they were headed. She assumed they would be going to another room in the house but instead Tam led her down the hallway and out the door, heading into the gardens beyond.

"Where are we going," she asked.

"You can't learn magic inside," he said. The best classroom is outside."

"Why is that?"

"Magic is intrinsically tied to nature. Essentially, it is the energy of the world in which we live. Every living thing on the planet has an energy of sorts. Call it what you will; essence, spirit, it is all the same. That energy is what makes up the basis of what we refer to as magic." They were now walking through the edge of the gardens, heading out into the large, green lawn. "When we use magic, we are borrowing the energy of the world around us. We use that energy to make it do something different or create something new."

"But if you continue to borrow, doesn't it take away the essence of everything? How do those things you borrow from continue to live?"

He smiled at her. "An excellent question! I can see you will make a very intelligent and curious student. Fortunately, after the expelling of that energy, spell, enchantment, whichever word you would prefer, has been fulfilled, we release the energy and let it return to its original source. In more familiar terms to you, the energy is a renewable resource. It can never run out so long as there are living things on this earth and so long as we return the energy from whence it came."

"Not that I would ever do this, but what happens if you don't return the energy?" Vy thought she already knew the answer to this but wanted to hear it aloud, just the same.

Something dark flashed briefly across Tam's face before he softened, no doubt understanding that she was unused to this and just trying to learn. "If the source of the energy goes without it for too long, it will wither and die. That's why we always make sure to return what we use before a full day has passed."

They continued walking as Viola pondered this new information. When they had moved some distance away from the gardens and further onto the lawn, Tam stopped and turned to face her. "Here is where we will have our first lesson." They were surrounded on all sides by the greenest grass she had ever seen. It was full and lush, and all she wanted to do was kick off her sneakers and walk barefoot, to feel the blades of grass tickling her feet. Thick woods lay beyond them on three sides, with the Inn behind them. "Now, I'm going to make a small plant grow here in this field. You watch me to see what I do and observe what happens."

"Okay, sounds good," she replied, wondering if she should have brought along a notebook. She hadn't thought about taking notes on magic. Perhaps, if she needed, she could make a quick run back to her car.

"Okay, here we go." He took a few steps away from her and stood completely still. Focusing his gaze on the ground in front of him, he stretched out his hands, palms down. Closing his eyes, he seemed to focus all of his attention, concentrating very hard on whatever he was trying to do. After a moment or two, she felt the hairs on the back of her arms begin to stand up. It was very slight and if she hadn't been paying such close attention to everything, she might have missed it. Suddenly, the tiniest of green shoots began to slowly emerge from the ground. Then, it was a tiny stem of a plant, then the next moment it had formed a bud. Within a matter of seconds, the bud had opened into the most beautiful flower she had ever seen. It resembled a tiger lily, with its six petals open and fanned out wide, but she'd never seen a tiger lily with those colors before. Each petal was a light orange at its base, where it met the pistil. The outer edges darkened to a fiery red-orange, which surrounded a deep purple in the middle.

Tam lowered his hands, looked back up at her and smiled widely. "Well, what just happened?"

Vy struggled to find words. "Honestly…I have no idea, but it was wicked!"

"That's magic," he quipped, grinning. "Did you notice anything?"

She thought for a moment, contemplating what she had just seen and felt. "Well, the hairs on my arms and the back of my neck stood up."

"Excellent," he commented. "And what do you think that means?"

"Um...I guess...maybe that was the energy? I could feel it?"

She didn't think it was possible, but his smile widened even further. "Exactly! As one who can wield magic, you are more in tune with how that energy feels and behaves, even if you haven't yet wielded it with your own power. When someone near you is manipulating that energy, you will sense it. I assume the feeling was very slight, even weak?" She nodded in affirmation of his words. "That is normal. You're still very new to this, even in knowing of its existence. As you learn more and get used to how this energy feels and how it reacts to your nudging, you'll become more sensitive to it."

"How long does it last," she asked, gesturing to the flower.

"Ah, another good question. The duration of a manifestation, to use a common word, depends on how much energy you put into it. This flower will only last a few minutes more as I didn't put much into its creation. Something larger, requiring more magic will last longer. Growing a tree, for instance, requires much more concentration and energy and will last for several hours, at least."

She nodded, looking toward the flower, the colors of which already seemed a bit faded. "Is it possible to grow something and make it last forever or at least years?"

"Of course, though it takes a very strong magic user and vast amounts of energy, which must be moving in a constant circle to the magic user, then back to the source, and so forth. I know of only a dozen or so throughout history who have been strong enough to maintain such a circle." He let her think about that for a few moments before moving on to the next part of his lesson. "Now, let's have you give it a try."

Her head whipped around as she stared at him sharply. "What? No, no, I don't think I can..."

"You'll never learn if you don't try, my lady." He smiled warmly at her.

"Nnngg…okay, that's fair. What do I have to do?" She was not at all sure about this. Honestly, she still wasn't sure she entirely believed she had this ability inside of her. She didn't have any memories about the story her father had told her, and she had no memory of any similar incidents. She still felt…exceedingly ordinary.

"What you need to do first is decide what you want to create. This," he said, gesturing to the blossom that was now starting to wilt," is an incredibly rare flower and its creation requires an experienced magic user. So, we'll focus on something you're more familiar with, at least for now. Close your eyes and think of your favorite flower. Picture it within your mind, in perfect detail. Think of how it smells, the colors and shape of the petals, the way it sits on its stem." He quieted and allowed her several moments to imagine the flower in her mind. When it felt long enough, he began again. "Are you ready? Can you picture it?"

"Yes," she nodded. "What's next?"

"Now, you want to stand in a position that is most comfortable for you. I recommend standing with your feet placed shoulder-width apart. It allows for the best possible balance and gives you a stable center of gravity." He demonstrated the stance for her and helped her perfect it. "Good. Next, pick a spot on the ground in front of you where you want to grow your flower. Focus on it, ignore absolutely everything else."

Viola found a small and particularly green patch of grass just in front of her and stared at it intently. She didn't have much faith that anything would happen, but she was going to try, just the same.

"The secret to performing magic is to draw that energy we talked about into yourself. To do this you just envision that energy flowing into you from the trees, the grass, or the water. All you need is deep concentration. Envision that energy, picture it in any way you like, a stream of energy flowing into you. Now, picture that energy moving through your body, into your arms, down to your fingertips. Stretch your hands over the spot you picked out."

Viola stretched her arms out over the ground just as he had done minutes before, with her palms face down.

"Perfect. Now, see that energy flowing from your fingertips out into the air. Focus it and picture it moving down into the ground, taking root and forming a tiny seed. Picture that seed opening, a tiny sprout emerging from inside of it, pushing itself upwards toward the surface of the earth. All the while keep in mind the image of your flower. Remember the colors, the smell, the shape of the petals."

The sound of his voice and his words were comforting, and Vy felt her nervousness beginning to melt away. She resolved to take this task seriously and put effort into its execution. "Imagine that tiny sprout, reaching for the sunlight. Picture it pushing its way out of the earth, a tiny bit more of green added to the landscape. Imagine a bud forming on top of the stem, and that bud slowly opens into your favorite blossom." Everything was silent for a few moments as Viola continued to concentrate, focusing everything she could on making that flower grow. After a minute or two, Tam continued to provide her with verbal encouragement. "Concentrate. Imagine it all in your mind and you'll make it happen."

     Viola was trying her best, concentrating just as hard as she possibly could. She chose to imagine the energy as a shimmering golden thread, winding its way from the trees, moving across the field and into her own body, then exiting from her outstretched fingers to coax the flower into blooming. Now that she thought about it, she wasn't entirely sure if she knew every step of a flower's germination process. Maybe she was missing something or not concentrating on the right things. Doubt began to wiggle its way into her mind and, making her think this really was all a mistake. Perhaps she was still dreaming. Perhaps the dream she'd had a couple of nights ago was still going on and she would wake up soon and have to go to school. Sweat began to bead on her brow as she felt her temperature rise a few degrees. Who knew concentrating on a tiny bit of plant life could be so difficult and draining? Just as she was about to give up and accept the fact that this was all complete nonsense, a tiny, *tiny* little green sprout broke the surface of the ground. She gasped, not believing what she was seeing. The green sprout had one tiny little leaf on it. It stopped reaching upwards to the sky, sat still for a moment, and then disappeared. She glared at the ground in frustration.

"What happened?!" She looked up from the ground to meet his eyes, worried she had disappointed her teacher with this failure.

But the look on his face indicated the exact opposite. He was smiling widely, nearly giddy with happiness. "You did very, very well, my lady! For your first-time using magic that was exceptional! Not many creatures could manage to do what you have just done on their first try!"

"But it didn't grow. The flower didn't bloom. It just…disappeared."

"You can't expect to grow a rose bush on your first day. You are still so very new to this whole idea. We'll give you a few minutes to rest and I'm sure you will do better on your second try." He paused for a moment, that smile not wavering for an instance. "I'm very impressed. You will be a promising student."

She thought for a moment. "I assume you know…who I am? Supposedly?"

"I do," he replied, nodding. "We all do. You're the reincarnation of Queen Evelina." The words fell from his tongue as if it was the most natural thing in the world.

"Well…if I'm this great faerie queen, shouldn't I be able to do this without struggling?"

The smile he gave her was bright, kind and caring. "It's true, in your former life you were incredibly powerful. And you'll get there again, but not yet. Right now, you're still Viola Campbell, who just discovered that the world she knew is so much bigger and more amazing than she realized." At this he gestured to the grounds around them and she followed his gaze. She suddenly noticed that what she had mistaken for various insects flying about the field, were far too large. One came close and she could see a small, humanoid shaped creature. Some kind of faerie?? Pixie, perhaps? Near the house she saw other creatures sitting on the porch or tending the flower garden out front. Behind the Victorian was another garden, this one for the growing of fruits and vegetables and in it, she could see several small things moving about. They were fairly far off and difficult to see clearly, so she squinted in an attempt to sharpen their image. She thought they kind of resembled the ceramic garden gnomes her father placed in his yard at home. As she continued looking around, taking it all in, Tam resumed his speech. "While there is a wealth of magical knowledge and ability within you, it's buried deep inside. Before you achieve that level of ability, you must accept who you are and unlock the power that's hidden away."

After finishing her survey of the grounds nearby she returned her gaze to Tam's. "You're essentially starting from scratch," he continued. "But with these lessons, and immersing yourself in this world, I'm sure it'll be no time at all before that knowledge and ability once more rises to the surface."

"Okay," she said, smiling. "Thanks for that."

"Not at all, think nothing of it. Ready to try again?"

She nodded. "Yes, let's do it."

"Just as you did before. Don't let anything break your concentration, not even when the plant bursts out of the dirt. Any break in concentration will disrupt your connection with the energy and render your magic moot. As you get more accustomed to magic usage, this will become easier and you'll even be able to multi-task while performing magic."

She got herself into her position, with her feet placed shoulder-width apart and held her hands over the ground. "Okay," she said, more to herself than in acknowledgement of Tam's previous statement. Taking a deep breath, she squared her shoulders and forced thoughts out of her head, focusing only on the image of her favorite flower. She pictured everything, just as she did before, within her mind's eye. This time, when she felt as though the plant was about to sprout through the earth, she closed her eyes tightly, concentrating as hard as she possibly could. In the quiet of the grounds she began to hear soft rustling sounds at her feet but did her best to ignore it. After another minute or two of not speaking, Tam broke the silence.

"Very well done, my lady." He sounded impressed.

She opened her eyes and saw before her a small, but flowering stem of bleeding hearts. There were only two flowers on the stem, but it was enough. The two petals that made up the blossoms were perfectly pink and folded downward into a heart shape, the white stamen hanging down beneath it. It had been her grandmother's favorite flower and Viola had loved it because of the memories she had with her. It was small but she had still managed to create a plant from absolutely nothing. "I did it." She tore her eyes away from the plant to smile happily at Tam, her own joy reflected in his wide grin. "How long will it last?"

"For the size that it is, the amount of energy you used, and your experience, I would say… probably around ten or fifteen minutes."

Her face fell slightly, saddened that it wasn't a particularly strong bit of magic.

He laughed loudly. "Don't be disappointed, m'lady. You've done very well. Certainly, the best first day I've ever seen, and I've taught many students over the years. Your magic is quite strong and soon you will begin to understand that as well."

"I hope you're right," she said, dejectedly.

"Don't worry," he said, smiling. "Let's try it a few more times and see how well you can do."

They spent about another hour and a half alternating between Viola trying to grow more flowers, Tam describing in more detail the fundamentals of magic, and taking a few breaks for Vy to catch her breath, compose herself and find her center in order to try her hand at magic again. The sun was just beginning to make its descent when Tam said it was time to call it a day. She had managed to go from her single stem of bleeding hearts up to a rose bush from which grew three different colors of rose: yellow, pink and the standard red.

"We'll head back inside so you can meet with Lady Rosalyn to plan your next visit." He gestured for her to go ahead and they began to casually make their way back toward the house.

"Will we be doing more flowers next time?"

"Hmmm...that's a good question," he said, taking a few seconds to think it over. "I think we'll try something a little bigger next time; perhaps a lilac bush or a small flowering tree of some kind. That will be a step up from what we did today, while not being too much of a drain on you and your developing skills."

She nodded, happy and looking forward to the next time she would be at the house, learning magic with the graceful, elegant and, frankly, handsome elf. They made their way down the hall but instead of going to the back of the house, they stopped about midway and entered the same parlor from earlier. Lady Rosalyn had relocated and was sitting in one of the single occupancy chairs. Her two guards, never far from her side, stood in the back corners of the room, just behind her. The corresponding chair placed opposite her seemed to be empty, though Vy could swear she heard a small, high-pitched voice emanating from the seat. At their entrance, Rosalyn looked up from what appeared to be a very serious discussion, an expression of concern showing on her face.

"Oh, I am terribly sorry, my Lady," Tam began. "I was not aware you had guests. We can come back." He bowed and turned to usher both himself and Vy from the room.

"Oh no, nothing to worry about, Tamnaeuth. Asteria was just telling me about some recent events but we have finished. You and Viola may stay."

The duo turned back towards her and Viola gasped aloud when she saw a small, purple humanoid creature rise up from the seat and hover above it, glittering wings beating madly. The tiny creature zipped across the room and hung in the air a few inches from her face. Now that the little thing was closer, Vy could see that it was like one of the tiny humanoid creatures that had been flying around the field earlier. This one had lavender skin and violently purple hair. Really big hair. The little creature wore no clothing. The skin was completely smooth and lacked any specific bodily features; no imperfections, no bumps and no protrusions, aside from the silver wings sprouting from her back.

"Lady Viola," it said with its small voice, "it is such an honor to meet you. I am Lady Asteria." Viola watched as the little creature bowed in midair. "I look forward to serving you in any way you may require."

Taken aback by this statement, Viola stumbled over her words, not quite knowing what to say. "Uuh...thank you. It's lovely to meet you, as well." She smiled at the purple woman, still unsure as to what kind of creature she was currently speaking. The tiny thing bowed once more to Viola and then to Rosalyn, bid them all farewell, then flitted out the door.

Rosalyn and Tam must have known just how confused she was because as she stared toward the door through which the little purple creature had disappeared, she could hear them attempting to stifle their giggles. She returned her gaze to the interior of the room and waited while they pulled themselves together. Rosalyn took a deep, calming breath then managed to form words.

"Asteria is a kind of pixie, Viola. They can be a little mischievous but nothing like the unpleasant creatures some of your authors have written about. She has never played any tricks on humans."

"Is she one of the creatures who live here all the time," Vy asked.

"Not usually. She stays with us for a while then disappears into your world for weeks at a time. She had just come from there to report some rather...disturbing news," Rosalyn explained, concern darkening her features.

"Is everything okay, my Lady," inquired Tam.

"I certainly hope it will be," she replied, "but that's a conversation for another time." She turned her attention back toward Vy. "And how was your first day of magical instruction?" There was a smile on her face, though it didn't quite reach her eyes, which remained darkly pensive.

"It seemed to go well, I think. I made a rose bush," she offered.

The female elf's eyes brightened at this and she clapped her hands together in glee. "Splendid! That's wonderful news! Great job, both of you!" Tam stood just off to their side, beaming with pride at her accomplished first day. "We must decide the next day for you to have a lesson," Rosalyn continued. "Charles tells me you have a school and work schedule, though he said if it is needed, you may take some evenings off from the bookstore."

"Oh okay, great!" Vy thought for a moment, going through this week's schedule in her head. "Let's see...I get out of class around three o'clock tomorrow afternoon. Would that work?"

Rosalyn looked to Tam, who nodded, saying, "Certainly. That would be fine."

"Excellent," Rosalyn exclaimed. "If you would, Viola, when you arrive tomorrow you may go straight to the lawn where Tamnaeuth can meet you. Normally, I would receive you myself but with the news Asteria brought me this evening I fear I will be indisposed for most of the day tomorrow. However, we shall meet again tomorrow evening to chat about your second lesson."

"Sounds great," Vy replied. She wished them both a good evening then made her way to the door. In the few seconds before the door closed completely behind her, she managed to overhear the first few words of whispered conversation between the Lady Rosalyn and Tam.

"How did she do," Rosalyn whispered frantically. "We're running out of time. Will she be ready?!"

Viola didn't get to hear whether she would be ready, or for what, as the door latched completely, cutting off the sound of their whispering voices.

CHAPTER NINE

Inside the top floor of the tallest building in the city's business district, a woman in professional attire stood peering through the large glass windows overlooking the harbor. Her hair was dark, aside from a thin streak of gray running along the right side of her head and was pulled back into a tight bun. She wore a powder blue shirt beneath a black suit jacket and skirt, with shiny black heels on her feet. Her lips were painted with bright red lipstick and her eyes were a stormy gray, which seemed to reflect her mood. She glared out at the moon rising over the water of Breitbach Bay, arms crossed in front of her chest. She had the look of someone who was tired of waiting.

Directly behind her was a large, wooden desk, the polished wood gleaming under the office lights. A high-backed leather chair sat behind it with two smaller chairs on the opposite side for office visitors. The rest of the large room remained unfurnished, aside from a few paintings hanging on the white walls and a leafy, green plant placed in a corner. The office was impeccably neat, not a stray piece of paper on the desk nor a rogue bit of fluff on the floor.

A tentative knock on the door broke the silence. "Yes," the woman replied, without turning from the window.

A petite woman in a purple dress covered with flowers and wearing a telephone headset poked her head into the office. "Pardon the intrusion, Ms. Moon, but Hoodah has returned."

The woman turned her head slightly but remained facing the windows. "And?"

"They tell me he was successful, ma'am."

At this, she turned around completely with an alarming, crimson-lipped smile stretching across her face. "Excellent." She made her way across the room toward the door, heels clicking against the tiles beneath her feet. "Radio down to them and tell them I'm on my way."

The small woman backed out of the doorway like a cowering child. "Yes, ma'am. Right away."

Shutting the office door securely behind her, the dark-haired woman strode briskly down the hallway, aiming for the elevator. Once the metal doors had opened and she had stepped inside, she turned to the control panel. Instead of pushing one of the floor buttons, she waved her hand in front of the panel, revealing a hidden compartment beneath the standard buttons. Inside the compartment was a single button, which she pressed with one long, pale, perfectly manicured finger. The elevator began to descend, the floor buttons lighting up with each level the elevator passed. The last button, marked 'B' for the basement, lit up, but the elevator continued to move along its path. After a few moments it finally stopped, the doors opened, and she exited into a bright, white hallway. At the far end, sat a single small, black desk, behind which, on the wooden chair sat a green creature, about the size of a toddler, with a protruding belly and limbs that were thin and spindly as sticks. He was wearing a simple brown loin cloth and hat, through which his long, pointed ears poked out. The woman had never been a fan of goblins, but they were fairly easy to please; just toss them something shiny every now and then and they were yours for the bidding. They could be rather malicious if they were angered, so she made sure to treat them with enough respect to keep them happy but still under her control.

"Good evening, Ikidrak," she purred. "I assume Hoodah is in with him, now?"

The goblin grinned at her gleefully, showing off its many sharp teeth. "Oh yes, miss," he cried, in a grating, raspy, high-pitched croak of a voice. "Wizard not happy, no siree!"

She returned his wicked smile. "Just how we like it, isn't it?"

He jumped up and down on his chair, clapping his little hands maniacally.

"Let's see him," she said, smiling at the little creature's antics. He laughed merrily and pulled a ring of keys from the desk drawer, jumped off the chair and skipped to the door located in the wall behind him. He turned the key, pushed the door open and suddenly screams of pain filled the hall. The corner of her mouth turned up in a wicked smirk as she walked forward into the room.

Shackled to a chair with chains was a middle-aged man wearing a dark blue shirt, charcoal gray jacket, black pants and dress shoes. His graying black hair was messy and tangled, one of the lenses in his glasses was badly cracked and a trickle of bright, red blood trailed down the side of his face. He was struggling to get free as an enormous creature, over eight feet tall at least, loomed above him, making a horrifying repetitive snorting-roaring noise that sounded rather like laughter. Its skin was a grayish green, it had a face that looked as if it had been smashed in; all pinched and squashed into its head. Its clothing consisted of a long loin cloth which may have been white at one time but was now stained with dirt and colors that looked suspiciously of dried blood. The troll turned and looked toward the door as the woman entered, giving her a large, toothy grin.

With the monster distracted, the man in the chair calmed slightly but still breathed heavily in fear, watching as the woman sauntered closer to him.

"Dr. Sawyer, how wonderful it is to see you. We've met before, though," she paused for dramatic effect, "I must say, you looked much better then."

"Ms. Moon," the man sputtered, recognizing the woman before him. They had met and run into each other several times at various events around the city. Experience told him she was a polite and kind businesswoman. The shock at seeing her in this dungeon or torture chamber was evident on his face. "Why are you doing this?"

She smiled widely at him. "Well now, *that's* a very interesting story," she said, slowly strolling around the room. "It starts a long time ago, you see. Many, many years ago I was just the poor daughter of a tailor. I spent most of my days learning his craft and was set to take over his small shop when I was ready. One day, I came upon something rather strange while on a walk in the woods." As she spoke, she continued to slowly walk around the room, the simple action having an incredibly menacing effect on the man chained to the chair. He did his best to follow her every move, straining his neck to watch her when she walked behind him. "What I saw was a group of very tiny creatures dancing in the middle of the wood. I moved closer to get a better peek and soon realized I was looking at a something I didn't believe existed. I had come upon a fairy circle, you see."

She finished another loop around the room and stopped just in front of him. "That day I realized that everything I knew about the world was false. I learned that magical beings existed, and it became an obsession for me. I spent all of my waking hours searching for more creatures, hoping to be a part of their world."

She sat down in the only other chair in the room, the one opposite him. "It took months, but I finally came upon some of them again. I happened to be walking in the area of the woods where elves were out hunting. I immediately went to them and though they tried to run from me, I had always been fast. They were far ahead of me, but I managed to follow them. I followed them all the way to their city, hidden deep within the forest. It was the most beautiful thing I had ever seen. It was as if the trees grew larger there and formed natural hollows for dwellings. There were bridges formed from entwined branches. The light filtering down through the leaves of the trees was soft and warm.

"They didn't want to let me in, but I wouldn't leave and spent a night outside just to spite them. Eventually, they opened the gates of their city and lead me to a great room inside the largest of all the trees. Inside was a beautiful woman. Her hair was red as sunset or a blazing fire. Her eyes were a piercing green, and she wore the most beautiful dress; the kind of gown I could only imagine ever being able to wear. It was a pale green, made of the lightest material, like gossamer, adorned with gold and jewels, and on her head rested a silver crown that seemed to be made of moonlight, itself." As she talked, the man's eyes began to widen with understanding and terror.

Her expression changed from one of fond reminiscing to envy and anger. "I spoke with this faerie queen and begged her to let me come live with them, to teach me to be as graceful as they were and to learn the ways of magic. Well, she wouldn't have that. She told me crazy lies; that if I were to even touch their magic it would destroy me. She said they were protectors of that magic, keeping it and people like me safe. She expressed sadness, saying she was sorry it had to be this way but for the safety of everyone it must be so." She shook her head in frustration, giving out a tiny snort of disgust. "As you can imagine," she started, leaning back in the wooden chair and crossing one perfectly nylon-clad leg over the other, "I was unimpressed by what she had to say. When they banished me from their city, I swore that the next time I went near that place, I would be claiming it as my own." Swinging her leg back down and placing her foot on the floor, she leaned forward, her elbows on her knees. "And now, I'm sure you know who I am, Dr. Sawyer. And you know that I am fully aware who *you* are," she growled, bringing her face mere inches from his own. "Who you *really* are."

He glared back at her, defiance written on every inch of his skin. "Melarue. You're Melarue."

"Indeed, I am," she sighed contentedly, standing up straight again. "It's been so long since anyone has called me by that name. And if I'm here, then you know who else must be around here somewhere; your precious Lady Evelina. And you, my dear little wizard-turned-history professor, you are going to tell me who she is in this life and where I can find her."

He let out a bark of laughter. "Well, you've just wasted a bunch of your time, then! I've heard that she's returned but I haven't been back to our realm in a few years. I've no idea who or where she is, now."

"Yes, it looks like you've taken quite well to the world of us humans," she sneered.

"You still refer to yourself as human, then. I would think that by now you've become more monster than that." he retorted.

"Oh, good one! Nicely done, professor. Brave one this, isn't he, Ikidrak?" The goblin laughed loudly and danced around. She turned back to the professor and began to applaud. "I commend you, sir. You are certainly one of the bravest I have interrogated in this room. However," she said, her applause abruptly ceasing, "bravado will only get you so far."

She paced back and forth in front of him for a few moments as she considered. "You see...if you can't give me the information I require, then what good are you?"

The professor continued to glare at her defiantly, though she could see that he was trembling slightly.

"I can't let you go, obviously. You now know the truth about me and where to find me. I can't have you running back to whoever is leading you now and having you spill the beans. I'd be attacked by some wee little pixie in no time! But to kill you...you were one of the greatest wizards the world had ever seen. Studied under Merlin, did you not?"

The man sat stiffly and refused to speak.

"Killing you would be such a waste of magical ability. No, we can't do that. Well…not yet, anyway. "

She stopped suddenly in front of him, placed her palm flat on his chest.

"First, I'll take your magic. No sense wasting it." She flashed him a wicked smile as she began to slowly curl her fingers inward, forming her hand in the shape of a claw, still positioned against his chest. The man began to look uncomfortable, as though he was in pain once more. She then began pulling her hand back from him very slowly. His pain seemed to escalate, and he began to struggle, attempting to twist away from her and to escape his bonds.

Attached to her fingertips were flowing streams of a silvery light, originating from his chest. As she pulled further and further away, he began to cry out and writhe against the chair and his bindings. Sweat beaded on her brow as she, too, began struggling to contain the magical energy she was drawing out of him. She growled and pulled back as hard as she could, the thin streams converging into one thick wave of magic, as it poured out of the man before her. With one final, powerful tug, she drew the last of it out of him, the silver wave diminishing as it was drawn toward her own body, her victim screaming in absolute agony. As the last silver tendrils left him, the man slumped forward, body limp and lifeless. She staggered backward and collapsed onto the chair she had recently vacated, panting and exhausted, her left hand clutched tightly around a gold coin she'd been holding throughout the entire ordeal.

"Whew, he was a tough one." The troll and goblin were both clapping their hands together gleefully. She took a few moments to catch her breath and collect herself, then straightened once again. She stumbled momentarily as she turned to leave the room, slipping the coin into her coat pocket. "Well done, Hoodah," she said. The troll laughed again, and she beckoned him to follow her with a curl of her index finger. "Come with me. You deserve a treat for that and then we'll see if the scouts have discovered anyone else you can bring back to me." Hoodah laughed his deep, roaring laugh and clapped his hands together again. "Ikidrak," she called, turning back to the goblin, standing closely to the man's body, "would you mind taking care of him?"

"Oh, yes miss! I can do that miss! Yessir, miss, Ikidrak take care of him real good," the goblin shrieked excitedly.

"Thank you. When you're done you may come upstairs, and I'll see that I have something for you, as well."

He let out a terrifying giggle. "Oh, thank you Miss! Ikidrak like things miss give him! Good Miss! Thank you, Miss!"

Ms. Arin W. Moon stalked out of the room and headed back toward the elevator and, once the troll had managed to squeeze himself into the tiny box, ascended the flights of the building.

The goblin unlocked the man's shackles, letting him slide down to the floor. He clucked his tongue once, muttering to himself, "waste of magic, it is. Too bad!" Before getting rid of the body, he raided the man's pockets, looking for anything shiny. He let out a squeal of glee, pulling out a shiny, new penny. He clutched it tightly in his little green fist and began to slowly drag the body away.

CHAPTER TEN

Viola got to school the next morning, said hello to her office mates as she dropped her bags off on her desk and pulled her coffee cup from a shelf. She trudged down the hall, still feeling rather tired from the previous day's events. Wielding magic, it seemed, was mentally and physically draining. The focus and concentration needed to draw out and manipulate the energy took a lot out of the user. Hopefully that would improve as she grew more used to it. In addition, she'd had a difficult time sleeping the night before, contemplating what those few overheard words of conversation meant. Judging from what they said, it sounded like something big would be happening, it would be happening soon, and she had a feeling she was a major part of it. This thought plagued her all night, making her toss and turn and get very little sleep. Her fluffy, black cat, Sirius, a stray that had adopted her rather than the other way around, grew so annoyed with her restlessness, that he bounded off the bed and left the room, in search of more comfortable places to sleep. Vy felt as though she was just going through the motions today, slowly making her way down the hall to the department office. In a sleepy haze, she entered the office, smiling and waving at the secretaries and heading straight for the coffee pot. She closed her eyes, breathing in the earthy smell of the dark liquid and felt her mood already begin to shift in a more positive direction.

After adding her cream and sugar, she went back to her office, clutching the warm mug in both hands, letting it's comforting embrace warm her from the inside out. Upon entering her office, she heard one of her office mates, Nick, sniff the air as she walked past.

"Oh my God, that smells so good," he said.

"Nectar of the gods and fuel for English majors everywhere," she said, raising her mug in salute.

He laid his hand over his heart in a most dramatic fashion. "Truer words were never spoken. I'll be back." He grabbed his mug from the shelf and took off down the hall, in search of sweet, sweet caffeine. She had a few moments to herself, so she plopped into her chair, gazed out the window and took the first sip. The coffee was pleasantly hot, and she reveled in the warmth as it traveled down her throat. The chill of winter was still hanging on in the air, even though it was technically spring by the calendar. The snow had all melted, the grass was turning green and flowers were starting to grow. It was, however, still chilly enough that hoodies and hot coffee were required in the mornings. This and fall were her favorite times of year. Summers on the coast of Maine could be absolutely wonderful but they could also be hot, humid and miserable. The way she saw it, you could always add another layer if you were cold, but you could only take off so many before you got arrested.

With the caffeine beginning to work in her system and waking her up from her stupor, she started to organize herself for the class she was teaching in twenty minutes. She'd somehow managed to finish grading all of her student's essays on Sunday, in between her first adventure in the magical realm and working at the shop. It was finals week, so she was really just meeting with them to return their final essays and discuss their overall experience in the class. It was a bit late in the semester for her students to be making the mistakes so many of them were making. She'd have to focus a decent part of their discussion on those errors. Just as she was piling her books and her student's essays into her arms, Liz walked through the door and mumbled a 'good morning,' also rather sleepily.

"Don't you have class right now," she asked. "What are you doing down on the first floor?"

"Dr. Sawyer never showed up," she shrugged. "I stayed up all damn night writing an essay for nothing," she grumbled.

"Well, there's a pretty nasty cold going around, maybe he's sick."

"Probably, but its finals week! You'd think he'd at least have sent out an email. I guess I'm just going to drop this in his mailbox," she said, waving several typed pages in the air. "Where are you off to?"

"You can't tell from the books and papers," she retorted, raising an eyebrow. "I have my last class to teach in a few minutes."

"Aaaah yes, fresh meat - oops, I mean *freshman* - English."

Vy rolled her eyes, grabbed her half-full coffee cup and started out the door, Liz trailing behind her. "Yes, freshman English. Just like your freshman History."

Liz narrowed her eyes. "Do not speak of such foul things to me." She paused a moment, then completely shifted the conversation. "Soooo, has Monty been down to ask you out yet?" She said it rather loudly, in the middle of the crowded hallway, attracting the attention of a myriad of nearby students, some of whom were probably familiar with the unbelievably good looking history grad student.

Vy coughed and sputtered on the coffee she had just sipped. "Sshh! No, he hasn't. Stop it!"

"Man, what is that boy waiting for? It's a good thing you look cute today, he could be down anytime."

Vy didn't want to admit to her that when deciding what to wear this morning she had opted for something that made her look fetching; a green sweater dress over yellow tights and tall, brown boots. She'd taken a little extra time with her hair and makeup that morning, as well.

"Just…stop it, okay? If it happens, I promise you'll be the first to know," she said, reaching the door to her classroom. She could see several of the students were already there, chatting with each other. Some looked like zombies, as though their coffee hadn't had time to kick in yet. There were still a few empty seats, and she instinctively returned her gaze down the hall to see if anyone else was on their way into class. She didn't see her students, but she did see Monty. He was an inch or two taller than the undergrads that surrounded him, his slightly messy hair standing out over the tops of the other heads. He was focused on where he was going but happened to look over in her direction. His smile was bright as he waved, calling "Hey, Viola!" Then, noticing Liz was beside her, he nodded to her and greeted her as well. He didn't stop to talk but continued down the hall, black messenger bag slung over his shoulder.

Vy stared after him for a moment or two before she heard Liz mock vomiting beside her. "Good Lord," she said, "it's like John Hughes just threw up all over your life."

Vy rolled her eyes. "Don't you have somewhere else to be? Get going, won't you?!"

"Sure thing, Molly Ringwald. I'll see you at lunch," she laughed, heading the opposite way down the hall. Vy shook her head and stepped into the classroom.

*   *   *

Vy and Liz were sitting in the university's cafe, eating lunch, happy they didn't have any essays or homework to grade for the rest of the semester. The cafe had been crowded when they arrived but was gradually starting to clear out so they could have a conversation without having to raise their voice over the din of the other patrons.

"So," Liz started, mouth full of chicken pot pie, "you didn't say for sure or not the other day. This weekend. You, me, Liam. The bar?"

"I think so. I've got a lot going on right now, but I should be able to make something work."

Liz furrowed her brows. "A lot going on? What're you talking about? The semester's over, mate! Something going on at the store?"

"I'm not really sure," she said, trying to come up with a story on the spot. "One of the girls might be leaving so I think Dad wants me to be there more often, in case I need to take her shifts or if she doesn't show up one of these days."

"Aw man, that sucks!"

"Yah. So, I may not be able to do much for a while until we figure out what's going on with that. Plus, I'm trying to get a head start on my thesis. Last thing I want to do is go out like one of my officemates last year; she was in the office past midnight most nights, trying to finish up." She was thankful she had been able to come up with something so quickly, though it nearly caused her physical pain to lie to her best friend. Why couldn't everyone just already believe in magic, so she wouldn't sound crazy?!

"Oh bollocks, grab yourself a tissue, quick," Liz exclaimed. "You'll need it to wipe up your drool!"

Vy's brows furrowed and she tilted her head, confused, when she suddenly felt a presence just behind her. Turning, she saw Monty coming around to face her.

"Hey Vy, Liz! How is your day going?"

"Oh, fine," Vy said. "And yours?"

"Pretty standard, but its fine, also." He took a moment to smile at both girls, in turn, looking to Vy second. "Hey, I'm fairly booked this week, what with papers and final exams and all, but I thought maybe you might like to go to that coffee shop next week? Any days that work better for you?"

She was not prepared for this and couldn't believe he was actually asking her to coffee. She assumed he was just being nice during their first meeting but here he was, asking her out while Liz kicked her leg repeatedly under the table. Trying to ignore the toe of Liz's boot smacking into her shin, she thought about her schedule for next week, hoping magic lessons wouldn't get in the way of anything. "Uuuh, sure. You said lunch, right? I could do Tuesday or Thursday. I'm done with teaching as of about an hour ago, but I'll still be around campus to meet with my advisor and do research."

"Great! I'll head down to your office around twelve thirty on Tuesday, sound good?"

"Sounds great," she said, her voice high.

"Excellent. I'll see you then. Have a great day, ladies." He smiled at them, gave them each a respectful nod and small bow, and then walked out of the cafe.

Liz didn't say anything at all, but she didn't need to; the smug look on her face said everything she was thinking.

"Don't even start," Vy said.

Liz affected an air of innocence. "To what are you referring? I don't understand." Vy just glared at her in response. Liz shrugged. "I *did* tell you to grab a tissue."

CHAPTER ELEVEN

Vy pulled into the driveway of the house, debating whether or not to ask Tam about the tiny bit of conversation she had heard the other day. She knew she wasn't supposed to hear it, and for that reason she shouldn't ask about it. However, she had a feeling that something big was in the works and would impact her directly. For this reason, she felt she had a right to know. As she trekked through the tall grass, she continued to contemplate, eventually deciding it was best if she didn't let on that she had overheard anything at all. She walked through the archway, around the gardens and headed out onto the lawn.

There was someone on the grass, but they didn't seem to have Tam's shining, silver hair. As she got closer, she realized it was Vince, who had come to her rescue a few nights previously. He was sitting on the ground, leaning against a tree on the edge of the lawn, his nose in a very thick book. When he noticed her approach, he picked his head up, smiled and waved. "Hi Viola," he called.

She smiled awkwardly and returned his greeting as she neared.

"Tam will be out soon. He's in a meeting with Rosalyn and a few others," he said, relocating his bookmark and closing the pages around it. "I'm glad of it, though. We didn't really get to talk much the other night and I haven't been here at the same time as you the past few days." He patted the grass beside him, inviting her to sit.

"Yes, thank you," she said, plopping down beside him. "I wanted to thank you for saving me from that monster, whatever it was."

"That was a kind of faerie. Some of them are capable of shape-shifting. That one decided to take the shape of a massive wolf, in order to scare you," he said, clicking his tongue in disapproval.

"Well, it worked. Now I know just how scary a real-life werewolf can be," she said, remembering the snapping of the bones and the terrible face of the creature, so close to her own.

"I've seen worse," he said. "And by the way, there's a difference between shape-shifters and werewolves." He winked. "Shape-shifters can take the form of a wolf or other creature any time they wish, while a werewolf has no control over the change. Just for future reference."

"Ah, okay. Noted."

After a momentary pause, he continued. "I wanted to apologize to you. I think I might have startled you the other day on the bus, at your school and the bookstore. It wasn't my intention."

"It's okay," she said. "Although, why *were* you following me all day? I'm curious. I thought you were some kind of creepy stalker, waiting for your chance to take advantage of me or something," she chuckled.

"Oh no, no, no, nothing like that," he exclaimed, laughing awkwardly. "No, I have a boyfriend, not that that's relevant to this conversation. Well, y'see...and I'm not sure I should tell you about all of this yet. It's a bit sensitive." He hesitated a moment, looking at her curious expression. "But I suppose...you have a right to know what's going on.

"Truth is, Viola, that there's been someone from this realm guarding you for your entire life; ever since they realized who you are. They've mostly kept at a distance; however, we've been getting reports of magical beings getting attacked in your world. They've been happening more and more frequently lately, and Lady Rosalyn thought it was a good idea for your guard to be increased, to monitor you more closely to make sure you weren't hurt or killed by something."

"Because...I'm this Evelina?"

"Exactly. You don't realize yet how important you are in all of this." His expression continued to get more and more serious.

"And... these...*attackers*, they're looking for me?"

"Most likely, yes."

Vy pondered this silently for a few moments. "I'm meant to do something, aren't I?" She looked at him to read his expression.

"Something is happening. That's why they're having meetings in there today; it's something to do with me, isn't it?"

He sighed deeply, facing the house but looking at nothing in particular. "Again, I'm not sure how much I should tell you of this. But...yes. Yes, it's to do with you." He sighed again, shaking his head and returned her gaze once more. "Viola, you are the reincarnation of Evelina, who was an incredibly powerful magic user and a leader of this world. You will be that powerful again and we'll need you and your power when the time comes."

"When the time comes for what?" She was getting very curious now, as her suspicions were being confirmed. "What, exactly, do I have to do?"

He sighed again and looked down, studying the cover of the book resting on his lap. "Evelina is a hero in this world, Viola. She stopped a great evil once before; an evil that promised to return in the future and finish what it started."

"So, that's what I'm to do; find this great evil and defeat it." It wasn't a question; she already knew the answer. She would have to fight and soon.

He opened his mouth to reply but was interrupted by a voice calling across the lawn. They turned toward the sound to see Tam walking towards them, waving and carrying a small bag. Vince's expression changed once again, a smile stretching across his face. He jumped up and started walking toward the elf, Viola following a few steps behind. They all met up on the vast expanse of lawn, a short distance from where Viola's first lesson had been.

"Good afternoon, my Lady," Tam said, bowing. "Are you ready for your next lesson?"

"Definitely!"

"Very good. Vincent, will you be joining us today? You are more than welcome," he said, smiling toward the young man.

"If I won't be in the way, certainly, I'd love to!" Vince beamed back at the two of them.

Tam nodded slightly. "Then, let's begin." Viola caught a secret look pass between the two men and realization dawned. So, Tam was the boyfriend Vince had mentioned! They were an odd couple, the elf and the man, to be sure; but they were also so very cute together and Vy couldn't help but smile at them.

"I've decided that we're going to attempt a tree today. Just a small one; a Japanese maple perhaps. To do this, you use the same method I taught you last time but instead you just envision a tree, rather than a flower. A tree, however, takes rather a lot more energy, so be prepared for that." He waved his arm as an invitation for her to step forward and give it a try, while Vince once more plopped down in the shade beneath a nearby tree.

As she did during the first lesson, she closed her eyes, breathed deeply and tried to clear her mind. She chose to create the image of a maple tree in her mind, one of the small ones that had grown on her grandparent's farm when she was little. Pulling the magical energy into herself, she expelled it downward and into the ground. She heard the familiar rustling of leaves; however, this time there seemed to be more. After another minute, she stopped pulling on the energy and opened her eyes. Before her stood a tiny maple tree which only came up to her chest; honestly, it was more of a maple bush than a tree, but she wasn't complaining. Tam was beaming at her, pride shining out from his eyes, while Vince was sitting straight up, staring at her and her tree, his eyes and mouth opened wide in surprise.

"Very well done, my Lady! Take a moment to rest and then let's try again. This time," Tam instructed," I want you to keep your eyes open. You need to be able to see the magic taking hold and not be distracted by it."

"Whew, okay." She picked a new spot for the next tree, breathed deeply, centered herself and began again. This time, she watched as the tiny sprout pushed its way out of the dirt, saw it thicken and lengthen, watched the limbs of branches take form and leaves begin to grow. The rustling came again as the growing leaves brushed against each other and the branches from which they sprouted. She ignored everything else going on around her; the presence of the two men, the chirping birds, and remained entirely focused on this little tree; on willing it to become taller and stronger. It grew to reach her knees and this time, she felt she could make it even taller than her first attempt. With her open palms angled toward the tree, she began to slowly lift her arms up, willing the tree to continue to grow. As it began to get taller with her influence, she couldn't help but feel excited, though she tried to keep that feeling at bay, not wanting to get too ahead of herself, and instead focused on making this tree a great one. She continued moving her hands upward, pulling the tree up taller and taller, until she was worn out and could do no more. When she stopped, the tree was a foot or two taller than she was and had a full, lush canopy of leaves. She bent over, putting her hands above her knees, to catch her breath.

"Viola, that was fantastic," Vince cried. "It looks great!"

"Indeed, you did very well, my Lady!" Tam's smile was very wide, his lavender eyes shining brightly. "Come, you need a decent rest after that." He picked up the bag he had brought with him and, opening it, revealed four bottles of cold fruit tea, wedges of cheese and a covered bowl filled with various fruits. Vy could see chunks of different melons, strawberries, blueberries, even pomegranate seeds. "I knew we would be working hard today so I brought us a snack to see us through. Nourishment will help you regain your energy to try again."

The three of them sat down on the grass, leaning against the tree she had just made, the trunk of which was quite thin, as maple trees usually are, so each of their shoulders touched another's. Viola leaned her head back, looking up through the leaves as she munched on a cut of cheese. "Do you think this tree will last long," she asked.

"This should last at least until nightfall," Tam replied.

She nodded. "I've been wondering," she said, "what else can magic do? I've grown flowers and now trees, but I know you can do other things with it. I saw what Vince did a couple of weeks ago, after all…"

"Oh, you can do plenty," Vince said. "Flowers and trees are just the basics. They enable you to make first contact with the energy of nature and learn how to properly wield it, how to move it within your body."

"That makes sense. I guess I thought minor charms and things like that would be the basics," she said.

"That's what your books and films would have taught you," said Tam. "The reality is that spells and incantations are just more complicated ways of doing what you've just done. The ones who use spells are those who were born with a connection to magical energy but not with the ability to wield it without effort. It happens sometimes. Spells, enchantments, and the like were created by those who had a connection to nature and its energy, but that connection wasn't quite strong enough to imbue them with natural magical ability. Your idea of wizards or witches who use spells are using the power of words to ask nature's permission to use the energy. Some are successful, like Vince here, but many are not."

"Can't anyone learn how to use magic, then?"

"Oh no, certainly not," they exclaimed.

"Why not? If the spells help one to do magic in the same way we do, couldn't everyone learn how?" She turned to both of them, expectantly.

"It's a tricky thing," Vince began. "The ability to sense and connect to that natural energy comes easily to the fey folk. Occasionally there are humans who exhibit the same ability but for the most part, they just aren't as in tune to the natural world as the fey folk are. It's very rare. Those who aren't born with that connection to the natural world have a difficult time sustaining that energy within themselves. On the rare occasion, humans are born with the ability to connect with that energy but aren't able to wield it in the same way as the fey folk. That's me. We are what you would refer to as wizards, witches or warlocks. We have that connection but because we aren't fey, we must use words to harness that energy for our use."

That made a lot of sense, she supposed. She chewed for a few moments and cleared her palate with a swig of tea, then decided to ask another question that had been burning in the back of her mind. "So, in the alley the other night, I didn't hear you say anything, but it looked like you were mouthing…something. You were speaking to nature, or…casting a spell, then?"

"You are correct," Vince replied. "I was speaking but doing so very softly, almost a whisper. I find that seems to work for me the best."

"Ooh, you're a wizard, Vince," she said in her best magical school groundskeeper voice. All three of them laughed at her teasing. "If you're human, how did you realize you could wield magic? How did you wind up here?"

"Thanks to Tam," he said, turning toward the elf with a small smile. "My early years weren't the happiest of situations. Due to a series of events, and several foster homes, I found myself living on the street when I was only fifteen. A few years ago, I was sleeping in an alley near the waterfront and ended up being attacked in a similar way as you were, though it was a different sort of creature. A small troll, I believe. Fortunately, Tam happened to be in the area and heard everything. He saved me that night and he could sense the magic within me."

"Yes, and you will learn how to do that as well," Tam added. "Once you have begun to really get used to that energy you will be so in tune with it, that you will be able to sense where magic exists and where it has recently been used. You can be out, walking down the street and if magic had been performed in that vicinity within the past twenty-four hours, you will be able to sense it. In addition, you will be able to sense the magical energy within another person."

Vince nodded in agreement before continuing his story. "I was injured so Tam brought me here, to Rosalyn. After she and her healers patched me up, she tested my abilities, found that I did, indeed, have magic within me, and allowed me to stay here. I healed for a few days and then Tam started teaching me how to use my abilities through the use of spoken incantations, words of power, which allow me to control the energy."

"That is so cool," Vy breathed in awe.

The two men chuckled. "I'm glad you think so," Vince said. "There are…certain members of the fey community who look down on those of us who are able to use magic without having faerie blood in our veins."

"Really? That's awful!"

"I'm afraid it's true," Tam piped in. "There is a fairly large section of the fey world who believe that humans who use spells and incantations are using an inferior form of magic and therefore, they believe the humans themselves to be inferior."

"It's not like that here, though. Not at the inn?" Everyone she'd met was so nice, she couldn't believe anyone would hold such prejudices against others. And yet…she recalled those suspicious stares…

Tam and Vince met each other's eyes briefly before turning back to her. "Unfortunately," Tam began, "there are a few fey living here who agree. Not many, mind you, but…enough."

"I'm so sorry Vince. That's terrible." She felt so awful for the man who had been so nice to her and certainly didn't deserve to be treated badly or looked down on.

"It's okay," he replied. "It could be worse. I get ignored a lot or overhear a few snide comments by some of the folks who live here but no one's attacked me. Others have it far worse than I do. And at least I have Rosalyn, Fulrin and Tam, of course." At this Vince reached over and gently squeezed Tam's hand briefly before reaching for his bottle of tea.

They ate and drank in silence for a few moments, until Vy had to ask the question that was burning inside her mind. "The few times I've walked through the house, I got the sense that…there were a few folks looking at me with suspicion…or something similar." She turned to look them both full in the face to gauge their reaction to her question. "I'm half human. The ones who don't like you for being who you are…do they not like me, either?" Tam and

Vince shared another of their meaningful looks. "So, that's a yes, then." It wasn't difficult to read their expressions.

Tam gave her sad smile before answering. "Unfortunately, you're not wrong in your assumptions, Viola. There are a few of them who don't have as much respect for you as they should, due to your parentage. Evelina was full fey, and they think her reincarnation should be the same."

Vy could feel it as her face fell, the boys confirming what she'd suspected. Vince quickly tried to cheer her up. "Don't be too upset, Vy. While there are a few who don't like us, there are far more who are welcoming and accepting. It's like any normal, dysfunctional family, really!" They chuckled and let the topic drop, but the knowledge still buried itself in the back of her mind.

Their break continued for a few more minutes, with Vy completely enraptured with their stories and magical knowledge, before Tam asked her to try again. By the time they had finished and were heading back toward the house, there were five new maple trees in the lawn, four tall and one short tree that was beginning to shimmer around the edges. Upon entering the Victorian, they headed toward the sitting room. Before opening the door, Tam knocked, hoping to avoid the intrusion from their first lesson. A voice from within called for them to enter and upon doing so, Vy was surprised to see the room full of people and various fey creatures. Lady Rosalyn was seated in the comfortable armchair as before, though now several more chairs had been placed within the room. Each of these seats was taken up by creatures ranging from small, some she recognized as pixies while others were new to her, as well as larger creatures including dwarves, gnomes and elves. Vy was surprised to see her father there, as well, seated beside three empty chairs, obviously meant for Tam, Vince and herself. Rosalyn greeted them and invited them to take the three open seats, which they did.

"I want to thank all of you for being here today," Rosalyn began. "The first thing I must do is to introduce all of you to Viola," she said, gesturing to the subject matter. "She is the one we have been waiting for, Evelina's reincarnation. She is currently learning how to wield her power and will soon be a very powerful magic user, as her instructor, Tamnaeuth tells me." At this, she smiled at Viola, who was feeling quite awkward indeed, seeing all eyes in the room intently focused on her. She did her best to sink back into her seat so she wouldn't feel quite as exposed. "Viola, these are all representatives of the many different species and clans of magics in the world. They were all very excited to meet you."

She went around the room, introducing each of her guests. Asteria was there, along with the Dwarven leader, Gordek, and a wizard named Gregory among several others. With introductions and pleasantries out of the way, Rosalyn's attitude and expression changed to one of a more serious nature. "Now, to business. As you are all aware, we have been encountering more and more attacks on magic users lately. All of you know what this means, of course. Melarue has returned." She paused as those gathered reacted to the news, several hushed conversations popping up throughout the room. When the murmuring quieted again, she resumed her speech. "It is my sad duty to inform all of you that Dr. Everett Sawyer has been taken and sadly, we must assume him dead." Several gasps erupted from all corners of the room as creatures expressed their shock and horror.

Her feelings of awkwardness momentarily forgotten, Vy interjected, "Dr. Sawyer? As in the History professor?"

Rosalyn turned toward Vy, as though suddenly making the connection that the grad student knew the man of which she was speaking. "Yes, the very same. Everett was a very skilled and very old wizard, spending much of his youth studying with the great Merlin." At this she turned back to the room at large, leaving Vy to comprehend yet another surprise. "The loss of such a man is great and will be felt throughout our entire realm."

She turned toward Viola, speaking directly to her. "Now, Viola, you may not yet be aware of this, but this is not the first time a magic has been taken. There have been several over the years, though the frequency has been increasing drastically over the past few months. When someone disappears, their bodies are inevitably found a few days later." She paused for a moment to take a breath and to center herself before continuing. "This also happened before; many years ago. The characteristics of these recent events are identical to those of the past. These kidnappings and murders are unique to one person, and that is Melarue. She takes someone with the intention of stealing their magic, which destroys the energy or soul within them. This, in turn, kills the body as well." Vy stared at her, unblinking, taking in all this horrible new information. "It's very old, very complicated and extremely dark magic. Long ago, Melarue found someone who was willing to help her. They taught her how to use this dark form of magic, then donated their own energy to her to get her started, storing it within an inanimate object she then drew the power from. The process is incredibly painful, and no one can survive it."

At this, she made her way over to Vy and knelt in front of her, taking Vy's hands in her own. "This is the woman you were born to defeat, Viola. As the reincarnation of Evelina, it is your destiny to fight her and defend us; your people and family." Vy felt Rosalyn's grip squeeze her hands reassuringly. "This is a lot to take in, I know. But we are all here for you and we will help you prepare."

Viola sat silent for a moment, considering what she had just learned. She was overwhelmed. Her future was already planned for her and it sounded dangerous and unhappy. However, she was now a part of this world and had begun to form bonds with these people. She hadn't known them for long, but she already felt a kinship with them, perhaps due to their shared abilities or magical lineage. While she was scared, she also wanted to be the person they believed her to be; she wanted to be Evelina for them, but she also wanted to be Vy. She looked around at their expectant faces and realized they wanted her to say something. She'd never been fond of public speaking, but she took a deep breath and tried her best. "This *is* quite a lot to process, I admit. Honestly, this is all absolutely terrifying, but I will do whatever I can, all that's within my power to protect and defend this community. Though, I am still learning, so any help you can give will be very much appreciated." She turned toward Lady Rosalyn. "How much time do we have before I will need to face Melarue?"

Rosalyn thought for a moment before replying. "Our prophecy doesn't include a specific date for your confrontation, but we must bear in mind that the more magic she steals, the more powerful she will become and the more magics we will lose. So, certainly, the sooner the better. Tamnaeuth tells me you are progressing very well in your magical ability, but you still have a long way to go if you are to defeat Melarue. She has stolen the magic of many, many people over the years and that energy is burning up inside of her. The hotter and brighter it burns, the more powerful she is however it also means she is struggling harder to maintain her sanity and to fight for life." Vy's brow furrowed in confusion. Tam and Vince had touched on that a short time ago, but she still needed more details.

"You see Viola," Rosalyn continued, "when a body that wasn't born with the natural affinity for magic attempts to use it, the body rejects it. Non-magics are those whose bodies and minds are not strong enough to sustain all of that extra energy. Melarue was instructed in ways to steal magic from others and use it as her own, but she can only do that for so long. Eventually, after all of that strain, either her mind or body, or perhaps both, will break. She may be stronger magically but physically, she is weak. If we get you to the power level you were at in your previous life, you will be able to defeat her and save our world."

Vy nodded and took a deep, centering breath. "Okay. How can I do that and how long will it take before I'm ready?"

Everyone around her smiled and expressed their gratitude for her willingness to play her part. They all conversed with each other in hushed tones, smiling in her direction, nodding their approval. Rosalyn held up her hands, requesting silence. "We are very grateful for your willingness to accept your role, Viola. You are already an incredibly strong woman, and we have nothing but faith in you. We will continue your lessons with Tamneauth for the time being but soon, I think it would be best if we take you to the location of that long-ago battle. It may help you to recover some of the knowledge, memories and identity which you lost that day." She spread her arms wide, including everyone in the room. "We will take only a few. I, of course, will go with you and certainly your father. Tamnaeuth," she said, looking toward the silver haired elf, "as her instructor, I believe you should come with us as well." Looking around the room at everyone in turn, she continued, "If there are others who would like to join us, please say so now. I will accept another two or three persons for this venture."

The dwarf she had met on her first day here, Fulrin, immediately stood up, followed by Vince merely a half second later. Lastly, Asteria, who had been meeting with Rosalyn a few days before began beating her wings furiously, along with a small fairy with whom she was sharing a seat. They both began gaining altitude above the chair, rising high enough to be on the same level as Rosalyn's head, both expressing their desires to join the party as well. Lady Rosalyn looked around at everyone, smiling. "Thank you all. I will be in touch with you to let you know when this journey will take place." With that, she dismissed everyone. People began standing and meandering out of the room, though Viola, Charles, Tam and Vince remained to talk with Rosalyn.

"Is the battlefield far from here? I just want to figure out travel logistics and plan for work and whatnot." Vy pulled her phone out and opened up her calendar.

"It is rather far from here," Rosalyn said, smiling. "But there won't be any need for major travel plans. With enough concentrated magic, we can create a door to get there in a matter of moments."

"Oh." Vy was slightly stunned.

"It's kind of like the archway we walk through when we come here, Vy." Her father was smiling at her, though she could see the anxiety in his eyes. Charles Campbell was not fond of this plan for his daughter to connect with her former self, it seemed.

"Very similar, yes," agreed Rosalyn. "Tamnaeuth, if you would, please begin teaching Viola how to perform the appropriate magic. We'll leave as soon as you're ready." She gave Vy one last encouraging smile before disappearing into the hall.

CHAPTER TWELVE

Viola looked at the clock on the wall, butterflies fluttering about madly in her stomach. It was quarter after twelve on Tuesday, the day Monty was supposed to meet with her for lunch. He had said he'd meet her in her office at about half past noon so he could walk in any second now. She pulled out a small mirror from her purse to make sure she looked okay. She was attempting to fluff her curls by hand when Liz walked into the office, no doubt here to harass her before she left with Monty. She whistled at her, to which Vy rolled her eyes.

"All ready for your big date with lover boy," Liz teased. "Our little girl is growing up!"

"Ugh. Honestly, Liz. Why are you here," she asked in mock irritation.

"Why, to torture you, of course! Would you expect anything less of me?" She posed, eyelashes aflutter.

"I suppose not." Viola snapped her mirror shut and dropped it back into her bag.

"Hey, if it goes well today, you should see if he wants to join us at the bar this weekend. It'd be fun." She leaned against Viola's desk. "That guy needs to get out and meet people. He doesn't socialize much." She pulled Vy's mirror back out of her purse and proceeded to check her own face with it as she spoke.

"I'll see how it goes and I'll give it a try," she replied. "I hope everything goes okay. He seems really nice."

"Oh, he is. I've had a few classes with him and he's super polite, though as I said before, not particularly talkative. Speaking of classes," she put the mirror on the table and turned to face Vy, "did you hear about Dr. Sawyer?"

Vy had most certainly heard about Dr. Sawyer but decided to play as though she had no idea what was going on. She wondered if his body had been found. "No, what's up?"

"Apparently, after he didn't show up to class at all last week, they decided to send someone to check on him. Turns out his house were broken into and he seems to have disappeared."

"No way! Have they started an investigation or anything?"

"I think they have, yes, but I haven't heard anything in regard to it. I hope he's okay. He's my favorite professor. He has such a dry sense of humor, makes all these amazing jokes in class."

Viola felt badly that in all probability Dr. Sawyer was already dead and there was nothing anyone could do. She debated spilling the beans to her friend; telling her everything, including what she knew about Dr. Sawyer. She had just decided to share her secret when Montgomery walked through the door.

"Hello, ladies. How are you both doing today?" He had dressed in a black sweater, the collar of his white shirt peeking out over the knitwear, with a pair of khakis and red Converse.

"Hi! I'm good!" Viola's butterflies started fluttering their wings at a maddening pace.

"Great! Yourself?" Liz seemed to have added on an absurd amount of bubbly to her personality. Vy hoped she wasn't about to say anything that would embarrass her.

"I'm doing quite well. Ready to head out, Viola?"

"Yes, I am," she said, picking up her purse.

"Will you be joining us today, Liz," he asked.

"Nah, thanks for the invite. You two kids go ahead," she said, grinning. "I'm meeting Liam in an hour anyway. I'll catch you later, Vy!"

She waved them off as they headed out of the office and down the hall.

"I hope you'll like this place," he started, "I've been there a few times. I think they may have the best coffee around. Certainly better than any of the chain shops around here."

"Great! Us English majors live on caffeine, so we're always looking for the best cup," she joked.

They climbed into his black car in the parking lot and were on their way, attempting the slightly awkward small talk that accompanies all first dates.

After a few short minutes, Monty parked the car on a side street near the waterfront, got out and quickly walked to the other side to open her door for her, while she was unbuckling her seatbelt and getting her things together.

"Oh! Well, thank you! You don't see that much nowadays," she quipped.

"You're very welcome," he replied, offering his arm to lead her down the street.

The coffee shop he brought her to was an adorable little cafe with plenty of drink options, a menu with sandwiches that sounded absolutely delicious and a case filled with a large variety of baked goods. They placed their orders; Vy a turkey sandwich with an iced chai latte and Monty a roast beef sandwich and a large coffee with cream and sugar. Vy didn't want to assume he was paying for her, so she began to dig into her purse to find her wallet, but Monty had already paid for everything by the time she had found it. She thanked him as they proceeded to the dining area and sat down to wait while their sandwiches were made.

"Now what, exactly, is chai?" he asked.

"It's one of my absolute favorite teas," she explained. "It's very spicy; loaded with cinnamon, ginger, cardamom, cloves and such. It's delicious."

"It smells amazing. I'll have to give it a try sometime! And here I am, just a plain, boring ol' coffee," he said, lifting his cup slightly in salute.

"Hey, there's nothing wrong with a classic!" She laughed.

After a few moments, the woman behind the counter called their order number and Monty got up to get it. He brought the tray back to their table, picked up her plate and set it in front of her. She thanked him and took a small bite of her sandwich as he picked up his own.

"Oh, wow! You were right, this is fantastic," she exclaimed.

"Yeah, I love their turkey sandwiches. That flavored cream cheese just makes the whole thing."

"Definitely," she agreed.

Their lunch was great, and they thoroughly enjoyed each other's company. They talked about Shakespeare and Elizabethan England, discussed their favorite movies, books, television shows, discovering they had quite a lot of common interests.

"So, are you originally from around here," he eventually asked. They had finished eating and were slowly sipping on their drinks.

"Yes, I am. My dad owns Pages down on Penobscot Street."

"Oh, the bookstore? I'm surprised I haven't seen you there! I love that place! To be fair, I haven't been able to go for a while, haven't had much time to read for pleasure lately. You know how it is. Grad school." He rolled his eyes comically.

"Ugh. Yes. It's ironic but as an English major I don't get much time to read. At least not for fun. All of my time is focused on textbooks and essays."

"Oh, I hear ya! It's the same for us History majors."

"Hashtag grad student life," she chuckled. "So, how about you? Are you originally from here?"

He downed the last of his coffee before replying. "We used to live up north in Aroostook County. We moved here when I was a kid."

"Really? I don't remember seeing you in school over the years."

"That's because I didn't go to school here. My mother wanted me to have, what she called, a prime education, so she sent me to a boarding school for my middle and high school years. I didn't get back here until I started my undergraduate work."

"Wow, and you decided to stay here for grad school?" She didn't know many people who willingly returned to the towns in which they grew up.

"I'm not really a fan of big cities, there are way too many people. Plus, I missed being this close to the ocean," he gestured to the view outside the large windows of the coffee shop. The waves were gently crashing against the sandy beach, which was mostly devoid of people. It was still just a bit too chilly for beach days.

"There weren't any bodies of water nearby to the school I attended. And I missed the leaves changing in the fall, the colors are so beautiful up here."

She nodded in agreement. "Absolutely. I love this area. I'm hoping to get a teaching job at the university, so I won't have to leave."

"I'm hoping for the same thing," he exclaimed. "Maybe in a few years we'll have offices on the same floor!" She laughed and said she hoped they would, then smiled back at him. After a moment of silence, he checked his watch. "So, you must be working on a thesis right now?"

"I am. I'm working on *The Tempest*, actually."

His eyebrows furrowed at the mention of the play. "*The Tempest*…not sure I've read that one."

"Oh, it's lovely," she exclaimed. "It's about a sorcerer who, along with his daughter, was betrayed by his family and stripped of his title. They were left stranded on an island and several years later, members of his family pass by in a ship. When he realizes who they are, he decides to use his powers, and a captive spirit, to shipwreck them on the island. He manipulates them and the situation, eventually regaining his title and getting his daughter married to the prince. In the end, he decides to throw his book of magic into the sea, vowing to never use it again."

"Huh. That sounds awesome," he said, smiling. "I'll have to read it sometime."

"Yes! You absolutely should! I highly recommend it."

"I will, I promise." He smiled brightly, then started as his phone buzzed in his pocket. He freed it from his pocket, read the message, then returned it to its place. "I suppose I should probably be getting you back, it's already a little after two."

"Yah, I suppose. I have to work at my dad's store at four."

They made their way back to the car, where he held her door open as she climbed in, then they drove toward campus. When he finished parking the vehicle, he jumped out and opened her door just as he had when they got to the coffee shop.

"I really enjoyed talking with you today," he said, smiling. "I hope we can get together again sometime soon."

Returning his smile, she enthusiastically replied, "Yes, definitely! I'd love that. Actually, Liz, her boyfriend, and I were planning to head to Joe's this weekend, the bar down on Main Street. Would you like to join us?"

"Y'know, I think I can probably make that happen," he said, mentally going through his schedule. "Here, let me give you my number and you can text me with all the details." They exchanged phone numbers and bid each other a good afternoon.

"I look forward to seeing you again, Vy. Have a great night and hopefully I can make it in to visit you at the bookstore soon."

"Thank you for such a great afternoon, Monty." Vy wasn't entirely sure what to do at this point. She was not a kiss on the first date kind of girl, but it felt like they should do something as a goodbye. It looked like he was thinking the same thing. In the end, he reached over and gave her a quick hug, which she returned gladly. He was warm and smelled of herbs and balsam.

As Vy walked to her car she couldn't help but relive the wonderful time she'd had and how great Monty was. She wondered how he was going to fit into her busy schedule of work, thesis writing and magic lessons.

CHAPTER THIRTEEN

In typical Friday night fashion, Viola was sitting behind the counter in her father's bookshop. That same guy from a couple of weeks ago was in again, this time he'd thought ahead and brought headphones to block out the conversations of old ladies looking at knitting patterns. She had considered asking him what he was working on, but he usually wore such a sour expression she was certain she would probably never read it. Looking around at the other patrons, she saw that the store was fairly busy tonight. The same trio of little old ladies were looking through the new knitting and crochet magazines, there was the grumpy author in the chair by the window, a cute little old man was perusing the history section, a teenage girl was looking through fashion magazines while her mother found the perfect romance novel and finally, another little old lady was going through the children's section, probably looking for gifts for her grandchildren. For eight o'clock on a Friday night, the place was downright hoppin'!

She had a textbook open on the countertop, immersing herself in the world of William Shakespeare, taking notes on possible essay topics for her thesis. She couldn't help noticing the similarities between the play and her life as of late. A man with powers he both loves to use and yet also wants to be rid of? Sounds pretty damn familiar, she thought to herself. When the bell rang, she raised her eyes to see Liz walking in, hand in hand with the infamous Liam. Some of the old knitting ladies were shocked to see his bright neon green mohawk, although she could swear one of them looked as though she was thinking of doing that herself. Both Liz and Liam were wearing black, Liz in a short black dress, black tights, boots and jacket, silver chains around her neck, Liam in a black t-shirt, black hoodie, small silver hoops in both of his ears, black jeans and black Converse. They seemed to both be standing over the line of punk and goth, one foot on each side.

"What's up, Shakespeare" Liz greeted. "You remember Liam?"

Liam gave a quick nod of acknowledgement. "Sup?"

"I do, hello Liam. Nice to see you again."

Liam gave a quick nod of acknowledgement. "Yah, you too." Not particularly talkative, this one.

"I didn't expect you guys to come here first," Vy said.

"Well, we figured we'd check and make sure that creeper guy from a couple o' weeks ago wasn't here to bother you." Liz took a quick look around the store. "Looks safe for the moment, eh?"

"Haven't seen him." She hoped he wouldn't stop by at any time when Liz was here. She would have some serious explaining to do if Liz caught her conversing with Vince, seeing as the last time Liz had seen him Vy had been absolutely terrified of the man.

"So, is lover boy coming tonight," Liz asked, no doubt meaning Monty.

"I think so. He asked me to text him around eight thirty or so, just to remind him."

"Well, it's close enough to eight thirty! Get on with it!"

Vy agreed and pulled her phone out of her pocket after making sure none of the customers were heading toward the counter.

Do you think you'll be able to make it tonight?

"There. Sent."

"And now we wait," Liz said, ominously. "Liam and I will wander around for a bit. Let us know when you hear from him." With that she and Liam headed towards the music magazines and were lost in them. She had to admit, the two of them seemed to work well together. Liam wasn't nearly as sociable as Liz could be, but she had a feeling being with Liz might drag him out of his shell. Conversely, she had noticed a change in Liz over the past two weeks as she seemed to be mellowing out a little bit. Yes, she thought they complimented each other quite nicely.

As she was chatting with and ringing up the cute little old man who had been in the History section, she felt her phone vibrate in her pocket. She was anxious to see what the text said but focused on the task at hand, easy to do with such a friendly and kind little old man. He had seen her Shakespeare book on the side counter and inquired about it. After she told him she was an English grad student he began to tell her all about the time he had spent in England with his wife and that they had seen a performance of Hamlet in The Globe Theatre. She was completely enthralled with the conversation from that point on. When they had finished their discussion the man left, though she hoped he would return soon so she could chat with him again. It was kind people like that who made a retail job much easier to endure. Next in line after him was the woman with the teenage daughter. The daughter was purchasing a rather racy edition of *Cosmopolitan* and Vy wondered if her mother had actually paid attention to the headlines on the cover. However, her mother then put three romance novels on the counter which, Vy had heard from others who had read them, were quite graphic. Well...you know what they say about apples and trees. After she had finished with them, she finally had a chance to check her phone.

Yes, I'll be there! You said around nine thirty, right? - Monty

There were those damn butterflies again. She shot him a quick text back.

Yup! I'll be out of work around nine and we'll head to the bar. - Vy

Sounds good! I'll see you there! - Monty

He added a smiling emoji to the end of the text. Strange, how a tiny yellow face made of zeros and ones could make her feel so giddy. She walked over to the magazines where Liz and Liam were standing, Liz with her arms wrapped around one of Liam's arms. Vy couldn't help but think how adorable they looked together.

"Okay, Monty says he'll be there around nine thirty, just about the time I'll get there after closing the shop," she informed them.

"Sounds like a plan," said Liz. "We were thinking of going to get something to eat. Want us to grab you something?"

She shook her head. "Nah, I've got some leftover spaghetti in the fridge out back. Thank you, though!"

"Okay, well have fun closing!"

Liam put the magazine they had been browsing back on the shelf. "We'll see you there, then," he said. Yup, definitely not much of a talker but that was almost perfect, actually. Liz usually did enough talking for both her and Vy. Someone who was a bit more like Vy in the talking department would be a welcome addition to their little group.

After they left, she quickly ran out back to pop her dinner in the microwave. She'd been to the bar on an empty stomach before. It didn't end well. She'd learned many valuable life lessons on *that* particular evening. While it was heating up, she stayed by the door that led to the backroom, giving her a good view of the counter and door, in case one of the patrons was ready to be checked out. Fortunately, no one came up by the time the microwave beeped at her and she took her dinner up to the counter, the intoxicating smell of garlic and marinara sauce trailing behind her. She ate carefully, making sure no one was coming to the counter when she was about to take a bite and made very sure that no sauce splattered all over her light blue shirt. In retrospect, she probably should have worn red, just to be safe.

She managed to finish her dinner before the last customer, the one she had officially dubbed "Grumpy Author," packed up his laptop and left the store. She locked the door behind him, quickly bustled around, picking up the last of the rogue magazines and books people had left on the tables and at the counter, then began counting the cash drawer and printing off daily reports. She had just finished counting all the dimes when she heard a tapping at the window. Looking up, she saw Monty standing outside, grinning and waving. She returned his smile and wave, and then held up her index finger, asking him to wait for a minute or two. He gave her a thumbs up and she returned to counting.

Getting everything in order, she put together the bank deposit for the next day, separated the money that needed to be returned to the register in the morning, bagged everything up and took it out back, where she locked it all up in the safe. She also deposited her now-empty food container into the sink. She'd take care of it later. Grabbing her favorite black jacket and her bag, she turned off all of the lights, shut the back door and headed toward the front of the store. As she walked, she began slipping her arms through her coat sleeves, preparing for the cool night air outside.

"Hey, I thought I'd meet you here," Monty said. "Since the bar is just around the corner a little way up, I thought we could walk. That all right?"

"Sure, that's fine, "she said, nodding. "I was planning to do that, anyway."

"Well, I would definitely rather you didn't walk alone at night. Maine doesn't have much of a crime rate, but you never know who might be out here," he said, offering her his arm, which she gladly accepted. "We live in strange times." She heartily agreed. He really had no idea just how true that was. They walked together in silence for a moment. The bar wasn't terribly far away so she was glad they were walking at a slower pace, it meant more time for just the two of them to talk and be together, rather than surrounded by all the drunks at the bar, amusing as they were. "So, how was work?"

"Oh, it was fine. Nothing too terribly exciting." She told him all about Grumpy Author and his extreme dislike of the knitting ladies and they both joked about the mom buying some rather explicit romance novels. As they walked, other shops along Main Street were closing up; the lights in the coffee shop Vy frequented during morning shifts were going dark, and the owner of the gift shop across the street was locking the door. The apartment windows from the second and third floors over many of the shops were lit, adding to the light already being given off by the streetlights.

"Sounds like Friday nights in a bookstore can be pretty entertaining," he quipped.

"Oh, yes. Its retail but at least I'm surrounded by books."

"Do you really need the job when you're a grad student and, I assume, teaching classes? The stipend should be enough to cover your bills, right?"

"It does, yes. I mainly do it to help my dad out. I've worked there since I was old enough to do so and he doesn't care if I do homework or grading while I'm on the clock. As jobs go, it's probably the easiest one out there."

The sidewalks weren't incredibly busy, so there were a few people scattered around, most of them probably headed to the bars, or getting out of a late dinner. The majority consisted of college-age students, so, most likely they were heading toward the three or four bars that dotted Main Street. It was now late May and though the days were starting to warm up, the evening air was still a bit chilly, the dregs of winter holding on for as long as it possibly could. Vy didn't really mind winter, but she was ready for the warmth of spring. As they neared the section of street where the majority of the bars and restaurants were located, the noise level began to rise drastically. With the Spring Semester over, many of the students had left the area already. Those who had stuck around for work or for attending summer classes were apt to do quite a lot of partying on the weekends, now that there weren't any assignments due. At least for another week.

"I take it we're meeting Liz and her boyfriend here," he inquired.

"Yes, they were grabbing dinner and then heading this way." He nodded in acknowledgement.

They entered the bar, which was fairly crowded for a Friday night and looked around for Liz and Liam. They finally spotted them in a booth against the wall, making out rather fiercely.

"Uh...let's give them a minute. Want to get drinks?" Vy could feel the color rising on her cheeks. How awkward.

Monty agreed that was probably the best thing to do for the time being. Hopefully the pair would be able to separate themselves from each other by the time Vy and Monty made their way to the table. After a few minutes, the bartender finally recognized their existence and made their drinks, which Vy offered to pay for this time. She'd never been one to feel comfortable with other people spending money on her on a regular basis. She was more into alternating or splitting the costs of date nights. They made their way back across the bar, happy to find that Liz and Liam had managed to pull themselves apart for a few minutes.

"Hey, Shakespeare, Monty!" Liz loved using her nickname for Vy at every chance she got. "Let the drinking begin!" She held her plastic cup full of some purple concoction up in the air, and they all toasted to the evening's coming festivities.

The four of them spent the next few hours talking, laughing, telling jokes, reliving awful school stories and having a great time. Vy and Monty chose not to drink all that much, even with Liz encouraging them to both get completely hammered. Admittedly, Vy did drink enough to feel rather tipsy but she was still capable of walking out on her own at the end of the night. Monty gave Liz and Liam a ride home to Liz's apartment, as they were both incapable of driving, and then drove back to the bookstore to take Vy to her car.

"Thank you so much for taking care of them," she said, indicating Liz and Liam. "She has an amazing tolerance but when she *really* has too much to drink, I worry about her."

"No problem at all! Happy to do it! I hope they'll have a way to get their cars in the morning, though." He snickered a bit at the thought. "You're okay to drive now?"

"Yes, it's all worn off. Promise!" She tossed her things into the passenger side of her car and turned around to say goodnight. "Thanks again for joining us tonight, it was really fun!"

"It was! Thank you for inviting me," he said, smiling. "Any big plans for the rest of the weekend?"

"Oh, not much," she said, knowing full well that in a matter of hours she'd be traveling through some sort of magical gate to an ancient battlefield. NBD, as they say. "I'm helping my dad out with some things at home," she lied.

"Same here, except with my mom," he replied.

"Wild and crazy weekends for us, eh?" She smirked.

"Oh yeah. You know it!" He gave her two thumbs up in an overly excited gesture, giving her a brief fit of giggles. "Well, I guess I'll see you at school on Monday, then?"

"Yup, all the research! Goodnight!" She was reaching for the door handle on the driver's side when he gently caught her wrist and turned her around to face him. Her heart began pounding out a samba inside her chest. Gently pulling her towards him, he slipped one hand around to the small of her back and placed one hand beneath her chin, gently bringing her face close to his. The kiss was soft and sweet, and he didn't pressure her into more. His kiss was simple and respectful, while still making her see stars. They broke apart and just smiled at each other, relishing in the moment, then Monty opened her door for her and held it as she climbed inside.

"Goodnight," he said, as soon as she was settled into her seat. He closed her door, then slowly backed toward his own vehicle, smiling at her until she drove away. She couldn't wipe the smile from her face as she drove home, impatient to text Liz and tell her about this recent update.

CHAPTER FOURTEEN

Vy woke shortly after nine the next morning, needing an extra hour or two to sleep off the drinks from the night before. She reached for her phone as soon as she was awake enough to form coherent thought, eager to see what Liz had to say to the texts she sent her the night before.

What?! Details, woman! Now! - Liz

She quickly typed up a response text, telling her about all that had transpired between her and Monty, though she didn't exactly have any dirty details to share, which would no doubt be very disappointing to Liz. Putting the phone back down on her nightstand, she began to get ready for the day. The plan was to meet at the old Victorian by noon, after which they would create the gate and travel to the battle site. After showering, dressing and taking care of girly hair and makeup details, she returned to her phone to find the disappointed text she was expecting from Liz.

Seriously? That's it? Text me when something important happens...

She smirked then proceeded to stuff everything she'd need for the day into her purse. Carrying her bag out to her car, she climbed into the driver's seat, and then headed toward her old childhood home. She and her father had decided to drive over together. He stepped outside the moment she pulled into the driveway and was already unlocking his car as she put her own into park.

"This could get to be a pretty intense day for you, Vy. I'm sure Rosalyn will have much to tell you regarding the battle," her father said from the driver's seat.

"How does she know so much about this? Are the events written down somewhere? I'd love to read the texts."

"Well, I believe they are, yes, but she was there. She actually witnessed all of it firsthand."

Vy turned to stare at him in disbelief. "What?! That's not possible. She looks like she's only a couple of years older than I am!"

"For many magical beings, the passage of time doesn't affect them in the same manner as it does human beings, particularly elves. They reach a certain point and stop showing physical signs of aging, staying young for many, many years."

"Then...how old is Rosalyn? How old was mum?"

"Your mother wasn't very old for an elf. She was around one hundred years old when we first met, though she looked to be the same age as I was."

"I mean...that's mildly disturbing."

He chuckled. "When you're still new to the idea, I suppose it is a bit. Yes, she had lived quite a bit longer than I had but for all intents and purposes she was in her twenties." He paused for a moment as Vy let that knowledge sink in. "As for Rosalyn, I'm honestly not sure. She was present at the great battle which she speaks of to you so often and I don't really have any idea when that occurred. She's probably at least a couple of centuries old."

"Wow. At least she's aged well." The two of them had a great chuckle at that while they drove through town, heading toward Sugar Maple Hill. A few seconds later another thought occurred to her. "Does that mean…I'll age differently, as well?"

"I don't really know, Vy-Vy." He didn't look at her as he spoke. "It's entirely possible."

They traveled the rest of the way in silence, both immersed in their own thoughts. The idea that she might look the same age for eons was a strange one. Wasn't it everyone's secret wish to remain young whilst still living an exceedingly long life? But if you had to watch all of your friends and family grow old and wither before your eyes…was it really something to hope for? After crossing under the archway, she saw Tam and Vince out on the lawn, walking back toward the building. Spotting her and her father from afar, they began to wave. They all met on the porch and exchanged greetings before heading inside. Once more, they proceeded down the hall toward the parlor. Inside, they found their small traveling group standing in the middle of the room, readying themselves for the trip. Rosalyn had chosen much less extravagant dress for the occasion, opting for a loose, cream-colored blouse, brown pants, and boots. Her hair was still piled elegantly on her head, however, exposing her pointed, elongated ears. The rest of the party was similarly attired in shades of brown and green travelling clothes. The pixie, Lady Asteria, however sported her purple skin and nothing else. They turned when the four new arrivals entered the room.

"Ah, Viola! A pleasure to see you, as always," Rosalyn gushed. "Are you ready for today's adventures?"

"Well...I'm as ready as I'm going to be, I guess!" She spoke with a brightness and energy she didn't quite feel but the desired effect was achieved, as Rosalyn's smile widened at her response.

"Excellent," she cried, clapping her hands together. "We will begin momentarily but first I want to explain where we're going and how we will be getting there, as we won't be travelling by everyday means." She gathered everyone close to her before she began her explanation. "The place we will be going to is a place similar to this house and grounds in that it coexists with the world of humans, but they are incapable of seeing it. To them, it looks like a wild swamp and the magical wards and enchantments around it make any human who ventures near it immediately desire to leave. Thus, we continue to keep it secret and safe from humans and those we don't want in the area. When we arrive there, we will see a barren field, dotted with grave markers. Once there," this part directed toward Viola, "I will lead you to specific areas around the field, showing you where certain events took place during the battle. Hopefully being there will help you to recover your memories of your former life as Lady Evelina. Everyone with me so far," she asked, looking around at those present. Everyone responded with a nod.

"Very good. Now, as the place we are traveling to is a place of magic, we must use magic to get there. I am glad that all of you volunteered to travel with us, as we will need lots of powerful magic to cast a traveling spell. We will go outside to do this, getting away from everyone else inside the house and where we can be the most in tune with nature. I will instruct more fully on how we go about doing this as soon as we are outside. So," she said, clapping her hands together again, "gather everything you want to bring and let us all meet out on the lawn in five minutes."

Everyone scattered, gathering up their belongings, while Rosalyn beckoned Vy closer to her. "Now, I'm not sure what will happen when you get there, Viola. As I said previously, it is our hope that being on the battlefield may help you to remember some of what transpired there. However, it's possible that you may not remember anything at all." At this she took Vy's hand in an encouraging gesture. "Whatever happens, I'm sure it will all work out well in the end."

"I understand," Viola replied. "I am as prepared as I can be for whatever happens…and I will deal with it as best I can, no matter the outcome."

"You are strong, Viola," she said, smiling. "Strong and very brave. We will all be there with you to help you through," she said, briefly squeezing Vy's hand before releasing it. "Now, come, let's go outside and get ready to leave."

They walked out onto the lawn, where everyone else was standing around, waiting to depart. Some of them carried small packs on their backs, all were dressed for a walk or hike. A few creatures were out on the lawn to see them off, including a couple of Fulrin's folk, some pixies, an elf and several of the gnomes who did most of the gardening.

"Okay, everyone. Gather 'round and let us create the gate!" Everyone closed in, forming a circle. "Now, everyone, take each other's hands and focus all of your energy into the center of our circle." Everyone reached for the outstretched hands of the persons on either side of them and closed their eyes, concentrating all their efforts on the center of the circle. Vy did as Tam had instructed her, focusing on imagining the energy of the lawn around her flowing up, through her body, down her fingertips and connecting with the hands of her father and Vince, then exploding inwards toward the center of their small circle and transforming into a doorway. She could sense the energy around her, coming from everyone else gathered there. The magic was overwhelming and felt as though it was completely encompassing their group. A strong breeze blew across the grounds and she felt her curls going wild around her face. When the wind calmed, there was a sudden POP! She was curious but didn't want to look around in case she broke her concentration.

"Well done, everyone!" Rosalyn cried. "A perfect gate!"

With that, Vy assumed it was safe to open her eyes. She didn't see anything out of the ordinary at first, just the people standing around beside and opposite her, and the grassy ground in between them. After a few seconds, however, she noticed something off in the air in front of her. While everything still looked mostly normal, she could see a strange shimmering in the air, which stretched along the edges of a large oval-shape in the center of their circle. Inside the oval she could see the grass of the field on which they stood. And yet…perhaps it was a bit greener? And taller?

"Okay, then! Let us be off!" Rosalyn let go of the hands she'd been holding and moved toward the strange shimmering. She paused momentarily to wink at Vy, who was staring at her, waiting to see what would happen next. She stepped forward and disappeared. So, that's what a magical gate looks like, Vy thought. Placing one under a garden archway somehow seemed more dramatic and beautiful than the one they'd just created. One by one, everyone stepped through the gate, Vy going just before her father, who went last. They had left the vast lawn and gardens of the Victorian and now found themselves on a wide, open field that stretched further than Vy's eyes could see. To her it seemed the green grass went on for miles, disappearing into the horizon beyond. The sky was gray and cloudy, as thought it might start raining at any moment. The field was mostly flat, though there were several smallish hills further away from them. The ground was covered in tall grass and scattered throughout were large, gray rocks of various shapes. Upon closer inspection, Vy saw that they looked like chunks of stone you might find in the ruins of a castle. Everyone else was looking around just as she was, taking in the new landscape on which they found themselves.

"And here we are," Rosalyn said, looking around at everyone. "Now, we must figure out where we are in relation to those long-ago events. As you can see, this battlefield was quite expansive." She turned away from them and toward the field, taking a few steps in each direction, trying to orient herself. Vy wasn't sure how she could tell where anything specific occurred, everything looked exactly the same to her eyes. "Ah, yes. I know where we are now," Rosalyn said, turning back toward them. "While the entirety of the battle stretched across this field, the more notable locations are further ahead. It's a bit of a hike but we should be able to make it across the field within an hour or so."

Everyone shouldered their packs and bags and fell to following Lady Rosalyn as she led the way forward on the battlefield. Initially, Vy didn't think it would take as long as the elf had indicated it would but as they got going, she realized much of that time was devoted to maneuvering around all the large stones dotting the field. Many of the stones were the size of small boulders and required only a few steps to get by while others were vast, requiring them to either go dozens of feet to one side or the other to get around it, or climb over them. A few minutes into their trek, Rosalyn called Vy to walk beside her.

"It's more than just mere happenstance that these rocks are placed where they are, Viola. Each of them represents where a life was lost in the battle," she explained solemnly. Vy looked around at the field with a new understanding and appreciation of the loss felt here, taking in the rocks and boulders that dotted much of the green landscape. Meanwhile, Rosalyn continued to speak. "The larger rocks denote the areas where there was a particularly high concentration of lives lost."

"There are so many," Vy observed, as she surveyed the land around them.

"Yes. A great many were lost. It was truly a terrible day, both for magics and non-magics, alike. There are markers for all of them." Vy could hear the sadness in Rosalyn's voice. She struggled to think of something comforting to say but when she looked around at the hundreds of rocks stuck firmly in the ground, nothing seemed good enough. Instead, she remained silent and continued to observe the landscape. Several miles off to the right she could see the dark green of a thick forest and to the left she thought there might be some sort of lake or even ocean in the distance.

They walked for roughly an hour and were starting to feel rather exhausted after climbing and stumbling around all the rocks, when Vy suddenly stopped. She couldn't identify what was wrong exactly, but she felt strange. The little hairs on the back of her neck were standing up, as though she could feel someone staring at her. Looking up, she saw that everyone was still walking ahead of her. She felt drawn to the spot where she was standing and couldn't bring herself to move her leg to take a step or call out to those ahead of her. She could only remain standing where she was, attempting to identify the cause of her discomfort. Looking around, she saw that she was standing in a grassy area surrounded by stones arranged in a circle.

Vince was the first to notice she was no longer with them. He turned around and saw the strange look on her face, recognizing immediately that something was wrong. "Viola? Are you okay?"

At his question everyone turned to look in her direction, then quickly made their way back to where she was standing, frozen in place.

"Something's...off. I'm not sure what it is," Vy said, when they reached her. She felt shaky, and apparently others could see it, as Vince moved toward her and took her arm to steady her in case she needed it.

"What is ..." Rosalyn stepped forward, starting to speak. "Oh. Oh, I see." Her gaze was pulled away from Vy and to the ground on which they were standing. She reached an arm out and prevented Vy's father from going to his daughter's side to check on her. "This is it. This is the spot we were looking for. This is where Evelina...where you," she said, turning her gaze back to Vy. "This is where you fought and died."

Vy stared back at her in silence, knowing full well that everyone else's eyes were trained on her. Her discomfort continued to grow as Rosalyn spoke. "This is where everything happened. Our queen, Evelina, faced off against Melarue during the battle and they each killed the other. Melarue performed her bit of magic just before she died from her wounds, and Evelina got caught inside the spell. That patch of earth in the very center of this circle is where Melarue used her magic to ensure that she would return, thereby creating the prophecy." She yet again took Vy's hands in her own. "I think this is why you feel so strangely right now, Viola. I think you can sense the importance of this spot. I think Evelina might be calling to you from the depths of your subconscious. She's trying to find a way out and you need to let her. Don't fight it. This is a good thing." She paused to look toward everyone else, all of whom were standing nearby watching and listening in on the conversation. "I think we need to give you space. We'll stand just outside the circle and let you figure this out. If you need us, we won't be far away, okay?"

Vy nodded silently and watched Rosalyn leave the circle, gesturing to everyone else to do the same. She smiled weakly at her father who wasn't even attempting to hide his concern. He sat down on a nearby rock and stared watched her intently, his leg bouncing nervously. Vince squeezed her hand tightly before letting go and joining the others. She watched him go, but after a moment she looked away, needing to ignore everyone else and focus on what she was feeling, in the hopes that it would help ease this odd sense of discomfort she couldn't seem to shake. It was as though a buzzing was going through her entire being. She felt as if she was on the verge of something incredibly important but at the same time she was filled with dread. She felt like she needed to get closer to the ground, while at the same time it felt as though she was being pushed away. She fought back against the need to turn and run, knowing she had to do this, that hopefully it would bring her a better kind of understanding. She wanted to understand the world she had been thrust into, her abilities and this other self, Evelina, who was part of her and yet not.

Whether through magic or her own inability to maintain her composure any longer, she dropped to her knees, placing her palms on the ground in front of her to steady herself. The moment her bare skin touched the ground everything changed. Wide eyed, she stared as the rocks and faces around her disappeared and were replaced by hundreds of warriors, ghostly and transparent at first, solidifying slowly before her eyes.

The last light of day spread across the grassy field; the sky red with the rays of the setting sun. There were no chirping crickets or singing birds to be heard in what should have been a usually peaceful meadow. Instead, it was full of the sounds of battle; metal clashing on metal, the screams of the injured and dying, the cries for help, the sticky, wet squelch of flesh being rendered, the pops and bangs of erupting magic. She was surrounded by all the creatures of her childhood fairy tales and her fantasy novels. Humans, elves, werewolves, goblins, faeries, gnomes, and she couldn't tell what else; each of them fighting with whatever weapon they could, be it blades, claws or magic. Countless creatures lay on the ground, injured; hot, red blood pooling in the grass beneath them.

In her peripheral vision Vy saw two women marching toward her from opposite directions. One had hair as black as the night sky, tan skin and dark eyes. She was dressed all in battered, black armor, carrying a great sword in her hands. The other had long, fiery red curls, her eyes shining silver in the setting sun. She had a pale complexion and was wearing a set of golden armor over a billowing red gown. The dark-haired woman smirked at the red head while the battle raged on around them.

"Come now, Evelina," she said, mockingly. "Was this really necessary? So much death...is this what you wanted?"

The woman in gold and red stood tall, not moving. "This is all *your* doing, Melarue. It is you who started this awful war. We did not want to fight this."

Melarue guffawed loudly before screaming at Evelina. "*WE* started this?! No, my dear, you and your people started this war! You started this with your prejudice and your desire to dominate humans! All these creatures' deaths are on YOUR hands!!"

Taken aback by the accusation, Evelina's calm was shattered. She glared at Melarue as she struggled to maintain her calm exterior. "No," she said, shaking her head. "No, we would never want to hold any sort of power over you." She spread her arms wide, gesturing to everyone around them. "We are all equals!!!" Before she could open her mouth to say any more, Melarue began screaming again.

"LIES!! ALL LIES!!! EVERYTHING THAT COMES OUT OF YOUR MOUTHS IS A LIE!!!" She shook her head back and forth as she began laughing hysterically. "We ask you to share your knowledge and your power and you deny us. You sit in your little gardens and your forests, performing magic tricks but if one of us, a human, ever asks to study your ways, we are rejected, pushed away. You cannot tell me we are equals when you don't treat us as such. YOU LIE!!" She screamed, lifted her blade, and ran toward Evelina. A moment before the blade struck, Evelina moved out of the way with lightning speed. The blade hit the ground, the point burying itself in the dirt, jarring Melarue. She jerked the blade free, then spun around quickly to once again face Evelina. Other creatures around them were beginning to cease their fighting and watch the interaction between the two women.

With a deep sadness in her eyes, Evelina tried once again to talk to Melarue. "Please, Melarue...we don't deny you our knowledge out of malice. Only those who are born with the ability to wield magic can do so safely. A human without that naturally born ability cannot keep control of the knowledge once it has been learned. Many have tried and failed. The magic, the energy, burns through the body and drives the person mad, changes them or kills them. You know this, you've seen it. It's burning *you* up even now and yet you still feel the need to wage this war against us? Why? Why, when it will accomplish nothing?!"

"Accomplish nothing?" Melarue's mad laughter started again. "You have no idea about what I can accomplish, Evelina." Holding up her hand, Melarue closed her eyes and focused while Evelina watched with her own eyes wide open in contrast. Melarue's hand trembled and sweat started to bead on her forehead as a small ball of light slowly began to form just above her open palm. Evelina watched in horror as the tiny ball of energy grew into a ball of flame, hovering over Melarue's palm. Melarue slowly opened her eyes and grinned widely at her. "You see, I've learned a great deal since I last saw you. I found a very wise teacher. And, as you can see," she said, playing with the flames burning in her hand, "I was a diligent student and I have learned much." She quickly threw the fireball toward Evelina's face, who just barely managed to jump out of the way in time. "Do you see?!" Her laughter reached a fever pitch. "Do you see what I can do, Evelina?!" She sent bursts of flame toward an elf on her left and a dwarf to her right, who both screamed in pain as the flames crawled along their skin. A third blast incinerated a faerie in an instant. Vy watched as the grass around Melarue wilted and blackened with each burst of flame, the casualty of energy stolen by someone who didn't know how to wield it properly.

Evelina quickly sent out jets of water to douse the flames on the elf and dwarf, but not before they had suffered serious burns to their flesh. "Stop this at once, Melarue! These creatures have done nothing to you!"

The fire reflected in her dark eyes, Melarue smiled calmly as she transferred the fire from her hand to her sword, engulfing the blade in a bright green flame. "I will not stop," she said quietly, "until you and your faithful magics," she sneered, "have been imprisoned or destroyed. I will not stop until all that is left of your kind are the few who see how wrong you are, the few who support our cause." She lifted her hand and, using her new-found knowledge of magic, grasped the throat of Evelina from afar, dragging her closer. When Evelina was but a hair's breadth away from her face, Melarue whispered in her ear. "And then all of us will know the secrets of magic and then everything you have done, all you have sacrificed to stop us, will mean nothing."

Evelina's arms hung at her sides, the fingers of her right-hand curling and twisting as she prepared her own attack. "I will not let you do this," she croaked through Melarue's magical grip on her throat. "You will condemn all the humans to madness, corruption or death. Why can you not see that we are trying to save you? Let me help you before it's too late and the damage you've inflicted upon yourself is beyond our aid."

Melarue's smile widened. "It is you who needs saving, little faerie princess." Evelina let out a scream of pain as the fiery blade pierced her right side. Cries of dismay sounded around them as faerie folk and magic wielders saw their leader injured. Melarue pulled the blade from Evelina's stomach and let the injured woman fall to her knees, blood and green flame escaping the wound. Melarue swiped a finger across the blade, blood dripping from her glove. Grinning wickedly, she leaned down to whisper once more to her foe.

"The flame of my sword is burning through your blood. You don't have long, little princess. Die, knowing that all you have fought against has been for naught." An evil grin spread across her red lips as she gloated above the fallen queen. "I will take what you have built and destroy anyone and any*thing* that gets in my way." She slapped Evelina's cheek, then stood, turned around and began to walk away. The creatures nearby were silent, some in abject horror and others in elation. A short distance away Vy could see a slightly younger Rosalyn, dressed for war, her battle with a large troll momentarily ceased as she watched what was transpiring, a look of emotional agony on the young fey's face.

Melarue was walking away, victory exuding from each step, when she heard a sudden intake of breath from those nearby. Half a second later, a sharp pain slammed into her back and sent her tumbling forward. She pushed herself back up and turned to see Evelina, barely managing to stand, one hand pressed against the bleeding wound in her side, the other outstretched in front of her, the glow of recently cast magic fading away. "What in the hell do you think you're doing?! You're finished!! Why fight and prolong the inevitable?!"

Trembling and gasping, Evelina struggled to remain standing. "Yes, that is true. I can feel the flames of your spell pounding through my veins. But I will *never* cease trying to stop you. You will damn your kind if I fail."

Melarue took long, quick strides back toward her. "Why continue when it matters not?!" She stopped suddenly, a few paces from Evelina, with a sudden muscle spasm. A look of confused concern crossed her face and she looked toward her enemy, who returned her gaze with sadness in her eyes. A second spasm dropped her to her knees as she cried out in pain. "What have you done to me?!"

"I have done what I had to do. I will not survive this day, but neither will you and without you, your movement will lose its fire and peace shall return to our lands, with as little loss of life as possible."

Melarue doubled over, wrapping her arms around herself, trying to calm the magic racing through her body. She gritted her teeth, groaning through yet another painful spasm, and then lifted her head once more to look in Evelina's eyes. "Then I shall cast a very special spell; a spell I stole from a dark magician. A spell of reincarnation!" Evelina gasped, unable to hide her surprise. "That's right, princess. I shall return again and finish what I've started." Another painful spasm wracked her body and she collapsed onto her side, maintaining eye contact, while she whispered an incantation under her breath.

"This is dark magic, Melarue. Don't let yourself be corrupted by it!" Evelina took a few steps toward the woman, teetered and fell forward into the grass, the loss of blood becoming too much for her to bear. Gasping, she clawed her way across the ground, trying desperately to stop the woman before she could complete such a dark spell. "Please, Melarue. Don't. Do not do this and corrupt yourself even further!"

Evelina reached Melarue and grasped one of the woman's arms in her hand, mere seconds before the woman finished her spell. Evelina gasped as she felt the spell spreading outwards, enveloping her in its sinister embrace, due to their physical connection.

Melarue felt it as well and grinned weakly as she understood what was about to happen. "See you on the other side, Evelina." She exhaled softly and ceased moving.

Evelina let out a weak "no," as a tear leaked from one of her eyes. Then, resting her head on the green grass, her eyes went dark, and she moved no more. Simultaneously, Vy felt a tear fall from her own eye. The image began to fade, the warriors becoming less and less corporeal. Vy thought she would be returning to the real world but instead of seeing her father, Vince, Tam, Fulrin, Asteria and Rosalyn reappearing in her vision, everything around her faded to black. Vy felt a terror she had never known before. All around her was just an unrelenting absence of anything. Just a deep, unbroken darkness.

Suddenly, two tiny pinpricks of light began to shine out, growing ever larger and moving closer. As the two lights grew nearer, they began to have more defined shapes: that of two human beings. The lights grew brighter and brighter until they started to hurt her eyes, then suddenly winked out, leaving two women in their place. To the left was Evelina, her red hair fluttering in an invisible breeze, wearing her golden armor and red ribbons over the red battle dress, smiling warmly toward Vy and beside her, on the right...

"Mom?"

Viola's mother, Helena, was dressed in a long, light blue gown, her gossamer wings open and fanned out behind her back, pointed ears poking out through her dark curls and her smile reaching from the corners of her mouth up to her pale green eyes.

"Vy-vy," she stepped forward, stroking her daughter's face gently. "You've grown into such a smart, caring, wonderful, beautiful young woman."

"Mom…" Vy put her hand over her mother's to find that it was real and soft and warm. "Mom, you're here. I've missed you so much." Vy threw her arms around her mother, relishing the embrace. She had been young when her mother died and had ached to feel her mother's arms wrapped around her. She felt her mother's hands caressing the back of her head, smoothing down her curls.

"I miss you too, sweetie. But I want you to know that I'm okay. I'm far more than okay. And I am so proud of you. Everyday. You're amazing, Vy."

Vy pulled away from her mother, who used the pads of her thumbs to gently wipe the tears from her daughter's cheeks. "You're really here?"

"In a way, yes, I am. I'm always with you, no matter where you go or what you do. You can't always see me, but I'll always be there, watching over you."

As happy as she was to reunite with her mother after so long, Viola had to turn her gaze to the other woman, her other self, Evelina. The woman's face was very similar to Vy's except lacking the freckles or blemishes Vy always glared at when she looked in the mirror. Her eyes were the same green as Vy's but perhaps more piercing and her red curls, which looked like tendrils of living fire, hung down to her waist, while Vy's stopped just passed her shoulders.

"And you...you're Evelina."

The armor-clad woman nodded. "Yes, I am. And so are you. I am you and you are me."

"And where are we?"

Evelina looked around before answering. "We're in a space between worlds. And in your head. And not. It's difficult to explain, but this is a place where we can meet safely."

Standing here in this strange place, with a woman who looked just like her standing next to her mother, Viola felt the weight of everything crashing down upon her. "I am so scared," she said to both of them, feeling tears welling up in her eyes. "This is all so crazy and so much; I have no idea what to do!"

"Just keep doing what you know to be right in your heart, Vy," her mother soothed. "Protect others, fix the wrongs you see in the world and listen to what your heart tells you."

Evelina stepped forward. "You can't stay here in this dream-world for much longer. You must go back. But before you do, you need to know everything; all of my memories, everything I have learned, all of it will be yours. And then you have to go back."

"And what will I be? *Who* will I be," Vy asked, tears threatening to spilling over yet again.

Both women smiled at her and at each other.

"You'll be you. And me. You'll still be Viola, but you will also be Evelina." The elf put her hand on Vy's left shoulder. "We are the same person, you and me. It will be scary and confusing. It will be difficult, but you are strong and brave. I have no doubt that you will overcome it and achieve success."

"And you are my daughter, Vy-vy. I'll be with you, especially when things get tough. I love you so very much."

The tears were flowing freely down her cheeks now. "I love you too, mom."

Vy's mother again wiped the tears from her cheeks, kissed her forehead then slowly faded away, leaving Vy wracked with sobs as she turned her gaze toward the warrior queen before her. Evelina stroked her cheek softly, then walked towards Vy. In this strange dream-world between realities, Evelina walked through and into Vy's body, a golden glow of shimmering magical energy surrounding them, then finally just her.

Her mind exploded in colors, sights, sounds and knowledge. She could see everything Evelina had ever seen in her life and the memories mingled with her own, as if they were one and the same. She understood the fundamentals of magic and how it worked, suddenly knew how to use the earth's energy to perform magical feats of the greatest magnitude. She felt as though she could see everything that ever was and ever could be, all at once. She was still Vy; she still loved Shakespeare, her friends, and her father. She still had the same likes and interests, opinions, and beliefs. But she was also Evelina. She was leader of a great kingdom of magics. She had centuries of knowledge and was filled with power and energy the likes of which Vy had never felt before. The force of it was too much and she found herself falling forward into the black, empty space before her. She blinked and suddenly she was back in the real world, staring at the grass beneath her. She could see the edges of rocks out of the corners of her eyes, and beyond that, the legs of her father and friends. She was panting, tears still leaking from her eyes, and she was trembling violently, but the discomfort from earlier had disappeared. After a moment she caught her breath and steadied herself, then pushed up from the ground and rose to her feet, turning to face the group behind her. Everyone was staring at her strangely, their mouths and eyes wide open.

"I'm okay, don't worry." Her voice was still shaking, and she did not blame them if they didn't believe her. She had assumed they were concerned for her wellbeing, but no one seemed to acknowledge her statement. She furrowed her brows in confusion just as Rosalyn began to take several small, uncertain steps forward.

"Lady Rosalyn," Vy started, "what…?

Rosalyn suddenly stopped and bowed her head low. "Evelina, my queen." Vy stared at her, struggling to comprehend, then looked up when she saw movement out of the corner of her eye, to find everyone else, aside from her father, bowing in the same fashion. While not bowing, her father's face still held an expression of shock.

"What are you doing? Why are you looking at me like that," she asked, looking toward her father. He started toward her, still staring, and reached into his pocket. Pulling out his phone, he swiped his thumb across the screen and clicked twice before handing the phone to her.

"We didn't see anything happen," he said. "You knelt down on the ground and stayed perfectly still for a few moments and then…just…" he trailed off, lost for words.

As she took the phone from him, she saw that he'd opened up his camera app. He'd put it in selfie mode, so she saw herself looking back at her. She looked for some sort of wound or something; perhaps she'd hit her head on a rock when she fell to her knees but could find none. She was about to ask again what their issue was, when she suddenly understood why everyone was staring at her. The major facial features were the same, but her skin seemed much more polished and smooth. Her green eyes held an unusual energy and sparkle, giving them an otherworldly brilliance. Her ears had elongated and grown points like mother's and Tam's, though they were much shorter. She could see their pointed tips poking out from underneath her hair. *Her hair!* The red was much more vibrant, and it had grown down to her waist. She was still herself and yet something more.

The sight was shocking and overwhelming to say the least. Perhaps even more shocking, was that she hadn't recognized it at first. In her mind she'd looked the same, because she looked like Evelina. But the image staring back at her wasn't Evelina; it was Vy. *Wasn't it?* She didn't know how to feel. It was her, yet it also wasn't. She was a confused mish-mash of memories and knowledge she couldn't seem to separate, and that absolutely terrified her. She wanted to allay their concerns, however, so she returned the phone to her father and looked to everyone else. They were still staring at her but were gradually standing up from their bows. She gave them all a small smile. Humor was always a good way to diffuse a situation and she'd used it as a defense mechanism plenty of times in the past, so why not now?

"So," she said, "looks like school's going to get weird tomorrow."

CHAPTER FIFTEEN

Arin Moon sat at her desk, paperwork spread across its surface. Numbers and figures filled the pages of sales reports and annual profits. She sat, contemplating their contents, ensuring things were progressing favorably at her company. The sky outside the window behind her was a light gray, the early morning sun having given way to a rainy Saturday. She usually didn't work on the weekends but was waiting for a report from one of her many secret employees; the ones who worked in the sub-basement. She thought she might as well look over figures for her seafood company at the same time. She picked up her mug of coffee off the black topped desk and raised it to her lips, savoring the aroma.

Suddenly, a flash of light crossed her vision, the mug slipping from her hand to crash onto the desktop beneath it, shattered porcelain and dark coffee spilling across the surface and staining the pages. The flash of light and brief stab of pain could only mean one thing - her enemy, the faerie queen, Evelina, had remembered who she was and was close to reaching her full power. Staring at the liquid pooling on her desk and dripping onto the floor, she knew she needed to step up her attempts to find her enemy.

Now that Evalina had woken and was closer to regaining her full strength, time was running out. Arin had intended to find the queen before she fully remembered who she was and destroy her before she could pose a threat to Arin's plans.

Pulling out her phone, she sent a quick text to her secretary, asking her to come in and get the mess in her office cleaned up. She then hurried out the door and down the elevator to the levels below. The elevator doors opened, and she saw before her the long hallway with the desk at the end, in front of the single door. Ikidrak, her goblin guard, was seated in the chair, his tiny feet propped up on the desk, his face obscured by a comic book. She said his name and he quickly jumped into action, throwing his comic book to the floor and whipping his feet of the desk, onto the floor.

"Yes, Miss. Ikidrak is here!"

"We need to ramp up our searches," she said, heels clicking briskly down the long hall floor as she walked. "Evelina has regained her consciousness, meaning she has remembered her abilities. With enough time, she will be stronger than ever and pose a serious threat to everything we have worked for so far. Who is out tonight and where are they?"

Ikidrak bolted behind the desk and pulled out a clipboard with several sheets of paper under the clip. "Let's see," he squeaked, running his long index finger down the list of names and dates. "Yes! Here it is, miss! Straakt is out, miss. Should be around York Street and Washington Avenue about now, miss."

"Good. Call him and everyone else back here. I need to have a meeting with everyone immediately."

"Yes, miss. Ikidrak do this right now, miss," the little goblin replied.

"Good. I want everyone in my office in an hour," she commanded. "Earlier, if possible!" She turned and stomped back to the elevator, heading back up to her office. When she arrived, the spilled coffee had been cleaned up, the stained and ruined papers thrown away and replaced with fresh copies. Beside these sat an empty mug and a carafe of fresh coffee. She spent the next forty-five minutes glaring out at the gray clouds and black waves beginning to crash more violently against the shore. A storm was coming inland, and she wasn't entirely sure if she wasn't conjuring part of it herself.

A knock on the door woke her from her reverie. "Come in," she snapped loudly.

The door swung inward, and she heard the sound of several sets of feet coming into the room. As soon as they had quieted, finding their spots within her office, she began to speak. "We have a very serious problem," she growled. "Evelina has awakened in this world. Who knows what that means," she asked, turning to face the myriad of creatures standing in front of her. There were several goblins, with their gray-green skin and pointed teeth, a couple of trolls who barely managed to fit through the door, the tops of their heads almost touching the ceiling, and short creatures that resembled goblins but wore red caps on their heads and brandished sharp weapons. Mixed among them were a few humans and a few who looked like humans but were…something else. Each of these were her military leaders, commanding forces made up of their own species and they were all staring back at her in silence. The fear was glaringly obvious on their faces.

"Well?!"

One of the creatures wearing a red cap cleared its throat to speak, while all the other creatures turned to stare. "It..it means," he stammered, "we didn't find her reincarnated host body?"

"Yes," she hissed. "Yes, that is exactly what that means. And how do you think that makes me feel," she asked, pacing in front of them. Her query once more yielded silence, bringing her rage to the boiling point. She snapped her head back toward the redcap, demanding, without words, to answer her.

"Erm...angry?" His voice was but a whimper.

"YES!!!"

Bending her arms and lifting her hands she turned toward the desk and, with a swiping motion, made all the sheets of paper fly off her desktop and into the air. Dragging her hands, palms outward, she directed the papers toward the creatures in front of her. All of them took several steps away from the redcap who had answered her questions. The redcap took a small step back, unsure how to react to the flying sheets of paper headed now headed in his direction. In the second before they reached him, they folded themselves into origami swords, their matte surfaces suddenly glinting dangerously under the office lights. As the papers fluttered against him, huge tears appeared in his clothing and scarlet lines erupted on his flesh. The creatures behind him looked away as he began to howl and scream with pain. Rivulets of blood started to flow out from the many gashes in his skin, new cuts opening every time the tiny paper weapons touched his skin. Blood and scraps of flesh began piling up beneath him, covering the floor in a puddle of gore. His screams increased in pitch and frequency, until he collapsed into the puddle of himself, his breathing ragged and strained, incapable of uttering another sound. The paper swords continued their assault until his desperate intake of breath ceased and the light left his eyes. The metallic sheen faded from the swords and they fluttered harmlessly to the floor, landing gracefully on top of the bloody heap beneath them, patches of red staining the bright white sheets.

"Now," Arin said, her voice barely above a whisper, "what are we going to do about my mood?" The creatures before her stared straight ahead, all of them afraid to make a sound. Turning, she walked away from them, toward her large office windows, calmly settling down into her desk chair. Placing her elbows on the desktop, she steepled her hands together, fingertip to fingertip, resting them against her chin. "Grunork," she barked, making one of the other assembled redcaps jump and nervously step forward. "You're my new captain. I expect you and your forces to deliver that faerie princess to me as soon as possible. I'm growing tired of incompetence."

"Yes, my queen," the creature whimpered.

"You're dismissed," she said, swiveling her chair around to face the gloomy late afternoon sky beyond the windows. They all began to silently exit the room, not daring to make a sound. "Send someone to clean this mess up and bring me a new plant." The plant in the corner of the room lay drooped over the sides of its pot; all life drawn out of its once green leaves, stolen by her in order savagely murder the redcap.

"Right away, my queen," said Grunork, Ikidrak bouncing just behind him.

Before the door shut behind them, she could hear a high pitched, rasping voice say, "Ikidrak wishes you congratulations on promotion! Tough job, yes. Last guy couldn't *cut* it!" The goblin's laughter trailed away as he closed the office door behind him.

CHAPTER SIXTEEN

Viola stared into her bedroom mirror for the seventeenth time that morning before leaving for school. Assuring herself that her glamour was perfectly in place, hiding her elongated, pointed elf ears, she grabbed her bags and headed out the door to catch the bus. She hoped the magic would hold throughout the day and keep her ears hidden. Her skin was now perfectly smooth and flawless. *Think of all the money I can save on makeup*, she thought. Over the course of the previous day, she had decided she wouldn't worry about the length of her hair. She could easily just put it up in ways that would hide the additional inches and if anyone *did* ask, she could just say that she'd got extensions over the weekend. The more intense red was easily chalked up to an appointment at a salon to color it. The only thing she was concerned about was those blasted ears. Rosalyn had told her she shouldn't worry about the glamour fading, as she was now capable of wielding much stronger magic. However, she still didn't entirely believe it was possible. Her last magic lesson hadn't been since before their trip and upon their return, they were all quite worn out and decided not to have one on Sunday. She'd applied to teach over the summer and had her first class this morning, after which she would be heading straight to the house to test out her new abilities. Thankfully, through the memories of Evelina, she now had the knowledge to perform more advanced magic, though Rosalyn explained that she would have to get used to everything before she was fully in control and had unlocked all that potential.

    The new memories were something altogether different. They were entirely new memories but simultaneously they felt like she'd had them all along but had simply forgotten for a time. Coming to terms with a whole other life and identity was maddening. She felt like two people inhabiting the same body, and yet both of them were her. Rosalyn said that with time these feelings would fade, and she would fully accept the identity of Evelina that lived within her. But Rosalyn couldn't know exactly how this felt. That morning she had woken up in her own bedroom in her apartment but had been briefly confused by her surroundings, not recognizing anything. It was as if she had woken up as Evelina and Viola had to reassert control over her own mind and body before she remembered where she was. It was a frightening and disorienting feeling.

    Staring out the window during this sunny and refreshingly warm day, she quietly watched the cars and buildings go by as the bus headed toward campus, ear buds jammed into her ears, blocking out the conversation of everyone around her. Doing this allowed her to stay lost in her own thoughts, contemplating the strangeness of the past 48 hours. She also wondered what was going to happen next. Now that she could remember the war, she knew that very soon, she would have to search for Melarue, who was already here somewhere, gaining strength and building an army. Inevitably, they would have to fight and Vy was scared she would be unable to win the war yet again. And if she couldn't, what would happen to everyone who lived in and around Sugar Maple Inn? Would she have to get sucked into a reincarnation spell again? She realized now that she had an entire world of people to save and protect. She'd never fought before, never had to lead before, hadn't really had much responsibility for other people, aside from helping her father after her mother had been killed. Emotional support she could handle, defending an entire people was a whole new ballgame.

 The bus stopped at the school's main building, which housed the several eateries, bookstore and mailroom for all the students and staff who lived and worked on campus. She walked through the building, ear buds still pressed into her ears, drowning everything out. She hoped she could get herself calmed down and acting normally before she ran into anyone she knew. Making her way across campus she managed to avoid contact with anyone, though she was certain she saw a fellow classmate out of the corner of her eye. She thought they had been staring at her and she began to worry that the points of her ears were visible. She checked the magic and sensed that the glamour was still holding, so she hoped they were just looking at her flawless "makeup" or maybe her messy bun didn't hide the fact that her hair was longer.

 She pulled open the door to the building and went inside. The halls were full of students milling about, looking exhausted and generally displeased to be there. She caught a couple of more recognizable students look toward her in surprise. It looked as though no one was in her office yet so, pulling her keys out of her purse, she quickly unlocked the door and ducked inside, shutting the door behind her, hoping to avoid any more of their stares. Dropping her things on her desk, she pulled out her mirror and looked over her reflection for any sign that her glamour spell might be fading. So far as she could tell, everything seemed to be fine, though her skin was still abnormally smooth and even. She took a second to add a couple more freckles, just to be safe. She was hesitant to announce her presence in the office and attract attention, but she didn't have much of a choice. She took a deep breath to steel herself, then flipped the light switch and opened the door, letting in all the sounds from the hallway.

"Mornin'," came an English accent, "what's happ…Vy?!" Liz was staring at her with an unreadable expression.

"Uh..hey, Liz. What's up?"

"Uh…is your hair longer? And redder?"

"Oh, you noticed?" She tried to laugh it off as if it was no big deal.

"It's kinda hard not to…even with it pulled up." Liz raised an eyebrow.

"I decided to do something different, and I got extensions and a color. Soo...what do you think?"

"Y'know…I think I dig it. It's different and a bit of a shock but…it suits you." Liz reached out and started to play with her hair. "Y'know, they say guys tend to like longer hair. With this, Monty won't stick to just snogging for too much longer," she cackled, winking at her conspiratorially.

"Oh, my word, Liz, *please*!" Begging her friend not to say anything more to further embarrass her, she pulled her into her office.

"So, what brought this on? You didn't say anything about it on Friday."

Vy shrugged. "I dunno, really. I just decided I wanted to do something different."

"Well, it is very different! Most definitely!" Liz kept looking her over, checking out the new look, finally nodding her approval. "I like it."

"Thanks! Though, I've had some weird looks in the halls today." She began opening her bag to get all of her things out for the day.

"Well…your hair is a shade of red not normally found in nature. I mean that is seriously red! And long."

"Oh, well. I'm still getting used to it, but I think I like it." She pulled out her books, notebooks and pens for her morning class. "I hope Monty will like it."

"Oh, believe me," she said, with meaning, "He will definitely like it. Rawr!" She held her hand up in a claw on her last word, to which Vy responded by rolling her eyes and heading out the door. Liz followed her out into the hall, as Vy was heading toward her Shakespeare class. "I expect a full report after your next date. I mean *all* the details." Vy rolled her eyes at her best friend. "When is the next date, by the way? You guys have been going everywhere lately."

"I'm not sure yet, actually. I haven't seen him since the bar the other night. We texted off and on over the weekend, but we haven't made any plans to get together yet."

"Hmmm. You need to get on this."

"Oh my gosh, Liz!" She stared toward her, open mouthed. "Aren't you getting enough action with Liam?! Why do you need to hear all the details of my love life?"

"Oh, Liam is fantastic! For sure! I am... exceedingly satisfied," she said, grinning wickedly. "But I think *you* need some satisfaction. This is the first guy I've seen you with since that jerk screwed you over. Literally." Her expression was one that conveyed her extreme irritation. Vy had been seeing a guy the previous year who she had thought was the one, her person. She had fallen so very hard for him that she had decided to take the leap and be intimate for the first time. She had grown up believing that sex was only something you did with someone you were truly in love with, and she wasn't one to sleep around or do anything until she had been with someone for a long time. The guy she had lost it to had turned out to be a pathological liar and cheater. About a month after she had given him everything she had, she found out that he had been sleeping with one of the women he worked with at a local restaurant. She was completely heartbroken and hadn't dated anyone after they'd broken up, her trust in people completely destroyed.

Since that day, Liz had been on the lookout for a new guy to fix her heart, trying to convince her that not all men were, as she had put it, "ass-faced cheaters."

"Well, thanks for bringing up those fond memories," Vy muttered, sarcastically.

"Hey, you've been closed off to love and all the fun things it offers ever since that wanker cheated on you with that bimbo of a waitress. Monty is a good guy; he won't hurt you the way that asshat did. Besides," she grinned, "he knows me, and he knows that if he ever hurt my best friend that I would kick his ass into next month!" Liz laughed while Vy rolled her eyes and chuckled, knowing full well that she probably meant it.

"Okay, I've gotta go," Vy said, as they reached the door of her classroom. "I'll catch you later, okay?"

Liz waved goodbye with a flourish. "Yes, ma'am! And think about what I said," she called, before flouncing down the hallway.

About a half hour into the class, Vy realized she was supposed to turn a project proposal into her faculty advisor by the end of the day. Unfortunately, due to dealing with all the new memories, the new lifetime that had suddenly become part of her person, she had forgotten to finish the paper. It was approximately halfway done and saved on her computer, which she had left at home today. As soon as class was over, she ducked out of the room as quickly as possible, rather than making herself available for her students as she usually did. She hurried down to her office, where two of her office mates had finally arrived from being on lunch breaks. They both freaked out over her hair and she thanked them for their compliments as she packed everything back into her bags. Normally, she would stay to do work on her class for the following day but now she needed to get home as quickly as possible to finish her proposal and email it into her advisor before heading to her next magic lesson.

On her way out of the building, she ran into Monty, who was heading in for class.

"Well, *hello* gorgeous! I love this!" He ran his fingers through her hair. "You look amazing." He leaned in and gave her a quick kiss on the cheek.

"Thanks! I'm glad you like it," she gushed, beaming. "I decided I wanted to try it out."

"Well, I love it! Hey, would you like to join me for a movie this weekend?"

"Sure, which one?" She hadn't seen any previews in weeks, being so busy with school, work and magic training.

"No idea," he grinned. "We'll figure it out when we get there?"

"Sounds like a great plan," she said, laughing softly. "Can't wait!"

"Great," he said, smiling. "Text me and let me know when you're free." He planted one more brief kiss on her mouth before saying goodbye and heading into the building, while she took off, walking quickly towards the bus stop.

On her way home, she thought about what Liz had said about her love life and, although she hated to admit it, Liz had a point. She had closed herself off since she'd been hurt, and she knew Monty was a great guy. They hadn't quite been dating long enough to where she felt comfortable taking their relationship to a new level but perhaps in another couple of months, she might be ready to jump into something a bit more serious with him. For now, she was happy just enjoying his company.

When the bus stopped on her street, she hurried to her apartment, climbed the stairs and spent the next hour and a half quickly typing up the rest of her proposal, before sending an email to her advisor, with the completed document attached. Shutting down her computer, she grabbed her purse and car keys, and then raced across town to the old Victorian.

CHAPTER SEVENTEEN

Walking out onto the lawn, she saw Tam and Vince already there, just as before. She waved to them as she drew nearer and heard them calling out hello toward her. She wondered if anything would be different today, given the events of the weekend. Ready to get to work, she hurried out to meet them. After exchanging greetings, she decided to get right to it.

"So, what's happening today? Anything different since...y'know?" She gestured to all of herself, giving the two men a good chuckle.

"Well yes, we *are* going to be doing things a little differently today, I think," Tam said. "With your new abilities, a flower or a tree is much too simple. Today, we're going to start battling. It will be the best option, given that Melarue is beginning to ramp up her efforts and attacks. Plus, it will give you an opportunity to gain a better understanding of the power to which you now have access. "

"Does that mean I'll have to fight her soon?"

The two men exchanged a look before turning back to her, Vince answering her question before Tam could speak.

"Most likely. Scouts on our side have noticed an increased magical presence in the area. They're no doubt amping up their efforts to find you." He gave her a pitying look before continuing. "So, I'm afraid we may have to have a guard around you whenever you're alone from now on."

"What?!"

"I'm afraid so, Viola." He breathed in sharply and shook his head. "Sorry. *Evelina*. My queen. If Melarue is increasing her efforts it may mean she knows that you have regained your memories and abilities, which therefore means that you are much more powerful and dangerous to her. No doubt, her goal was to destroy you before you had recovered your true self but now that you've regained those memories, she'll want to hurry and take you out before you've mastered them again." Vince put a hand on her shoulder. "Therefore, I've taken on the responsibility of creating a guard schedule for you."

"So... does this mean I have to have someone with me whenever I'm at school? At home? Out with friends?"

"Probably not while you're at school," Tam piped up. "It's highly unlikely Melarue will attack you while you're in public. Any time you might be alone or unprotected while in town, though, yes."

"Just like the night I saved you from that shape shifter. We're fortunate that I dispatched him before he could tell Melarue about your presence."

"Okay," she grumbled. "I have to be honest, I'm not a fan of this idea but I understand its necessity." She sighed, giving in, knowing she didn't have much of an option. "When does this start to happen, then?"

"Uh, well…it already has," Vince admitted. "There's been someone nearby, keeping an eye on you since last night."

"Fine," she said, shaking her head slightly. She wasn't a huge fan of this loss of her privacy but figured there was no point in arguing the matter. "Anyway, how do I fight?" She just wanted to get things moving along. If a showdown were imminent, she'd better start preparing for it.

"Right. First, Vince and I will demonstrate for you. Watch how we move, and you'll see how to block magical attacks and defend yourself, while still making an attack of your own." She nodded and sat down on the grass to watch.

They went through a routine once at full speed, then again more slowly, allowing her to see every angle of their magical battle. They were so graceful and sure of their motions that she thought it looked more as though they were dancing rather than fighting. Tam pushed his open palms out toward Vince and a stream of water shot towards him, sending him flying. Vince straightened himself and wiped the water out of his eyes, then, his hand facing downward as though he was pulling on something, raised it from the ground and sent a shower of small pebbles toward Tam. Vy thought she could see Vince's lips moving as he mumbled incantations to perform his kind of magic. Their movements and attacks seemed complicated and visually stunning, like wicked expensive special effects in a film, and yet somehow, she knew they were using weaker attacks in order to keep from hurting each other during these demonstrations. That knowledge must have come from the increased magic sensitivity she had acquired after their time spent in the battlefield. They continued in this manner for several minutes, showing her different attacks, followed by several methods of blocking and deflection.

They finished their demonstration, then trudged back toward her, looking rather worn out and, in Vince's case, dripping wet after being drenched by Tam's attacks. They flopped down on the ground beside her, breathing heavily.

"Whew! Well, I hope you learned something!" Vince hooted with laugher, throwing his head back and sending drops of water raining down onto her and Tam. She raised an eyebrow and pursed her lips in irritation at the unexpected shower, then, without thinking, waved a hand in his direction, bringing up a great wind that buffeted him until he was completely dried off. The intensity of the magic took her a bit by surprise. Normally, she would have had to maintain deep, unbroken concentration in order to do that, but this time it was nearly effortless. She found that knowledge to be exceptionally frightening. She looked down at her hands, wondering what else they were capable of doing. Vince took stock of his dried clothes and felt his hair, which, when not covered in gel, had a slight curl and was incredibly fluffy! It was now fluffily sticking up and out in every possible direction and stared at her, wide-eyed with horror.

Tam clapped his hands together once, laughing loudly at the state of Vince. "Oh, very well done, my Lady! Excellent!" All three eventually dissolved into a fit of laughter at the sight of Vince's hair. If it had looked wild and unkempt before, now it was in absolute chaos. Curly, fluffy chaos. When they had calmed themselves and managed to stifle their snickering, Tam tried to restore order to the day's plans.

"Now then, we should have you try out a few attack maneuvers." He took a moment to conjure up a large, thick oak tree several feet away from where they were sitting. "Now, head over to where we were fighting and try to attack that tree with anything you have."

She nodded and rose up from the ground, stretching out and loosening up muscles as she walked over to face the target. They hadn't had her attack anything before this, only creating trees and the like, so this was a bit new to her. And while she now had the memories and identity of Evelina within her, this was her body, Vy's body, and it hadn't yet performed this kind of magic. She had great power within her but needed to regain the muscle memory that belonged to Evelina. She took a moment to collect herself, replicating the same movements Tam had done a few moments ago, then sent a huge wave of water crashing into the tree. Before the wave reached the oak, it quickly disappeared, as she was surprised by the force of the magic she had just unleashed. She'd expected a small wave; what rushed forward from her outstretched palms was a massive surge of water, an overwhelming natural force. Had she continued to push, it likely would have destroyed the tree completely.

"What was that?!," she shrieked. "I've never done anything like that!!"

"Don't be concerned, Viola. That is going to happen. It is merely the true power that lies within you, the power you unlocked when you regained the memories of your previous existence. You just need to become accustomed to it." Tam paused for a moment, giving her a big smile. "I told you, you would be powerful!"

She was rather shocked that she had managed to perform such strong magic. Deciding to try something a little different, this time she used motions similar to that of Tam but focused on a different element of nature. Concentrating very hard, she turned to the target tree and released the magic she had built up inside her body. From out of her hands came a torrent of flame, which shot across the training area, hit the tree, completely engulfing it in flame, and continued hurtling on, heading toward a small gnome carrying a bag of potatoes from the gardens to the house for dinner. The gnome took off running, screaming in terror, leaving the bag of potatoes on the ground, where the fire licked at them for a several minutes before petering out.

The trio stared in awe at the place where the flames had been, the tree now a smoldering pile of charcoal and the potatoes steaming. Vy turned her open-mouthed gaze toward the two young men, who stared back at her.

"Uhhhhh..." she mumbled, struggling for words, "anyone want a baked potato?"

CHAPTER EIGHTEEN

"So, what do you think?" She and Monty were standing outside the theatre, looking at the movie posters on display. They had decided to go out for lunch on Wednesday and then to an afternoon matinee, when the ticket cost was lower than usual. It was a fairly small theatre, with only five screens, so their options were limited. This week they had a terrible looking romantic comedy, two horror movies, a superhero movie and an animated children's film.

"It's a tough decision," she replied. "Everything looks *so* good!"

He turned toward her, smirking. "Wow, I could actually *feel* the sarcasm emanating off you."

"Sorry," she said, laughing. "I'm not really sure. What would you like to see?"

"No, no, no! I told you the movie was your choice! Although, I guess if I had to pick, I'd go for..." he thought for a few moments. "I would say...either the horror movies or the superhero flick. Though, if you really want to see this one," he gestured to the romantic comedy, "I'll watch it."

"Ugh. You don't need to worry about that. I'm all set." She looked back and forth over the posters once more. Monty's phone buzzed in his pocket and he pulled it out, to read and respond to a text message while she was making her decision. He looked a bit grumpy, so she asked him what was wrong.

"Oh, nothing. Just my Mom. She knew I had plans today but still sent me a text asking me to do something for her."

'Oh…well, we can reschedule if you need to help her."

"Nah, no worries. I told her I wasn't available until tomorrow." He stuffed his phone back into his pocket rather gruffly. "Did you decide?"

"Umm…I think so. Let's do…this one," she said, finally pointing to one of the horror movies. "Though, I can't promise I won't hide under my jacket."

Laughing, he offered her his arm. "Don't worry," he said as she took it, "if you get scared you can hang onto me." He gave her a quick kiss on the forehead before they made their way inside to get tickets. Twenty minutes later they were sitting in the darkened theatre along with a couple dozen other people. They had been playfully throwing popcorn at each other before and during the previews, attempting to catch the kernels with their open mouths. Monty was quite good at it, but Viola had never been good at playing catch. After several failed attempts, which he got quite a kick out of, Monty had finally given up with the game and they had settled in to watch the movie. Once the plot had started to take off and the vengeful spirits began to make their appearances, she found herself turning her head away during particularly gruesome scenes, burying her face into his shoulder. After she had done this multiple times, chuckling, he put his arm around her and let her bury her face in his chest when she couldn't bear to look at the screen. She turned away several times but did her best to watch as much of the movie as she could.

After the credits finally began to roll, Monty apologized to her as they got up to leave.

"I don't think you enjoyed that movie at all. I'm so sorry, Vy."

"I would believe you," she said, "if it weren't for the fact that you're trying not to laugh." She poked him roughly in his stomach.

"Ow!" He was desperately trying not to crack a smile but with her accusation and poke to his middle, he could contain it no longer. "I'm sorry but you were just so funny!" He dissolved into laughter while she walked beside him, rolling her eyes. It was early evening but thankfully the days were getting longer, and the sun was still in the sky, though it was hanging low, and the dark of night was slowly pushing its way across the horizon.

"Yeah, yeah, laugh it up!" She smirked, shaking her head.

"I'm sorry!" He wiped his eyes and composed himself, clearing his throat. "Let me take you to the beach to make up for it."

"The beach? It's still early, isn't it?" She stared at him in disbelief. "Granted, it's June but it's *early* June...not exactly beach weather yet."

"Then, there won't be anyone there! It's cool, yes, but we have jackets. We'll be fine." She held onto his arm as they made their way toward his car. "We'll just take a quick walk, okay? It's quiet and peaceful there at this time of day. Just the sound of the waves hitting the shoreline." He talked as they drove the short few minutes down Main Street toward the public beach access. "I go there quite often to think or if I've had a bad day and need to relax or something."

After arriving at the beach, they left the car and took a walk alongside the water. With the breeze coming in off the water, it was, as she'd suspected, rather chilly. Vy was glad she was still carrying her hoodie around. She pulled the hood over her head and drew the strings tightly to cut out the chill and to keep her hair from flying about and smacking her in the face. They walked along the beach, talking and laughing about the movie, enjoying a bit more of each other's time before calling it a night. A few seagulls had begun to circle in the hopes that the couple had food to offer. The sun was beginning to set, and the moon was becoming visible in the darkening sky.

"It's beautiful out here at this time of day," she said.

"See? I love it here."

As they walked, she saw movement further away on the beach. She pointed it out to him, and they studied it as they got closer. All too soon they realized they were not the only ones who had thought to come to the beach that evening. Further down the shoreline there was another couple who, upon slightly closer inspection, seemed to be engaged in a rather tender embrace. Their steps slowed as the realization gradually dawned. Fortunately for them, the waves coming in were making enough noise as they hit the beach that neither couple could hear the other.

"It might be time to turn around and head back," she told him, feeling quite awkward.

"I think you might be right. Let's go before they realize they've been spotted." They took off quickly, heading back to the car, snickering with each other like school children. They hurriedly threw themselves into the car when they arrived, and Monty started the engine.

"Well, that certainly was a memorable walk," she laughed.

"It was! I'm sure it is for them, too!"

They continued laughing and chatting while he drove back to her apartment. Parking on the street outside, he turned toward her to say goodnight.

"I'm glad you're feeling better after the movie."

"Thanks," she said, giving out a little snort of laughter. "Hopefully, I don't have any nightmares tonight. I don't relish the thought of ghosts in my bedroom."

"I'd fight them off for you." They both flushed and Vy turned away shyly, his implied presence in her bedroom firmly planted in their minds.

Laughing softly in an attempt to ease the awkwardness, she thanked him. "How very noble of you."

"Well, I hope you have only the best of dreams," he said, a bit awkwardly. "I know you have plans with your dad tomorrow, but I'll text you. Even if it's just to make sure there weren't any ghosts in your bedroom."

"Well, thank you. I hope I'll have good news for you." She grinned. "Guess I'll talk to you tomorrow, then. Have a great night!"

"And you." He leaned over toward her, putting a hand behind her head to bring her face closer to his. He placed a soft kiss on her mouth. And then another. And another. Twisting in his seat, he brought his other hand over to her shoulder, then behind her back, the kiss deepening. She slid her right hand up along his arm and behind his head, tangling her fingers in his hair. He pulled her as close to him as he possibly could, given their positions in the car and the armrest between them. The kiss lasted for several moments, quite taking her breath away. When he finally broke away from her, he placed one last, soft kiss on her mouth before fully pulling away, breathing heavily.

Vy sat still for a moment, blinking in the darkened car, trying to get herself together. When the world around her stopped spinning, she reached for her bag with one hand, placing her other hand on the door handle.

"Goodnight," she managed to squeak.

"Goodnight, Vy. I'll talk to you tomorrow," he said, smiling rather wickedly.

She exited the car and made her way up the driveway toward the door of her apartment, the world dancing around her the entire way. Shutting the door of her apartment behind her, she got ready for bed, as if in a dream. Drawing the covers up over herself, she grabbed her phone off the side table to send a text to Liz. She was surprised to see that there was already a text waiting for her. She smiled when she realized it was from Monty.

Tonight was amazing. Can't wait to see you again. - Monty

She sent him a quick reply, saying she couldn't wait to see him again, either. Once the message had been sent, she opened a new message to send to Liz.

Best. Snog. Ever. - Vy

Placing the phone back on her table, she rolled over and went to sleep, looking forward to the text she would get in the morning and hoping to dream of that kiss.

CHAPTER NINETEEN

In the middle of a busy June full of teaching summer classes, working on her thesis, magic lessons and a few dates with Monty, Vy was seated in the school café, nose buried in an article about Shakespeare, when a black bag was suddenly slammed down onto the table in front of her. "Now, listen here, missy." Liz plopped down in the seat across from her. "Something has gone completely balls-up with you lately. Are you having some kind of a breakdown or gone full nutter?! First you suddenly start having things going on all the time whenever we would usually hang out. Then you were spending a ton of time with your dad, followed by the hair and now you've flaked on me for lunch. Twice. Are you pissed at me for some reason or is there something going on with you?"

Viola felt so guilty; there was so much going on in the magical realm. More and more magics had been disappearing over the past few weeks, meaning an increase in training appointments. She had spent the better part of the last three weeks at the old Victorian either in meetings with Rosalyn and the others or out on the lawn training with Vince and Tam. Exhaustion was setting in and she was finding it difficult to maintain the schedule. Now, it seemed, her relationships were beginning to suffer, as well.

"You're absolutely right, Liz. I'm so sorry. My life...it's been a bit of a mess lately." She marked the spot where she left off in the paper she was reading and quickly closed her laptop to give her best friend the attention she deserved. "I've had so much going on and I can't keep up."

"Then let me help you. I haven't seen you in days. Hell, I haven't got a text from you in days!"

"I'm sorry, Liz." Vy weighed her options, while Liz waited for a proper explanation. She really shouldn't tell anyone about her true identity, about the truth of magic. However, if the cost of keeping the secret was her friendships, she wasn't sure it was a secret worth keeping. She knew Liz was trustworthy. She'd shared plenty of secret things with her over the past couple of years and Liz hadn't said a word about them to anyone. Unfortunately, she hadn't known Liam quite long enough to determine how trustworthy he was. Without knowing, it would be difficult for her to share her secret with him as well. She'd been debating telling Monty but hadn't been able to get herself comfortable with that idea yet, either. Her father had handled it well when her mother had revealed the truth about herself, maybe Monty would be able to manage, as well. On the other hand, there was always the possibility that he'd run as far and as fast as he could in the opposite direction. Finally, she made her decision and looked back to the expectant Liz. "You're right. There *is* something going on, Liz, and I will tell you."

"Good." Liz shifted in her chair, giving Vy her undivided attention, waiting for the big reveal.

Vy looked around at the people filling the cafe. "Not here! How about you come over to my place tomorrow night? I'll make dinner, we can watch a movie and I'll tell you everything. Bring Liam and I'll invite Monty to join us as well."

"Better. What time?"

"How about five? Sound good?" Vy had it all planned out. She would have Liz and Liam over at five but tell Monty six. That way she could explain everything to her two friends. She'd like to tell Monty, but she just wasn't sure how he would take it. Perhaps in time, she'd be ready. Liz, however, she had known longer and was prepared for how she would react. Liz would probably think she'd gone completely around the bend at first, but Vy was sure she'd warm up to it eventually. Liz and Liam were a matched set so if she told Liz, Liam would know too, so…might as well just tell both at the same time. She wasn't completely prepared for that reaction, but it would be what it would be.

"Excellent. We'll see you then!" She stood up, picking her bags up with her as she did so. "Gotta head out. I've got a meeting with my advisor in five minutes."

"You do realize you're across campus and can't make it in five minutes, right?"

"Eh," she shrugged. "Maybe the meeting will just be *that* much shorter!"

"Wow," Vy chuckled. "Classic Liz!"

Liz bowed deeply and took off, slowly meandering toward her meeting.

Vy sucked in a deep breath. Now that she'd made the decision to tell them everything, she vowed to stick to the plan. For good or ill, in just over twenty four hours she would tell them everything. Now, she just had to tell Rosalyn, Tam and Vince that she would not be available for anything on Friday. Considering how hard they'd been working, she thought a break was well deserved.

* * *

It was quarter to five in the afternoon the following day, Liz and Liam could be arriving at any moment. She had just finished putting a large tray of lasagna together. Popping the heavy baking dish into the oven, she washed up all of the dishes she'd used during the preparation. Sitting on the counter, waiting to go into the oven fifteen minutes before the lasagna finished, was a loaf of French bread, spread with garlic butter. In the fridge sat a large bowl of salad, made of lettuce greens, spinach, tomatoes, onions, julienned carrots and she had purchased three different bottles of dressing to appeal to everyone's taste. Of course, she made sure there was plenty of wine chilling in the fridge as well. She'd had a bottle of unopened Moscato she'd received as a gift but given the conversation she was going to have with Liz and Liam, she'd bought two more bottles, just in case. Liz would undoubtedly bring something to drink as well, along with some sort of dessert she'd promised to bake. The girl was a wonderful baker. If Liz hadn't wanted to study history, Vy repeatedly told her she could open a bakery. She poured herself a glass of wine, and then went into her living room to sit on the couch and wait for them to arrive.

She'd finished a glass and gone into the kitchen to pour a second when there was a knock, or rather, a kick, on the door and the muffled sound of Liz's voice on the other side.

"Yo, Shakespeare! Let us in!"

Opening the door, she saw Liz and Liam standing in the hallway outside, laden with offerings of food and alcohol for the night's festivities.

"The party has arrived," Liz cried, as Vy opened the door enough to let them pass. Both Liz and Liam headed toward the kitchen to drop off their donations to the cause.

"Really? An entire party case of beer? I have three bottles of wine plus a six pack in the fridge already."

"Pffftttt!!!" Liz put a couple of bags and a container on the counter, which looked like it might hold a cake inside, while Liam opened the refrigerator door to put the 12-pack of beer inside it to chill. "The more, the merrier, right?!"

"Right!" Liam opened two bottles of beer, handing one to Liz. "You've got a glass of wine, so I assume you're all set right now, Vy?" He gestured to the glass on the counter, standing empty beside the opened bottle of wine.

"Yeah, I'm good. Thanks, Liam." She felt a bit overwhelmed by all the bags, containers and alcohol they'd brought with them. The kitchen was a flurry of snacks and drinks being unwrapped and placed on the counter and in the fridge, and Vy just stood by and watched as Liz and Liam took over.

"All right, I've brought a cake, ice cream," Liz handed a shopping bag to Liam, who pulled out a carton of ice cream and popped it into the freezer. "I also grabbed a bag of tortilla chips, salsa and queso," she said, pulling out the jar of cheese with a flair.

"What? Nachos and lasagna? That makes sense," Vy retorted.

"Of course, it does." She opened up the cupboard where Viola kept her bowls and began emptying the cheese into a bowl to microwave. "Nachos, like alcohol, go with everything." She emptied the bag of chips into a large serving bowl and put the salsa into another small bowl. Handing Liam the chips and salsa, she asked him to take them into the living room. The microwave dinged and Vy carefully pulled out the bowl of hot, melted cheese. She carried the bowl into the living room and placed it on the coffee table just next to the bowls of chips and salsa. Liz and Liam were already plopped onto the couch, starting to munch on the nachos, while Vy walked to the kitchen to grab her glass of wine. She took a deep breath, knowing that it was time to share her secret with them.

"C'mon, Vy. You'd best get in here before Liam eats all of the crisps!"

Vy started toward the living room, thought about it for a moment, and then grabbed the bottle with her free hand. She brought both her glass and the bottle into the living room, setting the bottle on the table but keeping the glass in her hands as she sat down.

"So, what's been going on with you, Vy? We've both been worried," Liz said around a mouthful of nacho.

She brought the glass to her lips and took a long draught of wine, suddenly realizing how badly her hands were shaking. Her stomach was a nervous mess of butterflies numbering in the thousands, but she took a deep breath and began. "Okay, this may be hard to believe but I promise it's the honest to God truth." She looked into their expectant faces, full of concern and curiosity. This was going to be much harder than she thought. Draining her glass of wine, she reached for the bottle and poured a third, then launched into her tale. She told them about the night at the bar, being saved from an attack by the shape-shifting faerie; saved by the very man who had been following her all that day. She told them about waking up in the stranger's car, her father in the front seat; about walking through the archway and into a completely new world, including every detail. Lastly, she told them about Evelina and her true identity, along with her destiny to fight against Melarue. After she had finished, she stared with bated breath, waiting for them to respond. They returned her stare for several moments, saying nothing, and then finally Liz turned around to exchange a meaningful look with Liam. She reached for her beer and chugged it, then finally turned back toward Viola.

"Wow, Vy. Just wow." She began shaking her head. "Y'know, I get it if you don't want to tell us. It's fine. But coming up with some crazy story like this just to cover your ass? That's ridiculous." She stood up abruptly, tugging Liam up as well. "Nice knowing you, Vy."

"Liz," Liam started, "she's your friend. Give her a chance."

"No! This is insane and I'm not having any further part of it!" Liz stomped toward the door, with Liam trailing sullenly behind her.

Vy had suspected she might need to prove it to them, so she already had something planned. Taking a moment to concentrate, she raised her arms up and stretched her hands to the ceiling. Liz and Liam were at the door when the snowflakes began to fall, causing them to momentarily pause their efforts to leave. They looked up toward the ceiling and around the room, their gaze finally landing on Vy, who was still molding the energy to her will. Now that she had their attention, she began moving her hands through the air, making the snow swirl around the apartment, finally bringing it all on top of the coffee table, where it formed a perfect snowman. It was just missing a carrot nose and button eyes. They stared at her, mouths agape, as she snapped her fingers and it all disappeared. Silence reigned for nearly a full minute as she waited for their reactions. They slowly turned their faces toward each other, then back to her.

"You...was that..." It seemed Liz was having a difficult time forming full sentences.

Liam made several small sounds in the back of his throat before finally finding control of his voice once again. "Did...did you do that?"

Vy nodded. The two looked at each other once more, and then turned back to her, their eyes alight with excitement, begging her to do something else. She thought for a moment, looking around the room for inspiration. When her eyes lighted on a potted plant she had sitting in the corner of the living room, an idea struck her. Working with the plant, she caused vines to grow out of the soil, the tendrils growing tall and strong. They began snaking and curling about the living room, stretching across her small apartment and into the kitchen. They grew up the walls and across the ceiling, tiny pink and white flowers erupting from amidst the green. She turned and was momentarily distracted by Liz and Liam's shared expressions of shocked delight. A loud crash made her swivel away to see that the vines had wrapped themselves around her TV and knocked it off her entertainment stand. Vy made a small gesture with her hand, compelling the vines to lift the TV back onto its stand and release it. While she didn't think the fall would have done it, the pressure from the vines must have been too much for the TV, causing a great spider web of a crack to spread across the screen. There was a moment of silence as the three of them just stared at the broken television.

"Well, dammit!" She pushed her hands away from her, sending all the vines creeping back into the pot from whence they came. "I really liked that TV."

"Wal-Mart or Best Buy or something will probably have a back-to-school sale soon," Liam said. Liz and Vy both turned to stare at him for a moment before Vy started to snicker at his comment. Liz snorted briefly, then snapped her head back toward Vy.

"Holy shit, Vy," she shrieked. "You can do magic!!!!"

"That's amazing!! Liam's eyes were still wide open in awe and shock, but he was grinning from ear to ear.

"Believe me now, I take it?" She smirked at the pair of them. They both responded with a resounding yes. "Good! Now, you can't tell anyone, you understand?!"

They both nodded. "Does Monty know," Liz asked.

"Not yet. I want to tell him, I'm just not sure when I should," Vy replied. "I want to make sure it won't freak him out too badly."

"He'll be okay with it, Vy. If he really cares about you, he'll be accepting of this," Liz reassured her, with Liam nodding beside her. "Besides, you have magic! How can that possibly be a bad thing?!"

"I mean it isn't exactly normal, is it? I was worried you wouldn't believe me, or you'd freak out when you saw what I can do."

"This is amazing, Vy. How could anyone freak out? At least, not for long." The existence of magic seemed to have unlocked Liam's tongue. Vy was shocked to hear more than one sentence leave his mouth at a time. As long as she'd known him, he'd always been so quiet. "This means that everything we've ever known, everything we've been taught to believe about this sort of thing, isn't true. It's all real!"

Liz and Liam both continued to gush to her as they processed everything. A quick glance at the clock told her Monty would be arriving any minute. She rushed to the kitchen to put the garlic bread in the oven, then turned back to her friends, who were still standing in the living room, just on the other side of the kitchen island.

"Can't you just fix the TV with magic, then?" Liz was heading toward her, tipping her beer bottle up, draining the last drops.

"Nope. There are different kinds of magic and every person has a different specialized area. My magic is very much based in nature, meaning I can do things like controlling elements, plants or even the weather, if I focus hard enough, but I think repairing TV screens is beyond me."

"Well, isn't glass just sand heated to a high temperature? I'm sure you could do it," Liam offered.

"Uuh…maybe…but I think I'll leave the repairs for a day when I'm not expecting more company at any moment."

"Fair enough." Liam nodded in agreement.

She took a quick look around to make sure all of the food was in order and mentally checked off all her to-do items. Returning her gaze to Liz, who was rinsing out her empty bottle in the sink, she asked, "Now, you won't be telling anyone, right?"

"We won't! Promise," they both agreed.

"Not even Monty?" She gave them a very pointed look.

"Of course not," Liz piped up. "That is absolutely one hundred percent up to you." Liz's expression darkened suddenly as she turned away from the sink to face Vy. "But... what about this battle? You'll have to fight? Will it be dangerous?"

Vy opened her mouth to respond when there was a knock at the door. "That's Monty. Don't say anything, please?" They both indicated their agreement, as she went to the door. On the other side stood Monty, holding a bottle of wine and a bouquet of flowers.

"Hey, gorgeous! It smells fantastic in here!" He leaned in to give her a kiss before walking further into her apartment, extending greetings to Liz and Liam. "Hey, guys! How goes it?"

"Great! Can I get you a drink, Monty?" Liz had the refrigerator door open and was digging for another beer.

"Sure!"

Liz put Monty's bottle of wine into the fridge and handed him a beer in exchange, then they all headed toward the living room.

"Whoa! Vy! What happened?!" Monty was gesturing to the damaged TV screen.

"Oh," she waved it off, making up a story as quickly as she could, "I was in here cleaning earlier and I bumped into the stand and knocked it off. I'll have to pick up another one at some point."

"Bummer," he said, closely inspecting the damage. "Well, at least you have your laptop. Thank God for streaming services, eh?!"

They all plopped onto Vy's couch to munch on the nachos, have a few drinks and to chat. Shortly before the cooking time was up, Vy excused herself and made her way to the kitchen to get everything prepared. She listened in to the conversation as she worked, laughing along with her friends and not thinking about battles, magic or centuries-old curses. After taking plates down from the cupboard, she pulled the salad out of the fridge and gave it a toss, then pulled the garlic bread out to slice.

"Do you need any help in there," Monty called.

"No, no, I'm fine! It will just be a moment or two and we'll be good to go!"

After slicing up the bread, she pulled the lasagna out of the oven and set it on the stovetop. Grabbing serving utensils, she got everything placed on the counter.

"Come and get it," she called. While they were loading up their plates, Vy dashed into her bedroom to grab her laptop. She set it up on top of her coffee table and opened up Netflix, then returned to the kitchen to make up her own plate. Once they had piled their plates with lasagna, salad and garlic bread, grabbed another beer or filled another glass with wine, they made their way back to the living room.

"Okay, so I know the screen is much smaller but if we sit around here we can all see. Shall we find something?" They eventually settled on a goofy comedy they had all watched as kids. Vy, Liz and Liam sat on the couch, Liz practically in Liam's lap, while Monty chose to sit on the floor, leaning back against Vy's legs. They spent the next couple of hours making jokes about the movie, eating far too much and having a wonderful time together. After several drinks they were all fairly buzzed but not completely inebriated. Vy told everyone they needed to switch to water for the next hour, so they would be able to drive home safely.

"Ugh! What a party pooper," Liz grumbled.

"Hey, I'm making sure you get home safely! I only have one bedroom and one couch. If you all have to stay, you're sharing the floor."

"Yeah, yeah. Thanks, mom." Liz rolled her eyes over her glass of water. "At least there's still cake!" She jumped up and rushed out to the kitchen, coming back a few moments later bearing plates and a knife, balanced on the top of a cake carrier. Placing everything on the table, she opened the carrier to reveal a one-tier cake of pastel green, covered with multi-colored flowers made of buttercream. Everyone gasped and complimented her skills before tucking into the delicious cake.

There turned out to be a bit more romance to their comedy than they remembered. One scene featured the female lead sobbing, a rare somber moment amidst the laughs. The woman had been betrayed by her significant other and was completely heartbroken. Liz, who had been providing a running commentary on the film, followed the tone of the scene and dropped the comedy in favor of a more serious topic of conversation.

"Hey, this is just like what happened to you, Vy! Y'know with that asshat."

"Yah," Vy said, laughing softly, though she hoped the boys wouldn't catch on.

"What asshat?" Alas, Monty had been paying attention.

"Oh, a couple of years or so ago Vy was dating this manky bugger of a guy. Totally used her."

"What happened," Monty asked, looking up at Vy, who tried to wave it off.

"He was nothin' but charm most of the time and eventually convinced her to give it up to him. Soon after that he bailed on her."

"Really, Liz?!" Vy squeezed her eyes shut and rubbed her forehead. Sometimes Liz didn't think about whether something might be best left unsaid. Oh, well. It was out now, nothing to be done.

"I'm so sorry, Vy." Monty was looking up at her when she opened her eyes.

"It's okay. Honestly, there were several others who told me to break it off. They had a feeling he was no good but sadly, I fell for it."

"Not before he broke your heart," Liz quipped.

"Yes, thanks for that, Liz. I think you've said enough. You know how chatty you can get when you've had too much to drink." She gave Liz a kick and glare that told her to shut it.

Monty reached up and took hold of her hand. "That's awful, Vy. I promise I would never do that to you."

"Damn right! 'Cuz you know I'd kick your ass for it," Liz cackled.

Vy rolled her eyes and Monty smiled up at her before turning back to the movie, still holding her hand.

After an hour or so Liz and Liam decided it was time to head home and started packing up their stuff.

"You're sure you're okay to drive?" Vy hadn't seen them drink any more after she told them they had been cut off, but she wanted to be sure.

"Yeah, I'm good. Hey, we'll leave the last of the beers and ice cream with you, okay? I'm taking the cake home, sorry."

"No worries," she said, laughing, as Liz plopped a couple slices of cake into a plastic container which she left on the counter. "Thanks for coming over! I'm glad we were finally able to do this." They both agreed and suggested they all get together and do it again in the near future. "Definitely!"

They all said goodnight, then Vy closed the door behind them, turning around to see Monty leaning against the kitchen counter, smiling.

"That was a blast, Vy. Thank you so much for inviting me."

"Thank you for coming! I'm glad you had fun."

"Let me help you with all this," he said, gesturing to the mess in the kitchen and living room.

"Oh no, that's fine. I can take care of it!" She had the habit of never accepting help when she was playing the role of hostess.

"Vy," he said darkly, "I'm not taking no for an answer." He gestured to the casserole dish containing uneaten lasagna, with sauce and cheese cooked onto all sides, the platter of garlic bread, bowl of leftover salad and the pile of dirty plates, silverware and wine glasses filling her sink. She clicked her tongue, looking at the mess.

"Okay, fine. Good point."

Together they packed up the leftovers and put everything in the fridge, then washed all the plates, utensils, cups and the platter on which the garlic bread had rested.

"We can just let the lasagna pan soak for a bit. It's the only way all of that sauce and cheese is coming off."

"Sounds like a plan," he agreed. She poured one last glass of wine and then they both went back to the living room where she flopped down on the couch beside him. He put his arm around her, and she curled into him.

"Y'know, it's quite obvious this is the home of an English major," he said, gesturing to the full bookcases on both sides of the living room.

"To be fair, nearly half of them are movies, not books."

"True, but you still have more books than I've ever seen in one place at any given time, aside from a bookstore or library." He looked around at them all for a few moments. "Have you read all of them?"

"Oh gosh, no! No, the bad thing about working in a bookstore is that there are always really great deals, plus all employees get a discount on top of that, so I find a new book almost every day I work. At some point I'll be finished with grad school and be able to read for pleasure again."

"Same here," he chuckled. They sat in silence for a moment or two while Vy sipped on her wine and he read through the book and movie titles on her shelves. Then, he turned to her suddenly with a sober expression on his face. "Vy, I'm sorry about the guy you were with before me. And I'm sorry that Liz brought it up, she really shouldn't have."

She felt herself flush slightly at the memory. "It's okay. It was a bad situation and it took me a while to get over it but I'm okay now. And, I think Liz only mentioned it because of the movie and all the beer she'd had before then. Also, so she could threaten you."

"Threaten me?! Why?"

"Well…she told you she'd kick your ass if you did what he did to me, didn't she? I mean…she already damn near broke your nose with a door, so…" She grinned as he chuckled.

"I mean…fair enough! Still, I'm sorry it happened. That guy was an idiot."

She smiled up at him and leaned in for a quick peck on his lips to show him that all was well. They chatted for another half hour before Vy stifled a small yawn.

"I suppose that means I should go," he said, rising from the couch.

"I'm so sorry," she said. "Wine makes me sleepy."

"Don't worry, Vy! It's late. I totally understand." He picked up his jacket off the back of a chair and headed toward the door, Vy following behind him. "Have a goodnight."

"You too," she smiled.

He leaned in to give her a quick goodnight kiss, which turned out to be a tad longer than expected. Before long they found themselves with their arms wrapped tightly around each other, Monty's hand at the back of her head, tangled up in her hair. Suddenly, Vy found herself pressed against the door as his kisses left her mouth and traveled across her cheek and down her neck. She ran her hands up his back and pulled him closer, sliding one hand beneath his sweater to rest her hand on his back. He made a small noise in his throat and now his mouth was on hers again and she could barely breathe as his kisses deepened. Without pulling away she reached one hand behind her, groping the door to find the knob, which she locked as soon as she'd found it. With one hand still behind her head, he returned her gesture and slid his other hand up the back of her shirt, gently digging his fingertips into her back.

They finally broke apart, both panting softly, in need of more air. Maybe it was the wine or the conversation she'd had with

Liz a few weeks ago, or maybe even the presence of the bold, strong faerie queen who was now part of her, but she took his hand in hers, giving him a pointed look and led him away from the door and further into the apartment. They passed the kitchen counter and living room couch, heading toward a door which had remained closed all evening.

Vy's bedroom walls were a pale blue, on which were scattered a few pictures here and there. Against one wall sat a small vanity table which held her makeup and perfume. Across from this was her bed, draped with a white bedspread and decorative pillows in blues and rusty orange. Monty took little to no notice of her decorating, however, as she led him toward her bed, pulling him up onto it after her. He lay down beside her and their lips found each other's once again as she slid her arms around him and began tugging at his sweater, untucking it from his jeans. His hot breath warmed her neck as he trailed kisses down the side, pulling the collar of her shirt down to kiss her bare shoulder. Sliding her hands up under his shirt, she gently dragged her fingernails down his back, eliciting a gasp from him as he momentarily tensed.

Pushing her back, he carefully moved over her and looking down at her, he stroked her cheek softly. "Are you sure," he asked, breathily.

She smiled and took his hand, leading it to the buttons of her shirt. "I'm sure." He let out a sigh of contentment as, with one hand, he began to work at her shirt buttons, and leaned down to once more press his mouth to hers.

CHAPTER TWENTY

The first thought that entered Viola's mind upon waking was that she could smell bacon. She rolled over in bed and saw the disheveled sheets and blankets on the opposite side and she smiled at her second thought. Sitting up, she realized that the smell of bacon was indeed real, and that she could hear the sounds of cooking coming from beyond her bedroom door. She climbed out of bed and pulled on a robe over her t-shirt and shorts, then made her way out to the main living area of the apartment. Monty was turned away from her, working over the stove, whistling quietly to himself. He had dressed, though his shirt hung loosely from his shoulders, indicating that he hadn't buttoned it all the way up. She quietly walked up behind him and leaned on the kitchen counter, watching him.

"That smells fantastic," she said, making him jump. She couldn't help but laugh upon seeing how she had shocked him. He turned around to look at her.

"Vy! You were supposed to sleep so I could bring this to you," he pouted.

Now she felt a bit badly for ruining his surprise. "Aaww, I'm sorry."

"Oh, it's okay. Maybe next time," he smiled at her wickedly and she could feel the blush rise in her cheeks. He laughed and left the stove long enough to give her a quick kiss. "You're beautiful." He turned back toward the stove quickly, not wanting anything to burn.

"What are you making," she asked, after recovering herself.

"I found some bacon in your fridge, so I've almost finished that and next I'll start on some eggs. How do you like them? Scrambled? Fried? Sunny side up?"

"Oh, anything is fine. If you go with scrambled, I have some cheese in the fridge. Do you like cheese in your eggs?"

"Can't say I've ever tried scrambled eggs with cheese."

She stared at him in silent shock for several silent moments. "Oh, you poor thing. We're gonna fix that right now!" She went around the other side of the counter to root around in the fridge until she found a bag of shredded cheddar. "As soon as you've got the eggs in and scrambled up, add some of this in and let it melt as the eggs cook. It's how my dad always made them when I was growing up. It's so good!" She stayed next to him to help him finish making breakfast. "I can throw some bread in the toaster? Would you like some?"

"Sure!"

She busied herself with making toast and coffee while he finished the eggs. They sat down to eat, and she laughed as he discovered the delights of cheesy scrambled eggs. As they ate, she considered whether or not she should tell him the truth about herself. He'd whispered to her in the darkness last night, saying he loved her. Surely, if he meant it, he would accept her for who she truly was. Sipping on the last of her coffee, she decided it was now or never. Heart pounding, she took a deep breath and opened her mouth to speak.

Suddenly, his phone began buzzing from inside his pocket. He quickly pulled it out, silenced the beeping and stared at it for a moment as he read the text message. She thought she saw his expression darken but it was gone so quickly she wasn't sure if she'd just imagined it. "Aw, man. I'm so sorry, Vy," he said. "My mom has some stuff going on today and I need to give her a hand." He sighed, plunging the phone back in his pocket. "I'm afraid I'll have to head home. I was hoping to stay with you for a while today." He looked extremely disappointed and apologetic as he finished buttoning up his shirt and prepared to leave.

Vy sighed inwardly, giving up on telling him anything today. Instead, she began clearing their breakfast dishes off the table, while he grabbed his sweater from the bedroom. She set everything in the sink, noticing that he'd already washed the lasagna pan she'd forgotten about the night before. He emerged from the bedroom, pulling his sweater on over his head.

"I can't tell you how sorry I am, Vy." He leaned in to kiss her goodbye. "I'll call you later, okay?" He kissed her forehead, stroked her cheek, looking on her with tenderness in his eyes. "Love you."

She beamed happily. "Love you, too. Talk to you later." She closed the door behind him as he left and sighed, happily. She went to the sink to tackle their breakfast dishes. Just as she'd filled the sink with hot soapy water, she heard her phone go off, the message alert sounding from her bedroom. Her phone wasn't on her side table where she usually put it at night. After a few minutes of searching, she finally found it kicked under the bed, still crammed into the pocket of her jeans. She was surprised to see that she had three messages.

Emergency. Need you here as soon as possible. - Vince.

We need to go to Rosalyn's. Call me - Dad

Did you get any? - Liz

Rolling her eyes at the last one, she opted to reply to it later. She quickly pulled together clothes to wear and hopped into the shower. Evidently, the dishes would have to wait.

* * *

Walking into the house, Vy was shocked at the heightened activity. Creatures were running back and forth through the rooms and up and down the hallway, calling out directions and orders. Vy saw Fulrin trotting out of a room to the right and caught his attention.

"What's going on?"

The dwarf looked at her with a mixture of concern and excitement in his usually jovial eyes. "Melarue has discovered our location and sent us a message; her forces are coming. Tonight, we fight!" He pounded his chest with his fist, obviously eager for battle. With that, the dwarf took off down the hall, heading toward the dining room, Vy following shortly after.

Upon entering, she saw a huge gathering of people and creatures, all talking and looking at maps and books. Her father was there, next to Vince and Tam, all three of them hovering over a parchment spread out on the table. At the head of the table stood Rosalyn, dressed once more in her traveling clothes, listening as one of the faeries spoke to her, both wearing serious expressions on their faces. The room was noisy, a cacophony of voices all talking as one and she couldn't discern one from another, everything blending together. As she moved further into the room Rosalyn must have seen her out of the corner of her eye and looked up toward her direction. She was usually a very cheerful woman, however today her face was one of focused determination. She excused herself from the faerie she was talking to and came around to the front of the table.

"Viola, I'm so glad you've arrived." She took Vy's hands in her own, looking grim. "I'm sorry for the state of things. It is very serious business we conduct here today, I'm afraid."

"Yes, I see that. What's happening?"

She sighed deeply, leading her by hand, further into the room where everyone was congregated. The decibel level began to decrease as they took notice of her arrival. Rosalyn led her to a seat at the back of the room, sitting next to her so they could speak somewhat privately. "I must ask a very dangerous thing of you, Viola. I hope that you can channel Evelina's essence within you completely because we are going to need her strength, power and leadership today. Melarue is coming. She kidnapped one of our own and sent them to us in the wee hours of the morning to deliver a message."

"What message is that," asked Vy. Rosalyn was being so morbid and cryptic; it was simultaneously irritating and panic-inducing.

"It was terrible," she said, taking a moment to compose herself so the tears brimming in her eyes wouldn't overflow. "A brownie called Fabin was deposited on the sidewalk outside the house around four this morning. He'd been terribly hurt by magic as well as human weapons. His flesh was marred with many puncture wounds and deep gashes. The blood loss was incredible, and he was left with only enough magic energy to keep him alive long enough to deliver her message; a threat, which indicated she would be pursuing all-out war with us in the immediate future."

"Do you have any idea when this will happen?"

"Unfortunately, her message did not point to an exact time," she replied, shaking her head from side to side. "We are thinking it wouldn't be any earlier than midnight tonight. Her magic is powerful, due to stealing so many individual magical signatures over the years, but it wouldn't be strong enough to transport her forces directly here. They would have to travel through non-magical means. Given the creatures she used to fight us in the past, I doubt very much that she would want them to be seen by people in town. She'd want to avoid being noticed as much as possible."

Vy nodded in agreement. "Yes, that makes sense. How did she know to drop Fabin on *this* sidewalk? I thought she didn't know where this place was."

"She shouldn't have. The only thing I can think of," Rosalyn posited, "is that one of her scouts happened to be in the area when someone went under our enchanted archway. They wouldn't know how to go through it because the magic surrounding it is incredibly powerful but if they saw that someone disappeared under it..." She let the idea trail off. "Or she may have extracted it from one of our allies whom she's taken. Even the strongest of creatures can break when in distress." Both women shared a look, neither wanting to think about the implications of that thought.

Vy remained silent, taking a moment to ponder. She noticed that many of the people and creatures in the room were now looking toward them. She saw her father, staring intently at her, the fear in his eyes visible even from across the room. She was filled with a desire to inspire courage in him and everyone else present. She was supposed to be their queen, she needed to lead them and protect them. However, despite the newly discovered memories of Evelina, she was still rather new to military strategy. Fortunately, she understood that a good ruler knows how to use her advisors. "Okay, then. What's our next step?"

Rosalyn gave her a sad smile before standing up, indicating to Vy that she should follow. "Our next step is to prepare for battle." She and Rosalyn walked over to the long dining room table, where several of those gathered had been poring over old maps and documents. "These are descriptions of all the enchantments and magic guarding this place and these," she gestured to the maps spread out across the wooden surface, "are maps detailing the layout of our lands."

Vy looked at the maps with curiosity, unsure of which lands she was speaking. She saw the sketch of a large building in the center of one map, with a wide area of green land, surrounded on three sides by a wide area of forest. Beyond that was a vast expanse of green, which seemed to be a sort of field or meadow. As she looked on the drawings, realization suddenly dawned on her. "Wait...this is here! This," she exclaimed, putting her finger on the house in the drawing," is this house! All this land exists around here?" In her travels around the property, she hadn't gone much further than the woods surrounding the great lawn. She had thought there wasn't much beyond the trees aside from more trees. If these maps were accurate there was a huge area of land hidden behind them.

"Yes, indeed," was Rosalyn's reply. "All of this space is protected by our magic. There are many who choose to live in our little bubble realm but do not want to live in the house. Some choose to be even closer to nature, sleeping under the stars, making their homes in hollow trees and caves. This land out here," she waved her hand over the area beyond the woods, "is for that purpose. Most of this land is a large meadow. Over here, near the river, are a few caves hidden in the hills, the perfect environment for some of our more reclusive residents."

Vy looked over the maps, surprised at the amount of land they actually had. "Well, then." She lifted her face to look at everyone, all of whom were staring back at her expectantly. Until now she hadn't thought much about how they looked to her as a leader, and admittedly, she wasn't sure how to be the leader they needed, especially under these circumstances. She took a deep breath and began to address everyone for the first time as their queen. "I must admit to you all that while the memories and essence of Evelina resides within me, I am still coming to terms with these two identities. In the end, I still feel that I am Viola Campbell. I am not an expert in military strategy and will appreciate your help in preparing for this." She looked back to the maps in front of her before continuing, still shaking from her brief foray into public speaking. "I think the first thing we should do is to set up a line of defense. Where do we think she and her forces will enter from? The archway? Would she be able to do so with those enchantments in place?"

Rosalyn visibly grimaced as she responded, saying, "If she knows the exact location of the archway, then with enough time, she could work through the enchantments. It wouldn't be easy, but it can be done. And with all of the magic she's stolen coursing through her blood." She let the sentence trail off.

Fulrin spoke up next, apparently volunteering for the position as head of magical military forces. "The archway'll probably be the most obvious, but we shouldn't assume this'll be 'er only attack point. If she found one way in, she'll find more of 'em. Alla this area over 'ere," he said, waving his hand over the wide meadow, "could be open ter attack. We should think abou' stationing forces 'ere and over 'ere." He ran a hand over several different areas on the map, indicating each location.

    Lady Asteria, the purple pixie, who had flown over to stand on the corner of one of the maps piped up in her tinkling voice. "I can direct a quarter of my fellow pixies and sprites to the main entrance and disperse the rest all along the back perimeter. We will be able to fly high enough to see them from a mile off in any direction and can quickly get messages back and forth between the different troops!"

    "Excellent, Asteria, that will be very helpful," Rosalyn encouraged.

    "We should probably contact everyone who lives in this outer area of the property, as well as those who live with the humans in the city and nearby. I get the feeling we'll need everyone we can get," Vy offered.

    Rosalyn agreed and called for several messengers to be sent throughout the city and outlying country areas, as well as sending three or four to the woods and meadow nearby, requesting aid and warning the inhabitants of what was to come. They continued discussing where to break up different forces, which areas needed the most defenses. About halfway through the meeting, Rosalyn instructed the cooks to prepare a large meal for everyone, saying they should all enjoy a meal together before they went to battle. Her true sentiments remained unspoken but were heard by all just the same; she wanted everyone to share a meal and time together, in case some of them didn't survive the night. They all agreed it was in their best interest to magically light the entire area. Anyone going by the house would see nothing but the decrepit, old inn against the darkening sky but once beyond the magical border, the inside would be bright and sunny to allow their forces to see better in battle. An enchantment this powerful required all of them to stand outside and focus their magic together. By the time they finished their planning meeting, they all felt reasonably confident in the positioning of their forces.

  At six in the evening Rosalyn dismissed them and they all went outside, where a long line of tables had been set up for everyone to enjoy their meal together on the green lawn. The tables were filled to capacity with meats, cheeses, vegetables, fruits and pastries, tea, mead and coffee. Everyone who called the old Victorian and its surrounding lands their home was in attendance, even the creatures that always seemed to be in the kitchen when Vy had been there. Seated amongst them were also those who chose to live in the human world for most of their days. Introductions were made between Vy and everyone she hadn't yet had the opportunity to meet. With each introduction she couldn't help but think of the man who called himself Dr. Sawyer or the brownie called Fabin, two members of this magical family whom she would never get to meet. Though they were all talking, laughing and eating cheerfully, the dread of battle and uncertainty of death hung over them, a dark shadow marring their sunny day.

As they ate, joked, laughed and talked together, Vy couldn't help but notice some of the guests were being ignored by others or treated unkindly. There were those same expressions of suspicion or anger that had become so familiar to her from some of the inn's inhabitants. The offending parties must have only been putting up with the human presence due to the need for numbers in battle. She immediately made it a point to sit amongst the humans and engage them in polite conversation and didn't give a damn about the looks she received from other members of the group further down the table. The people she talked with seemed relieved and overjoyed that she was speaking with them. It broke her heart to know that they could feel so out of place amongst people who should be their closest friends. She was listening intently to a wizard named Gregory, who was telling her about his own theories on the origin of magic, when Rosalyn announced it was time to finish up and get moving.

When the food was gone and the glasses empty, the dark shadow that had been hovering over them fully began to settle in, their happy moods devolving into varying levels of fear, dread, worry, stress and determination; everything hidden behind brave masks, ready for whatever came next. Rosalyn instructed everyone to begin their preparations for battle. The first step was to clear the tables, which a horde of gnomes fell to immediately, along with several others; a few flying fairies and pixies quickly ferrying dishes back inside the house. Vy was helping to move a table when Rosalyn, Tam, Vince and her father came over to her.

"We have something for you, Vy-Vy. Come with us," her father said, looping her arm through his own. They led her back into the house and up the stairs to the second level, where she had never been before. The second floor was decorated in much the same fashion as the first, with beautiful oriental rugs and vintage paintings, however while the first floor seemed to be focused in a red and gold color scheme, the second floor was of blue and silver. Vy had always loved the color blue and she thought pairing it with silver was pure genius on the part of the interior designer. Rosalyn led the group down the hall and unlocked a door on the right, gesturing for them all to go inside. Vy, still holding onto her father's arm, looked around the room, which was ringed with cases containing what must have been various relics and powerful items. In the very center of the room, stood the red dress and golden armor she had seen in her visions.

Letting go of her father's arm, she walked up to it and laid her hands on the cool metal, some part of her already knowing how it would feel; the weight of it, how it felt to wear it, how chilly the links of chainmail felt against her skin where it made contact. The chest plate bore the image of a golden sun, while a trail of flowers wound its way from the right hip, around and up to the left shoulder plate. Peeking out from below the shoulder plates and tasset, which was positioned beneath the waist and would cover her down to her mid-thigh, was an unbelievably light-weight dress of golden chainmail. Underneath that was a thick-woven red dress to protect her skin from the metal. Sitting on the floor beneath the suit of armor was a pair of gold-plated, knee-high boots. The Evelina half of her admired the suit with fondness, while the part of her that was still Viola experienced the old armor for the first time, thinking how very thankful she was that it wasn't like the ridiculous bikini-like armor of video games.

Stepping back from the suit, she turned toward the other four, who were watching her from just inside the door. "This is...," she found herself incapable of finishing the sentence, but Rosalyn gave her a small nod of affirmation.

Vince took a step forward. "We thought you should wear it tonight, given the history." She nodded her understanding, but remained silent, still working it all out and putting things together inside her head.

"You remember how to put it on?" Vy nodded in response to Rosalyn's question. It was a feeling she was still getting used to; having copious amounts of knowledge she hadn't had two months ago. It was simultaneously fascinating and unsettling. "Very well, then. Come," Rosalyn said softly, ushering Tam and Vince out of the room, "we'll see you downstairs when you're ready." The three of them left the room, shutting the door behind them, leaving Vy alone with her father.

"Here, kiddo. Let me help you with all of this." He lifted the armor up off of its display, handing her the two dresses. "Here, you can change behind there," he gestured to a screen in the corner of the room. "I'll get all these pieces of armor ready for when you're done."

In a bit of a daze, she did as he asked, ducking behind the curtains to kick off her sneakers and pull off her top and skirt. She decided to keep the black leggings on underneath both dresses; the thick red one and the one made of chainmail. She pulled both on over her head, one after the other. Stepping back out from the curtains, she alerted her father that she was ready and began putting on her boots. Next, her father went to her to help her fasten on the different pieces of her armor, starting with the tassets to protect her thighs, and ending with the shoulder plates.

"What do you think of that," he asked, stepping back to get the bigger picture.

"Um...it's quite a bit lighter than I would have expected."

"No doubt that's the magic," he chuckled. He took a deep breath as his facial expression darkened. "Vy, I know you have the armor but that doesn't mean you have to be right out front in battle. You can organize and tell the others what to do from the back of the lines."

She mulled over his words for a moment. The truth was she was terrified. She'd never done anything remotely like this before and part of her desperately wanted to run and hide herself away somewhere until it was over. She wanted to be like Prospero and let the sea take her spell book and magical staff into its dark depths, never to be seen again. But wearing the armor also made her feel more like Evelina than ever. She felt strong and ready to face whatever was about to come at her. She wanted to protect the people she'd met and with whom she'd grown close over the past couple of months. She sighed and met her father's gaze once more.

"I'm sorry, Dad, but I can't. And you know I can't do that." She took his hands in hers, trying to offer him some comfort and to calm his fears. "I've only known them a short time, but I care about these people. And apparently, I'm also supposed to be their queen, which means that I have to help defend and protect them. I wouldn't feel that I was doing that to the best of my ability if I was hidden in the background."

He nodded. "I knew you would say that." He smoothed her hair and kissed her forehead before giving her one of his classic bear hugs. "Your mother would have done the exact same thing. She'd be so proud of you. And so am I." He broke the hug and held her at arm's length to look at her face. "I'm going to fight with you and do my best to stay close to you and protect you, but I need you to be careful out there, okay? I can't lose you."

She felt the sting of tears welling up in her eyes and could do nothing to stop it as a couple of them escaped and rolled down her cheeks. "You be careful, too, okay? Because I can't lose you, either. I'll be fine," she forced a laugh, trying to play it all off, "I'm Evelina, after all. I've got this."

"Of course you do," he said, nodding and forcing his own laughter and smile. "Though, I still won't be upset if you decide to stay in the back." They both chuckled as he pulled her in close for another big hug and a kiss on her forehead. "I love you, Vy-Vy."

"I love you too, Dad."

CHAPTER TWENTY-ONE

Her father found a set of armor that he could use, and while he was putting on some of the simpler pieces, Viola grabbed her phone to send out a couple of messages. Her stomach was in knots, the thought of battle was terrifying. She had her father beside her but there were two people to whom she needed to say goodbye, just in case things didn't go well.

Hey Liz, war starts tonight. You're an amazing friend and I love you. You and Liam should get married. Hope I'll see you tomorrow.

Hi Monty. She thought for a few minutes about what to say to him. There was so much she wanted to type but he wouldn't understand any of it. In the end, she decided to go with something simple. *Just wanted to say I love you.* She tucked the phone back in the pocket of her hoodie, hoping she would be fortunate enough to be able to check them later.

After her father had put on his own set of armor, he and Viola went back downstairs. Rosalyn, Vince and Tam were at the bottom of the staircase, waiting, and each of them turned their awed faces toward her as she and her father descended the stairs. She felt a bit awkward with the three of them staring at her but that feeling grew stronger as all three went down on one knee to bow before her. She thought she had finally got them to stop doing that. "Everyone...please. Don't."

They looked up at her and slowly rose to their feet. "I apologize, Viola," Rosalyn began. "It's just been so very long since we've seen this armor on anyone and now that you have merged yourself with Evelina, you look exactly like her. It...took me aback for a moment." Viola thought she heard a small crack in Rosalyn's voice and saw the trace of tears in her eyes as she and her father made it to the bottom floor and stood beside the other three. She wondered if Rosalyn and Evelina had been friends in that other life. She'd have to examine her memories at another time, when she had time to look at the ones that weren't focused on war and usage of magic.

"There's something I've been curious about," she said, getting back to the matter at hand. "How does armor keep me safe from a magical attack?"

"Gold is a very strong metal," said Rosalyn. "It is naturally capable of providing a small amount of shield protection against magic. Also, while Melarue is sure to have magical creatures in her army, the last time we met in battle, the majority of her forces were made up of humans. Without having magic to defend themselves, they resorted to using things like swords, axes, any type of blade. If you're concentrating on an attack or defensive enchantment, the armor will protect your body from these weapons."

"Fair enough," she replied. Oh, great. There would be stabby weapons, too. "What time is it?" Their magic was keeping the darkness away, so it was impossible to tell what time it was, given the sunlight pouring in through the windows.

"About nine thirty," Vince said. She could see the same nervousness she felt being reflected back at her from his eyes. She nodded, taking a deep breath.

"Okay. I'd like to get into positions, then. I'd rather be there early and wait for an extra hour or two than to get there too late." Instructions were sent out to get everyone mobilized. Viola and Rosalyn lead their small group out to join the others on the meadow beyond the woods. Three fairies traveled with them, in case they needed to send out any messages to forces in other locations. The meadow was a sea of green, the grass swaying slightly in the soft breeze. They trudged across the field, taking their positions among the other troops along the northern border, near the caves where the less sociable creatures made their homes.

They stood together in silence, waiting to hear the flutter of fairy wings coming to deliver a message, or the many footfalls of an approaching army. Vy was thankful they had decided to use their magic to prolong the sunlight; she thought it would be far worse to be standing here in the dark, trying to discern movement through the trees. She instructed everyone to sit and rest for as long as they could; an approaching army would be heard long before they were seen, so everyone could be on their feet, stretched and into combat positions long before they needed to engage in battle. Some of their forces were trying their best to entertain themselves while they waited for news and perhaps to get their minds off of the impending battle. Vy found herself completely enthralled by a small gnome who seemed to be knitting. She had to raise an eyebrow at the sight, wondering exactly how such a small creature had ever learned how to knit. The needles were almost as tall as he was and they were clicking away madly, the work of blue yarn growing slightly longer with every passing minute.

The furious fluttering of tiny wings began to sound through the air, distant at first but getting closer. They all looked in the direction of the sound, as a tiny green pixie drew close enough to become visible. The little thing was beating her wings just as fast as she could, speeding straight toward Vy and her group. Vy took several steps in the pixie's direction and held out her hand, catching the tiny thing as she landed, completely spent from her flight.

"Willowblossom! What is it," Vy asked, gently.

The little pixie was standing in the palm of her hand, bent over, hands on her little thighs, trying to catch her breath. "Melarue's...army...coming," she panted. "The archway," she said, pointing back toward the direction of the house. Vy intended to ask her for more information but the sound of another set of wings distracted her. Looking up, they all saw a tiny fairy descending from where she had been positioned above them. Unlike Willowblossom, this one didn't have to work as hard to reach them, merely allowing herself to fall gently back to earth. This time, Charles reached a hand out to catch the little thing as she came in to land.

The little blue-haired fairy touched down in his palm and immediately began to speak. "Melarue and her army are coming through the woods from that direction," she said, pointing to the thicket of trees just to the right of the caves. "They're probably about a half hour away." Vy wasn't entirely surprised; it made sense to attack from multiple points, in the hopes of finding your enemy off guard. Unfortunately for Melarue, Vy and her team of magical creatures and humans had planned for this.

Turning to the three fairies that had traveled with them, Vy began to act as leader, the Evelina side of her taking over. "Please head to the other stations to find out if they are seeing any advancing troops but don't tire yourselves out; we'll need your help. Have one of their fairies report back here to us." The three fairies started flying off to the other forces stationed around the border. "And thank you!" She turned back to those around her. "Well...here we go."

The silent minutes dragged by, each tick of her father's watch like the reverberating pound of a bass drum. The gnome had tucked his ball of yarn away, though Vy had no idea where he could have stashed such a thing, and assumed he had bigger-on-the-inside pockets. The two knitting needles, however, he was brandishing in each of his hands, like miniature purple swords. She wasn't sure how effective they would be in battle, but she appreciated his enthusiasm. Roughly fifteen minutes passed when the sound of wings were heard again, cutting through the silence.

Each of the fairies arrived within minutes of each other, two of them reporting sightings of Melarue's army. Vy looked to

Rosalyn, waiting for her to give out instructions to all of the nearby troops. When the elf stood silent, returning her gaze, Vy realized she was meant to address all of the troops within close proximity. Up to this point, the largest assembly of magical creatures she had addressed had been the dozen or so people in the dining room earlier that day. Public speaking had never been her favorite class so, of course, fate would have it that she would find herself in a position that required being in front of large groups of people. She already had enough butterflies in the pit of her stomach so what the hell; why not add a few more?! She quickly threw together a speech inside her head, and then took a few steps away from her small, close-knit group.

      Willing her butterflies to settle down a bit and attempting to force down the anxiety-induced vomit threatening to come up, she began to address her troops. "Everyone, I have just been informed that we are very nearly surrounded. Melarue has sections of forces advancing on us from the archway, from the river area and coming toward us. We should be seeing her troops coming through the trees behind me in another fifteen minutes or so." Her voice was shaking, and she cleared her throat awkwardly, as all manner of faces stared back at her, looking uninterested and thoroughly unimpressed. Her father, Rosalyn, Vince and Tam were all looking to her encouragingly. "I must admit, I have never led a battle. I have never been a queen, and all of this is very new and terrifying. But in the short time that I have been among you all, I have grown to love you and this world. I may not be the greatest military strategist the world has ever seen, and I may not be the fastest thing on two legs, but I promise that I will fight for you. I will fight with you to keep us and our way of life safe." As she spoke, her gaze moved around the field in front of her, taking in the faces of all those listening to her. They were beginning to warm up to her speech and she thanked the stars above for allowing her not to screw up what was probably the most important speech she would ever make in her life. She saw fear in their eyes but determination and courage, also. She hoped that when they looked into her eyes, they saw more determination and strength, rather than the fear trying to claw its way out of her insides.

"I admit that I am afraid," she called out to them. "But I have faith. I have met all of you, I have dined with you, I have laughed with you and I know you. I know that you will give everything you can tonight. I know that you are all strong and brave and will not back down from this fight. And, above all, I know that we shall not be defeated!! Tonight, we will empty the mead stores in celebration of our victory!"

Cheers erupted around her as humans and creatures raised their hands and weapons into the air in support. Either that, or they just really wanted to get wasted on all the mead. She couldn't blame them, really. Mead sounded fantastic right now. The whooping and hollering eventually quieted and they stood still as statues, awaiting their approaching enemy. Within minutes, the sound of many footsteps crashing through woods could be heard in the distance. Vy's heart was pounding so hard she could hear the blood rushing through her ears as she pulled on her golden helmet. As the first line of troops became visible, Rosalyn, Tam and Vince positioned themselves so they were ready to act quickly, prepared to attack or defend. Out of the corner of her eye, she saw her father raise a shining, silver sword. She hadn't even been aware he knew how to wield a blade. The little gnome was in a fighting stance, his knitting needles raised high. She adopted a stance similar to that of Tam and Vince, prepared to let loose all the magic at her disposal.

The advancing troops stopped a few dozen feet away from them, as though daring them to make the first move. The group wasn't large, probably around five dozen in total, meaning they had about fifteen or so more combatants than Vy's side. There were a good many human foes, but they were far outnumbered by a myriad of magical creatures. She saw strange, short, thin-limbed green creatures with long, pointed noses and teeth sharp as daggers, a couple of greenish-brown skinned creatures, towering above the rest, a creature that looked as though it was made purely of fire and many others were hidden behind various types of armor. The one who appeared to be their leader was wearing a suit of red armor, fashioned in the style of a classical, medieval knight. They were too far away for Vy to see any distinguishable features and the red helmet hid the face, so she wasn't sure if this was Melarue or not; only time would tell. Both armies stood still and silent, facing each other, waiting for someone to make the first move. Above all else, Vy would have preferred them to come to a peaceful agreement, rather than resorting to violence. She refused to have her army make the first move.

"We are prepared to accept your surrender," she called across the empty space between them. "No one needs to die today."

Words hadn't worked for Evelina all those years ago, but she still needed to try.

"Indeed," came the deep, muffled voice of the red knight. The knight, evidently, was male and not Melarue after all. "Loss of life would be regrettable. We will be happy to accept *your* surrender."

Vy shook her head, refusing to respond. "I don't think they're willing to listen to me. I'm afraid we won't be able to avoid battle," she said to Rosalyn, who nodded in agreement. She called back across to the opposing force. "We will not be surrendering this evening. But we will fight, if we must!"

The red knight gave a slight bow. "Then let us begin!" With a wave of his hand he signaled his forces to begin their assault. A moment later, balls of light were screaming toward Vy's side of the meadow. She and half of the other magic wielders present worked on creating a barrier to deflect the attacks, while the other half began sending their own spells to the other side. In the meantime, the red knight and his forces moved forward a couple of feet before erecting their own barrier. The battle continued in this manner for the next several minutes, each side trying to get something through the other side's defenses, until one of Gregory's spells managed to get through the red knight's weakened barrier. Suddenly, a large, thick vine sprouted up from the ground, enclosing three of his troops. It took about half a second for both sides to realize what had happened and then all hell broke loose. The red knight let out a loud battle cry, holding his sword aloft, the point aiming directly toward

Vy. After a brief pause, his army pumping themselves up, he launched himself toward her, his army following directly behind.

"FORWARD!!" Vy screamed out the command and seconds later she, and her friends and family were running toward Melarue's army, weapons and hands raised. The little gnome was surprisingly fast, a streak of red and blue flashing forward into the melee of war. The front lines met with the clangs of metal on metal, the pops and crashes of magic going off and the cries of those who were injured. Vy found herself fighting one of the small, green creatures with the long, pointed noses. While its magic wasn't overwhelmingly strong, the spells and attacks it was throwing her way were quite painful, her flesh of her arms and legs stinging horribly with each contact. She was doing her best to dodge his attacks, while trying to set off her own. The creature was quite fast and easily avoided her spells, his thin little limbs easily twisting out of the way just in time. After several minutes and a few scratches on her exposed skin, she'd had quite enough of their fight and she conjured a large wave of water, which crashed over the creature.

The second the water made contact, Vy immediately froze it, keeping him trapped within a large chunk of ice. This surprised her; she didn't think she'd known how to do such a thing. Perhaps during battle, she was more Evelina than Vy, the elf's essence taking over the human one. That thought scared her, but she didn't have time to dwell on it, quickly moving around the frozen creature to face her next foe. A short distance away, she saw her father engaged in battle with one of the tall, brownish-green-skinned creatures and immediately ran in his direction. She lifted both of her hands in front of her, then dragged them through the air, aiming her palms toward the creature, sending a torrent of flame spiraling through the air toward it. The force of the impact knocked him backwards, giving Vy time to run over to her father.

"You okay, Dad?" She had to yell over the din of battle for him to hear her, despite their close proximity to each other. They were surrounded by fighting on all sides. Vy could see Tam and Vince facing off against a group of creatures which looked rather like angry and mutated brownies, while Rosalyn was locked in battle with two more of the creatures like the one she'd just frozen.

"I'm fine! Are you okay," Charles shouted back. She nodded, though she didn't like the large cut across his cheek. The troll had pulled himself back up during their short exchange, preparing to charge. Her father raised his sword beside her, while Vy started focusing on her next attack. Swinging his blade, Charles managed to destroy the wooden club the troll had been using to whack him, sending splinters and wood shards flying. Throwing his useless club to the ground, the troll roared and raised his arms up, preparing to slam his fists down onto their heads. Vy was scrambling with her magic, trying to put it together, realizing it may have been a bit too complicated for the current situation. She began to panic slightly, when suddenly the troll let out a roar of pain and fell to the ground once more as Vy and her father watched, confused. A little gnome quickly climbed up and over the troll's body, wrenching one of his purple knitting needles out of the troll's calf, flicking it to remove the troll's blood. An interesting and wonderful idea popped into Viola's head and she quickly began working on new magic. She wasn't sure if she could do it but if Evelina was indeed taking over during the battle, perhaps she was capable of anything. The little gnome had planted himself on the troll's chest and was smacking him in the face repeatedly with the knitting needles, not causing much in terms of damage or pain, but it had to be incredibly annoying, at the very least. It also provided a good distraction while Vy's magic took hold and the troll rapidly shrunk and transformed into a sheep, covered in soft, fluffy, brown wool. "For your knitting," Vy called to the gnome, who saluted her happily, then rode the new sheep off in search of his next foe.

    A trio of strange little creatures with razor-sharp teeth and bloodied hats ran toward them, teeth gnashing together. Charles swung his blade toward them and managed to catch one, a deep gash erupting across its chest, while the other two dodged and sped toward Vy. She whipped around, narrowly avoiding one of them but screamed out in pain as the other sank its teeth just above the top of her boots and deep into the flesh of her calf. The pain forced her to the ground, while the little beast gleefully reared back to attack again. Fortunately, a stray spell from a nearby battle sent the creature flying, allowing Vy to push herself back up and crash another water spell over both of the creatures, quickly freezing them.

    There didn't seem to be any enemies immediately near her, so she took a moment to have a look around the battlefield. It brought a great amount of sadness to her heart to see so many people and creatures fighting to the death. The green grass was dyed in shades of pinks and reds as fighters from both forces lay bleeding. There seemed to be an equal number of injuries and casualties on either side, though, at least from where she stood, it looked as though there was slightly more damage inflicted upon Melarue's forces. Speaking of the woman, Vy wondered where on the battlefield Melarue was located. She'd have to keep an eye out for a faerie or pixie and ask if they could find her and report back to Vy. She wondered how the troops in other locations were faring. Rosalyn was across the field sending sparks and glowing streams of magical energy in the direction of her opponent, the last of the brownie-like creatures. Vince and Tam were still fighting alongside each other, taking on another troll. After taking care of one of the creatures that had tried to attack her, her father was already a couple dozen feet away, fighting against yet another redcap.

    A terrifyingly loud noise sounded behind her and, turning around, she saw a plume of purple smoke rising back beyond the trees leading to the house. Instinctively, she took off running, tearing across the meadow to find out what was happening. She dodged past several nearby battles, sending a few magical blasts toward enemy forces as she went, doing her best to help all of those who were fighting. Upon reaching the tree line, she looked back to see the battle still raging behind her. As she did so, she noticed the red knight had caught sight of her and had broken away from the melee, quickly cutting down the distance between them. She darted into the trees, hoping to lose him in the thick woods. She hoped the woods' leafy canopy and the shadows it created would hide her.

    Unfortunately, the sunlight trickled in a bit more than she would have liked, eliminating much of a chance of cover for someone trying to disappear. She heard the snapping and cracking of branches being broken behind her as the knight reached the tree line. Putting on an extra burst of speed, pushing through the pain in her leg from the redcap's bite, she raced to the other side, following the purple smoke which she could pick out between the branches.

Bursting out of the trees, she was horrified to see the lawn, gardens and house in absolute chaos. A much larger force had arrived here and was locked in battle with her soldiers. There was far more reddened, blood-stained grass than there was green. Bodies of humans, goblins, brownies and fairies lay in terrible angles all across the lawn, while several dozen more clashed swords or loosed magic at each other. The purple smoke was coming from the garden, where a terrible spell had been set off. A large, scorched plot of ground where the roses once grew was surrounded by blackened, burning vegetation. The side of the house that was closest to the gardens was also rather scorched from whatever had happened. The porch lay in shambles, planks of wood thrown haphazardly along the ground. The well toward the back of the lawn was nothing more than a pile of rocks. She started forward, eyes roving the field as she decided where she was most needed, when she heard a crash behind her. Looking around, Viola saw the red knight emerging from the trees, heading straight toward her. She readied herself and got positioned in a fighting stance, ready to release more fire magic the second the knight began to attack. She frowned as the knight stopped suddenly, several feet in front of her. She was confused as to what was going on but began concentrating on her attack, visualizing the torrent of flame bursting from the palms of her hands. She watched as the knight slowly reached up to push the visor of his helmet up and away from their face, revealing his identity. Vy steeled herself, wondering who or what would turn out to be Melarue's right hand man. The knight finished lifting the visor and moved his hand from his face.

Vy's concentration was completely shattered. The man in the red armor had the bluest eyes she had ever seen, staring back at her widely; the jawline of a god and dark hair, messy from sweat, poking out from beneath his helm.

"Monty?! What..."

The question was lost on her lips as the loud boom of a second explosion shook the ground and reverberated through the skulls of everyone nearby. Half a second later, Vy's vision was nothing but a white flash as blinding pain coursed through the back of her head. A moment later, everything went dark.

CHAPTER TWENTY-TWO

The sun was rising in the world outside of their magical bubble, so Rosalyn and the others began pulling magical energies away from their manufactured sunlight. The battlefield dimmed slightly when they were returned to the natural light unaffected by magic, however the sky was brightening with every passing minute, allowing them to see the destruction around them. The meadow in which they stood was a gory mess of the injured and dying. Rosalyn limped away from where she had been standing, catching her breath. The worst of the fighting had ceased about an hour and a half ago, Evelina's army overcoming Melarue's. Now, they were tasked with the horrific job of treating the wounded and mourning the dead. Rosalyn limped slowly toward a man in blood-stained silver armor.

"Charles." As she spoke his name, Vy's father turned around. They both spent a few seconds looking over each other's wounds. Both were covered in bruises and sporting several decent-sized cuts and gashes. Rosalyn had a terrible burn on her thigh, which sent waves of pain through her leg with each step. She had also managed to twist the ankle of that same leg while running across the field. Thanks to his armor, Charles wasn't badly hurt, aside from his own cuts and bruises, though he also looked rather singed. "Are you all right," she asked.

"As good as can be expected. You?" He gestured toward the nasty-looking burn on her thigh. It needed a good cleaning and bandage; otherwise it would no doubt become infected.

"About the same," she replied. The two looked around at the battlefield. In the early morning sunrise, the field was eerily quiet; the only sounds the soft whimpers of those who were in pain and the crunching of grass and leaves under boots as those well enough to help made their rounds through the field. Rosalyn took a few moments to heal the worst of their cuts, burns and scrapes, then Charles offered her an arm for support and helped her walk to the people nearest them.

Vince was carefully pulling tiny splinters and shards of wood out of Tam's injured leg. The process was slow and bloody and very painful, Vince apologizing with every piece he pulled from the elf's flesh. Tam would nod and shut his eyes tight against the pain of the wooden shards scraping back along his injured flesh as it was pulled out, releasing the blood that had begun to pool beneath it. They were both covered in cuts and burns, Vince also sporting a nasty case of frostbite on the right side of his face, after a run-in with an ice sprite. Charles and Rosalyn slowly made their way over to them to see if they could offer any help. Carefully sitting down beside him, Rosalyn looked over the mess of wood, blood and flesh that was Tam's leg. "Tamneauth, how did this happen?"

Gritting his teeth, he told her of how he and Vince had been winning a fight against one of the trolls when a spell had missed its target and smashed headlong into the troll's club. The force of the impact sent shards of the club flying in all directions. Vince had a few splinters bury themselves in his limbs but Tam, who had jumped in between the troll and Vince, had received the full brunt of the explosion.

"I can heal it for you quickly, Tam," she said, "but to do so, I will have to remove all of the shards and splinters. And it will hurt. Terribly." The elf was more pale than usual and looked incredibly weak as he nodded his assent.

"Please."

"Very well. I'll try to do this as quickly as possible," she said, smoothing his dirt and blood-stained silver hair. Vince shifted around and took hold of Tam's hand, offering him support. "Okay, Tamneauth. Three...two..." Closing her eyes and focusing her energy, she used her magic to find every piece of wooden splinter and shard in his body and magically drew them out all at once. Tam writhed and let out a cry of pain as the pieces were pulled from his flesh en masse. It broke Rosalyn's heart to hear the pain in his scream and his labored breathing, and she found it impossible to stem the flow of three large tears that escaped from her closed eyes. Once all the pieces had been removed, she focused on stemming the blood flow and mending the flesh back together. There had been several large chunks of wood that had caused major injuries from his mid-calf up to his thigh. She focused mainly on these larger wounds, using magic to knit the torn flesh back together. After a few moments, his sounds of pain ceased, and his breathing began to calm. He was still exceptionally pale, but he heaved a sigh of relief, opened his eyes and took her hand in his.

"Thank you, My Lady." His voice was exhausted and weak, but grateful.

She smiled down at him. "You are so very welcome, dear, dear Tamneauth." Looking back up to Charles and to Vince, she included all of them in the next part of their conversation. "Have any of you heard anything? How many people have been injured? Who didn't survive? Do we know where Viola went?"

Vince replied, still gently squeezing Tam's hand as the magic continued to heal his leg. "I'm not sure of exact numbers but it seems their forces took a more extensive hit than ours, though we have still lost far too many good men and women today."

"Have we heard anything from the other stations," she asked.

"A few fairies and pixies flew in a short time ago," Charles said, "and it sounds as though they fared much the same as we did here. Majority of losses to the other side, though we've lost quite a few of our own." He gazed down at Rosalyn, a look of sadness and concern on his face. "What I hear from the house isn't good. We should get over there soon." Lifting his eyes, he looked toward the smoke still rising above the trees, anxiety creeping into his voice. "The last time I caught sight of my daughter she was heading that way."

"Then we should go there at once," nodded Rosalyn. They helped Tam stand and he leaned on Vince as the group of four made their way through the field. Though she desperately wanted to find Vy and see that she was okay, Rosalyn couldn't help stopping to assist the seriously injured as they made their way toward the old Victorian. They came across a dwarf who was sprawled on the ground, clutching his belly. A quick inspection revealed two daggers embedded inside his middle, up to their hilts. They crouched around him as Rosalyn tried to ascertain the level of damage. She used her healing magic to sense what was going on inside the poor dwarf, who was breathing raggedly and seemed to be struggling to maintain consciousness. After a moment, she lifted her eyes to meet the others' gaze. The expression in her eyes spoke volumes; the poor dwarf was beyond her abilities to heal. They stayed by him, comforting him, telling him everything was going to be fine, while Rosalyn held and stroked his hand. Eventually, the light in his eyes dimmed and he sighed softly. Briefly pressing her lips to his forehead, Rosalyn placed his hand around his sword and laid it down on his chest before closing his eyes and turning away from the horrific site. A short distance before the woods they saw a small mound of bodies, another group of redcaps, all dead, piled in a heap. A sheep was nosing at one of the redcaps, bleating mournfully. They were passing by when Tam suddenly stopped them.

"I see something under there," he pointed. They all looked toward the sheep and could see a thin piece of purple metal sticking out from beneath the pile, a tiny hand clutched loosely around the base. "I think it's Nigel."

Charles pushed four lifeless redcap bodies away, revealing the little gnome lying in the bloodied grass beneath them. The tips of his knitting needles were spattered with blood, as was his clothing and even his white beard. One of his little arms was bent at an awkward angle and he lay unmoving. Tam's right hand flew to his mouth in shock as Vince hung his head in grief beside him. Charles sighed sadly and gingerly slipped his hand beneath the gnome's body to pick him up. Nigel's little blue eyes suddenly snapped open and he looked up at all of them as they started to laugh with joy. "You're okay," Charles said to him, beaming. "You've got a broken arm, but we can fix that." He beckoned Rosalyn over, who quickly focused energy into his little arm, resetting the bones.

"There now," she said. "You should be right as rain in no time. Take it easy, though. It will still be a bit tender." The little gnome didn't say anything but blinked his eyes once before smiling back up at her through his white beard and moustache, letting himself be carried in her arms as they continued on their way. He gestured to his new sheep to follow them and held tightly to his precious knitting needles; giving them a pat every now and then to be sure he still had both of them.

It was slow going, with two of them still limping from their injuries. Rosalyn had done what she could for a majority of the damage, but they still needed time to heal and their injuries continued to pain them. They made it through the thickest part of the woods and as the trees began to clear they started to see some of the damage that lay ahead of them. Through the trunks and branches they could see more bodies strewn about everywhere, the lawn turned bloody in several patches. Off to the side they could see several gnomes and a dwarf fighting off the last enemy, a giant troll. The troll was very nearly done. They could see that he was struggling and starting to tire. They tried to put on a little extra speed to their limping in order to help the ones who were fighting. The glow of several bursts of magic flew through the air toward the creature, which teetered for a moment then fell backward, his opponents scattering out of the way. The magics checked to make sure the troll wouldn't be getting back up then slowly turned away, walking and hobbling toward the center of the lawn. Rosalyn and her little group were now close enough to be heard so she waved a free hand in the air and called to them.

"Hello! How did everything-" She stopped speaking as they emerged from the woods, the trees no longer obscuring their vision. The once beautiful house now resembled the abandoned version on the other side of the archway. It was scorched and blackened, glass littering the ground around it from the blown-out windows. Planks of wood were tossed around the lawn in various broken patterns, the posts from the porch had been thrown across the lawn, and bits of the decorative flourishes from the house's exterior were everywhere. Mixed among all of this were shingles from the roof, which had been completely destroyed, as though an explosion on the third-floor attic had ripped it wide open. Underneath the layer of broken bits of wood, glass, shingles and shattered paintings, vases, clothes, and decorations from the interior of the house, were those who had been killed or injured, from Evelina and Melarue's armies alike.

Rosalyn sank to her knees on the ground, the pain in her leg momentarily forgotten, consumed only by the devastation she saw before her. She stared around, mouth agape, at a loss of what to do. The little gnome in her arms stared ahead, locking eyes with his kinsmen across the grounds, gripping his knitting needles tightly. Tam was overcome with grief and sadness, letting tears fall freely and silently. No tears fell down Vince's cheeks, though his grip around Tam's shoulder tightened while he stared ahead, saying nothing. Charles stared at the house in silent horror for a few moments, then, the terror rising within him, looked to the nearest ally, a brown-haired dwarf with a short beard, who sat on the ground, staring blankly at the ruined garden.

"Where is my daughter?" The dwarf looked up at him with big, sad eyes but said nothing, so he asked once more, raising his voice ever so slightly and punctuating each syllable. "Where is my daughter; your queen?"

The dwarf squeezed his eyes shut, sighing deeply. "She was 'ere when the house exploded," he started. Everyone near them turned their attention to what he was saying, their hearts, especially Charles', pounding in their chests. "She got 'it by somethin' when it happened, and she fell." He looked up at Charles, tears and regret in his eyes. "I tried ta save 'er. I did. That feller in the red tin can, he took her afore I could get 'ere. She was lyin' on the ground an' he just picked her up and disappeared through the archway. I jus' couldn't get to 'im fast enough." He put his head in his hands, trying to stem the flow of tears.

Charles backed off a few steps then sat down on the ground, himself, utterly dazed. "She's gone. They took her, she's gone."

Rosalyn went over to him, putting her hand on his shoulder. "We'll get her back, Charles." She turned to look at everyone gathered near, at the decimated house and at the scorched, wrecked landscape, with tears and determination in her eyes. "We'll get everything back."

CHAPTER TWENTY-THREE

Vy gradually regained consciousness, her first sensations that of a cold surface beneath her and a throbbing pain in the back of her head. She groaned and lifted a hand to touch the spot on her head, only to find that her wrists were weighted down by something else that was cold and hard against her skin. In addition to the pain in her head she felt a stinging sensation on her face and forearms. Finally finding the strength to open her eyes, she found herself lying on the floor of a large, perfectly square room with white walls and a white floor. Her armor had been taken away, aside from her boots, and she was wearing only the red shift dress and her black leggings. In the center of the room was a single wooden chair with a set of shackles chaining it to the floor. Along the room's perimeter were several members of her army, bound against the wall with similar manacles. Fulrin was directly across from her and seemed to still be unconscious. A couple spots away from him was Asteria, who was awake and struggling to get free of the chain wrapped around her body. Nearby was the wizard called Gregory, whom she had met just a few hours ago; maybe a day, she wasn't entirely sure how long they'd been here, leaning against the wall with his hands tied behind his back, awake and taking in everything he could about the room.

Looking to her own wrists, she realized the cold sensation she had felt earlier belonged to a set of metal shackles clamped around them. Upon seeing the many cuts and scrapes on her arms, the stinging of the injuries became more pronounced. A sharp twinge on her cheek told her that her face resembled her scratched arms. She struggled to release her hands from the shackles but to no avail, as they were far too tight, no matter how much she wriggled her hand or squeezed her fingers together in an attempt to make her hand smaller. Giving up on the use of her less than stellar physical prowess, she concentrated on using her magic to release her restraints. She spent several moments searching for any energy she could use to release herself from the restraints but could sense nothing. Trying again, she attempted to use her own energy as a source. She imagined the energy flowing through her body, into the palms of her hands and out of her fingertips, as she quickly uncurled her fingers to release the magic. Opening her eyes, she looked down to discover that absolutely nothing had happened, much to her confusion and chagrin.

"It's no use," said the old wizard. "I've been awake for a half hour and tried everything I could think of; the shackles won't come off. There must be some sort of guard against magic in this room. Some enchantment or another."

"Where are we," Vy asked, struggling against the metal shackles to feel the large bump on the back of her head. It was very sore to the touch and felt slightly damp. When she pulled her hand away there was a little bit of sticky red blood staining her pale skin. Fortunately, it seemed as though the injury wasn't too terribly deep and that she hadn't lost a dangerous amount of blood. She wiped the blood off onto her red battle dress.

"I'm not entirely sure," he replied. "Though, I assume we are prisoners of Melarue. No doubt she'll be making an appearance soon."

Muffled grunts and twitching limbs indicated that Fulrin was starting to wake. Vy watched him wake from his injuries while running through the last memories she had before waking up in the strange room. Everything was a bit of a blur, all the images rushing together as her mind worked it all out, but she had a feeling something terrible had happened to her. As they began to separate and clear, she remembered running through the woods, the smell of last winter's fallen leaves that crunched beneath her feet. She remembered that she had been trying to get to the house, something had gone horribly wrong and she was on her way to assess the damage and fight if it had needed defending. The helmet of the red knight flashed in her mind and she remembered what the terrible thing had been. She ignored Fulrin's cursing and shouts as he woke up and became aware of his surroundings. Instead, she focused on the memory of the red visor being lifted, revealing Monty's piercing blue eyes and handsome face staring at her just before things suddenly went dark.

"Don't cry, my queen," said Fulrin from across the room. "We won't let 'er do anythin' ter ya." He had ceased his cursing and was now staring at her with concern. She hadn't even been aware that she was crying but with his words of comfort she suddenly felt the warm, wet tear creeping down her cheek. She wiped it away with the back of her hand, chain and shackles rattling with the movement. Her heart was falling to pieces inside her chest as confusion, rage and a deep sadness coursed through her. The man she'd fallen in love with had been working against her the entire time, fighting on the side of her enemy. She wondered how long he had known of her true identity. Had he known who she was the day they met? Had their entire meeting been planned? Had the past few months, had *last night* meant absolutely nothing? For the second time, it seemed, she'd given everything away only to have her heart broken. Had he been reporting to Melarue about her the entire time? Perhaps he had followed her to the old Victorian once and discovered the location of the magical realm. Perhaps he'd been involved with injuring the poor brownie left on the sidewalk. The betrayal was heart breaking. She felt used and completely devastated, but now was not the time to deal with those feelings.

There was a clicking sound as the latch on the door began turning. Someone was opening the door on the other side. Wiping another stray tear from her cheek, she stood up, along with the old wizard and Fulrin, while the fairy stood on the floor, her wings trapped under the chains wrapped around her body. Vy wished she had spent those few precious moments looking for a way out or tried to rip the chains from the wall instead of mooning over another boy who had hurt her. A small gap opened up between the door and the wall, wide enough for a small creature to bound into the room. He was a little green goblin, with long, pointed ears and nose, sharp teeth and stick-thin limbs. He bounced his way gleefully into the room, cackling softly and twirling a dangerous looking knife in his hands.

"All wakeyed up, I see, yes. Have good naps, yes?" He cackled, dancing toward them menacingly.

"What do you want," Vy growled at him. His head snapped toward her and he grinned widely, showing off his numerous sharp teeth.

"Oh, Ikidrak want something very precious, yes. Veerrry precious," he cackled. "Ikidrak here for samples, yes. Test your magic, yes, yes!" He walked toward her, spinning the blade against his long index finger. "Ikidrak get your sample first, missy."

Vy held onto her chains with all of her might, ready to kick the hideous goblin the second he came near. "You can try," she snapped.

"Oh, Ikidrak no need to try, miss, no." He held his left hand outstretched toward her, his elongated thumb pointing toward the floor, then gradually twisted his hand to the left and she felt herself being pulled back into and pinned against the wall. She tried to push away from the cold, white tiles but couldn't move at all. He hopped over to her, grinning madly. "Ikidrak have magic, miss! Ikidrak needs only a little bit." With that, he quickly drew the blade of the knife across the palm of her hand, a thin red line forming as it passed. He giggled as she let out a hiss of pain and with his left hand, magically pulled the blood away from her palm, using the energy to shape it into a small, liquid ball that looked quite like a morbid soap bubble, which he then made to float down into the pouch at his waist. He proceeded to go around the room and do this to each of them, each time forming a tiny, floating bubble out of their blood, and magically floating it into his pouch, mumbling and cackling to himself the entire way. When he had finished with Fulrin, he bounced back toward the door and before leaving, waved his hand across the entire room, releasing the four of them from their enchantment. Each of them fell to the floor as they were freed, causing the little goblin to let out his loudest cackles yet, as he shut the door behind him.

"What was all that about," the little purple fairy cried.

"I have no idea," the old wizard said. "'Test the magic', he said. I'm not sure why she would need to test it." He looked over toward Viola. "She'll already know who you are. As soon as she sees you, she'll recognize you."

"Mayhap the little green one didna get the memo," Fulrin grumbled. He was in a bit of a bad mood, no doubt from waking up covered in cuts and bruises upon bruises, in addition to being in a strange, white dungeon where a strange little green thing was drawing blood from his hand. Vy completely understood.

Pushing her heartache to the back of her mind, Vy tried to pull on the chains attaching her to the wall. She'd seen movies in which the captured main character somehow managed to free themselves by pulling the chains out of the walls. As she tugged, she realized that chains in movies were horribly misrepresented. Chains don't just come free of the wall if you tug hard enough. She quickly gave up on this venture, trying to look about the room for other options.

A short time later, the click of the door came again, this time opening wider. Into the room strode a woman with dark hair, wearing a black pantsuit, black heels and a red silk shirt. Behind her, following at a distance, was Monty, dressed in the same sweater he'd been wearing the day they first met. Vy met his gaze briefly, stiffened and then proceeded to ignore him. The woman bore a wide, lipstick covered smile as she gazed around the room, while Monty looked only at Viola, who vehemently refused to look in his direction. Instead, Viola glared at the woman in the suit, recognizing her immediately from her former life.

"Melarue."

The woman's crimson smile widened. "Indeed, I am. Though in this world I'm known as Arin Moon. And I would recognize you and that blaze of red hair anywhere, Evelina." She slowly sauntered over to where Vy was chained to the wall. "It certainly has been awhile, hasn't it?" Viola remained silent, glaring back at her enemy, unblinking. Melarue laughed. "Things are a little bit different this time around. I've had quite a life in this new world, you see. I own a very successful seafood business, I live in the largest house in town and now I have a son." Vy's eyes widened with realization as the woman gestured to Monty, who was standing just behind her, asking him to come closer. He took a few steps and Vy noticed he'd stopped looking toward her and was now staring intently at the floor. "This is Montgomery. I'll begin teaching him magic as soon as this is all over but in the meantime, he has turned out to be a fine soldier for the cause. You may remember him," she teased, coldly. "I'm told he's the one who found you on the battlefield and brought you to me." He raised his eyes to look at her now, but she couldn't read the emotion hidden within their icy blue depths. They didn't house the same gleeful malice his mother's eyes bore. Looking into those eyes, and at his full lips which had whispered words of love to her in the darkness; to see him broke her heart all over again. Vy thought they looked sad, perhaps even guilty. Good. He should feel that way.

"You will be saddened to know," Melarue started again, beginning to saunter slowly and victoriously around the room, "that while your forces technically won the battle, mine still caused damage to your world that will take years to recover from. Your gardens have been burned to ash, your great, big Victorian mansion has a crater the size of Aroostook County on the top floor." Vy and the others all filled with concern for their friends, though they tried not to let their emotions show. "True, your forces destroyed many of my own but that doesn't matter a bit, now that I have *you*." She grinned, roughly patting the top of Viola's head, sending waves of pain through her neck and upper back, where she'd been struck in battle.

"You show no remorse for your lost soldiers?" Viola couldn't believe how nonchalantly Melarue had dismissed the death of her forces.

"Why should it matter? The majority of them were non-magic using humans. They couldn't be any more unimportant! The only thing I wanted was to get you here and in that, obviously, I was successful."

Vy couldn't contain her disgust, letting it out in a disgusted puff of breath. "You care nothing for the people who died for you today?! Just so long as you got me?!" She shook her head in revulsion. "I would never have done such a thing. That is reprehensible!"

"Yes, yes," Melarue rolled her eyes. "The great and pure Queen Evelina, whose moral compass always points due north," she scoffed, mockingly. She paced back and forth in front of the chained-up Viola. "But, let me ask, in which direction did your compass point when you denied humans the ability to wield magic?"

Vy felt the Evelina part of her welling up, ready to answer her foe. "We had no choice! Your human bodies aren't designed to withstand that energy. The magic, the energy of it would burn you up from the inside out!" Vy watched as Melarue continued to pace, her face growing red with the rage boiling up inside. "We weren't trying to deny you anything. We were trying to save you," she said softly.

"Bullshit!!" Melarue had stopped pacing to glare at her directly. "You weren't trying to save us," she hissed, mockingly. "You were just trying to keep us from having access to all that power, all that influence. You wanted to rule over us!" Vy opened her mouth to protest but Melarue continued to talk over her. "Don't bother trying to deny it. The truth was plain as day. You wanted to hoard the power then and you're still doing it now. All of you," she turned to look at the others in the room. "But I found a way, didn't I?" She cackled wickedly. " I found a way to claim some of that magic back for myself." She began to slowly walk around the room, stopping in front of the old wizard, just a few feet away from Vy. "Would you like to see what I can do now that I have gained that magic?" She placed a hand on the wizard's chest, then slowly began to draw it back toward herself, the fingers and thumb pointed toward the old man, as though she was pulling something. After a moment a golden shimmer of light began to emerge from the man's chest while his breathing became labored and he struggled against the pain. She pulled back a little faster and he cried out as the magic was ripped from his body. The second the scream was uttered, she let go, allowing the magic to rush back into him, knocking him into the wall.

"Gregory! Are you okay," Vy cried. The man was leaning against the wall, panting while Fulrin had resumed pulling at his restraints, grumbling loudly and cursing Melarue's name. Monty stood back near the chair in the center of the room, watching everything with wide, open eyes.

"I would say he's probably not okay, dear," Melarue purred. "You see...I'm told that when magic is ripped from the body and soul of a magic user, it is *unbelievably* painful. Indescribably so. I hear that you can feel it as the energy is being sheared away from your very essence. The physical pain is incredible but the mental and emotional pain caused by a piece of your very soul being torn from you, that's the part that kills you," she turned, grinning wickedly.

"Please," Vy begged, tears beginning to blur her vision. "Please, don't do this. What could it possibly accomplish?!"

"Oh, my dear Evelina," she purred, "it will hurt *you*. And that is just delicious." She hissed the last word at Vy, then turned and slammed her hand back onto the wizard's chest, pulling the magic from him once again, this time with more ferocity. Gregory screamed out in agony, thrashing against his restraints, sweat beading across his forehead. The golden energy flowed out of him and into Melarue's palm faster and faster. Vy's tears were spilling over her cheeks as she begged the mad woman to stop, while Fulrin cursed and tried to get out of his shackles and Asteria screamed out some less than ladylike language. Monty's eyes were dancing back and forth between his mother and Viola. As before, Melarue returned the wizard's magic to him by slamming her hand against his chest as hard as she could. He fell back against the wall and slid down to the floor, weeping audibly. "Oh, what a rush," she cried, catching her breath. "Let me tell you, Evelina, there's nothing like the feeling of tearing someone else's magic away from them."

Vy was on her knees, sobbing, begging for her to stop, her hands worrying at her bonds. Melarue let out a howl of laughter as she marched over to Vy, grabbed her by the hair and jerked her head back to look up into her face. The action sent pain running through Vy's head again, Melarue's fingers pressing into the painful, bloody spot where she'd been hit by debris. Across the room,

Monty was clenching and releasing his fists, silently watching events unfold.

"You will watch this," Melarue growled, "knowing it is all on *your* head." She roughly released Vy's head, and then used a bit of magic to keep her frozen in place, ensuring that the young woman would be unable to look away.

"Please stop this," Vy cried. "You have me; you don't need to hurt anyone else!"

"True, but it's just so much fun, dear." The woman ignored her pleas, turning back toward the wizard.

"Git offa 'im!" Fulrin's chains were clanging as he pulled and swung them from the wall, yelling curses at Melarue, who ignored him as well. She stood in front of the broken man, turned once more to grin wickedly at Viola, and then slapped her hand to his chest one final time, drawing the magic out of him with all her strength.

Vy thought his screams had been terrible before but they were nothing compared to the pain in his voice now. Watching him die so horribly; to have his magic, a bit of his soul, violently ripped from his body was too much for her to handle. She screamed for the woman to stop, her throat going raw as tears coursed down her cheeks. Straining, Melarue grasped her wrist with her other hand, steadying herself as she began to shake, drawing his magic out completely. As the horrible moments passed by, the man's screams grew more and more pained until they suddenly went silent as the last tendrils of golden magic pulled away from his chest, disappearing into Melarue's right hand. At the same moment the enchantment on Vy broke and she was able to look away, weeping onto the cold floor below as the man took his final, shallow breath, collapsing onto the floor. Melarue staggered and laid a hand against the wall to support herself as the man's magic coursed through her body.

"'Ow dare you! You bitch!" Fulrin's grief was evident through his anger and cursing, the fairy was hysterical, shrieking out a tirade of curses while Vy sobbed, her tears pooling on the cold floor in front of her. Melarue was standing still, catching her breath from the effort of stealing the man's magic. Monty stood where he was, breathing heavily, saying nothing while the little goblin stood nearby, his face broken by a wide, toothy grin. Still panting slightly, Melarue straightened up, letting out howls of laughter.

"Oh, he was a strong one," she exclaimed, holding her hand up as if she could see the magic pulsating beneath her skin. She walked toward the fairy, snapped her fingers and the little creature was released from her chains. She tried to fly away but was caught almost immediately by the woman, who glared down at her then with a quick motion, ripped the wings from her back. The little fairy screamed in pain as silver blood began to ooze from the open wounds. Throwing them to the floor, Melarue placed a black heel on top of the shimmery, lavender wings and twisted her foot back and forth, crunching them beneath the toes of her shoes. "Ugh. Disgusting. That is quite enough of you," Melarue growled, drawing a long, perfectly manicured fingernail across the fairy's throat. The creature went silent and limp in her hand as she bled out, silver dripping down Melarue's fist. The woman opened her hand and the tiny body fell to the floor in a heap, silver blood spreading across her crumpled wings.

"You're a monster," Vy rasped, face still full of tears.

Arin turned to face her slowly, an evil grin across her face. "Oh no, my dear. It is *you* who are the monster; you and all of your little magic friends. You hold the power to take away life within the palm of your hand and you hold it close, claiming dominion over the rest of us. Well, not anymore." She lifted a hand, making Vy rise to her feet as Fulrin began to yell and beg to leave her alone.

"You leave 'er alone! Come over 'ere and get me, you evil 'ag" Melaure sneered at the dwarf's words, but ignored him and continued advancing on Vy, who hung by an invisible force, the toes of her boots scraping along the floor.

"You, who have denied me," Melarue continued. "Denied me your power, your grace, your strength. Well, it's my turn now and it is going to be glorious." She opened her palm, stretching it out toward Vy and began to haul the magic from her.

Vy had never experienced pain as intense as this. It felt as though she was being torn in two, as if one half of her entire body was being cut away from the other. The physical pain was tremendous but the mental agony of being separated from half of herself was indescribable. She couldn't think, she couldn't speak. It was as if a thousand blades were stabbing into her en masse, tearing away chunks of flesh, mind and soul. It felt like every layer of skin was slowly being flayed from her body, as if every single bone was breaking over and over again. She was no longer Viola and she was no longer Evelina. She was just pain. Deep, physical, emotional, mental, spiritual pain. In addition to the muffled sounds of Fulrin's cries, she could hear a scream and knew it must be hers, but she couldn't feel the air pushing up and out of her throat. She couldn't see, aside from the flashes of light and darkness. She knew only agony and suffering, filled with loss and sorrow as a part of her was cut away.

And suddenly it stopped.

Panting, she opened her blurry eyes to see Monty holding the chair that had been attached to the floor, having just swung it at the back of his mother's head. Arin lay unconscious on the floor next to Vy, who had collapsed the moment the connection between the two women had been broken. The cool floor was comforting and refreshing after all she had just endured. Dropping the chair, Monty rushed to her side.

"Vy, are you okay? Talk to me, please!" His eyes were wide and shining with unshed tears. One arm was behind her supporting her weight and holding her in a sitting position, while the other was gently touching her face, wiping blood away from the cuts on her cheeks.

"Wha..." She looked up at him, struggling to form coherent thoughts. Out of nowhere he suddenly seemed to care about her again, when only minutes before he had been standing by as she and her friends were tortured. She was still weak from her ordeal, but she found enough strength to push away from him and stand on her own, though she wobbled and had to lean against the wall for support. "Stay away from me," she growled.

"I'm so sorry, Vy." He obviously intended to continue speaking but she silenced him with a single look. Biting his lip, he moved to his mother's prone form and lifted a set of keys from her person. Returning, he unlocked her chains before moving across the room to release Fulrin as well. "I'm releasing you. I'm sorry I didn't do it before." He turned back to Vy, eyes still shining. "I will lead you out of here and you can take us both as your prisoners," he said, gesturing to the goblin, who, when noticed, paused his search for shiny things on the dead and unconscious bodies.

Vy could sense that the wards on the room had failed when Melarue had fallen unconscious and she tested the magic, producing a tiny bit of flame in her hand. Fulrin gently picked up the body of the dead fairy as Vy stretched a hand out in front of her, palm facing Monty, a small fireball dancing before it. "Why should I take you prisoner after everything you've done? I could just kill you now and get it over with," she snarled. Fulrin looked up in shock and Monty nodded slightly, sorrow and shame still visible on his handsome face.

He bowed his head, seemingly resigned to his fate as she stared at him through the flames burning in her palm. She was hurt and angry. He'd played her hard and, like the fool that she was, she'd fallen for it again. He'd fought against her in battle and had probably killed some of her friends and newfound family.

"I'm so sorry," he said again. "I never should have brought you here."

She could see Fulrin's wide, tear-filled eyes staring at her, unable to read what she was thinking. She stared into the flames silently for a few moments, pushing the feelings of sorrow and rage away, trying to replace them with sense. She closed her fist abruptly and turned away.

"Fulrin, could you please get those chains and bind these two up?" She gestured to the chains and shackles that had once been attached to the chair. Fulrin gingerly placed the tiny fairy body inside a small pouch at his waist, securing the bag tightly, and then proceeded to arrange the chains around Monty and the goblin, Ikidrak, ensuring that their hands were bound tightly in front of them. Meanwhile, Vy stood over Melaure's unconscious form, deciding what to do. Given the chance, Melarue would have killed Vy in a heartbeat, no questions asked, and some small part of Evelina was encouraging Vy to do the same; to end it once and for all. But Vy shook her head. She didn't feel right about taking the life of this woman. Not like this. It felt wrong, somehow. But she and Fulrin didn't possess enough strength to bring back two prisoners and two prone bodies. She couldn't leave Gregory here in this awful place, and he meant so much more to her than this woman did.

While she was pondering, Fulrin finished shackling Monty and the goblin, then joined Vy. "Wish I 'ad me axe," he said, then began to lift his heavy, booted foot, with the intention of bringing it down upon the unconscious woman's head.

"NO!" Vy held out a hand to stop him before his boot could make contact. The dwarf looked up at her, confused. "We can't. Not like this. Leave her for now, we have more important people to return home." She gestured toward the pouch at Fulrin's middle, where the body of Asteria now lay, and toward the wizard Gregory, who lay sprawled on the floor behind them.

"But, yer Ladyship," the dwarf began to protest.

"No," she said firmly, cutting him off. "I know she'd do the same to us if the roles were reversed but I will not be like her. Besides, we have some leverage over her now." She nodded her head toward the goblin and Monty. "I still hold out hope that we can reason with her."

Fulrin grumbled under his breath but turned away from the woman and set about getting the wizard into a sitting position, easier to pick up and carry. Vy righted the chair, took another loose set of chains and bound Melarue to it. She knew it wouldn't hold her for long once the woman was discovered but it would still keep her trapped for a while and wound her pride some.

"Is there anyone or anything outside of this room that we need to be concerned about?" Vy looked to both the goblin and her former lover.

"There are people and creatures here who work for my mother, but I can get you out of here without them noticing. She doesn't like to have many people around when she's...interrogating."

"Fine. You'll go first," she threatened.

Fulrin picked up the limp body of the old wizard and hoisted him over his left shoulder, glaring at Melarue.

With Monty and Ikidrak taking the lead, followed by Vy, who had the ends of the chains wrapped tightly around her arms to keep them from running, and finally Fulrin, carrying Gregory's body over his shoulder, the group made their way to the door. "Be aware," she grumbled, "if you try anything, I am prepared to hit you with magic. You will *not* like it, I promise you." Monty nodded ahead of her and carefully opened the door. He led them out into a long, white hallway, passing a desk just in front of the door to the room from which they'd just left. The only exit from this hall was the elevator, inside of which they all squeezed, Monty pushing the button to take them up to the main floor.

When the elevator doors slid open, they found themselves in the darkened first floor lobby of an office building. They stepped out into the quiet room and began to make their way across the empty space, heading toward the doors. The only sounds were their footfalls on the tiled floor and the soft jingling of the chains as they moved.

"Don't try anything funny," Vy whispered into Monty's back.

The sound of a door closing on the second floor brought them to a halt, all four of them freezing in place. Heavy footsteps began making their way to the top of the stairs, setting Vy's heart to pound with fear and she silently instructed everyone to hurry. A man with a flashlight and security uniform began to descend the stairs, whistling as he slowly walked, swinging his flashlight around.

"Hey," he called, suddenly catching them in the beam from his flashlight, "what do you think you're doing here?!" Vy quickly shot a bolt of magic toward him, knocking him over. She saw a plant placed in the corner of the foyer and made vines begin to grow out of the pot and up the stairs, then wrapped him up tightly, tucking his arms into his sides and binding his legs together. A wide leaf grew out of it and plastered itself to his mouth to muffle any sounds he might make to alert others of their presence. With the guard incapacitated, Vy and the rest of the group quickly ran to the door, bursting out onto the street as the first hints of dawn began to brighten the dark sky.

CHAPTER TWENTY-FOUR

Rosalyn, Charles and the others were gathered inside the house, trying to make sense of the damage caused by the explosion. The force of the blast had made paintings fall off the walls and shattered windows, scattering glass shards everywhere and knocked over just about every piece of furniture or decoration inside the house. The little gnome, Nigel, hobbled around the room, using a knitting needle as a cane, picking up sheets of paper and debris, listening quietly to the conversation going on around him.

"We need to get our forces together and go find them immediately!" Charles was still in his armor, several hours after the fighting had ceased, eager to find his daughter and the three others who had been kidnapped earlier that day. "Every moment she's with that vile woman is a moment she could be suffering. She's probably torturing them as we speak, if she didn't just up and kill them immediately!"

"I understand your eagerness to get her back, Charles," Rosalyn said, "but we need to go about this properly. We are fortunate to have gained knowledge of Melarue's identity in this lifetime, thanks to one of her dying soldiers, so now we have a few locations where we can find her. However, more likely than not she is aware that her identity has been revealed and she will no doubt have set up her own precautions." Charles grunted with dissatisfaction and impatience. Nigel hobbled silently out of the room to investigate a commotion he heard down the hall.

"She's right, Charles," Tam piped up. He was seated on the large armchair normally inhabited by Rosalyn. His injured leg was propped up on an ottoman and Vince was nearby, keeping a watchful eye should he need anything. "We can't just run in, as you say, guns blazing. We need to approach this in such a way that there is little chance of our failure. We all want to get Vy and the others back," he said, soothingly, "but if we run straight in without a well-drafted plan, we won't be doing her any favors."

Charles flopped into the chair beside him, resting his elbows on his knees and his face buried in his hands. "You're right. I know you're all right." He sat back in his chair, rubbing his tired, stubbly face with one hand. "It's been nearly twelve hours since the battle ended. Who knows what could have happened to her in all that time?"

Rosalyn walked over to him, taking his hand in hers. "She'll be okay, Charles. She's strong." She gave him a small smile, trying to offer him some sort of comfort.

They all looked up as the gnome hobbled back into the room, his knitting needle cane clicking frantically as he did his best to hurry, while pointing into the hallway with his free hand.

"What is it, Nigel?" Vince was leaning against the dining table, which they had just turned right side up.

Everyone in the room stared in amazement as an exhausted, bloodied and bruised, but very much alive Vy and Fulrin entered the room, leading a goblin and a young man on a chain.

"So..." Vy said, breaking the silence and looking around the disaster of a room. "Looks like we missed some things."

Charles launched himself off the armchair and raced across the room, pulling his daughter into a giant bear hug. "Vy! Thank God you're alive! I was so worried!" He pulled away and proceeded to look her over, checking her injuries for anything serious. "Are you hurt? Tell me, are you okay?!" The man was frantic; thrilled his daughter was standing in front of him but worried about what had happened to her during her time at the hands of her enemy.

"Dad, I'm okay, I promise!" Finally getting him to calm down, convincing him she was fine, she moved to address Rosalyn. "These two volunteered to be taken as our prisoners after they helped us escape." She gestured to the two in chains as her audience stared back and forth between them in confusion. "The goblin is called Ikidrak and...and the other...is Montgomery Stevens-Moon, Melarue's son." She couldn't bear to call him Monty; it felt too close, too personal, after all that had happened. Out of the corner of her eye, she could see him shift slightly when she used his full name, including his mother's last name. Charles' eyes widened briefly, and then narrowed into a scowl, recognizing the name of

Vy's boyfriend, whom he had heard of but had not yet had a chance to meet.

Rosalyn looked at the young man and goblin, the confusion and surprise evident on her face. "Er...very well, then. Vince, would you mind taking them downstairs into the basement of the house? And post a guard by the basement door, please." Vince bowed slightly, before taking the chain from Vy's hand and leading them out of the room.

She watched them leave, Monty turning around to meet her eyes once before he rounded the corner and lost sight of her. Turning back to those remaining, she looked to them for answers. "What happened here? Last time I saw it, the house looked a bit scorched, but it was still mostly intact."

Rosalyn escorted Vy and Fulrin to the chairs at the back of the room, which they gladly accepted. "I wasn't here when it happened," the elf said, "but I'm told it was Melarue. Apparently, she joined the group near the archway roughly halfway through the battle and immediately took aim at our home. She fought her way in here, set off some sort of violent spell, then immediately took off through the archway."

"That must be what happened when I got knocked out. There was a loud boom and then something hit me in the back of the head." As she said this, her father immediately went behind her to inspect her injury. "Can we use magic to repair it?"

"Oh, certainly. Though I'm afraid it will take quite a bit of effort. We'll need quite a few of us to do it." Rosalyn shook her head sadly, before turning to the question of the hour. "But more importantly, please tell us what happened to you!"

Vy and Fulrin launched into their story of what happened when they were captured and their experience in the basement dungeon of Arin Moon's waterfront office building. They detailed the horrific deaths of the wizard, Gregory, and of Asteria and how Montgomery had knocked his mother unconscious when she had begun to steal Vy's magic. Charles made a small hissing sound as he sucked in an angry breath when hearing of what Vy had gone through, and though he still looked angry, he seemed to soften ever so slightly when he heard that Monty had saved her at the last minute.

"Well," Rosalyn could sense the tension radiating off of Charles and changed the subject in an attempt to ease it. "Well, I suppose we need to figure out what to do next. Top priority at the moment will be getting the two of you checked over and getting some healing magic started. I don't like that bump on your head. The next thing will be to fix the house. There's rain coming this evening and we already have enough damage and injuries to deal with, without flooding and slippery surfaces."

They all agreed this was probably the best plan, and after Vy and Fulrin's injuries had been bandaged and healed, they went outside to round everyone together. Positioning themselves all around the exterior of the house, they focused their magic on the damaged third floor and blown out roof. It took quite a bit of effort, but after several minutes, the large group of magics managed to gradually reform the roof, using magical winds to lift broken planks of wood from the ground, sending them soaring upwards where they knitted themselves back together to form the roof once more. The shingles all flew back into place with several soft thuds, sounding very much like hundreds of large raindrops hitting the roof. The shattered glass tinkled as the shards flew back together to form windows inside the gaping holes of the building. About ten minutes passed as they all pitched in to help, with the few present non-magics standing back several feet, watching the process and calling out directions to help them place wood and shingles in difficult to see angles. Finally, they all lowered their hands and stepped back to look the house over, pleased to see it looked almost as good as it had two days previously. A new coat of paint would do it some good, though. If they'd had the energy, or if they weren't mourning the loss of so many friends, they might have cheered, but instead they simply nodded thanks to one another and filed back into the repaired house.

    The work had taken a bit out of them and they all needed to have some rest before they could proceed any further. Rosalyn suggested everyone sit down and discuss their next moves. Most of them hadn't eaten since their dinner the night before, so the gnomes bustled into the kitchen to put a meal together for everyone. Somehow, Vy assumed it was only due to the wonders of magic, everyone was able to find a seat at the dining room table, with plenty of room to spare. Intending to take one of the seats along the side of the table, Vy began to pull out a chair but was stopped by Rosalyn. With a smile on her face, the elven woman led Vy to the seat at the head of the table.

"This is your rightful place, Viola; Lady Evelina." Giving her a small bow, Rosalyn backed away, leaving Vy to take the head seat, while others watched her happily from around the room. Glancing at her father, she saw unabashed pride beaming from his smiling face. They loaded up on a delicious egg and vegetable dish, breads and cheeses, fruits with honey and the ever-present iced tea and mead. Vy poured herself a very tall glass of mead and laughed inwardly as she watched several others do the same. It had been a rough couple of days. They all deserved it. As they ate, they discussed their options.

"Melarue's forces were fairly wiped out in the battle so it is unlikely she will attack again in the immediate future," Rosalyn said, addressing everyone from the seat to Vy's left. "However, as we also have her son locked up downstairs, it is entirely possible she may come to retrieve him. Either action is a possibility."

Many spoke up with suggestions or comments and they talked of strategy. Vy tried to pay attention, but strategy had never been her strong suit and she found her thoughts drifting elsewhere. Instead of troop placements and intrigue, she thought of Monty, chained up below the room in which she was currently sitting. When Vince had returned from the basement, he had informed them all that he had used their chains to bind the two captives up downstairs. She found herself hoping he wasn't in any pain, though she tried to tell herself she didn't care. He had used her, broken her heart and worked against her on behalf of her enemy. By rights she shouldn't give a damn about whether or not he was suffering.

But dammit all to hell, she did care. Their meeting began drawing to a close, with plans laid out for preparations in case Melarue decided to attack them again in the near future. Extra guards were to be stationed at all possible entrances into the estate, including two gnomes who would hide in the bushes near the road. They discussed setting up trip wires that followed the length of the perimeter, invisible to the naked eye, but when activated would send a signal back to the house, alerting all inhabitants that someone had arrived. As everyone began to get up from dinner, Viola took two plates from the table and began putting small helpings of bread, cheese and fruit onto each of them. A couple of people in the room glanced her way, curious expressions on their faces, though they didn't ask anything of her. Rosalyn met her eyes and nodded slightly, seeming to understand the battle raging inside her head and heart. Vince saw the plates and nodded toward them.

"What's with that?"

"I thought our prisoners would appreciate something to eat." Of everyone in the present group, only her father was aware of her relationship with Monty and she intended to keep it that way; at least for the time being. Vince nodded once more, agreeing with her actions.

"Would you like a hand taking them down? Would you like someone to go with you?"

"No, I'll be fine. Thank you, though."

"Okay." He didn't look particularly comfortable with this, and neither did Fulrin, who had been sitting near Vy and overheard the conversation. "Well, I've asked two dwarves to guard the cellar door, so if you need anything just yell and they'll be down to help you within seconds. They're small but they're sturdy."

She nodded, smiling, as she lifted the plates off the table, carrying one in each hand. "Thank you, Vince, I appreciate it." Balancing the two plates, and a small jug of water, she left the dining room, went down the hall and headed toward the cellar door, where two dwarves stood on either side. To the left was Gargen Firepick, a dwarf with a rather large and bulbous nose, the blackest hair she had ever seen and bright, smiling brown eyes. He seemed to always be in a cheerful mood and was fond of frequenting the local bars in the evenings. Beside him stood his brother, Korir, who looked so similar to his brother that the only way to tell them apart was how Korir kept his beard, arranging it in several tight braids that hung down over his chest, while Gargen let his fall freely.

"Evenin', my lady," Korir rumbled merrily in his deep baritone. "What can we do fer ya?"

"I'm bringing some food down to our prisoners. Would you let me pass, please?"

"Certainly, my lady," Gargen piped up. "Would you like one of us to go down with ya?"

"Oh no, thank you. That won't be necessary," she replied, smiling. "I think I can manage."

The brothers exchanged a look, their thick, dark eyebrows furrowed together in concern. "Do you think that wise, Lady? They tried to kill ya, after all..."

"I'm sure Vince managed to get them chained up well enough. I'm not worried." She watched as they shared another loaded look, worry passing silently between them. "I'm sure I'll be fine but if it makes you feel better, I can leave the cellar door open. If anything goes wrong, you'll be the first ones to know. How about that?"

She watched as a tiny bit of the fear and concern in their faces melted away. "That'd make us feel much better, your ladyship!" Gargen smiled at her brightly, while Korir leaned over and opened the door for her.

"Thank you very much!" She slipped past them and began making her way down the cellar stairs. It was noticeably cooler down here compared to the rest of the house but still not entirely unpleasant. It was the coolness of a Maine cellar, a welcome relief in the summer months, a herald of winter in autumn. She descended the stairs carefully, ensuring that she didn't dump the contents of the plates all over the floor in front of her. As she moved further down the stairs, the two prisoners came into view, more and more of their bodies being revealed as the floor from the level above became the cellar ceiling.

Vince had chained them up against the wall to her far left. There they sat, the man and the little goblin, surrounded by crates of household supplies. Monty looked up at her with big, puppy dog eyes and she desperately wanted to believe the sadness and regret shining inside of them. The goblin continued to grin at her rather maniacally.

"I brought you both something to eat," she said, setting the plates and the water jug down on the floor in front of them. The goblin grabbed for it with a relish, while Monty slowly reached forward, bringing the plate to rest on his lap with a quiet 'thank you.' He began to put pieces of food into his mouth, chewing them slowly, while hanging his head, staring only at his plate. Vy saw an old wooden chair nearby and pulled it closer, setting it directly in front of the two prisoners. She sat silently, watching Monty and Ikidrak who, unlike his human counterpart, was shredding the meal to pieces with his razor-like teeth, grumbling all the while about the lack of meat. She thought she saw Monty start to raise his eyes towards her a few times, then quickly lower them back to his plate, seemingly unable to meet her gaze. She continued to watch in silence, waiting for the two of them to finish. The goblin seemed unaware of the tension building inside the room as his pointed teeth made quick work of the meal. He seemed to enjoy it despite the lack of meat. Meanwhile Monty chewed maddeningly slowly. She didn't begin speaking until his plate was nearly empty and the goblin was leaning back against the wall, sucking fruit juices from his fingers.

"Why?"

His hand paused a short distance from his mouth, cheddar crumbles falling from his fingers to plop back down onto his plate. Sighing, he set it off to the side before looking up at her.

"I didn't know, Vy. I truly didn't," he insisted when she snorted and rolled her eyes. "My mother raised me with a mixture of fear and hatred toward those who were born with magic. She said they were cruel and selfish and any one of them would rather slaughter a human than walk beside them down the street." He lowered his eyes, shaking his head. "I believed anyone, or any creature born with magic in their blood was a threat."

"But Melarue used magic. How is it that her magical ability was acceptable, even though it was stolen magic?" She glared at him while the goblin, who was still licking sticky fruit juice from his fingers, was staring at her intently.

"She told me they were strong and the only way to fight back was to use their own weapons against them. She found a way to pull magic from the creatures she interrogated and managed to increase her abilities. I…" he stumbled for a moment over his words. "I...I didn't know the process killed them. She worked hard to learn how to use magic and give us a fighting chance against creatures more powerful than us. That's how she justified the things she did. I accepted it completely because she's my mother and I love her. She taught me all about magical creatures, showed me the most amazing, fantastical things, taught me how to fight and she said one day she would teach me how to use magic, as well." He paused for a moment and sighed. "She also told me there was a woman who was bent on destroying her, that she had tried to kill my mom in another life, and she would try again. This woman, my mother said, was incredibly dangerous, with a deep-seated hatred for humans and a plan to kill us all. The only way to defeat her was to capture her, steal her magic and, if necessary, end her. Mother said that was the only way we, meaning humans, could survive."

"And now?"

"Now," he started. "Now, I'm not sure what to think." His gaze had returned to staring intently at his plate of cheese and breadcrumbs.

She could feel rage and sadness rising within her and after a few beats, she could no longer contain the force of her emotions. Standing quickly, she paced in front of the chair for a few seconds before the anger and grief consumed her and she kicked the chair back across the room. "Dammit, Monty," she yelled. "I watched too many friends, people I loved, die over the past two days! The place I've come to call home, torn apart! I was chained up, not able to help when friends were being tortured! And then *I* was tortured, with a pain so great I thought my very soul was being torn from my body. I have endured so much hell over the past forty-eight hours and damn it all, you are going to give me a proper answer!" She hadn't intended to raise her voice so much but by the end of her rant, she knew the two dwarf brothers could hear her upstairs. The door creaked as one of them pushed it open further and she heard one of them call down to her.

"My lady? Is everything okay down there?"

"Yes, everything is fine, Korir. We're just having a little chat. I'll be up shortly." She didn't tear her eyes away from Monty's as she spoke. Her tone indicated there was no room for discussion, so the dwarf responded with a "very well," and pulled the door back, leaving the slight opening they had agreed on previously. "So? What's your answer?" She forced herself to remain calm, her voice even and soft. "How do you feel about your mother's beliefs now, after what you've learned?"

He took a few moments to answer, squeezing his eyes shut as he struggled to find the right words. "I...I didn't know it was you, Vy. I had no idea you were the one my mother was searching for until yesterday, when I got close enough to see your face."

"And yet, you still took me to your mother to be tortured?!"

He shook his head violently from side to side. "I know, I know! I was so confused. I'm *still* confused! Everything mother taught me, everything she showed me that proved your kind were awful, destructive, hateful creatures…" He trailed off and raised his head to meet her eyes once more. "But I know you, Vy, and you aren't like that at all. You are good and kind and wonderful. I know you would never do what my mother said you would. And what she did to that old wizard…I couldn't let her do that to you." Vy felt a small spark of hope flare to life in her heart. "But at the same time…she's my mom." The spark strangled itself into ash.

"I see." She reached for their empty plates and water jug, carefully piling them up in her arms. "Evidently, you just need more time to sort out what you're thinking. I'll leave you be." With that she headed back up the stairs, blinking back tears and ignoring Monty as he called her name over and over again.

CHAPTER TWENTY-FIVE

Everyone stayed at the inn that night, Vy collapsing happily into bed and sleeping well past her usual wake up time. Alarms were tripped around ten in the morning, indicating that someone was walking up the driveway toward the broken down, decaying facade of the house. Within seconds, the house was flooded with the cacophony of hundreds of creatures scrabbling for armor and weapons, racing downstairs, upstairs, down the hall, and out the door. Vy followed closely behind Rosalyn as she dashed toward the doors, all the while Vy couldn't help wondering exactly how Rosalyn could move so quickly in her gown without tripping unceremoniously throughout the house. They stopped on the porch just in front of the stairs, creatures fanning out behind them and to the sides, filling the porch. Meanwhile, others raced out the back door to stand on either side of the house, as additional reinforcements. They had a few seconds to wait as the newcomer made their way from the end of the driveway toward the portal that would bring them to the other side. One moment they were staring at the colorful garden, devoid of any human life and in the next breath a young man stood under the ivy archway.

He was roughly in his early to mid-twenties, with sandy hair. He wore a business suit which looked rather disheveled, as though he had been in a fight only moments before, his jacket and pants dusty, tie sliced off halfway down, a trickle of blood slowly tracing its way down the side of his face. He looked terrified and Vy wondered if Melarue might have taken out her anger on the poor fellow before sending him here. He blinked, eyes widening at the bright, lush garden and pristine house in front of him, surrounded by an army of men, women, elves, gnomes, dwarves and fairies. He hesitated for a moment then forced himself to move forward, closer to the house. Vy couldn't sense any trace of magic emanating from his person, so she assumed he couldn't be that dangerous. Perhaps just a simple messenger. As he drew closer, she could see his eyes darting back and forth, taking in the array of weapons before him, deciding who was a magic wielder, who was the most dangerous, and the most lethal. He passed the borders of the garden, a few feet away from the bottom of the stairs when Rosalyn began to speak.

"That is far enough." Two elves moved forward to stand between the man and the stairs, preventing him from ascending. Vy found that she actually felt sorry for him. The fear in his eyes was painfully evident.

"I...I bring a message," he stammered nervously. "A message from Arin...from the Lady Melarue. She demands you return her son to her, along with the tyrant, Evelina."

"And if we refuse?" Rosalyn's voice was clear and resolute.

She didn't think it was possible for his eyes to widen any more, but at Rosalyn's question he somehow managed to do so. His gaze shifted to the two elves just in front of him, their sharp spears pointed towards his chest. "Th-then...then she promises you all much suffering and particularly slow and painful deaths for Evelina and her second in command, Rosalyn."

Vy moved closer to the stairs. "Where and when, exactly, did she want Montgomery and I to be handed over?"

She watched his face as he realized who she was; the reincarnated form of Evelina. He displayed a mixture of horror and admiration. Melarue obviously had this confusing effect on everyone with whom she came into contact. The young man spoke again, directly to her. "There is a small beach outside of town, hidden by a copse of trees just off the road. Only those who know where it is can find it."

She nodded. All the locals knew how to find Somerset Beach. In the summer when the town was flooded with tourists and the locals wanted to escape, they would carefully sneak to the hidden beach. There was very little sand, the majority of the shoreline consisting of sharp rocks and pebbles, slimy and slippery with salt water and the droppings of seagulls. Visitors had to be sure of their footing or expect the sharp points of the rocks to pierce their skin if they were to slip and fall. It wasn't the most glamorous of Maine's beaches, but it was indeed beautiful, just the same. Vy had often taken careful walks along the beach, collecting rocks of interesting shapes and colors, sea glass of various shades of blues and greens as the salty breeze whipped through her hair.

"I am familiar with this beach," she piped up.

The messenger looked up at her, the expression in his eyes unreadable for the first time in the encounter. "She would like you to make your surrender at three a.m. tomorrow." He waited a moment as Vy nodded once more, before venturing his question. "Should I tell my Lady Melarue to expect you there?"

Vy said nothing, weighing his words. After a moment, Rosalyn's voice broke the silence.

"We will never give Evelina over to Melarue. You can tell your mistress to keep her terrible offers to herself!" She shifted her gaze to address the guards. "You may escort this young man off the premises!" With that, she turned and marched back into the house, obviously very upset by the offer presented to them. When the elf had turned her back, Vy quickly conjured a small butterfly out of the air. Its blue wings beat furiously as it fluttered off in the direction of the young messenger, currently being led back toward the archway. It darted back and forth in front of his face, irritating him until he moved a hand to swat it away. As he did so, the butterfly suddenly changed into a small strip of paper which stuck to his hand. For a moment or two he waved his hand quickly, trying to get the paper to come off. When it didn't, he finally took the time to inspect it. Vy watched as, after several seconds, the paper burned up, sending a tiny blue trail of smoke up from the man's hand. He looked back and locked eyes with her the second before he passed through the arch.

Satisfied that he had received her message, she turned back around and headed inside the house. She could hear Rosalyn grumbling as she made her way down the hall, toward the parlor. It was evident that Rosalyn wanted to be alone and Vy was perfectly fine with that, as she had her own things to do now that the majority of the excitement was over. She ascended the stairs and made her way up to the second-floor room, which had once contained her golden armor. At the thought, she realized she hadn't seen that armor since she had lost consciousness during the battle. She assumed it was thrown to the ground somewhere in the sub-basement of Melarue's office building. As she walked, she looked around at the house, on the lookout for anything that hadn't been repaired correctly during the magical reconstruction from earlier. It seemed their magic had done the trick, although she wasn't sure if her eyes were playing tricks on her or if certain sections of the intricately patterned wallpaper didn't quite match up to the one beside it. Walking into the room, the first thing she noticed was that somehow, through some unexplainable magical means, her armor was resting in its case, shining under the lights, as though someone had just finished giving it a good polish. Knowing full well she hadn't been wearing the golden suit when she made her escape from Melarue only a few hours beforehand, she had no idea how it could possibly be sitting in its case, as though it hadn't been bombarded with weapons and magical attacks the previous day. She decided this was one of those times when it was better not to question and instead just smile and nod.

After accepting the sudden appearance of her armor, she began to search the room, looking for the clothes she had changed out of before battle, in the hopes of finding her long forgotten cell phone. She'd been exhausted after arriving back yesterday and hadn't bothered to look for it, preferring to eat and sleep, instead. The last message she had sent to Liz had been a bit cryptic and she couldn't imagine what her friend had texted back to her in response. Poor Liz must have been freaking right the hell out. After several minutes of searching and turning up nothing, she realized exactly what they had missed during their reconstruction. She mourned the loss of her phone and one of her favorite shirts, then proceeded back downstairs. It had been about fifteen minutes and she hoped Rosalyn was feeling more receptive to a brief interruption.

She found the elf still seated in the parlor, gazing out the window in contemplation. She rapped lightly on the open door, bringing Rosalyn out of her reverie.

"Oh, hello Viola. Please, come sit," she said, gesturing to a nearby armchair.

"Thank you but I was actually hoping it would be okay if I left for a while? After everything that's happened, not knowing how bad the battle was going to be and if I would live to see another day, I'd like to go see my friends for an hour or two. Is that all right?"

Rosalyn smiled at her. "Of course! Though, I do hope you'll be back in time for the meeting." At Vy's look of confusion, she continued, "I've just called it. I sent a couple of the gnomes around to let everyone know. They must not have got to you, yet. It will be held over dinner, at five-thirty. We must decide what to do next. When that messenger tells Melarue we have no intention of handing you over to her, she will no doubt begin planning and putting into motion her next attack on us. I have guards posted everywhere, even further into the center of the town, so we will know the second she begins advancing toward the house, but it may be time for us to make the first move."

Vy nodded enthusiastically. "I couldn't agree more. I'll make sure I'm here in time for it."

After bidding Rosalyn goodbye, she made her way back down the hall toward the main entrance. Walking through the garden was lovely; the warm sun beaming down on her, a soft breeze blowing through her hair, keeping everything from getting too hot. She passed through the archway and into the gray, drizzly day beyond the magical borders. As she neared her car the realization hit that she had left her keys in her purse, which had been upstairs in the armory room. She highly doubted her purse and keys would have survived the attack when her phone and best shirt hadn't. There was a spare key stashed in a drawer in her apartment, but it was of no use to her now. She sighed heavily, then began walking back toward town. Hopefully, Liz was at home.

CHAPTER TWENTY-SIX

The second after the door swung open, Vy was being pulled inside while Liz shrieked at her with a voice so high in pitch, she had trouble making out words.

"Whoa, whoa, whoa, Liz...take a moment and say that again. I couldn't understand you." Now that she was inside the apartment and Liz had stopped pulling on her, Vy could see what terrible shape Liz was in; her hair was pulled back into a messy ponytail, the strands looking matted and frizzy like she hadn't washed or put product in for a couple of days. Dark makeup smudged around her sleep-deprived eyes and the black nail polish on her bitten down fingernails was chipped and peeling. Liam, staring at her, open mouthed, was seated on the couch in front of a wooden coffee table, the top of which was obscured by layers upon layers of papers with "MISSING" in large, bold letters at the top. Vy could see a large picture of herself staring back at her from each page, with contact information written underneath.

Though she was still breathing rather heavily, and clutching tightly to Vy's arm, Liz seemed to have stopped hyperventilating and was beginning to calm down enough to be reasonable and coherent.

"Okay," Vy said, turning back to her friend, "try that again."

She sucked in a massive mouthful of air and held it for a moment or two before letting it out in a rush. "Where the BLOODY HELL have you been?! You send me this cryptic-ass text and disappear for two days!!! I called you, I texted you, I left you about a thousand voicemails and got NOTHING!!!! WHAT IN THE ACTUAL HELL, VIOLA??!!!" She was quickly approaching the panicked, high pitched stage from before.

"Okay, okay. Just calm down." She made her way toward Liz's kitchen. "Let me brew us all some tea and I'll tell you everything that happened." Upon reaching the kitchen, Vy had to pause for a few moments to untangle herself from Liz, who still had her hands wrapped tightly around Vy's forearm. Liam followed them over and helped her get Liz into a chair by the kitchen island, then sat beside her, rubbing her back lightly as Vy busied herself with making a pot of tea.

*   *   *

About forty-five minutes and two pots of tea later, Vy had finished telling them about the battle, her incarceration in Melarue's hidden sub-basement and her most recent conversation with Monty. They had listened to the entirety of her story with eyes opened wide, interrupting only rarely to ask a question. Liz had eventually calmed down and Vy was grateful to Liam, who stayed close beside her. It warmed her heart to watch them interact with each other. She was truly happy for Liz, and had a growing love for Liam, who was turning out to be avery good for her best friend.

"What a filthy wanker!" Liz shouted. Vy had just finished discussing Monty's betrayal. "I am so bloody pissed at that tosser. I thought he was a nice guy! I had no idea he'd turn out to be a giant ass. And working for the enemy! Vy, I'm so sorry."

Vy shrugged. "It's okay. It sucks but it's okay. I'll get over it eventually." Vy knew she wasn't convincing any of them that she was fine; least of all herself.

"It most certainly is not," Liz grumbled, "and if I ever see that prat again, I'm gonna give him a piece of my mind! How could he do such a thing?!" Liz was flailing her hands around expressively, to the point that Liam reached in front of her to gently push her full mug out of the danger zone.

"Dude is an ass, Vy," he piped. "That was a seriously dick move on his part."

Vy nodded in agreement. "Oh, I know, believe me." Across the kitchen island, Liz was still seething and Vy knew she had to take her friend's mind off of everything that had happened. Now that she was finally seeing her best friend again after two of the worst days of her life, she didn't want to dwell on the tragedies of the past forty-eight hours. "Listen, I don't want to talk about any of that anymore." The other two looked up at her with shocked expressions. "I know. I realize this is probably the biggest thing to ever happen to me, but it was awful, and I just want to move past it.

Yah?" They both nodded in agreement and she could see some of Liz's tension dissipate, though she could still sense their concern. They would want to come back to this one day, no doubt.

After a few moments of silence, Vy realized she had to be the one to initiate a distracting activity. "Y'know what? I've been focused on magic lessons, battles and school for months. The fall semester starts in a few weeks and I haven't done anything fun. I haven't even looked at a video game in ages. Shall we?" She gestured toward the old Nintendo 64 and the pile of games in front of the TV. Liz and Liam exchanged a look and she could tell they weren't buying her act; they knew she wasn't as calm and cool with everything as she wanted them to think, but they turned back to her, grinning.

"Please," Liam started. "You ladies will never beat me at Mario."

"Challenge accepted! What do you say, Vy? You and me against Liam?"

"Sounds great!" She beamed at them.

They ordered delivery pizza for lunch and finished off all the Mountain Dew and beer left in Liz's fridge. Liam beat both of them at Mario Kart, easily defending his title of reigning champion. The rest of the afternoon was spent without mention of Vy's magic, the war, or Monty. She just relished the time she was spending with her two closest friends, enjoying every moment spent in their company.

Around four thirty, she announced that she had to get going.

"What? Where?" The stress and concern were once more visible in Liz's eyes. Not wanting to alarm her poor friend any longer, Vy chose to tell a little white lie. At least she hoped it was just a little white one, rather than a massive, seething dark one.

"Don't worry, guys! Seriously. We're all meeting over dinner tonight just to go over things. No more fighting, I promise."

"What *things*," Liam asked, suspiciously.

"Just post-battle things. We must decide how, exactly, we want to proceed. It will mainly be a debrief of the fight from the other day. We won't be taking any sort of action tonight, I promise."

With the two of them feeling slightly more at ease, she was able to extricate herself and get back on the road toward the old Victorian that had become her new home.

* * *

She didn't really pay much attention at dinner that night, feigning interest and participation. She nodded when it seemed appropriate, furrowed her eyebrows to look as though she was concentrating, but in reality, her mind was elsewhere. Towards the end of dinner and the conversation, they had decided to do nothing overnight, aside from having plenty of guards surrounding the area, but planned to mount an attack on Melarue at dawn the following morning. The plan was to wake at four in the morning, get dressed in armor and gear, and arrive at Melarue's building by the time the sun crested over the ocean. That sounded like a good plan to Viola.

As everyone stood to leave, Vy caught her father's arm.

"Hey, I was thinking we could go to Scoops tonight. We haven't gone for a father-daughter ice cream date in months." She beamed up at him with the smile that always melted his heart.

"Sure, Vy-Vy. That sounds great!" He smiled back brightly.

They took his car into town, parked in the public parking lot and walked down the street toward the main beach. Scoops was a smallish little ice cream shop that was located near the biggest beach in the area, the location so chosen due to the large numbers of tourists on the beach each summer. The shop remained open even throughout the winter months, mostly so the locals could enjoy an ice cream without the ridiculously long lines of the summer season. There were six round tables that sat four people each, the surrounding chairs a bright, candy shade of orange. In the back of the shop stood the counter, half of which was devoted to a case holding all of the hard serve ice cream flavors. Vy ordered a chocolate and peanut butter parfait, while her dad got his usual: the classic banana split with extra hot fudge. The blonde teenager behind the counter took their money; her dad wouldn't let her pay, despite her protests, and made up their orders. They accepted them, their eyes widening with childish excitement at the vast amounts of sugar they were about to consume, pulled several napkins from the dispenser on the counter, then found a table.

Normally, the little shop would be full of tourists, enjoying a cold treat on a hot day, but they were delighted to find that it was a rare slow summer night. There was only one other occupied table in the restaurant; a young man and woman who were most likely on one of their first dates as a couple. Vy thought they looked adorable together, grinning at each other like school kids over their sundaes.

"So, what made you want to come here," her dad asked.

"I dunno," she shrugged, plunging her white plastic spoon into the chocolatey, peanut buttery mess inside her parfait cup. "We always used to come here, and we haven't been here in a long while. Guess I was feeling nostalgic."

He smiled at her as he tried to keep his hot fudge and melting ice cream from flowing over the rim of the boat-shaped plastic dish. "I can understand that. Happens when you get old."

"I'm not that old!" She feigned a shocked anger at his comment. "You realize if *I'm* old, that makes you an antique! You're practically a relic!"

"Why, yes I am!" They both laughed loudly at their customary age joke, then spent several minutes chatting about random, happy topics while enjoying their ice cream. He laughed as she told him about her epic Mario defeat earlier in the day. After a time, her father's mood seemed to sober. She noticed he wasn't eating his banana split so much as swirling the hot fudge into the melting ice cream.

"Dad? You okay?"

He let out a heavy sigh. "Are *you* feeling okay? With the war and everything?" He paused a moment to let his questions sink in but continued before she could respond. "It'll be okay, you know. I realize it seems like a lot to handle, with Melarue's threats and promises but we won't let her take you. She won't be able to hurt you, I promise that."

"I know, Dad. I'm not worried about what she could do to me, but I *am* worried about what she could do to you and to everyone else at the house. I don't want her to hurt anyone because of me."

"Don't you worry about that, Vy-vy."

"I have to worry about it. Evidently, I'm queen of this world of magical creatures, meaning they look to me for protection and guidance. I have to do all I can to keep them safe from harm. That's my new job."

"And we will. Rosalyn and I will help you throughout all of this, I promise."

She pretended that his words brought her more comfort than they actually did, not wanting him to know the worry she truly felt. "Then I will take whatever counsel the two of you and everyone else can give me. I'm not sure I'm prepared to lead an entire realm."

He reached across the table to take hold of one of her hands. "It's a weight I never wanted for you, but you already know that. It won't be easy, leadership can be incredibly difficult. I'll be there to help you, along with Rosalyn, Tam, Vince, Fulrin and everyone else. We'll all help you learn how to lead and advise you in any and all situations. You won't be alone in this, okay?" The smile he gave her across the table was one full of love and encouragement. Despite her misgivings, she couldn't help but return his infectious smile.

"Thanks, Dad. I'll appreciate all the help I can get, and I know you'll help me make the best decisions for everyone."

"And uh…what about Monty? That's the fellow you've told me about, isn't it?"

She sighed. "Yes. That's Monty. I'm not sure, Dad. He's Melarue's son and he took me to her. He stood by while she tortured and killed my friends, and while she tortured me. But then he hit her with a chair before she could finish me off, so he saved me. This is just…so confusing." She ran her fingers through her hair, a habit she exhibited when she was tired or frustrated.

"Well, personally I'm pretty damn pissed that he took you to Melarue and let that happen to you. But at the same time, I'm very grateful to him for getting you out of there." He paused to sigh and collect his thoughts. "I dunno, Vy. He may not be that bad. Considering who his mother is, and how awful she can be, I'm not surprised that he didn't know what to do when he realized who you were. I'm not saying that excuses what he did," he said quickly, when she opened her mouth to protest. "I'm just saying that…if he was willing to whack his own mother in the head when you were in danger, well…he's probably got a lot that he's trying to figure out. I wouldn't jump back into a relationship with the guy but don't push him away until you know who he really is, okay?"

She mulled his words over for a minute, then nodded and gave him a soft 'okay.' She let the moment hang in the air for a beat, then, needing to break the tension; "Now, your ice cream is practically all melted. You might want to do something about that." She used her spoon to point toward the plastic bowl of melted ice cream that once was a banana split. In the end, she had to laugh as he brought the plastic boat-shaped dish up to his lips to drink the melted treat. She teased him and laughed about it all the way back to the Victorian.

Upon arriving back at the house, Viola soon announced that she would be going to bed.

"Really?" Her dad looked at her, concerned. "It's barely nine. Are you feeling okay?"

"Yeah, no worries, Dad. The past couple of days have been exhausting. I'm just still pretty worn out from it all." She planted a kiss on the top of his head before gently mussing his graying hair. He was seated in one of the large armchairs in the parlor, along with Rosalyn, Tam and a few others. The small gnome sat in the corner, knitting needles clicking furiously as something long and light blue grew out from the needles. "I just need to sleep."

"Okay, then," he said, wishing her a good night's rest. She bid everyone else a good night then made her way upstairs to where the bedrooms were located. She passed the door to the armory and the door next to it, stopping in front of the third door in the hall, painted in the purest shade of white she had ever seen. Opening the door, she looked in on the room she had been given to sleep in the night before.

Each room in the house seemed to have its own color theme and she was very fortunate that she had managed to get a blue room, which was her favorite color. Each of the four walls was painted a light, powder blue, the wall opposite the door included a large window that looked down over a section of the garden below. The bright white windowsill was wide enough to sit on and read or look out at the scenery. Against the wall on the right stood a large, four-poster bed with beautiful dark blue and silver bed covers. Beside it stood a dark wooden end table, which matched the wood of the dresser across the room. A sizable vanity table stood between it and the closet door, which was painted the same white as the windowsill. The bed had been the most comfortable bed she had ever been in, the perfect temperature and softness. She usually had a difficult time falling asleep at night, taking up to a half hour or more before she finally drifted off but, in this bed, she was out like a light seconds after her head hit the pillows. She hoped it would be just as easy to fall asleep tonight.

After rummaging through the bag she'd brought from her apartment, she found a t-shirt and pair of shorts to wear as pajamas. She changed, crawled into bed and reached for the alarm clock across the bedside table. Pulling it close to her, she saw it was, indeed, shortly after nine. Early, even for a planned dawn battle. No wonder her dad had questioned her about her bedtime. Setting the alarm, she set it back on the table, turned out the lights and snuggled down, hoping it wouldn't take her too long to fall asleep.

CHAPTER TWENTY-SEVEN

BEEP BEEP BEEP!!

Viola quickly turned off the alarm before it woke anyone else up. She dressed quietly and speedily, choosing something comfortable; a pair of dark blue jeans and a black t-shirt. Pulling on a black hoodie, her backpack and red sneakers, she slowly turned the doorknob and gently pulled the door open before peering down the hall. All was quiet and dark, aside from a few dim lamps on the walls, to light the way for late night bathroom trips. Taking the stairs carefully so as to avoid any creaks and groans of the wood, she made her way downstairs. At two a.m. everyone was in their beds, sleeping peacefully. Everyone, that is, except for the two dwarven brothers, who were in the midst of their latest shift of keeping watch in front of the basement door. Rounding the corner, she pasted a smile on her face to greet the two brothers. "Hi, Korir, Gargen!"

The two dwarves bowed to her slightly, something she still wasn't entirely used to or enjoyed. "M'Lady." They straightened and Gargen, his brow furrowed in concern asked, "what are ye doin' awake at this time o' night? Is everythin' okay?!"

"Yes, I'm fine. Just couldn't sleep. I thought I might have another chat with our friends downstairs. I have a few more questions which are keeping me awake. I'd like to have them answered." The two men eyed each other, obviously hesitant. "I survived last time," she offered, "I'm sure I'll make it this time, as well." She smiled brightly at them, trying to allay their fears. Although they still looked unsure about it, they stepped aside so she could open the door to the basement. Closing the door behind her, she was enveloped in semi-darkness. She took the stairs carefully, making her way into the basement proper. The dim light coming from two glowing orbs near the ceiling was just enough for her to avoid knocking anything over. Focusing a tiny bit of energy, she gave the orbs a little nudge with magic and they glowed a bit brighter, giving her a better view of the room around her.

Monty was asleep on the stone floor, looking quite uncomfortable. She could hear his soft, deep, rhythmic breathing as he slept. Seeing him lying there reminded her of the night they'd spent in her apartment, of waking up in the middle of the night to his arm draped over her, of his warm breath hitting the back of her neck, how completely content she had felt. She squeezed her eyes shut and shook her head, hoping the action would send the memory rattling away into the dark recesses of her mind, never to return again. Opening her eyes, a flash caught her attention, coming from the right side of the room. Ikidrak was awake, sitting up and grinning at her, the light from the orbs glinting off his beady little black eyes and sharp, needle-teeth. She tried to hide the shiver the sight elicited from her, but the goblin saw and his grin widened even further.

Ignoring the creature, she stepped toward Monty, eager to get moving. "Hey," she said quietly, gently nudging him so as not to startle him. "Hey, you need to wake up." After several seconds, he opened his eyes sleepily and stared up at her. A smile flashed across his face before he remembered where he was. Looking around, he realized it was still quite late, then turned back to her, his eyebrow raised in a question. "I'm taking the two of you out of here," she explained.

"What? Where are we going?" Monty obviously could tell something was up, but she couldn't tell him her plan. Not yet. She had a feeling he wouldn't approve and might try to alert everyone else.

"We're leaving and that's all you need to know. Unless you'd *rather* stay here..." She let the thought hang in the air and die, knowing neither of them had left this basement, aside from a couple of bathroom breaks, in nearly twenty-four hours. Monty didn't say anything and Ikidrak continued to sit silently in the corner with his horrible grin. Vy took a quick look around the basement. The two men, human and goblin, were no longer bound as the council had all agreed it was unnecessary; with two guards posted outside the cellar door at all times, it would be near impossible for them to escape. However, she didn't want either of them escaping from her as they traveled, so some kind of binding would be prudent. She didn't see any ropes, chains or anything else she could use as a method of binding. The cellar was used as a storage area for supplies, the majority of the room being filled with crates of fruits and vegetables, bags of potatoes or flour, wheels of cheese and several small pots containing seedlings. As her gaze landed on the tiny green stems poking up from their orange terracotta pots, an idea began shaping itself inside her head. Grinning to herself, she crossed the room and chose one of the seedlings, placing it on the floor in the center of the cellar floor, where she had the most open space. Monty and Ikidrak watched as she stood and stretched her right hand out over the pot, staring intensely at the tiny green shoot. Slowly, she began to raise her hand, fingertips gracefully trailing upward as she lifted her wrist. She repeated the motion two or three times, then the tiny green shoot began growing. Monty stared in fascination as the seedling's base grew to about an inch wide and the top of the plant grew taller and taller. Eventually, it grew far too tall to remain standing upright and fell to the side, snaking along the floor as it continued to lengthen.

    Within moments, there were several feet of long, green vine curling around the cellar floor. Vy began to bring the magic to a close, slowly rotating her wrist around in a circle while the growth rate of the vine began to slow and gradually come to a stop, the thickness narrowing with each centimeter. Grabbing hold of the plant, she gently pulled it from its small, orange pot, the width at the base now only as wide as the original seedling. The vine suddenly and quietly separated, Viola holding the end of it which was swinging gently over the small seedling resting in the terra cotta planter, as if it hadn't just grown several feet in an extraordinarily short amount of time. Coiling it around the length of her forearm,

Vy got the wandering vine under control and began looping the end around Ikidrak's wrists.

"I'm sorry," she said, keeping her eyes from meeting Monty's, "I can't have either of you wandering off. It's very important that I get you both where we need to go."

"And where is that, exactly?" Monty looked at her with concerned curiosity as she brought the vine toward him and began wrapping it around his wrist. She made the mistake of making eye contact with him for the briefest of moments, kicking herself for feeling the affection nudging at her mind and heart.

"You'll see."

"Vy...somehow, I don't feel like I'm going to like this plan of yours. I don't think we're off for a jolly stroll to get ice cream."

She couldn't stop herself from smirking at that one; even Ikidrak hissed with laughter a few feet away. "Oh, you never know. Perhaps there's a shop open somewhere. At two in the morning." She tightened the final loop around his wrist and anchored the other end around her own, connecting all three of them. "There, all set," she said as she looked at them both, in turn. "It's time to go." Leading them by the end of the vine, Vy took them up the stairs, pausing a moment to reach into her pocket for something before opening the door.

Gargen and Korir turned at the sound of the door swinging open, their mouths stretched in a wide grin, which quickly disappeared as they saw Monty and Ikidrak behind her.

"My lady, what -" Gargen was cut off as Viola blew a puff of pink powder into both the dwarves' faces. Seconds later they both slumped to the floor. Tugging hard on the vine, Vy quickly moved her two prisoners down the hall toward the front door. Blowing more powder into the face of the guards outside, the trio made their way from the porch and into the garden.

"What is that," Monty asked.

"Sleeping powder, it is," cackled Ikidrak. "Basic magic. Very old."

"Correct. I picked it up at a shop today, run by an old wizard," she explained.

Vy then shushed the pair of them, knowing there were more guards around. "Stay quiet," she whispered as they continued through the garden path. "There's another set of guards just on the outside of the archway entrance. After that we should be good."

"Vy, where are we going?" Monty had planted his feet and wasn't allowing himself to be moved, no matter how hard she pulled. "If we're hiding from guards and blowing sleeping powder into their faces then you weren't granted permission for any of it, and that worries me!"

"Monty, we don't have time for this! The effects of the powder won't last long, and we need to get out of here before they wake up. Come ON!" She pulled on the length of vine as hard as she could and though he had to put effort into resisting, he stood fast. Worried the vine would snap or another guard would suddenly come upon them, she finally gave in to his wishes. "Ugh! Fine," she hissed. "Your mother proposed a deal. I'm taking you to her."

In his shock, she managed to get him moving again, Ikidrak grinning madly all the while, as if he thought this whole interaction was the funniest damn thing he'd ever seen. They passed under the flower and ivy-covered archway, Viola already prepared to blow more powder into the faces of the two guards on the other side. "There," she said, as the last two guards dropped to the ground, fast asleep. With those two, we'll be all set." She checked her watch; half past two. They needed to move it. As she led them past the aging, dilapidated house, so different from the stately, brightly lit mansion they had just left, Monty was finally able to finish his train of thought.

"You mentioned a deal. You're giving me back to my mother, which will make her happy but there must be more to it than that. What was her proposition?"

"She has promised the cessation of violence against my people in return for my delivering you," here she paused, "...and me." As Monty protested, she continued her brisk pace, leading them to the road and into the dark night.

CHAPTER TWENTY-EIGHT

The town of Lyndon was dark and silent as Vy drove toward the coastline. After leaving Liz's apartment, she had stopped by her own home, used the spare key hidden under the doormat and retrieved the key to her car. She had managed to get Monty and Ikidrak into the backseat of the vehicle, despite Monty's protestations and his efforts to resist. Due to his arms being tied at the wrists, he was unable to use his hands to brace himself when she was trying to get him inside the vehicle, so a good, quick shove is all that was needed to get him inside. Ikidrak seemed to find the whole situation ridiculously amusing and gladly hopped into the car by himself, grinning with glee the entire time. Thankfully, her car had a child lock feature in the backseat, so neither of them could open the doors. Vy glanced down at the clock; 2:43. The effects of the sleeping powder would be wearing off in another five or ten minutes and then the entire house would know what she'd done. It didn't matter. By that time, she would have already parked the car near the beach and met Melarue, after which, whatever happened would happen.

"You can't do this, Vy! I know what my mother is like and how much she hates you." Monty was frantically trying to change her mind, begging her to turn the car around. "She'll kill you, Vy. Please, don't do this!"

"I have to, Monty," she said, slipping back into the familiarity of using his nickname. "If I don't, then she'll kill all those people and creatures back there and it will all be my fault. You saw what happened to Gregory and Asteria. I will *not* have anyone else's blood on my hands. If you're right, and she kills me, then I'll at least die knowing that I saved the rest of them. And even you." He was persistent in trying to change her mind but though she heard everything he said, she refused to respond to any more of it. Keeping silent, she focused on the dark, empty streets as she made her way across town toward the beach.

She parked the car in a public lot across the street, positioning it as far from the road and as deep into the shadows of trees as she possibly could. The last thing she needed was for a cop to drive by, see a car parked in the beach lot at three in the morning and get themselves in the middle of whatever was about to take place. Monty seemed to have resigned himself to her will as they crossed the empty street, no longer protesting and attempting to change her mind. Through the darkness she could see a white square, which was the sign directing an adventurer to two nearby hiking trails through the woods, one of which branched off and led to the hidden beach. She led them to the correct path and, once they were far enough into the trees to not be seen, pulled a flashlight from the pocket of her hoodie, so they could see their way on the path. She could hear the wwsshhh of the water as it hit the shore, tiny waves crashing against sand and rocks.

They quickly made their way down the darkened walkway, being careful to watch for tree roots and branches that may have covered the ground before them. Gradually the trees began to thin, and they could spot glimpses of moonlight reflecting on the water off toward their right, through breaks in the foliage. The path before them began to open up, the ground slowly changing from leaves, twigs, branches and trodden earth into sand and stones, becoming rockier the closer they got to the beach. Eventually the trees thinned out completely and they were left with the stunning view of the Maine coastline in the wee hours of the morning. The light of the waning moon reflected off the rocks of the beach, still wet from last night's high tide, and off the water beyond. The light was beginning to dim, however, as tendrils of incoming storm clouds began stretching across the moon's face.

Down by the water, facing out to sea, stood a lone, dark figure. Vy inhaled sharply, knowing exactly who it was standing on the beach by themselves in the middle of the night. Monty decided to make one final plea as they began to descend the low hill leading onto the beach proper.

"Please, Vy. Please, I am begging you. Don't do this." His voice was a frantic whisper, spoken softly so as not to attract the attention of Melarue.

She didn't reply but gave him a look that told him to shut it or else. Their footsteps on the rocks echoed around the small beach, causing the dark figure to turn toward them. The facial features were difficult to see in the dim light, but Vy could sense the grin spread across those painted red lips. Melarue stood still, watching and waiting for the approaching trio to come to her. Vy crossed the width of the beach with her two captives in tow, her gaze never wavering from the shadowed figure ahead of her. She finally stopped their small train a few feet away from Melarue, close enough to make out her features in the darkness. She planted her feet amongst the stones and pebbles, and stood motionless, waiting to see what the woman was going to do next.

"Well, well, well," Melarue purred. "I see you've held up your end of our bargain, Evelina. You've returned my son to me and brought back my goblin. That last part wasn't necessary but I appreciate it just the same." She spoke sweetly and politely, but the unexpressed rage and disdain dripped from her lips like so much honey. She extended her hand and beckoned for Vy to move closer, indicating she should place the end of the vine into Melarue's hand. "Give them here."

Vy looked toward her two charges, meeting Monty's gaze for the first time in the past few hours, before turning back to the woman smirking wickedly before her. "You'll keep your promise in this, right? I bring you Monty and the goblin and let you have me, in exchange for you letting my friends and family live."

Vy thought she saw a glimmer in Melarue's eye and her smirk widen slightly. "But of course! I would never renege on a promise."

Vy hesitated for a moment, studying Melarue's expression. She wasn't entirely sure she trusted what the woman was saying but if she didn't do this, it meant inevitable suffering and death for the people and creatures she'd come to know as friends and family. At least this gave them a chance. With a wave of her hand over the end of the vine she was holding, it disappeared, leaving Monty and Ikidrak free to do as they pleased. Melarue's grin widened.

"If they attack me, however, I will, of course, be forced to retaliate." She smiled menacingly at Vy, as the young woman clenched and unclenched her fists. After a few moments, the goblin took a couple of steps forward, slowly moving back to his mistress' side. Monty, however, remained standing beside Vy. The smirk plastered to Melarue's face flickered for a moment as she turned her eyes toward him.

"Monty. Come stand by your mother, dear."

He remained exactly where he was. "What happens to Vy?" Vy couldn't help but turn to look at him, hearing the hardness in his voice. He was staring at his mother's face, his eyebrows knit together in a frown of angry determination.

"Well, dear, as you know, she's caused me an awful lot of trouble over the years. She's one of the big reasons I came back, after all."

"But what happens to her?"

"What does it matter?! Now come stand with me, Montgomery." Her sickly-sweet red smile began to fade.

Ikidrak had paused between Melarue, and Vy and Monty, watching the other three during the exchange.

Still standing firm, Monty asked the question a final time, putting extra emphasis on each and every word. "What. Will. You. Do. To. Vy?"

Melarue dropped all pretenses, letting out a soft snort of laughter. "Well, I should think it quite obvious, darling...I have to steal her magic and kill her."

Vy could see Monty's muscles flex as he clenched his teeth. He stared back at his mother for a second or two before moving to stand in front of Viola. "Then, no, mother. I will not stand with you."

"Monty," Viola squeaked behind him. "What on earth are you doing?!"

"Yes, Monty, dear. What *are* you doing? First a chair to the back of your mother's head, which we *will* be discussing later, and now this?" Melarue was glaring at her son and the young woman he was protecting.

"All my life you told me how horrible this woman was, how badly she treated you in the past and how terrible and cruel her people were. Well, I've spent the last day or so among those people and even though I was their prisoner, I was still fed and well taken care of. I had the opportunity to speak to a couple of them when they brought me meals or let me use the bathroom, and I was treated respectfully. I watched them interact with each other and overheard conversations and all I heard from them was kindness. And I've known *her* for months," he said, gesturing to Vy with his head. "And I know her to be one of the kindest, sweetest, nicest people I have ever met. She has such a big, loving heart and I broke it because I believed the lies you told me. I won't see her endure any further pain if I can prevent it."

Melarue stared back at Monty and Vy thought she could actually *see* the woman's rage boiling over. She couldn't see Monty's face, now that he had taken a protective stance in front of her but she could see that his entire body was tense and seemed ready to defend her if the need arose. His words and stature did nothing to alleviate her confusion regarding where they stood as a couple. A mere two days ago, he was fighting on the opposite side and now, here he was talking about how wonderful she was and standing between her and his mother. This certainly wasn't going as she had expected.

"Get out of the way, Montgomery. I don't want to hurt you," Melarue growled.

"I won't move, mother. I can't bear to let you hurt her again." He paused a moment, his jaw working as he began to form his next words. "I love her."

Vy felt a layer of ice around her heart melt at his words and she was even more confused. She thought back to the conversation she'd had with her father over ice cream the night before. He had fought against her people, he had taken her to his mother, knowing who she was, and he had stood nearby as she and her friends were tortured. And yet, he had knocked his mother unconscious to allow them to escape and now here he was, standing between her and the woman who wanted her dead, defending her against his own mother. Beneath her feelings of anger, sadness and betrayal, she still felt those feelings of love and admiration trying to force their way in.

Melarue visibly stiffened, taking a deep breath. "Very well, then." She sighed, turning towards the water for a moment then suddenly, without warning, seaweed shot from the water's edge and wrapped tightly around Monty, encasing him in a slimy, green and brown cocoon. The only parts left exposed were his head and his feet. Unable to maintain his balance while wrapped in seaweed, he began to tip over sideways. Vy did her best to catch him and laid him on the ground.

"I'm terribly sorry about this, my dear, but I simply can't have you in the way and I *must* be rid of this thorn in my side."

Vy was pulling at the seaweed, trying to free him, but the plants kept springing back into position whenever she made any sort of progress. The wind was suddenly knocked out of her as something large and solid slammed into her middle, knocking her backward onto the rocky beach. She pushed the large rock away from her and sucked in air with deep, frantic gulps. She could hear Monty screaming her name, asking if she was okay and above his deep bass, a higher pitched cackling.' Melarue was laughing gleefully at what she had just done and if Vy wasn't so preoccupied with the pain in her midsection, she would have responded by *gleefully* flipping the woman off. So, this was how it was going to be. She'd desperately hoped to avoid this but what could she do?

Pushing herself up into a sitting position, she waved her hand and pulled a wave of ocean water into the beach, drenching Melarue and knocking her to the ground. In the meantime, with Melarue distracted, Vy took the opportunity to get to her feet. Monty was still struggling against his bonds and though she wanted to help him, she knew there wasn't enough time for it.

"I don't want to fight you, Melarue. I truly believe we can negotiate terms of peace."

"Peace?! You want peace?!" As she picked herself up, wet and bedraggled, Melarue shrieked at her in response. "You gave up the option for peace when you denied me all those years ago! You think I would suddenly decide that everything is *peachy keen*?!" She thrust her arms forward and sent a ball of fire toward Vy, who quickly ducked out of the way and pulled a bit more water from the sea to extinguish the flames. As she moved, a chain that had been hidden beneath Melarue's pristine blouse fell loose. The chain held dozens of coins which glinted menacingly in a flash of distant lightning. Viola saw several dead fish rise and float upon the surface of the water, the price for the magic Melarue was draining from the earth.

"You aren't thinking clearly, Melarue! The magic inside of you is blinding you to the truth! It's already burning you up inside! I can see it!" Melarue was shaking so violently she was practically vibrating, and a strange light shone behind her eyes. "But there might still be time! Please, Melarue, I'm trying to save you!" Vy could sense the presence of Evelina inside of her but this time it wasn't as if they were two separate entities, they seemed more connected, as though they were finally beginning to mesh into one being. She understood that Melarue was on the verge of being overtaken by the magical energies coursing inside her and Vy was scrambling, trying to find a way to stop it.

"You liar!!" Melarue lifted her hands as countless rocks and pebbles rose from the ground and hovered in the air for a moment before she sent them spinning towards Vy. Drawing energy from the trees on the hill, Vy quickly drew their roots in her direction until they burst from the ground, intertwining to form a wall in front of her. The rocks crashed harmlessly against the wall in front of her and when she stopped hearing them thud against the ground, she released her hold over the tree roots and let them shrink back to their original size and places.

"You're using too much magic, Melarue. You aren't just borrowing the energy, you're stealing it and holding it within you. If you keep this up, it'll destroy you. Please, *please* I'm begging, let me help you! Let me help you understand." She held her hands out in supplication, trying desperately to get the woman to see reason. The wild look in Melarue's eye was growing more and more deadly by the minute. They were wide and angry as she panted for breath, Vy beginning to worry that the woman was starting to lose control. Vy noticed Ikidrak ducking to avoid stray rocks that flew his way and Monty trying to roll out of the way of a few, himself. Vy could tell the magic Melarue was burning through was also burning through her as well, and soon the amount of energies coursing through her would be too much for the woman to handle. It was far too much for her to sustain. That much energy held inside one being wasn't going to end well. She was on the brink of madness or death. If only Vy could get her to calm down, to stop pulling those energies through a body that wasn't built to hold them, she could save Melarue from herself.

"Oh, I understand perfectly," Melarue growled, her eyes flashing as she glared at Vy. Without taking her eyes off her enemy, Melarue clutched her coin necklace in one hand and reached the other out to sea and seemingly began to pull on an invisible rope. Brows furrowed, Vy turned to see what she was doing and was shocked to see the storm clouds coming into land much faster than they should have been and growing larger and more violent as they did so.

"No. No, Melarue, no!!! That's far too much! You'll never be able to handle it!" Vy remembered calling forth a storm once when she had been Evelina. It had been incredibly draining, even for her, in the prime of her strength and power, and she'd had to rest for days afterward. She was terrified to think of what could happen to someone whose body wasn't prepared to handle that much energy, especially one already as compromised as Melarue's.

A strained yet wicked smile spread across the woman's face. "You just watch me, little fairy princess," she growled. Vy could see how much she was starting to struggle but the storm drew closer, droplets of rain beginning to pelt at her skin and hair, wetting the already slick stones even further until the storm was right on top of them and the rain came down in buckets. It was hard to see through the heavy precipitation and Vy narrowly escaped being sliced to bits as Melarue sent rain droplets sharp as glass in her direction. She just happened to catch a strange sort of glint coming from a few drops, then took off running back toward the trees just in time. The wet, slippery rocks made it difficult to make much progress, but she managed to get far enough away to only get a few cuts on her right arm, despite slipping and falling onto the rocks below.

She barely had time to catch her breath before Melarue's next attack came at her, as the water swelled, climbing further and further inland. She assumed it would start to slow as it reached Monty, but the water kept coming closer and closer, Vy realizing that Melarue was now prepared to even put her own son at risk, in an attempt to destroy her. Whether this was from the madness building within her or if she really truly did not care about the young man, Vy could not tell.

"Melarue! Arin, stop! Monty!" She gestured toward him as the water creeped ever closer to his trapped body. By now he had noticed it himself and was trying to squirm his way back up the beach toward the hill and trees. "Melarue! He'll drown!" Melarue, however, wasn't listening. She was focused completely on Vy, ignoring the rain and sweat mixing on her face and the yelps of her son as he struggled against the incoming water, all the while fondling that damn coin necklace. Ikidrak, being free of any sort of bonds, had already taken off, racing toward the trees. Melarue didn't even seem to blink as she stared Vy down. Her concern growing with every passing second, Vy finally chose to drop her guard and do what she could to save Monty. Tearing across the beach, slipping on the wet surface the entire way, she raced toward Monty as quickly as she could. Despite his squirming and wriggling, he hadn't gained much ground and it looked as though some of the seaweed binding him had gotten stuck around a group of rocks. He was unable to move and the water was rapidly nearing his head. It was at his chest, his shoulders, his neck. The slippery surface of the beach made speed a struggle, Vy reaching him just as his nose and mouth disappeared beneath the water. Pulling with all her strength, straining against his weight, increased by the water and wet seaweed, she tugged him as far away from the water as she could.

The water kept gaining on them as she struggled to get him away from it. Pulling with all her strength, she couldn't seem to get far enough ahead of it to ensure their safety.

"Vy, please, just go! Leave me! You've got to get out of here!" Monty was doing his best to try to help her, pushing against the rocky beach with his feet, but with his tangled seaweed bindings it just wasn't enough.

"No, I will not leave you here! I'll get you out," she shrieked, straining against his weight. The water was rising faster now, and she knew they were running out of time. She slipped on a particularly slick and loose rock and fell to her bottom, rocks jabbing her in her legs and seat. She tried to catch her breath and continue to pull him away, but the water was coming in so, so fast. Her muscles were on fire, exhausted from the effort of pulling Monty to safety. There were scrapes on both sides of her hands from slipping on the rocks, and she had a terrible gash in her right leg, a souvenir from one of the glass raindrops Melarue had thrown at her earlier. She tried to lift him again but couldn't find the strength to do so. "Monty, I... I can't. I don't know what to do." She started to cry, still trying to find the strength somewhere inside to pull him away.

"Don't worry about me, Vy, please. Please, *please* get away from here." He looked up at her with the shine of tears in his eyes, his head resting against her chest.

Shaking her head, she did the only thing she could think of as the water rose up above her knees; she wrapped her arms around him and kissed his cheek, tears falling from her eyes to his shoulder. "I'm so sorry, Monty" The water rose up and over their chests, and up to their chins.

"I love you, Vy. I really do."

"I...I love you, too."

They both squeezed their eyes shut, resigning themselves to the inevitable. They sucked air into their lungs and held it. She felt the cool water rush over their heads and suddenly, without warning it was gone. Opening her eyes, she saw that their heads were surrounded by an air bubble, which kept them from drowning.

"How…?" She looked around when a gray-green hand tightly grasped her arm. Ikidrak had appeared from the trees and formed the air bubble around their heads. *Huh*, she thought to herself, *why didn't I think of that?* She blamed it on the panic of the moment as the little goblin pulled her and Monty away from the water as hard and as quickly as he could. He was surprisingly strong for such a small creature and was making significant progress at getting them away. She had no idea why he had suddenly seemingly switched sides but she started to help his efforts by using her feet to push herself and Monty back from the surface. When they were far enough away, she stood and helped the goblin pull Monty up and over the hill. She got him settled on the less rocky part of the beach, near the edge of the tree line.

"Why did you help us, Ikidrak? I don't understand."

The little goblin smiled his toothy grin at her. "Ikidrak listen to what Master Montgomery say. He was right. Magic lady and friends much nicer than the Mistress. Treat Ikidrak nice and give him good food. Aside from no meat. And big house cellar more comfortable than box where Ikidrak sleep in Mistress' glass house."

Well, there you go, Vy thought. Treat someone with kindness and respect and look at what could happen.

"Coin necklace around Mistress' neck," he continued. "Coins were touched with blood Ikidrak took from prisoners. Coins are like keys. Hold magic inside Mistress."

Viola's brow furrowed as she tried to understand what he was saying. "The coins are keys. Oh!" Realization suddenly dawned on her. "Ikidrak! You mean the blood you took from us, from everyone Melarue has killed, that blood was put into the coins? And the coins are locking all of that stolen magic in place?! That means that if Melarue's connection to them is broken, it will release the hold on the magic and it would all return to the earth!" The goblin nodded enthusiastically. "That's wonderful news!" Quickly thanking Ikidrak, she turned back to Melarue. If she could break that chain, sever the connection, all the stolen energy buried inside the woman would be released and return to the earth where it belonged. She could save Melarue, all of her friends and herself. Focusing her energy, she brought forth a great wind that pushed the water back out to sea. She wouldn't have thought it possible, but Melarue's face had managed to fill with even more rage in the past few moments.

"I truly don't want to fight you but you're leaving me with no choice," Vy called across the storm. Spreading her arms wide to the dark clouds above, she pulled hail down from the sky, which rained down over Melarue, leaving red welts on her exposed skin. For the first time in several minutes, Melarue finally broke her stare at Vy and raised her arms to cover herself; protection from the small icy stones. Vy hoped the attack would cause her foe to have second thoughts about continuing their battle. The hailstones that made contact occasionally broke the skin, leaving angry, bloody scrapes behind. When Vy broke off the connection and the hail stopped falling, Melarue lowered her arms to reveal a glare full of hate the likes of which Vy had never seen. She felt truly terrified of the woman for the first time that night.

Melarue suddenly seemed to look through her at something beyond Vy's sight, something which made her wicked grin return once more. Vy was hesitant to turn, fearing it was a trick meant to distract her while Melarue sent something even worse toward her. Then, she suddenly heard shouts and cries behind her, and she instinctively turned to the sound. Coming down over the hill was Lady Rosalyn, her father and several of the other people and creatures from the house. Vy cursed loudly; they must have been on the beach far longer than she'd realized. Rosalyn and the rest of the inhabitants of the Old Victorian had already woken from their slumber, some of them magically induced, and discovered her missing. They'd figured out exactly where she had gone and what her plans were. She ignored their cries and protests, returning her attention to the woman across the beach.

"Viola, what have you done?!" Charles' voice rang out through the storm.

"I'm doing what I have to, Dad. Stay out of this and keep everyone safe!" Before they could protest, Vy used the energy from the storm to create a barrier keeping Charles and the rest from getting in the way of her fight with Melarue. She heard her father protesting, shouting at her to pull the barrier down and let them help but she continued to focus on Melarue, trying to ascertain what the woman might do next.

"It seems we have an audience now, little one," she sneered. "Why don't we give them the show they came here for!!" She stretched her arms to the sky and Vy copied the motion, trying to focus some energy on her next move. Thunder began to rumble, and she started when a bolt of lightning shot through the ground close by. The reflexive scream she let out made Melarue laugh hysterically. "Was that a bit *shocking* to you, dearie?! Prepare yourself! There's plenty more to come!" Flashes erupted all around as bolt after bolt crashed around her, while Melarue laughed maniacally. Even being connected with nature and being able to sense the electrical energy before the bolts struck, it was all Vy could do to avoid getting hit, but her hair was still frizzing up horribly and she could feel the buzz of the electricity in the air.

"You can't keep this up for long," she called to Melarue. "You won't be able to sustain it!" She threw herself to the ground to avoid another bolt that erupted from where she had just been standing, and felt rocks cutting into her palms and forearms. She couldn't protect herself, distract Melarue and get to the necklace all at once. "Please, I want to help you! Please stop this now!"

Melarue let out a low growl and threw her arms to the clouds once more. Beyond the dark clouds the sky was beginning to lighten, dawn approaching from the east. Staring intently at the skies above her, Melarue pulled on another invisible rope, pulling harder than she ever had before until suddenly a bolt shot from the sky straight into her own body.

"No!" Vy screamed and started to race toward the woman but she was pushed back by the force of the energy before her. Ahead, Melarue was glowing with the energy of the lightning, sparks bursting from her body, falling onto the sands below. Though she must have been in pain, Melarue laughed loudly as she channeled the storm's energy into herself. Vy was shocked; she'd never seen anyone take the entirety of a storm into themselves, even during her life as Evelina. She had no idea what was going to happen and was at a complete loss of what to do. The raw, electrical energy of the storm was keeping her back, not letting her get any closer to Melarue, though she was trying desperately to find a way through. All it seemed she could manage now was to try to stay out of the way of the sparks and anything else Melarue might send toward her.

"Watch this, everyone! I'll show you the kind of power I am capable of and I'll let you watch as your precious little queen is killed by me for a second and *final* time!" Melarue cackled wildly as another bolt crashed into her, turning her into a glowing ball of electric energy. She moved her arms out in front of herself, her open palms aimed directly at Viola. Everything happened almost instantaneously but to Vy it seemed that time was slowing down. A bolt of lightning shot out from Melarue's hands a short distance, crackling as the end moved ever closer to Vy. She heard shouts coming from all directions behind her, picking out a specific voice every now and then; her father and Monty screaming her name, Rosalyn begging her to let them help, Tam and Vince telling her what to do next.

She began to crouch, ready to jump out of the path of the bolt, hoping it wouldn't veer toward her. Drawing on energy from the trees and ocean around her, she began lifting the rocks of the beach into the air, hoping they would provide a shield against the lightning. If her movements were off by even an inch, that might be it for her. It was, however, the best and only plan she had. Whatever happened would happen. There was nothing she could do now. Melarue's laughter reached a fever pitch when suddenly the bolt in front of Vy disappeared and the sparks and glow coming from Melarue's body faded away. The woman's laughter ceased suddenly as she looked toward Vy, confusion evident upon her face.

Also confused, Vy stared back at her, trying to understand what was happening, hundreds of rocks and pebbles hovering in the air before her. Melarue pushed her hands forward towards Vy several times without anything shooting out from them. Letting out a growl that morphed into a battle cry, she tried again, and sparks began to shoot out from her hands, returning the smirk to her red lips. The sparks, however, quickly shorted out and stopped again. Melarue brought her hands up to her face to look at them, brows furrowed in confusion and frustration. Vy watched as a strange look suddenly crossed the woman's face. Melarue reached to her neck, fumbling about her throat. She lifted the chain of coins and inspected them, quickly locating one that had been damaged. It was split almost in half, possibly from the force of the lightning she had called down upon herself. She looked at the jagged edges of the coin in horror, then dropped it to the ground in front of her as sparks began to shoot out of her body at random intervals. She started to shake again and sweat poured down her face. Short, small explosions of lightning and energy pulsated from her body, coming in faster and faster bursts. The face that once wore a self-satisfied smirk was now a mix of bewilderment, pain and fear.

  Vy rose to her feet; exhausted, pained and bleeding, beginning to understand what was happening. Ikidrak had been right about the coins containing magic. She could see golden swirls of energy escaping from the damaged coin and turning back against the wearer of the necklace. Vy's plan had been to sever the chain and remove the intact coins from Melarue's body, thereby ending the connection she had with the stolen magic. She would then safely return that stolen energy to the earth from whence it came. With one of the coins damaged and the magic inside it not being returned properly to its source, instead the magic was rushing back toward the closest connection it had. Melarue was being overwhelmed by all the magical energy she had stolen from beings over the years. Viola started to run, hoping that if she could still remove that necklace, or if that failed, attempt to draw some of that energy into herself, Melarue could be saved. The woman had started screaming, all thoughts of war forgotten as the energies burned away inside of her.

'Please, please, please, please, please,' Vy chanted to herself as she tore over the rocks, hoping she could make it in time. "I'm coming, Melarue!" Stretching out her hand, she reached for Melarue, who was stretching her own out toward her enemy. Vy's fingertips brushed against Melarue's for a brief moment when a sudden blast of energies and light sent Vy flying backward, crashing hard into the rocky beach. Covered in cuts and bruises, pain radiating from every inch of her body, Vy managed to painstakingly push herself up into a sitting position to see what had happened.

Several yards away Melarue lay sprawled on the ground, steam coming off her body as the rain pelted her overheated form. Vy stood weakly and limped toward her, carefully lowering herself to her knees to check on the woman before her. The magical life energies coursing through the woman's body had overtaken her, destroying her from the inside out, then returned to the earth the moment Melarue was gone and had made contact with the ground beneath her. Vy watched a few golden tendrils of magic leaving the prone woman's form and disappearing into the ground below. She checked Melarue for breath and felt none. Picking up the woman's limp wrist, she felt for a pulse and felt none. Sitting down beside her, she focused on all the energies she could find in an attempt to heal her. She poured energy from her hands into Melarue's chest, directing it to her heart, hoping to bring her back. After several minutes of straining to force the energy into the body, she could no longer maintain the connection. Exhausted, her hands dropped to her lap as she turned to look toward the sound of hurried footsteps. Monty's seaweed bonds had loosened and were falling off, and he and Ikidrak pulled at the remaining pieces, while everyone else rushed forward, Vy's barrier failing due to her exhaustion.

Her father and Lady Rosalyn were suddenly at her side, checking on her wellbeing. She was worn out, overwhelmed, injured, disoriented and completely unable to focus on what they were saying to her, barely even able to recognize the faces surrounding her. Suddenly Monty's face pushed through the crowd and through the haze of everything around her, she could hear him asking if she was okay. She couldn't find the words to answer his question, her vision growing dark and speckled, but she raised her hand to rest against the side of his stubble-laden face.

"I'm so sorry, Monty," she heard her voice say, thickly. "I tried...couldn't...save her."

Then everything went black.

CHAPTER TWENTY-NINE

Vy could hear voices nearby, fuzzy and difficult to understand through the haze of waking up. She felt sore, unable to locate any part of her body that hadn't been stabbed, scraped, pelted with rocks or had rocks shoved into the flesh. She felt completely exhausted, even opening her eyes was turning out to be a struggle. The voices, through the fuzz and haze, sounded familiar but she couldn't identify any of them or understand the sounds they were making. Some of them sounded concerned and some of them seemed to be arguing. As she began to slowly regain consciousness, things began to clear, the voices becoming more and more recognizable with each passing second. She resisted opening her eyes because she was just so very tired. She knew the second they saw her eyes opening she would be bombarded with questions about her injuries, about what happened; she'd be sassed for going off on her own without telling anyone and she didn't think she was ready to deal with all of that. She just wanted to stay quiet, snuggled into the soft, warm bed she now recognized beneath her, the comforter drawn up to her chin. As the fuzziness melted away, she kept her eyes shut tight, listening as the voices and words became clearer.

"Do we think it's safe for him to be in here," her father asked, concern coloring the edges of his voice. "We're not really sure how he's handling what happened."

"I understand sir, but he insists that he will come in to see her. He refuses to leave until he's able to see that she's all right." She couldn't put a name to the owner of this voice, but she could recognize the accent as that of a faerie, no doubt someone who'd been told to guard her room.

"This debate isn't good for her," Rosalyn said gently. "If it means that she can have peace and quiet, I say we let him in, Charles." There was a pause as her father must have made a face and given her an angry look. "I share your reservations," she soothed, "but it may be best for Viola's well-being. Should she wake up to yelling and fighting after having endured what she just did, well…I can't imagine that would help her recovery in any way." Another pause, while she heard short noises coming from her father as he tried to construct a coherent sentence.

"I'm not opposed to him seeing her, I'm just not sure today is the best option," he cried, finally finding his words. "This is all still too fresh and he's hurting. He might get her all riled up or try to hurt her for what happened yesterday. We don't know what kind of state he's in right now!"

"We'll all be here and none of us will let that happen. He's only asked to come in and see that she's okay. He didn't specify being able to get close to her. We won't let him get anywhere physically near her and should he try to harm her in any way, we're all here to stop him by whatever means necessary, magical or otherwise." Rosalyn's voice was calm and reasonable as she tried to alleviate Charles' fears. She addressed someone else in the room, whose voice Vy was unable to discern from the others. "Go and bring him in, please, but bring Gargen and Korir in with you, as well." Vy heard a door close in the room and her father began to grumble softly about the admittance of whoever wanted to see her, but this time keeping his voice down so as not to disturb her. "We'll have the two brothers on either side of him at all times. Should he try anything or look suspicious in any way, they'll be there to grab him immediately."

Vy could almost picture Rosalyn standing beside Charles, patting his shoulder and trying to calm him down. She toyed with the idea of keeping her eyes shut and continuing to feign sleep but, in the end, decided she wanted to see who was there with her and to find out whatever she could about what happened after she'd passed out. And she wanted to know these things before this unnamed visitor arrived. She opened her eyes and saw that she was back in the blue room in the Old Victorian. Someone had dressed her wounds and tucked her into bed, wrapping the covers around her to keep her warm. To her immediate left sat her father and Rosalyn. Scattered around the room were a few other faces she recognized. Seated on the bed around her were Vince and Tam, Fulrin, a small pink pixie and Nigel the gnome, furiously knitting more of the seafoam green creation, while watching her intently. The moment her eyes opened, the little gnome dropped his knitting needles on the bed and began to jump up and down lightly, while enthusiastically pointing towards her. Seeing his excited and animated movements, everyone followed his gaze and his pointing finger to see Vy, awake and looking around. As expected, she was immediately ambushed as everyone who wasn't near the bed rushed forward and those who were near or on the bed leaned in close to her.

"Vy-Vy, are you okay? You've been asleep for a whole day! I've been so worried about you!" Her father was leaning in, kissing and stroking her forehead, traces of happy tears rimming his brown eyes.

"Viola, my dear, how are you feeling?" Rosalyn was leaning in, holding her hand.

Overwhelmed with all the faces coming at her, she looked at them confused, lifting a hand to weakly wave them back, a request which no one seemed to be acknowledging. Vince, finally catching on to what she was asking, took her waving hand and held on before addressing everyone.

"Give her some space! She just woke up, let her breathe a little." She met his eyes and mouthed a weak *thank you*, to which he responded with a wink. Tam was beside Vince, holding his other hand tightly and smiling down at her.

Her gaze swept the room, taking in everyone's faces, some worried and some smiling brightly at her, she finally stopped on her father's and Rosalyn's.

"What happened?"

"Well, my dear," the elf began, smiling brightly. "You did it! You won the battle and saved us all." Those surrounding her bed all smiled and nodded, murmuring agreement and appreciation.

She frowned at this, fuzzy memories starting to fill her head. "But I didn't. I didn't fight her, I just…I tried to help her." The details of the battle's final moments started to clear and she remembered most of what happened. "Melarue. Did she survive?" She remembered flashes of bright light and the pelting rain, but she couldn't remember the outcome. "I tried to save her. Did it work? Or was I... was I too late?"

The looks on everyone's faces told her what she needed to know. "I see. I failed."

"Don't be sad, Vy-Vy. She would have killed you and everyone else. In the end, you would have had to fight her anyway."

"No, Dad. I didn't want to kill her. Sure, she's done terrible things and she deserved punishment but not that. Not that." She trailed off as she got a sudden remembered glimpse of the fear and suffering in Melarue's eyes. The thought broke her heart.

Rosalyn nudged her way closer to Vy, past Charles. "Viola, what you witnessed was indeed terrible. That's why, as Evelina, you denied her magic. This is what we went to war for, to stop things like this from happening. It was terrible, and I respect you for trying to save her in the end." Vy opened her mouth to argue but was interrupted as the door swung open, revealing Korir and Gargen, escorting Monty into the room. Vy was a mix of emotions upon seeing him. She was happy, so very happy, that he'd come to see her but then the realization that she'd fought his mother and that his mother had died, hit her like a ton of bricks. She wondered if he was here to check on her, to see if she was okay, or if he was here to cry and scream at her, for taking his mother from him. If that was his intention, that was fine; he was certainly entitled to that. She felt she deserved whatever she had coming to her.

Everyone moved over slightly to give him some room as he approached the bed, while still staying close in case he tried anything. Her father hesitated, determined to remain where he was, close by her head, but Vy reassured him with a nod and Rosalyn took him by the hand, leading him toward the foot of the bed. Monty reached the bed, kneeling beside it and taking Vy's hand. Garden and Korir eyed the action closely, ready to act if he should attempt to harm her.

"Are you okay," he asked, brushing hair from her face with his free hand. His face bore a few scratches, most likely from stray pebbles flying around the beach, and his eyes were rimmed with red. It looked as though he might have been crying a short time ago.

"I'm okay. Sore, but okay." There was an awkward moment of silence as they both searched for words, Vy finally breaking it, voice full of emotion and eyes brimming over with tears. "Monty, I'm so sorry. I didn't want it to end like that and I tried to save your mom from herself. I tried so very hard, but it wasn't enough." The exhaustion and emotions of the day were too much and those few tears dissolved into all out sobs as she continued. "I'm so sorry. It's all my fault and I understand if you hate me and I won't be upset if you never want to see me again. Just know that I tried. I tried. I tried." She ran out of words to convey her remorse and instead gave in to the flood of tears which demanded release. They were the culmination of everything; the many truths she'd learned, the secrets she'd kept, the training, the battle, the pain and the absolute exhaustion she felt deep in her soul.

His own eyes were shining as he let go of her hand and moved to sit on the bed beside her, pulling her into a hug. Vy felt more than saw everyone in the room tense and move ever so slightly closer but there was no need. She sat limply in his arms as he rocked her from side to side, stroking her hair and shushing her softly.

"It's okay, Vy. I know you tried and that's what matters." He pulled away from her and wiped his eyes with the back of his sleeve before looking her straight in the eye. "I'm not mad. Yes, I'm wrecked by the loss of my mother, but I've done quite a bit of thinking over the past few days while I've been amongst all of you. I love my mother but her ideas about the world and about you and your people were wrong. What happened to my mother is not your fault, Vy. She was a victim of her own selfishness and nothing you could have done would have prevented what happened."

Looking toward everyone else who filled up the rest of the room, most of whom had seemed to relax for the first time since he'd entered, he continued. "I'm sorry for everything my mother did to all of you and I'm sorry for everything I did to you in her name." He stood up from the bed and backed away a few steps, his eyes locked onto Vy's. "I've done terrible things to you and to your people and I hope to someday make up for that. Worst of all, I ended up hurting you. Despite everything that has happened over the past few days that says otherwise, I really do love you Vy and if you'll let me, I'd like to keep loving you. If you don't want that, well...I won't deny it will break my heart, but I'll understand. At the very least, I need to make amends for what I did to you as a boyfriend and as a leader."

He knelt to one knee and held his arm across his chest, placing his fist over his heart. "I pledge my fealty to you, Lady Viola, reincarnation of Lady Evelina." There was an audible intake of breath from everyone in the room, including Vy. "If you accept my oath, I promise to serve you in whatever capacity you may ask of me, to fight for you and protect you and your people until you so choose to release me of my position or death take me."

His voice sounded rather shaky as he finished speaking and he swallowed hard, remaining entirely still while he waited for her answer. Silence filled the room as everyone stared back and forth between Monty and Viola, waiting to see what she would say. Vy felt awkward and uncertain. As Evelina, having someone pledge themselves to her would have happened on a somewhat regular basis. Evelina would know how to react. But suddenly, Vy realized...she was Evelina. It seemed the two had finally become one entity, and, as awkward as it would have felt to the old Vy, the new Vy knew exactly what to do. She looked toward Rosalyn, who gave her a small smile. The elf gave her a reassuring nod, silently encouraging Vy to be their leader again. Vy weighed her options regarding Monty, taking time to internally debate all the pros and cons. After a few moments, the tension visible in Monty's hunched shoulders, Vy cleared her throat to speak.

"Montgomery Stevens, I accept your pledge and welcome you to our little queendom. You will be a valuable addition to our community." Looking toward the room as a whole, she decided to push on with her new role. "The past several months have been unbelievably stressful and the past few days have brought us fear, danger, war and grief. But we have also seen strength, courage and resilience. The immediate threat has been dealt with and we are now free to live without the constant fear of attack. However, we've also lost loved ones," she caught Monty's eye as she finished her sentence, "on both sides of this struggle. As your...queen...it feels so strange saying that," she quipped, dropping the formal language of a ruler for a moment and giving everyone a bit of a chuckle. "As your queen, I say that the first thing we should do, now that we've entered this time of peace, is to give a proper burial to all those we have lost in this conflict. Everyone," she said, turning to give Monty a small smile of acknowledgement. He gave a quick bob of his head in recognition.

"An excellent idea," Rosalyn replied. "And very well said. Shall we begin making the arrangements for say...tomorrow afternoon, Lady Viola?"

Vy nodded. "Yes, that would be fine. In addition, should any member of Melarue's forces wish to do as Monty has done and join our side, they are welcome to do so."

Rosalyn gave a slight bow, smiling brightly, obviously proud of how Vy was handling this moment. "A wise and kind offer, my Lady. In the meantime," she continued, raising her hands and gesturing to everyone, "Let's leave our queen to get some rest. She still has a lot of healing to do. I'll send up something for you to eat, Viola. You must be famished. Come, come!" Everyone began to file out of the room, coming forward to give Vy a slight bow on their way out. Vince and Tam came in close to squeeze her hand and give her a smile; Charles gave her a kiss on the forehead and headed for the door, where Rosalyn was waiting, the two last guests walking through the door frame. Monty waited until the last minute before he rose from kneeling on the floor, walked in close and gave her a kiss on the hand before quickly bowing and exiting the room, Rosalyn and her father watching all the while, and closing the door behind them.

Vy, however, thought she'd had quite enough rest, since evidently, she'd done nothing but sleep for the past twenty-four hours. Still sore, she gently kicked off the blankets and pushed herself up from the bed to limp across the room and look in the mirror. Despite the healing magic she knew had been performed on her, the scrapes and bruises were still visible, the worst of them covered by bandages. There was a particularly nasty gash on her forehead just above her right eye which she hadn't realized was there. She wasn't even sure when it had happened, but it looked red and angry. Her face was still a bit grimy with dirt and sea salt, pale lines cutting through the grime, footprints of all the tears she'd cried. She shook her head and rolled her eyes, mortified that so many people had just been in the room to see her like this. 'Oh well,' she thought. 'What can you do?'

A knock sounded at the door, and she bid whoever it was to enter. The door opened to reveal Ikidrak wearing a chef's hat and an apron that read 'Kiss the Cook,' bearing a tray laden with a bowl of something that smelled fantastic, a tall glass of cider and chunk of bread.

"Ikidrak? What are you doing here?!"

He grinned his wide, sharp-toothed smile at her. "Ikidrak is good cook. Asked to come with magic folk now that Mistress is gone."

"And they just let you?"

He shrugged. "Ikidrak is not idiot. Work for whoever give the best offer. Ikidrak hurt by old Mistress sometimes. Here, get good food and warm place to sleep. People nice, no pain for goblin-folk!"

"I see," she said, the hint of a smile spreading across her face. "So... you worked for Melarue because it was convenient for you at the time? But...Ikidrak, we don't do the things that Melarue did. There won't be any magic stealing or torturing going on here."

"This okay. Ikidrak prefer cooking over torture, anyway! Smell much better!"

Vy couldn't help but to laugh out loud. "Okay, then. What's for dinner?" She gingerly sat down in a cushioned seat by the window, Ikidrak placing the tray on the table beside her.

"Soup with lots of vegetables! Ikidrak think you need meat but elf lady say simple food only." He shrugged. "When you feel better, Ikidrak make you good food!" He turned and bounded out the door, leaving Vy grinning and chuckling behind him. She took the cover off the bowl and welcomed the scent wafting up to her nose. It was a steaming hot broth, loaded with carrots, onions, beans and a few noodles. It smelled amazing and tasted even better. It didn't take her long to finish it all. Evidently Rosalyn was quite right about how hungry she'd been. She felt much better with a full stomach and the prospect of a warm shower. She hobbled her way into her private bath and got the water running. After a long shower she dressed then bustled, as best as she could with her tired and sore limbs, down the stairs and into the main rooms to help with the planning for tomorrow. At some point, she thought, she'd have to introduce Ikidrak to the many wonders of pizza.

When she entered the parlor below, everyone was seated around, chatting casually, starting to discuss tomorrow's events. Even Monty was there, seated in an armchair, looking slightly uncomfortable in his new surroundings. His spirits lifted slightly when she walked in and he hopped up to help her over to the chair he'd just vacated. She plopped into it unceremoniously as the little gnome, Nigel, came running over to her, bearing an ottoman for her to rest her leg upon.

"Thank you so much!" She smiled down at the gnome, who beamed back up at her and sat down close to her ottoman, pulling his knitting out of his pockets. A sheep suddenly trotted into the room and settled down beside the gnome, who reached out his hand to give the animal a quick pat. Vy blinked a few times, realization dawning, then looked toward the others, who were smiling at her and trying to hide their snickering. "But that...how?" She pointed to the sheep that was formerly a troll. The magic should have worn off by now, yet here it was!

Tam chuckled before answering. "Magic can be a strange thing, Vy. We just think we understand it and then it throws us a curveball, as you would say." He leaned over to pat the sheep, as well. "I suspect that this creature prefers it's new life to it's old one and doesn't want this magic to end. Sometimes, that's all magic needs - a passionate wish." At this, the little brown sheep bleated happily at them, nuzzling it's head against Nigel's leg.

Rosalyn requested a tea service be brought in while they planned tomorrow's events, and Vy found that she was excited at the prospect. A bowl of broth and a hunk of bread were all she'd had to eat since the chocolate and peanut butter parfait at Scoops. She was ravenous. She hoped there would be fruit, cheese, some kind of protein and lots of mead.

Several minutes later, Ikidrak bounced happily into the parlor, pushing a tray laden with tea, cider, mead, cheeses, breads, cold meats, fruit and cookies. He began placing everything on the table as Rosalyn was addressing the assembled guests.

"I'm not sure if Gregory had any family in the outside world. We'll have to check into that and, if he did, we must invite them, as well." She paused to take a breath in between sentences when someone cleared their throat loudly, as though to draw attention to themselves so they could speak. They all looked around at each other, curious as to who had interrupted, when Ikidrak stepped around the side of the table and stood in the center of the room.

"Gregory is wizard, yes? Mistress killed him same night she had Miss Vy?"

"Yes, that's right, Ikidrak. Along with Asteria, the purple faerie," Vy replied. The tone the goblin was using indicated he had something more to say regarding them and her eyebrows furrowed in perplexity.

"Mr. Gregory and Miss Asteria not really gone, Miss. Ikidrak save them."

Vy sat up straight in her chair, and she sensed others do the same, all at attention. "What do you mean? They're gone, Ikidrak. I watched Melarue kill them that night."

The goblin grinned widely at them, a sight that, no matter how many times she saw it, Vy knew it would always be unsettling.

"Goblin magic very strong," he said, reaching into the pouch at his waist. "Blood magic. Not have time to put blood into new coins. Ikidrak can bring them back." He pulled out two vials, containing the small blood bubbles he had created the night she'd been imprisoned in Melarue's sub-basement dungeon. Vy didn't understand but Rosalyn suddenly clapped her hands together, happy tears forming in the corners of her eyes.

"Of course," she exclaimed. "I didn't realize you'd done this! Oh, what a clever little goblin you are!" Ikidrak beamed at her and gently handed the bubbles over to Rosalyn's outstretched hands. "These contain blood and magic belonging to Gregory and Asteria. With this, and Mister Ikidrak's help, we can bring them back!"

Vy wasn't sure she understood the workings of blood magic; apparently Evelina had never studied the workings of it either, but she could put two and two together. Evidently, the blood Ikidrak had taken from each of them in Melarue's dungeon was to be magically infused into the coins she had worn around her neck. After tearing the magic from a creature, Melarue would pour that stolen magic into the corresponding coin, keeping a massive well of magic at her throat. She didn't understand the mechanics of it all, but she did know that Ikidrak was capable of bringing back at least two of the people she had lost. The little goblin, with his terrifying smile, had just made her unbelievably happy.

CHAPTER THIRTY

Vy sat on the front porch swing, watching the sky darken as the sun disappeared below the horizon. After his announcement, Ikidrak had followed them to where the bodies of the dead had been left to rest while they made preparations for their burial. Goblin magic looked incredibly complicated and Vy made a mental note to herself to learn more about it in the future. Ikidrak managed to restore life to both Gregory and Asteria, though he was unable to return her wings to her. This was a huge adjustment for the pixie, but she was dealing with it as best she could. They were both grateful for what Ikidrak had done for them and were happy to see another day; even happier to know that Melarue was no longer a threat.

They'd spent the evening hours planning and this afternoon they'd held a beautiful memorial celebration for everyone they'd lost during the battle, including the creatures fighting on Melarue's side and even Melarue, herself. Vy had said a few words, letting Rosalyn do most of the talking as she'd known these people and creatures for much longer. Besides, Vy was still sore and exhausted; she wanted to be the center of attention as little as possible. They had even extended invitations to Melarue's forces, most of whom attended, and many had requested to join Vy and her people, hoping for a better life than the one they'd had. Vy fully intended to give all of them a chance and would officially welcome all of them at a later time, in a more appropriate setting than a memorial service for lost friends.

    She even managed to get permission for Liz and Liam to attend, mainly because she'd thought the last time she'd seen them had truly been the last time and she was anxious to see them again. It took a bit of convincing, but Rosalyn acquiesced, after Vy promised that her friends would pose no threat to their way of life. Liz had broken down into tears when she saw how beat up Vy was and both she and Liam were horrified that Vy had gone to a battle, fully expecting not to return. She'd gotten lectures from both of them, then they promptly made arrangements to spend another day gaming, drinking and eating lots of carbs, and getting properly caught up on the happenings of the magical world. Then Liz had asked her if Monty would be joining them and Vy didn't know how to answer.

    After that, Liz had gushed about the dress Vy was wearing; it turned out that Nigel had been making one for her. The dress was a beautiful light blue, the bodice expertly knitted and beaded by the little gnome called Nigel, and the skirt made of a shimmering fabric soft as gossamer. The sleeves matched the overskirt, which was a sheer silver. A silver belt hung low on her hips, a pearlescent brooch ringed with a silver setting sewn into the fabric, with tendrils of the sheer, silver fabric trailing down the front of the skirt. It was the finest thing she'd ever worn, and that included the three-hundred-dollar dress she'd worn to her senior prom. When Liz had finally stopped trying to touch every inch of the fabric, Vy had left them in the dining room, chatting with her father and marveling at the world in which they now found themselves.

They'd decided to have a feast after the service, in an attempt to cheer each other up through food and camaraderie. A couple of hours in and everyone was still inside eating, drinking, sharing funny stories about those they had lost and reliving grand moments of battle. Vy had needed a break from the noise and decided to wander out to the porch. She had plopped down on the white porch swing and began to rock gently, listening to the sounds of talking and laughter inside while she watched the colors of sunset paint the sky, lost in her own thoughts and a glass of mead in her hand.

"Mind if I join you?"

She looked up to see Monty standing beside the swing, bearing his own glass of mead.

"Of course," she said, gesturing for him to take a seat. He sat down beside her, taking over the work of slowly rocking the swing back and forth. They sat quietly for several minutes, but the silence was neither awkward or uncomfortable. Vy didn't feel like she had to find something to say to fill the empty space and knew that when he wanted to talk, he would.

"I meant what I said to you yesterday, Vy. I really do love you."

"I know, Monty. And I think I still love you, too. But everything that's happened over the past few days…I'm just going to need some time."

"I know," he sighed. "I didn't realize it was you during the battle, not until I got close to you near the house, and with my mother-" he trailed off. "I was so confused, Vy. On the one hand there was my mom who had instilled this entire belief system in my head about Evelina and her evil, selfish, cruel subjects. And on the other, there was this amazing woman who, over the past few months, had shown me such kindness, compassion and love. I was wrestling with the two versions I had of you, the one I'd been told about and the one I had known. I was a mess. And I know it's no excuse. I shouldn't have allowed it to go on so long and I will be asking your forgiveness for that for as long as I live." He turned toward her and she could see the pain in his eyes, lit up by the pink light of the setting sun. "Can you forgive me Vy? Someday?"

"I understand what you're saying, I want you to know that. I don't hate you, the fact is that, even after everything that's happened, I still have very strong feelings for you. But, you also have to understand that all of this, everything that happened, it's all so much to take in and to process. You *are* wonderful. Y'know, aside from when you're swinging a sword in my direction," she quipped, trying to make him laugh. The corner of his mouth lifted slightly and for now that was enough. She reached over and took his hand. "I do still love you, Monty. But I'm also recovering. I can't promise you I'll be okay tomorrow or a week from now or even months. I need time."

"I completely understand, Vy." He looked off toward the sunset as he worked out what to say next. "I'm still working out my own issues, as it is. I loved my mother. I still do. But so much of what she taught me turned out to be untrue. And I love you," he said, turning back to her once more. "I'm struggling to find a balance between everything I've known to be true and what I've come to realize over the past few months and days."

"Guess we're both a mess," she snorted.

"That's true. But please, Vy, don't think I enjoyed watching you suffer. The entire time that my mother was doing those awful things to you in that basement, I kept running through everything in my mind; everything she'd told me about Evelina and what I knew from being with you. In the end, I had to trust my own gut and heart and had to get you out before she hurt you any further. Please don't doubt me, Vy. I promise I really do love you and I regret everything that happened in that awful room, and on that battlefield."

"I don't doubt you, Monty. You made a few terrible mistakes, but we've all done that. For the most part, you've been on my side, showing me love and care. I *have* noticed. I just need time. Time to...to deal with everything and heal from it."

"You can lead. The entire thing, it's all up to you."

She smiled at him and gingerly reached for his hand. He returned her smile and took her hand in his, their first step toward healing. They watched the last rays of the sun fade as the stars shone brighter in the darkening sky. This time last year she was gearing up for her second year of graduate school and working in her dad's bookstore. She didn't do much in terms of fun, aside from going out for drinks or watching movies with Liz. Thinking about it, her life had been pretty darn ordinary.

Now, she could wield magic, had gone into battle twice and won. She was a queen, complete with fancy dresses, crowns and making life-changing decisions. She didn't know what was yet to come. In a few weeks she'd return for her last semester of grad school, having her degree in hand by Christmas. She wondered if there was time to switch to a creative thesis; she could write the story of everything that had happened over the course of the last year. She had to smile at the idea of someone picking up a book and having no idea the events they were reading had actually happened, the characters and lives within its pages all real. Perhaps she could use what she'd learned about leadership over the past few months and what she would learn in the months to come, and could teach others, becoming as great a role model as Lady Rosalyn. Above all, she hoped the peace they'd attained would last but sadly, history often proves otherwise. She wanted to erase the prejudices within the magical community, so they could all work together. Some folks wouldn't be happy about that, she knew, but she wanted to end that practice as quickly as possible. Whatever lay in the future, she had a host of beloved friends and family who would stand by her side and she found that she wasn't scared of anything.

The world was full of magic and wonder, and that was the most important thing in the universe.

Printed in Great Britain
by Amazon